WHAT GOES AROUND

WHAT

GOES

AROUND

SUSAN
DIAMOND

WILLIAM MORROW
An Imprint of HarperCollins*Publishers*

FIRST EDITION

Library of Congress Cataloging-in-Publication Data

Diamond, Susan.
    What goes around / Susan Diamond.—1st ed.
      p. cm.
    ISBN: 978-0-06-113781-5
    ISBN-10: 0-06-113781-2
    I. Revenge—Fiction.   2. Female friendship—Fiction.

PS3604.I157 W48 2007
813'.6 22   2006043309

---

07 08 09 10 11 ❖/RRD 10 9 8 7 6 5 4 3 2 1

For Larry,
who would have enjoyed this adventure

ACKNOWLEDGMENTS

While the story, characters, and philosophy in this book are mine alone, I am greatly indebted to Annette Basalyga, Judith Daniels, and Phyllis Eliasberg—poet, magazine editor, TV reporter—for their ever-ready help and impeccable judgment on all aspects of its final form, from specific words to general procedure.

Like the women in the book, we're all dependent on a circle of close friends and attachments. Mine also includes Caron Block, Karin Grant, Anne Roark, Molly Selvin, Shelley Shapiro, and Nancy Yoshihara, who constantly fielded random questions on (but not limited to) law, medicine, real estate, food, wine, technology, and life itself; my daughter, Erica Johnson, who was good company and encouragement in hard times; and my mother, who, like Polly's mother, is always here for me.

Several people generously shared their special expertise: Rob Giannangeli on tax rules and rulings, Judy Marriner on horticulture, Katinka Matson on publishing, Deirdre Hanssen on title and cover design, and my son, Lionel Johnson, skillful and infinitely patient in making my computer serve me well.

I'm grateful also for my agent, Molly Friedrich, who is not just top-notch but wise and witty, the best combination, and my editor, Carolyn Marino, who has a fine eye and taste, a real editing pencil, and a most efficient assistant, Wendy Lee.

Finally, my thanks to the *Los Angeles Times* for my many years there and the space to write the columns that provided Polly with ideas for her letters.

PROLOGUE

When it was all over, the five women would marvel that it had taken a death to change their lives. They stood in a row—Polly, Charlotte, Dinah, Justine, Kat—under the opaque glass ceiling of the Columbarium-in-the-Canyon, looking up at Ginger's niche high on the Wall of Inurnment. There was little to see: Ginger's husband had ordered the bare minimum, just name and dates, to mark her place.

Initially they stood in silence, subdued by the confines of the place. The ceiling panels flooded the long room with light, but the glass was bottle green and the twelve-foot walls were windowless, giving the whole vault a cool underwater feeling that removed it even more from the world outside. Also, they had already grieved so long for Ginger that when they finally spoke, they talked less of her and more of everything that had happened in the past half year and how, as Polly said, it had all started with a death.

"Not just a death," said Kat bitterly, "but a murder." She alone was weeping.

"Not at first," said Polly. "Just a death and a mystery. No wonder we felt like we were in a novel. That's how they all start now."

"Pursuing killers is all that's left to the modern hero," said Charlotte. "Except that ours was more like a quest than a pursuit, a quest for vengeance."

Dinah, abstracted since they'd come, had nonetheless been listening. "What's amazing to me is what it did for all of us," she mused. "So much for the classical idea that revenge is a goal that destroys you."

"I thought we agreed that what we did was more justice than revenge," said Justine, something tremulous in her careful voice.

"Whatever it was, we did it," declared Polly, turning to leave, "and we got them good. Ginger was right about seizing power wherever you can."

Kat, who was tall enough, reached up to run her fingers over the bas-relief letters of Ginger's name. "Ginger would have loved the whole thing," she said softly, and followed her friends out into the California sunlight.

1

For seventy-four years the Palatine Club had held a weeklong August retreat at Poderoso Pines. It was the longest-running tradition in the oldest men's club in California. They had missed 1942, what with the pressure on businesses to produce war matériel, but not a single season during the Depression years.

Now there was a dead woman on the bridle path beyond the east grove, and the retreat, only half over, was in danger of being ruined.

She was fully clothed, if not according to the dress code for women guests at the club's town house in the city. This was the country, after all, and she was not an invited guest. No women were allowed at Poderoso Lodge. Fortunately she was outside the fence.

For much of the night, she had lain belly-up on the dark forest path, like a fish floating in a bed of kelp. Now and then the moon broke through the clouds, but the pines were tall, the Douglas firs thick in this part of the woods, and what little light reached the forest floor only dappled the path like moonlight on moving water.

She was slight, her limbs splayed out at what could have been painful angles. There was no visible line between skin and clothing, her fair hair and skin very pale and the folds of her dress rippled out around her. A high-heeled sandal was tethered to one foot by its ankle strap. Several times she seemed to sigh, unless it was a breeze moving through the cooled forest. The edges of her dress lifted and settled, and leaves shifted around her body on its soft pallet. Sometimes her hands stirred, made little sculling motions by her side and then were still; sometimes her feet twitched.

Through the night no one saw her. Even if someone had caught a movement or a shape, it would have been thought an illusion, a trick of the eye and the hour. Many of the people there were already quite drunk. Besides, the area was secure, the atmosphere protected, and a body, dead or dying, was unfitting.

Over the years the Palatine Club had made its mountain acreage a place of ease and beauty, replacing the original rough outbuildings with grand resort architecture, then continually beefing up the furnishings with more mahogany and leather. It looked rich and private, the kind of enclave to which the entitled return every year, every generation.

It was carefully kept that way. The club rented it out a dozen times a year for select gatherings up to a week long—corporate retreats for upper management, business-school seminars for young presidents, a governors' conference. A writers' workshop, a jazz festival, even a museum curators' colloquium were rejected as mere amusements. For three weeks in midsummer, the place was opened to the families of members. Then the badminton and croquet and horseshoe sets were brought out, the swings set up, the stables contracted out to a wrangler company, and the canoes and rowboats mended and painted and piled on the docks and boathouse shelves.

Year after year the same families returned to the same cottages for their assigned week—the same every year, with the same assigned tables in the lodge dining room. For those weeks only, the patios and driveways at each cottage were strewn with tricycles and strollers, towels and swimsuits drying in the sun. The Adirondack chairs were brought down from the terrace of the lodge and scattered by twos and threes around the lawn that sloped to the lake, and there the mothers sat and watched the children playing in the shallows along the beach. Briefly the club grounds were lively with shouts and laughter, the rhythmic bounce of balls on clay, the smack of birdies against racquets, splashing water. Like many such places, it seemed inviolate, untouched by time or wear, the summer nights and long afternoons engraved in the memories of the children and their children's children, who never dreamed of going elsewhere.

When the men came to the August retreat, it was like conference time again, with the lingering flavor of summer camp. The horses were gone, and the strollers and swings, but the nets stayed up and racquets were available. Floats still bobbed on the lake, and corrals on either side of the wood pier were filled with small boats.

The night the woman lay on the path beyond the fence was calm but hardly quiet. Down the path, over the chain link fence and across the field, there was the sound of drums and the glow of torches at the lakefront. All the cottages and cabins were silent, each recessed in its woodsy grove like the cottage of the seven dwarfs. Above the lawn the main lodge was dark, its porch deserted, the sconce lights dimmed. Everyone was at the lake for the evening ceremonies. Men in white shirts lined the banks and sat on the grassy slope. Others manned the flotilla of dinghies, canoes, and rowboats that rocked gently out on the water.

Perhaps a dozen in brown monks' robes, hooded, stood at the water's edge near the pier.

Drumrolls, a burst of light, and a chant—"Atlas, rise! Atlas, rise! Atlas, rise!"—came from the several hundred assembled men. Klieg lights snapped on, illuminating a figure at the end of the pier, crouched in the vapors that swirled out from dry-ice machines. Slowly he got to one knee, then to his feet, apparently straining under a huge and shining white globe a yard in diameter. It was a professional body, oiled and bulbously muscular, one arm extended down behind him and one up in front to balance the orb on his upper back and neck.

"Atlas, rise! Atlas, rise!" The chant was louder, faster. Dramatically he raised the globe above his head and turned three times in the spotlight, vapor swirling to his waist. He held the pose, and a baritone voice, amplified, intoned, "Atlas, Atlas, take your rest, weight of world may you divest / And briefly here amid the Pines will rest as well the Palatines."

"Atlas, rest! Atlas, rest!" the crowd chanted, and the big man lowered the globe to the dock, where it disappeared in the vapor, rolled away lightly and easily by unseen hands. From the waistband of his loincloth, Atlas drew a set of wooden pipes, put it to his mouth, and walked off the pier and into the trees as the spotlights dimmed and the audience cheered and whistled and the sound came back on the night air.

Beyond the pier, some three hundred yards out in the lake, flames rushed skyward from a stage made of two wooden floats tied together and anchored to the lake bottom. Within a semicircle of torches toward the back of the stage, a group of robed and hooded brethren turned up the gas on a big fire pit embedded in fake gray boulders and pine boughs at center stage. They were starting the traditional fire ceremony, a celebration of the year past and dedication to the year ahead, with declamations in both Latin and English, punctuated by dramatic bursts of colored flames.

Out on the sloping grass lawn, some watched intently, some chatted, and some, done in by hours of drinking, just sagged against neighbors. But all, to a man, had demonstrable stature and strength. They were lawyers, executives, and government officials, captains, commanders, and chiefs. One could have put together dozens of boards of directors from the assembled group, with little overlap. For over fifty years, such men had come to the annual retreat to put aside adult responsibilities and return to the simple vulgarity of camp life. They could play at being noncompetitive because they had already prevailed in competition, and their presence at this bucolic summit proved it.

The August "High Camp" was a departure from the club's activities in the city, centered on a downtown brownstone open for lunch and dinner, press conferences and financial briefings—all conservative and exclusive and, unlike High Camp, not much fun. The retreat was even more welcome because the club was embattled, fighting antidiscrimination suits filed by three Jewish lawyers and a group of businesswomen. To these, club lawyers had responded that they did have Jewish members (one of whom turned out to be an Episcopalian since his marriage thirty years before and the other proposed but never actually admitted) and that women would be uncomfortable as members, given the nude swimming in the basement pool and the bawdy club revues. And invoked their right of privacy, right to freedom of association and assembly, and right to run around at High Camp in their underwear and urinate against trees.

For the duration the annual camp in the Pines was safe. And since the question of fairness now rested with the courts, it could be a very long duration.

It was at the end of the fire ceremony, midway in the festivities, that the woman in white had been carried out of one of the far cottages and through the woods to the edge of the property. By then even the laggards had gone down to the lake, and the upper groves were deserted.

There was no one to see when two men clambered over the wood stile and, holding her under the arms and knees, lowered the woman to the forest path on the other side and dropped a small purse next to her. No one heard the disturbance a little later in the cottage on the other side of the hill and behind the lodge. There was the sound of snuffling, but muted, as if someone were pressing his face into a pillow in his bunk. Once he sobbed aloud, and another voice hissed, "For Christ's sake, Cannon. Cut it out."

The two began to argue, voices rising, and a third voice said sharply, "Stop. It's done, done and over. It's nothing." The weeper began to remonstrate, and the sharp voice cut him off. "I said it's nothing. She's nothing . . . nothing."

Over the next hour and a half, the high mood of the lakeside gathering collapsed into buffoonery. There were water tricks, pie jokes, a blackface number, and several sophomoric skits in drag. And the evening closed with a toga-clad Diogenes lifting high his lantern and scattering dollar bills over the water. There was no clapping, just laughter and a murmur of talk as the men rose from the grass and moved up the slope to the lodge.

A thin night wind curled through the trees. The moon, directly above the pines, shone straight down to splotch the forest floor.

The woman on the path shuddered several times, and the thin fabric of her dress fluttered at her upper legs, her shoulders. Just before the first light seeped up from the horizon, she sighed. With a sudden deflating of the torso, she sank deeper into the leaves, and on this last breath all animation left her.

2

The law came to Poderoso Lodge at breakfast. It was a linen meal, like lunch and dinner, served in the same cavernous dining room with its huge, high ceiling beams, trophy heads of buffalo, longhorns, and bears, and a fireplace that could accommodate five standing men. Service began at seven, and by nine the big room was filled with sunlight and men in deck shoes and Levi's Dockers, some of whom had been up since before six-thirty, when the stock exchange opened in New York. Given the light and the view of the lawn and the lake, many took their coffee through the French doors to the porch that ran three-quarters of the way around the lodge. The men's voices rose above the clink of china cup on saucer, but they weren't loud: There was something about the setting that encouraged hush.

Terry Fleming always drove up the road from town very slowly. The stately approach to the old lodge seemed to demand it. It was not that he was cowed, although most locals were, and he did feel some awe for the site—the century-old lodge with its big gray stones, its seven chimneys, the tall, paned windows, and the long drive that wound up the hill under a dense canopy of old pines and fir. The woods were no deeper here than anywhere else on the mountain, but local people were used to homes set within twenty feet of a gravel road, with various items of machinery and transport rusting at the side of the lot. To them these were summer homes to end all summer homes, many of the "cottages" several times the size of most houses in town.

The town police chief, Fleming was a year-round resident and by definition a "local," but he had first come to Poderoso Pines as a summer kid in a summer home that his parents rented every year when their children were young. He understood about summer homes and the privilege accorded those who occupied them. He even understood big stately homes, having gone to a college where the main streets were lined with fraternity houses, including his own. But he had wanted to be a lawman since he was little, and college had suggested no more interesting life. Besides, he wanted to live in a high forest town like Poderoso Pines, so when a job there opened up after he was three years out of the Los Angeles Police Academy and wilting on the streets in mid-Wilshire, he took it.

Thus he now found himself driving slowly up the hill in the town's one police car, a '91 Chevrolet Caprice, accompanied by Wiley Shortt, his very young, very local deputy. Wiley was neither wily nor short. He was basically an Adam's apple on a stick, several inches over six feet and only a few inches thick. He was also somewhat slow, inclined to constant and plodding review of recent events in his effort to take them in.

"So it was round about seven they picked her up," Wiley said, thinking it over. "Anybody up at the big house know what was wrong with her?"

"Wiley," said Fleming patiently, "it was Romero who found her. The gardener. He knows a dead person when he sees one and isn't about to stop and discuss it with the rich boys. He just brought her to the fire station in his wheelbarrow, in case there was a spark left to work with."

He sighed, not happy with the breakup of a crime scene but glad the club management hadn't gotten there before he did. Fleming had no animosity toward the club, though there were always some members who came into town of an evening and got offensively drunk in the not-so-smart watering holes on its outskirts. He wasn't even critical of the annual retreat, with its silly ceremonies, buffoonery, and famous peeing-against-trees.

He figured it was the participants' onetime, condensed version of a year of Friday nights, in which a bunch of men who'd known each other long and well would get together to play cards, cracking jokes and belittling women and bragging of deals they'd pulled and ball games whose outcomes they'd predicted. Maybe for the rich there were no such Friday nights, just dinner parties and fancy benefits and art auctions, and for such men the summer retreat was a rare opportunity, thoroughly exploited.

Truth to tell, Fleming felt sorry for them in their three-piece suits and, feeling sorry, didn't feel subservient. He was careful of them, like most of the locals—an accommodation justified by the revenue they gave the little town. And he was easy with that, and with the club's officials, having worked out a relationship in which he was not obsequious but deferential and the club officials were not deferential but respectful of his authority.

"Jesus, look at the wheels," said Wiley as they pulled into the parking lot. Wiley was too new to have established any relationship with the club management. His only experience so far had been picking up drunken club members at local taverns and taking them home, where their assigned steward, summoned by the concierge, hauled them off in a golf cart without comment.

"They're rich, Wiley," said Fleming, swinging his legs out of the driver's seat and shrugging his arms into his uniform jacket. "Rich people have rich cars." And he started up the front steps.

The lobby was almost empty, except for a man in madras shorts lingering over the morning newspaper and another, already in his city suit, at the front desk arranging an early departure. The concierge, off to one side, was sun-streaked and handsome, one of many actors who worked the retreat. Fleming knew him slightly. He'd attended a meeting with town officials the week before the retreat, and he'd come into town two days ago to thank the fire department paramedics for their quick response on a possible heart attack.

The concierge came forward immediately. "Lieutenant Fleming," he said with a little nod, barely disturbing the blond hair brushed lightly across his forehead.

"'Terry' is fine, Carl," said Fleming, as always. "Little problem here. Romero found a woman lying on the path just outside your east fence early this morning. Dead. Cause undetermined at this point."

"Young? Businesswoman?" Carl asked quietly, glancing back toward the lodge office. "Anyone know her?"

"Mid-thirties, thirty-seven, in fact," said Fleming. "A very nice thirty-seven. Nice shape. Nice clothes. A blonde, your color."

"What happened?" said Carl. "Should I get the boss?"

"Well, you might tell him," said Fleming. "We'll be roping the area. It's an unexplained death, after all, and maybe a crime site. And we'd like to talk to anyone who might know anything or saw or heard anything last night. So you should ask before anyone leaves, of course, including him." He nodded toward the man checking out. "I'm sure you understand."

"Of course," said Carl. He clasped his hands, the universal gesture of service.

They studied each other, each wondering how much he should say or ask.

"Any ideas on her identity?" asked Carl.

"Well, she had an L.A. ID in a little purse, not much more," said Fleming.

The concierge couldn't suppress a sigh of relief. Bad enough a dead woman on the property, or near it. A dead local woman could be a disaster. "Well, that's not surprising," he said. "Probably here on the usual business this time of year. But why in the woods?"

Fleming shrugged and turned away. "Call me," he said.

"Right." Carl, in a half bow, watched them leave.

"They took it seriously?" asked Wiley as they crossed the parking lot.

"They'll take it seriously," said Fleming, opening the door of the Caprice.

"Too bad you don't have one of those beauties," said Wiley, taking a last look at the BMWs and Jaguars.

"Yeah," said Fleming, "Too bad. But I got peace of mind."

Milo Till and his guests had one of the larger cottages. The Palatine Club, for all the solidarity of its membership, didn't belabor the principle of equality. There were several levels of accommodations. Some were quite rustic, with the kinds of kitchen appliances and plain furniture and hooked rugs found in summerhouses. Others, behind the same stone and cedar walls, were luxurious suites, with leather furniture, fur rugs, étagères filled with crystal and china.

Milo Till got one of the latter because he was important in California, both financially and politically. A land developer, a venture capitalist, a wheeler-dealer with a gift for playing tax codes, regulations, and trade law to his own advantage, Till was also a heavy investor in political campaigns and politicians. He was a short man, but slim and straight, given to thin-striped Oxford shirts and preppy fabric belts. He had curly black hair and an affable face that belied a very declarative voice, an authoritative mien, and a well-known control over a considerable number of people and institutions.

He had been coming to the retreat for fifteen years. For six of them he'd brought Mitchell Reinhart as one of his guests. Reinhart was a divorce lawyer and successful in California and beyond, the first lawyer of choice for men with extensive assets to protect. When he was quoted in the press, as he was whenever the subject was divorce, his name was usually followed by the phrase "known as Mr. Divorce." The two men were actually friends, and business bound their friendship even closer. Till had been through two divorces, both Reinhart products. Reinhart had shares in two downtown hotels, a Valley mini-mall and some undeveloped foothills, all Till products. When Till's associates had marital problems, he got them onto Reinhart's calendar. Many of Reinhart's clients became partners in Till properties, which one would only know if one knew where to look and under what names.

Till's relationship with L. Walker Cannon, his other guest, was another matter, less a friendship than a useful association with potential for greater future usage. Personally, intellectually, even politically, Cannon was a cipher, but being well-born and well-married, he was seized on by more substantial politicians and thrust up the ladder to higher office. He was now a state senator, running for U.S. senator and beyond, and Milo Till was one of his handlers.

It was Reinhart, lingering over coffee, considering a scotch, who overheard Fleming's inquiries and, with no visible sign of haste, hurried the news back to Till. Barefoot and in shirttails, Milo Till began pacing the room's perimeter, chewing the inside of his cheek. Cannon sat stiffly in the center of a big leather club chair, his loafered feet crossed at the ankle, his thin hands fluttering nervously in his lap.

"I'll talk to them," said Till finally, halted in the middle of the room.

"Why?" Cannon stammered. "No one knows. No one saw. You said so."

Till and Reinhart looked at each other.

"Walker, it has to be met," said Till evenly.

"Can't you pay someone?" asked Cannon.

Reinhart looked at the ceiling, looked at Till, dropped his head to his chest. Nothing in Till's posture or gaze changed.

"Walker, it has to be met head-on," he said again. "Just remember, both of you, all of us: She wasn't here on the grounds. Wasn't. Here."

"It wasn't even us." Cannon was agitated, one heel chattering against the hardwood floor, his hands fluttering before his face. "The point has to be that it wasn't us. We don't know her."

"Dear God," murmured Reinhart.

"No," said Till patiently, addressing a child. "She wasn't here. You give something, but you keep it simple."

Till had worked out the details by the time he drove into the center of town and parked across from the police station. The town of Poderoso Pines was Y-shaped, with six to eight shops on each arm of the Y and the main highway running down the stem and out of town. It was a mix of old businesses, updated businesses, and new boutiques. The architecture was still small-town, with clapboard or log facades, and many buildings had porches, balconies, and paned glass windows, like old-fashioned drugstores.

It was a peaceful and profitable coexistence of old and new, of long-time merchants like Kranke's Plumbing and Berte's Café and trendy new boutiques like Bread Alone and Rhinestone! The rural and the chic ran side by side down one arm of town and up the other, and at the town's center point were the *Mountain High Times* weekly paper and the police station.

Given the proximity of the two offices, and the usual lack of both crime and news, it wasn't surprising that Oz Elkind, the paper's editor, was sitting in the station. Indeed, he was such a fixture there that no one but Milo Till was surprised when he made no move to leave and the financier found himself addressing three people instead of the one he expected.

Fleming and Shortt sat at opposite sides of the big desk behind the counter. Elkind slouched in an old club chair between the front door and the tray table that held the coffeepot and paper cups, his long, thin legs stretched across the door.

When Fleming came to the counter, Till introduced himself as a club member and said he understood there had been an accident and they were seeking helpful information about a woman found dead outside the club compound. "I might have something to add," he said, "though my knowledge is limited. I was with her for some of yesterday evening." He watched as Fleming wrote down his name.

"I met her at Reilly's, the usual thing," he went on. Wiley nodded, indicating his familiarity with the usual thing. "She said her name was Ginger, she was attractive, we had a few drinks, we came to an arrangement."

Wiley nodded, acknowledging more of the usual thing.

"A few hours, five hundred dollars. She had a motel room." Terry Fleming raised his eyebrows. "We didn't get there, of course," Till continued. "We got in my car, drove around a bit. She could talk, actually. Said she was up from L.A. We stopped at that overlook—Vista Point?—on the hill road, fooled around a while, you know. . . ."

Wiley knew. He nodded.

"Then we got into an argument about the sum we'd agreed on. Next thing I know, she was out of the car and stomped off without her money. Any money."

He paused, but nobody spoke. Elkind was studiously pushing back his cuticles. Wiley Shortt was nodding slowly, judiciously, pursing his lips.

"Yes?" prodded Fleming.

"So I went after her, we argued some more, I walked back to the car, waited a bit, then drove up to the club, figuring she'd go back down the road to the village. That where you found her?"

"Not far," said Fleming, and let another silence fall.

"So what do you think happened?" asked Till. "Was it a fall? A car?"

Fleming carefully aligned the sheets of paper on which he'd been writing, then realigned them under Till's gaze. "We can reach you through the club, Mr. Till?"

"Absolutely," said Till. He stood a minute more with his hands on the counter, then left.

Wiley Shortt came around the counter and stood at the front window to watch him leave. "You know," he said thoughtfully, "that one's got the spiffy car *and* peace of mind."

Elkind watched Fleming staple his few sheets of paper, put them into a manila file, and put the file in a desk drawer. "You going back to the lodge?" Elkind asked.

"Nah, he's it," said Fleming. "That's all we'll get from them."

"So what are you going to do with her?" asked Wiley.

Fleming's decision was quick. He liked his life. He had taken courses in criminal justice, he knew the law. He had weighed good and evil. But it wasn't that simple. Or maybe it was even simpler: He liked his life.

"Don't have to do anything," he said. "She's got an L.A. ID on her, like lots of them; these guys don't want Riverside gals. L.A.'s got nothing on her, but neither do we. And they have a coroner. So we'll ship her down there."

"I dunno," said Wiley Shortt, stroking his hairless jawline. He had been a deputy almost a year and seen nothing more violent than a visiting team member pulling a knife at a high school basketball game and three wife beatings, all the same couple. "Seems to me we could have a murder here," he opined, "given the remote setting, the hour, the bruises, the man-woman thing."

"Come on, Wiley," said Fleming. "To have murder you need four things. You gotta have a bad guy, you gotta have a victim, you gotta have someone who wants to catch a murderer, and you gotta have someone who cares whether it was murder. We got this fine upstanding citizen here, we got a dolly, and we got us. As for someone who cares, we don't know. If someone like that comes forward in L.A., we just backtrack. No sweat."

3

The six women had been meeting every Monday for over a year, and the death of Ginger Pass was the first thing they'd ever discussed that involved no questions of perception and posed no problems of handling. It was incontrovertible, all the more solid because there was so little information.

She was dead. They didn't know the how or the why. The discovery and identification of her body had been on the news, but details were as scant as when the news left Poderoso Pines. Stunned, they struggled to put the what and where together with the person they'd known.

"Are we the only ones who knew she was a hooker?" asked Polly, who had laid out supper for her children and hurried in wearing her usual jeans and white button-down shirt, her curly red hair pulled behind one ear with twine.

Polly Crother was a young widow and fairly merry, though it

demanded some effort. Naturally direct, she had come to take pleasure in being blunt during her eight years alone, without husband, parents, or siblings to embarrass by her behavior. There's no need to be harsh, she could hear her mother's voice say now. She ignored it.

"Don't say 'hooker,'" said Justine, her face tightened to porcelain by distress. A county administrator, Justine Teyama was so careful with her words that by the time she chose them, the conversation had often passed her by.

"Come on, she was one," said Charlotte DeLong, always impatient with positive thinking in a life she considered at best neutral. She was forty-eight, the oldest in the group, a lawyer aged further by constant immersion in the afterlife: She specialized in estate planning.

"Ginger wasn't afraid to acknowledge her trade either," she added. "Not in Harold's circles, of course."

"It doesn't matter what she was, at least to us," said Polly, working her clump of hair around and around her hand. "We knew her apart from her work, if I can call it that, and her home life. We also suspected that of the two, she preferred hooking to Harold."

"But what happened to her?" asked Kat, who had been weeping off and on since they'd arrived, so that both her face and the front of her blouse were mottled by her bursts of tears. Katharine Hurley was as generous as she was beautiful. And beautiful she was, tall and fluid, with long, muscular arms and legs and broad shoulders and heavy-falling blond hair—the best advertisement for her own health clubs.

Affectionately, they called her "The Body," used to watching her leap from her chair, pace the small room in front of them, then fold herself to chair level again. She did so now, unself-conscious as always, and starting to cry again as she crossed to the window and pulled the blinds up.

They were on the second level of a two-story stucco building of suites set hacienda style around an atrium. All the ground-floor offices opened onto a colonnade and those on the second floor onto a balcony above. In the middle was a tropical garden, probably neatly manicured when it was planted forty years ago but now so dense that a stone bench and rock garden were almost buried in maidenhair fern and birds-of-paradise and were visible only from above.

A modern "office complex" in its day, it now seemed lovely and old world, one of many such buildings scattered around Los Angeles that had not yet been torn down for a fourplex cinema or a mini-mall. It had stayed as offices, with such a common clientele that Dinah, who was impatient with trendy fields of mental health, dubbed it the "Dysfunction Arms" and seized every chance to mock the various enterprises. A successful dermatologist who was bored with both dermatology and success, Dinah Milanskaya found dysfunction rather like her own field, offering the inquiring practitioner only moments of insight, and those never blinding.

From their own window, they could look in on various businesses catering to a variety of dysfunctions, from out-and-out psychosis to simple sloppiness. There were therapists, whose blinds were kept half tilted to obscure any view of the occupants in the big leather chairs and couches. There were also groups like their own, united only by sex or age or personal schedules that left them free at a particular time. Others shared specific problems, such as smoking, drinking, eating too much or too little. And on the first floor, near the gated entrance, there was a large, light office, all teak and white cabinets, in which two women in sleek pantsuits gave popular seminars on "clutter control," in daytime hours focusing on household mess (closets, dens, home offices) and on office mess at night.

The window was wide and tall, and while Kat wept noisily, the other four women stared into an Al-Anon meeting across the way or watched the evening sky turn deep pink over the building's tile roof. Lotte, the therapist who ran their group, sat quietly, looking from one to the other.

It was Lotte's belief that she should be a moderator, prodding discussion, occasionally halting it, but letting them go where they would. She was a matronly woman garbed in youthfulness. She pulled her gray hair back at the nape of her neck or twisted it up under two wood barrettes, and was given to wearing ribbed cotton tights in earth colors and huaraches and blouses with frog ties and, once, something so like a blanket that they argued for weeks whether it was in fact a blanket. Behind her back Dinah called her "the last rose of the sixties," but she was smart and thoughtful and experienced and, so far, had held her analyst's biases to a minimum.

Death, however, was not a situation that drew the best from her. "What doesn't matter is what happened," she finally said, covering her awkwardness with a tutorial stiffness. "We have to grapple with its meaning to us. The fact is that Ginger's death wrote an end to our relationship with her and we can only deal with how that affects us."

Kat began to cry again. Polly muttered, "Good Lord," and put her head into her hands.

"Lotte," said Dinah, not holding back her irritation, "when we started this group a year and a half ago, you had just come out the other side of the recovered-memory movement. As you know, it gave us some pause that you had been deep into that stuff. We only got over it by reminding ourselves that you had the good sense to drop it. But you keep having these periodic little breakdowns into jargon, and that gives us lots of pause, like now."

No one spoke. Lotte counted her fingers, recounted them, then looked around the group for comment or further censure. "I understand how you all feel," she said slowly. "Perhaps we should forget group today."

She seemed flattened but not injured. They had an easy relationship, Lotte and the group, partly because they'd argued this out sometime ago, partly because this was not a typical group.

It had started with nine. Three had been looking for something else—more, perhaps, or maybe less—and dropped out in the first few months. The six who continued were, as Lotte said, an unusually cohesive group. As individuals they had obvious similarities. All presented well, as she put it. They looked good and had comfortable, enviable lives. Work was an important part of it, though not (they all said) the only important part or even (some said) the most important.

But they all worked, with the possible exception of Ginger, and they had learned midway through their first year that she, too, was working. She had joined in group discussions but provided little personal information, most of it concerning her home, her husband, her stepdaughter, now in community college. They knew only that she'd once been a model but never advanced beyond the convention circuit—the equivalent, she said wryly, of being an old-time Betty Crocker girl who threw cake mixes to a milling crowd.

She'd met Harold Pass at an outdoor show in Las Vegas. She was dressed as a cigarette girl, circulating with a tray of sample fishing lures. Harold was ten or twelve years older than Ginger and on his third marriage. He was also quiet, serious, and rich, all qualities that appealed to Ginger immediately. He had built a very successful business designing and installing animated billboards—huge displays of blinking lightbulbs in which giant champagne glasses filled with liquid and emptied, giant eyes winked over and over again, and moons rose, traversed an electric heaven, and disappeared at the other end of the billboard.

From that he developed an even more lucrative sideline, making panoramic animated marquees for nightclubs and casinos. High above the street, his endless lines of bright showgirls kicked their way across the front of Reno's Pink Garter. Kangaroos and wallabies hopped across the pediment of the Down Under in Las Vegas. A stagecoach pulled by six horses with flashing hooves rolled over and over again across the entrance of Denver's Pony Express tavern.

Harold worked all the time and mostly in other cities, but he didn't want Ginger to work, and he wanted her home whenever he was. She was therefore alone much of the time and at loose ends. At least the other women in the group assumed she was at loose ends, and, taken in, like everyone else, by her smoky-blond hair, her careful makeup and perfect nails, her focus on Harold's activities instead of her own, they'd offered helpful suggestions for how she might occupy herself. They suggested political action, charity work, volunteering as a docent at the art museum—all of which seemed laughable later.

Finally, exasperated by her polite lack of interest but still sympathetic, they asked her exactly what she did with her time. And sitting there in her aubergine silk Armani suit, her legs in their cream hose, feet shod in Bally pumps and crossed at the ankles, she told them, "I fuck men."

They greeted this information with some disbelief—nothing to their subsequent shock that Ginger actually liked the work. Indeed, she regarded it as work, not that she needed money. Harold, as Polly once commented, didn't offer quality support, but he did provide quantity. He was rich even beyond the dreams of Hollywood, though he had no ideas or interest in how to spend the excess.

Ginger, however, had a money sense. Certainly she was very much aware of her own market value. She billed her evenings at fifteen hundred dollars and her nights, when she took one on, at twenty-five hundred—rates, she said, that were pretty much the top of the market. In a good month, when Harold was away a lot and she was busy, she could take in twenty thousand dollars, of which her share was 65 percent or thirteen thousand, with what she called her "agency" getting the rest. She could probably have taken the same amount from their joint accounts without comment from Harold, but, as she noted sardonically, she had more scruples about squandering his money than his conjugal rights.

What's more, and contrary to current sociological belief, she didn't regard her kind of service as a loss of power. On the contrary, she saw it as an exercise of power, the only actual power she had, and she had no use for the standard feminist credo about the exploited prostitute. Less acted upon than acting, she felt in control. She said go, she said come, and men, lots of men, followed blindly.

Here, too, she seemed the exception to the group. The others, for all their apparent success and influence, felt that their progress forward had stalled to the point of derailment at this stage of their lives. Every one of them looked good, looked fulfilled, but they had a pervasive sense that they hadn't ended up where they wanted to go and had no idea how to move on.

Ginger, if anything, seemed calmer and more comfortable with her life than the others. She joined in the discussions, had sympathetic and practical comments on the questions everyone else posed but asked nothing for herself. Once they knew what she did, she would make humorous references to the scheduling problems of a double life or sharp and insightful little remarks about the temperament of men, but she showed no real concern over her circumstances. When pushed, she admitted only that she was a bit lonely and was there for the company. But when someone—probably Charlotte—commented understandingly that the kind of women she met in her work weren't really her type, she said, "Maybe I am their type. Or maybe the type isn't what you think."

Whatever her true type, Ginger hadn't interested Lotte as much as the other women had. Like most therapists, Lotte did better with doubt and fear than with Ginger's easy accommodations, and Polly was inclined to forgive her seemingly inhumane reaction to Ginger's death.

Now, waving aside the therapist's suggestion to terminate the day's meeting, Polly said gently, "It seems to me, Lotte, that the prime question is not what Ginger's death means to us. It is what happened to her. She wasn't suicidal. She was healthy. She was on a job. She was going out of town—she didn't say where, but she was definitely up and looking forward to it, in her weird way. Considering."

"It wasn't weird," said Dinah. "And even if her life was weird, she liked it. She wasn't depressed about it. She wasn't even depressed about Harold anymore: She didn't dislike him and seemed to be okay with the way she'd worked things out."

"Then why was she here?" asked Kat.

"She probably realized that, clinically speaking, it was weird," said Dinah.

"Did she die in some weird way?" said Kat. "I mean, do we know?"

"It just said she was 'found dead,'" said Justine. "There was only a short news story, mostly because of her husband's name. Nothing in the obituary listings. Nothing about any sort of service."

"Do you think we could get her death certificate?" asked Kat.

"Not until it's filed," said Charlotte. "Though maybe you could get to it, Justine. It's a county office, whatever county it was filed in—where she lived or where she died."

"Listen," said Polly, "we don't have to get sleuthy, at least not yet. Why don't we just ask Harold?"

"I don't know about that," said Justine. "Isn't that like meddling?"

"No, it's concern," said Polly. "It's caring. We're her friends."

"I'm not sure friendship's a concept Harold can comprehend," said Charlotte wryly.

"We'll go there personally," said Polly. "What can he do, shut the door in our faces?"

Their only experience with Harold was at Charlotte and Avery's New Year's open house the previous January. He and Ginger had come late and left early, and he'd stood by himself at one side of the arch between hall and living room and didn't move, talk, or eat. He was a pale and chilly man, and oddly grim for someone in such a whimsical line of work, as if the creation of flashing lights and bright moving figures had sapped all the levity from his person. Muted as she was in his presence, Ginger was his only coloration.

Lotte rose, slipping into her heavy leather sandals. "I really should excuse myself at this point," she said. "I understand the feelings of the group at this juncture, and your need to do something, but I'm uncomfortable with the action you're taking."

"We understand. Your business is reaction," said Charlotte. "You have every right to be uncomfortable with action, whatever it is."

So Lotte left, telling them they were free to use the room, which was usually vacant before and after their meeting. In fact, she'd chosen that particular room because it wasn't popular, being far from restrooms, phones, the file room, the little library a dozen therapists shared. It was one of the best things about Lotte, that she was compulsive enough to leave nothing to chance.

Her footsteps came back to them clearly, moving around the balcony, down the stone stairs at the opposite corner, out the heavy gate, which clanged shut, shaking the floor under them. Everyone immediately looked at Dinah. "It's nothing," Kat said quickly, reaching across Ginger's empty seat to put a hand on Dinah's knee.

"It's the gate," said Justine at the same time.

"I know," said Dinah, who was terrified of earthquakes. The slightest movement of a building upset her. "Was that one?" she'd gasp, wild-eyed, instantly washed of color. "Was that one?" And she'd grip the sides of her seat as they rushed to assure her that something other than a quake had jarred the building or rumbled over the street outside.

"Better not be an earthquake," Kat would add sometimes, and they'd all laugh, knowing that Kat herself, for different reasons, was afraid of any public accident—earthquake, flood, auto crash, mugging, a fall. Kat had breast implants, which she had come to hate, and, hating them as she did, she was convinced that if she lay dying, dependent on valiant efforts at resuscitation, the paramedics' paddles would bounce off her chest.

They sat now for a while after Lotte left, in general agreement that they couldn't just sit out Ginger's death. "We owe her," said Polly, "because we knew her double life. I'm not saying we knew the real Ginger or anything, but we probably knew as much as possible." She stopped. "I don't know what I mean."

"In any case, it's not right she should just be written off," said Kat, not crying now.

Everyone nodded. No one knew how they should act on it.

"Well, first," said Dinah, "we need information. You don't know anything unless you know how someone died."

"But we have to be prepared," said Charlotte. "In my experience— though I guess you all know this already—death isn't necessarily an end. It's more often the beginning of the true story."

Justine had borne a look of consternation throughout the discussion. "I don't know," she said. "I just don't think we should upset her family."

"Oh, for pity's sake," said Charlotte. "I'll call Poderoso Pines tomorrow and see what they'll say." She turned to Polly. "You want to do Harold?"

"What a thought," Polly muttered.

"I'll go with her," said Kat quickly. "Barnaby can hold down the fort."

As a decision it wasn't much, but it gave all in the group a feeling of decisiveness.

For Polly that feeling didn't dissipate, though she spent a long evening thinking of Ginger, "found dead" who-knew-where. Much of that time, she sat at her computer composing a complaint letter—her usual way of fending off memories and using her habitual sleeplessness to some advantage.

The other women in the group had recognized immediately that Polly wrote letters as ministers preached, as doctors treated, as lawyers filed suits. It wasn't the most active way of righting wrongs, but Polly had a bent for examination and a talent for complaint and had refined both to a craft, writing at least one letter a week and keeping careful files. Since the death of her young husband, she had understood well that one was powerless against certain blows of fate or the wholesale violence and tyranny in the world. But from her own house on a Hollywood hill, Polly could at least challenge the unfairnesses in daily life, the power of one person over another, a business over its customers, a government over its citizens.

This particular night she was writing to the state senate's transportation committee:

> There are over 8 million car phones in use today and their users operate them unregulated, though such people are as dangerous as drunk drivers.
>
> We all know people who've bashed into the car ahead while dialing a number. We've all seen freeway drivers drift into another lane while talking on their phones. For anyone who hasn't, I offered at your July hearings the example of my own husband, killed at an intersection because someone driving a car was also dialing on his car phone.
>
> Once just for the rich, car phones are now widely advertised and marketed. They generate lots of discussion, but it's all about gimmicks, price, and service, not their safety.
>
> In Britain anyone seen talking on a phone while driving can be immediately fined for not driving "with due care." Here that driver has to be speeding or weaving or tailgating as well to be stopped, although even the product instructions say one "should not use" cellular phones while driving.
>
> No one does anything to change this situation—not the DMV, not the insurance industry, certainly not the phone vendors, to whom it's just business as usual. So it's up to you legislators. If you can regulate seat belts and ban the use of stereo headphones while driving, you can certainly handle this.
>
> Sincerely yours . . .

This was a subject on which Polly had especially strong feelings, but it still got her standard format. Anecdote, statement of current situation and basic problem, paragraph of comment and/or demand. She tinkered with it a bit more and printed it out.

Good enough, said her mother, but you're wasting your time. No one cares.

Let's not get into that again, said Polly. No one cares enough about anything. People get away with murder.

It depends on who's murdered, said her mother, always after the last word.

No, said Polly, it depends more on who did it.

4

Charlotte made her calls to Poderoso Pines the next day—to the police, the newspaper, the San Bernardino medical examiner, and a local lawyer she knew slightly. The day after that, she reported the results to everyone, catching Polly about to drive her children to school.

"It's in the jurisdiction of L.A. County," said Charlotte without greeting or preamble. Charlotte omitted amenities as she omitted vowels in personal memos: She tried to keep the chores and exchanges of daily life stripped to their minimums.

"So getting something from Harold matters even more now," said Polly, but Charlotte had already hung up the phone. "Good-bye" was one of the words she thought unnecessary.

The Crothers lived high in the Hollywood Hills on one of the looped cul-de-sacs that formed the final upward tendrils of city streets far below. The landscape was all scrub and chaparral, sere and lion-colored much of the year, in contrast to the tropical plantings of the urban streets.

It was nothing like Seattle, where Polly grew up, but it still reminded her of the rain forest in the Olympic Peninsula. There, trees that had fallen and rotted on the moist forest floor became "nurse logs," putting down roots all along their length and sending saplings upward. The saplings then put out branches, and the branches put out twigs, and the twigs finer twigs, all stretching leafy tips to the sun. Similarly, Hollywood streets shot up the canyons from the crosstown boulevards, and then those streets sprouted branches up the canyons. From those sprang finer streets, up the canyon walls, narrowing and twisting as they followed the topography to the ridges above.

Polly ascended several levels on her way home from the schools—Andrea's in an old residential area of spacious homes and Jeremy's in a commercial area close to downtown—climbing up and up and then out into open air, above the shade of the live oaks and sycamores. Feeling the morning sun, she thought of Ginger's fondness for sun and warmth and light, of how she'd made a little ritual of opening the curtains and raising the blinds as soon as she arrived at Monday meetings.

The house was empty, so Polly could give in to her unsettled feelings and drift from one morning chore to another. She brought the garbage cans in from the street, went through old mail, opened the dining room drapes to let light fall on her plants, going down a few stairs to the kitchen, up a few stairs to the den, up a half flight to the children's rooms. The house was stepped down the hill like an Alpine funicular—one of its charms when she first saw it, later one of its failings, given the uneven indoor travel. More vertical than horizontal, there was no real backyard either, but a series of decks and side terraces at each level, and at the bottom a strip of garden the width of the house and five to ten feet deep. Many houses were like that in the hills, clinging to the slope where there was a slope, cantilevered out from the hill where it was nearly perpendicular.

The Los Angeles real estate business was the most creative in the country. Not put off by the paucity of usable land amid the gorges and ridges of the canyons, local Realtors enthusiastically sold land that was so vertical that in some cases they were really selling airspace. Nighttime justified their hype. From almost every point in her house, Polly could see houses similarly perched on the canyon sides, their lights running all the way down the hillsides to spill out on the wide plain of city lights below, far from the separate world of the canyon.

By noon Polly was at her desk, had moved twenty-five hundred shares of stock and made fifteen thousand dollars. Look, Mom, she exulted, I made fifteen thousand dollars. Money isn't happiness, her mother said dryly, and certainly not that little money. But it was pretty good for an hour's work at a home computer, and Polly's pleasure couldn't be punctured.

Her computer skills were minimal. She treated her IBM like an ATM for investments: It offered her access to current information on all the financial markets and to her brokerage, which executed her remote commands swiftly. It was a discount operation, but capable of brisk and attentive service for a good customer. No one there had any idea that the volume of orders they handled on this one account issued from a widow in a purple sweatsuit working at a PC on her sleeping porch.

In fact, Polly had neither background nor inherent interest in finance. She had gone from graduate work in history to law school but never took the bar exam because the law didn't deal with right and wrong as much as she'd hoped and justice had too often seemed to turn on strength, cleverness, or chance.

Still, she was dedicated to working for fairness. "The Caped Crusader," her husband used to call her. He meant it nicely, admiring her notes and files on consumer problems and business practices, enjoying her battles with banks, stores, credit bureaus, and the phone company— all a personal crusade to impose some slight order on an amoral marketplace and, by extension, on life itself. You can't right every wrong, he'd say fondly, but you sure can figure out why it happened.

In fact, you can't always do that either. Consider Polly's husband, who on the Sunday he died had waved good-bye at the kitchen door, forever frozen in her memory framed by the screen door, his features blurred by the mesh. It was barely even a parting. He was there, then he wasn't, gone from the Earth in that kind of instantaneous transport she'd always associated with the Virgin Mary's assumption into heaven.

Unheralded by angels, unaccompanied, Dan was assumed into heaven barely noticed. He had left on his bicycle at noon, dropped by his office and a nearby juice bar, biked up and around Mount Hollywood, and was headed home when he was hit by a speeding lowrider and tossed twenty feet up toward his final destination. As it happened, the lowrider had itself just been clipped by a man dialing a number on his car phone. The car was hot, its teenage driver took off, and Dan was dead, a situation unlikely to change while the police conducted a high-speed freeway chase after what television called "the suspect."

By eight that night, Polly had left the children with a neighbor and gone looking for him, following the imagined crumbs of his usual trail from home to office, from office to juice bar and up around the mountain, then to hospital, police station, and finally the morgue. There he waited for her, fully identified, his wallet and keys in a Baggie by his elbow. Law student that she was, all she could say, all she could think was, This is actionable.

Probably it was. But still he was gone, leaving her just thirty-one and alone with two small children, a lot of plans to reorganize, and a tremendous loss.

Not that loss was new to her. Her parents were dead before her young husband. Her father, who was handsome, fleet, outdoorsy, and athletic, had died from the feet up. He'd gotten a number of chigger bites at the start of a pack trip and characteristically ignored them. By the trip's end they'd become infected wounds, and finally a necrosis that moved up his whole body, visible and thoroughly resistant to treatment. Her mother, with equal appropriateness, died from the head down. Intellectual, rational to a fault, and somewhat disputatious, she had Alzheimer's before she was sixty. They'd seen the first sign of it when they found her in her beloved garden, surrounded by flower stems and strips of material, weeping because she didn't understand why she'd cut up her skirt with the gardening shears. At the last it affected not just her thought but her speech, her most salient characteristic. She just trailed off, taken from life in midsentence: "You never know when . . ." or "Be sure to . . ."

Oddly, Polly remembered them better than her husband, and even mourned them as a greater part of her. She missed Dan for himself, of course, but as time passed, Polly missed him most as someone with whom she had a community of interests. Nothing fancy: not politics, philosophy, even finances. It wasn't even necessary he be responsive. Just someone to whom she could say, "Andrea was really funny yesterday" or "The dishwasher broke again." And he might say, "What? Still up?" or "I took a twenty from your wallet."

Basically, we're all alone, her mother said. Yes, said Polly, but I liked the illusion of company.

About love she actually remembered very little: their first romantic weekends, some recent afternoons, a rare night out of town without children. These memories might not even have been accurate. It so disturbed her to have few specific memories that she built on them each time she called them up and no longer knew what was real and what was invention.

Not that she needed love. She was surprised how little it mattered once it was gone—so little that she didn't seek or even seize new possibilities when they were offered to her. The popularity of widowhood was quite unexpected. It wasn't mere popularity; it was pursuit. To men, and to people looking out for male friends, Polly was more appealing now than she'd ever been in active competition. Apparently a woman's sex appeal, so unfairly tarnished by divorce, was freshened by death. One was clearly a tragedy visited upon her; the other was assumed to be deserved in some way.

She felt no lack of money either. Thanks to Dan's grandmother, there were trusts to cover the children's colleges. A term life insurance policy had paid $1.25 million (a benefit doubled for accidental death). Another policy through Dan's business paid $600,000. And his two partners in the computer business, longtime friends, had arranged to "buy Polly out" of Dan's share with a monthly percentage of the gross and a balloon payoff in ten years.

On a whim born of grief, loneliness, or boredom, Polly took the $600,000 insurance benefit and began to buy and sell stocks. She had handled money before, not much, but more than her husband, who had an entrepreneurial talent for making money, not for passively multiplying it. She bought treasury bills, municipal bonds, and some shares in computer companies Dan had admired. They were all secure ventures, modestly profitable, forward-thinking and focused on product. They grew, their sales shot up, and so did their stock. As it rose and split, rose and split, she began to think one could make a living from this.

Within three years, she'd doubled the $600,000 and felt confident enough to take the rest of the money into her own hands. The more she played, the more she enjoyed it, imagining she stood on an athletic field, making moves that immediately translated into flashing scores. Sometimes she increased the excitement by playing against the clock, giving herself tight time limits to search, research, and purchase.

The trick was to be neither timid nor greedy. She allowed herself some speculation but decided at the time of purchase how long she'd hold the shares and how much profit was enough—a one-third increase in price within a half year, say, or 25 percent in a quarter. At that point she sold, even if the price was still rising. She also kept half a million in a well-managed fund, just to get the company's analyses of industry trends and the general economy. It did well, making 10 to 15 percent before tax, but she did better, making 15 to 40 percent.

Money is power, she'd always been told, but for her it was just independence, providing a sense of accomplishment that needed no one's endorsement. She got the same lift when she finished tasks in her kitchen, her laundry, her garden, even though they had no market value.

Kat came early, jabbing the doorbell so the chimes sounded a half-dozen times. "Coming, coming!" called Polly as she ran down from her office to her bedroom, from bedroom to front hall, then opened the door, instinctively flattening herself against the wall as Kat charged in.

"Hi there!" said Kat, already moving down the hall toward the kitchen, pausing briefly at the big walnut mirror over the hall table to lean forward and push back her streaked blond hair. "I know I'm early, but I figured you'd give me some coffee—decaf, please, it's after two—and we could figure out how we'd attack Harold, that okay?"

The house could barely hold Kat Hurley. The steps between rooms, the stairs, the turns, the constant change in levels confined her to small motions, when she was meant for straightaways, for free runs down long halls, the chance to step out. It wasn't her size, though she was almost six feet. It was her pace and forward motion. She was a country girl, brought up in bare feet and sunny fields, used to running with the dogs and the horses, to chasing the cows.

In fact, she had been a runner—a miler and a champion hurdler who saw in the trophies an all-American way to get to college and then to the big city and then to many more cities. After a few years of competition, however, she saw the limits, both financial and physical, of athletic achievement and turned to modeling, first swimsuit calendars, then live shows, again in swimsuits. A more compelling sight in motion than in pose, she specialized in runway work—not the best-paid fashion career but enough to fund the business that was her final goal.

She now owned and operated a chain of seven fitness clubs in Southern California. Huge complexes, they offered exercise and sports facilities, services ranging from physical therapy to facials, restaurants and juice bars, boutiques for clothing, athletic equipment and makeup. She'd made a lot of money and a good marriage with a trainer who also had a business head on his sculptured body. And now, at thirty-six, with no unrealized goals ahead, she felt she'd lost her center, her roots, and all sense of purpose.

She tended her body well, she told the group, if just for looks now, because her looks helped sell her club. Ironically, that principle had also led her to ruin herself physically. It was the breasts. In the early years of the business, when she was no longer an athlete or a model and had started using her body only for image, she had let herself drift over the line into pure vanity and had gotten breast implants.

She had only a few months of pleasure from the novelty. She couldn't race because the breasts got in the way. She could hardly exercise. Her weight was wrong, her center was off. She still ran laps and sprints and even hurdles just to stay able, but she was constantly uncomfortable. In the eyes of the world, she "looked great," but she described her body as useless—the first proof Dinah ever had, she said, that life was not automatically easier for the very beautiful.

Now Kat moved around the bedroom while Polly dressed. She fingered the toiletries on the dresser, trying on one ponytail holder and another, opening the drawers and riffling through scarves, as if she were in a college dorm or a backstage dressing room. Sometimes she stopped to stretch a leg muscle against the doorjamb, unable to keep from conditioning one body part or another at all times.

"It's not polite to keep preening your body in front of someone who doesn't have one," said Polly from the closet door.

"You do have one," said Kat. "It's just that no one can see it the way you dress. Besides, a body's all I have."

"Well, you're getting strange. You're like a man, flexing his muscles for the hall mirror when he thinks he's alone."

"Admiring your muscle," said Kat, "isn't the same as admiring your looks. God gave you one. The other is man-made, and hard work at that." She ran a bronze lipstick around her mouth and blotted. "Did you ever see Ginger look in a mirror?"

"I don't think she was vain," said Polly. "She always looked great in a country-clubby way—that beige hair, the beige suits, the beige stockings. But once it was all assembled, she didn't seem concerned. She was just wrapping her wares as attractively as she could; we all do, but more self-consciously."

Dressed in linen slacks now, Polly matched up the leg seams of her blue jeans, smoothed them over a hanger, and put them in the closet with her other jeans, lined up from dark colors to light. "Maybe really selling yourself—not your club or the clothes you're modeling but your very self, like Ginger—is uninhibiting."

Apparently, however, it wasn't very fulfilling. After all, they'd tell Ginger when she claimed to be content, she had joined this group, indicating that she'd welcome some revision in her life. What's more, she was neither stupid nor unrefined, Charlotte would remind her, and she probably knew perfectly well that prostitution was not a normal or a socially acceptable response to having a busy husband. To which Ginger would give a charming shrug and concede that she supposed not, but it seemed to work out well enough.

"The question," said Kat, "is did Harold know?"

"The bigger question is did he care?" said Polly, fitting her wallet, credit card case, comb, and Kleenex packet into a purse not much larger than the group of items.

"The fact he didn't seem to care proves he didn't know," said Kat.

"No," said Polly, "his not knowing proves he didn't care."

"Very neat," said Kat. "What does it mean?"

"Well, Barnaby knows what you're doing all the time, and if he doesn't, he asks. He probably asks a lot, because he thinks you're interesting, maybe even fascinating. Because he cares. Same thing."

To Polly's relief the children came home, a few minutes apart, just before she and Kat left the house. She was relieved also that her friend was there. If Kat filled her house with noise and energy, the children drained it, usually producing such an emptiness that she was left floating in a vacuum, all her warmth and energy and enthusiasm sucked down a black hole.

The children were her most recent loss, not really gone like everyone else but suddenly lost to her. Her son, Jeremy, always an independent little boy who since preschool had sought no help, kept his own counsel, and released few details of his life, was at twelve almost incommunicado. He was mostly an assortment of noises—squirks and brays and a repertoire of tuneless songs.

When directly addressed, his most alert response was a long, blank "Huh?" More often he did an elaborate vomiting pantomime with a relish displayed in no other activity. He clutched his throat, his stomach. He swayed and staggered, rolling his eyes between violent heaves. Even when not present, he was easily located, because although he was unspeaking, he was hardly silent. The snorts and brays went from room to room, now the kitchen, now the closet, with no letup for eating, or homework, or watching TV.

If the request that set off one of his dumb shows was not urgent and she had the time and composure, she would watch him, studying him as a naturalist studied a toad or insect. Stepping back from her motherhood, she wondered how many mothers disliked their young sons, whether many found the behavior of an adolescent male even faintly familiar, whether any felt adequate to the task of raising boys.

Her daughter, Andrea, was another matter—her precious daughter, who she'd believed would be precious, and hers, forever. Amiable, affectionate, appreciative, even neat, she had been a perfect child, the daughter a woman dreams of from the moment her dreams include daughters. And she in turn loved Polly, and said so, and wanted always to be in her company. But then, the night she turned thirteen two years ago, she also turned silent, sullen, and withdrawn. She became a vegetarian, a pacifist, ferociously agnostic. Once generous and polite at home, she no longer had a word or a thought or any apparent care for Polly or Jeremy.

In her worst hours, usually two or three in the morning, when Polly was awakened by an emptiness almost visceral, she'd think, These children are not enough for me to live for. And she'd weep that she had nothing better and nothing else.

Kat, however, was delighted to see them, as she was delighted to see everyone. Andrea came in first and stood in the door, her curly reddish hair draped around her head like an O-Cedar mop, her limp gauze skirt flowing down to dirty high-top sneakers, above it a brass-buttoned band jacket she'd found in a thrift shop. All this Kat was able to ignore as Polly could not, immediately finding something to admire.

"Oh, wow, cool bag!" she said, reaching out to touch the gray canvas pouch Andrea had gotten on one of her regular visits to the army-navy store. USN U GAS MASK ND MARK IV, it said on the front.

"It's from the army-navy store," said Andrea. "It came in two sizes. I got both."

"Hi, honey," said Polly.

"Hi," said Andrea, and was gone down the hall, dragging a panel of Indian gauze in her wake.

Standing side by side in the middle of the room, the two women heard her footsteps go up the stairs and her door close. Then the front door slammed, and more footsteps approached. Jeremy appeared, standing outside in the hall, partly hidden behind the door frame. He had something akin to hiccups; at least his shoulders were shaking up and down, punctuated by some kind of nasal snorts.

"You remember my friend Katharine Hurley?" said Polly.

"Kat," corrected Kat, taking one long, liquid stride forward and shooting out an arm. Jeremy shook hands, did a fair imitation of Woody Woodpecker, then took off down the hall making trombone sounds through pressed lips.

Polly sighed and picked up her jacket. "This look okay?" she asked Kat, examining herself in the dressing-table mirror.

"It doesn't matter what you wear to an arm-twisting," said Kat, who was herself in slacks and a blazer. "Remind me: Why are we doing this? Did you see a lot of Ginger outside?"

"None of us did," said Polly, taking her keys off the doorknob as they left the room. "But something's wrong here and somebody has to care, and I think this group was set up as a collection of somebodies who've agreed to care. Besides, advertisements to the contrary, Ginger was really a pretty nice person."

Kat took a last dip to check herself in the hall mirror. "You have to admire the fact that she picked her sport and excelled at it," she said, without apparent sarcasm.

"Unless that's what killed her," Polly answered as they emerged into the dusty sunshine of midafternoon.

5

Harold Pass had been left alone in a Beverly Hills house that would certainly need a new mistress, and soon. Like all the houses on the street, it could have accommodated not just one but several families. It was in the middle of a long, curving block between two major boulevards, with palm trees four stories high on both sides and each home a mansion as perfectly groomed as a movie set, which in fact some were. Producers rented them to shoot photos of exteriors for a movie or television sitcom, or a series of interior scenes. Even that was no problem for the residents, who were often traveling or staying at a second or third home and, being rich, wouldn't turn down another two thousand dollars a day.

Polly and Kat had the street almost to themselves, except for the gardeners' pickup trucks. The residents' cars, all Mercedeses and BMWs and Lexus sedans, were crowded into their circular drives and bricked parking areas.

"Were these people her friends?" wondered Kat as they rolled along. It wasn't really a question. Neighbors weren't necessarily friends anywhere, and in Beverly Hills neighbors were rarely neighborly, despite the narrow space between houses. People didn't hang out wash anymore, and only maids and gardeners stepped out into the backyards on weekdays. No one borrowed eggs or cups of sugar: Even those who cooked never ate sugar or eggs anymore.

"I'm not even sure if we were her friends," said Polly. "To be honest, I'm not so confident that Harold will know us. If they had friends together at all, it was probably this type of people, though you wouldn't know it by her."

Polly was glad they'd come in Kat's Ford Explorer, which was new, clean, and the type of car popular with women who could buy whatever they wanted. Kat said she chose it so she could transport exercise equipment from club to club. But she really wanted the four-wheel drive "just for the macho feeling," she admitted. ("Macha," said Charlotte. "We're female.") At any rate it was good to have four-wheel drive in case you were ever stuck in the sand in the desert, even if you never went there. And Kat liked sitting on a high seat above traffic: The perch stretched both her long legs and her confidence, and when she climbed down, she took that sense of position with her.

"Ginger wasn't to this manor born," said Kat, squinting through the tinted windshield at the house numbers on the curb. "Wasn't she from North Dakota or Idaho?"

"Milwaukee," said Polly. "If you mean the houses, we were none of us born to such manors."

"Here it is," said Kat. She came to a slow stop in front of a mottled brown stone manse from the English lake country, with casement windows, a gabled entrance, and on one side, a roof of waved shingles sloped almost to ground level. On the other side was a stucco garage with a flat roof, obviously a later addition. Junipers flanked the front windows, and a flagstone path curved unnecessarily back and forth up from the street, knee-high boxwood on both sides.

"Wait a minute," said Kat, who'd climbed down and was about to lock the car. Familiar with the tactics of Beverly Hills, whose parking restrictions were so complex that the city was guaranteed an enviable revenue base from parking fines alone, she walked back to the nearest signpost. It was typical: Residential permits had to be displayed for unrestricted parking; there was no parking at all between noon and 4:00 P.M. on Wednesday; one-hour public parking from 8:00 A.M. to 5:00 P.M. daily, and no public parking again on Friday and Saturday between 5:00 P.M. and 11:00 P.M.

"Get back in the car," she snapped, striding around to the driver's side again.

They climbed back in. Kat shoved the gearshift into drive and swerved noisily into the long driveway at one side of the house, separated from the main lawn by more hedging. They left the car down near the street, coming around the sidewalk to the front path. Kat was irritable now, which only exaggerated her normal, rather animal walk—easy, even powerful, but unpredictable, with sudden hops, dips, sometimes a deep, languorous leg stretch. She couldn't resist a low hedge like this one, hopping over and back twice between the sidewalk and the big carved front door.

"Damn boobs," she muttered as Polly pushed the bell. Chimes sounded.

They expected a servant, maybe male. They got Harold himself, after a lengthy period of listening to someone on the other side of the door fussing with latches and bolts and pulling on the doorknob. He was probably unfamiliar with the mechanism, being so rarely there.

Harold traveled constantly and alone. He went to Reno and Miami and sometimes Rio and Tokyo, all without his wife. "No place for a woman," he'd say, unaware that Rio and Miami and even Tokyo came to her and laid themselves at her feet, or between them. Ginger claimed she never thought about the irony; it was just business. As for Harold, what a waste that life sent Harold to these lush and lively climates, when he came back as chilly as he'd left.

This week, however, his wife had died, and he was home. He was in shirtsleeves—a button-down oxford with thin red stripes—and gray slacks, a dress belt, and tassel loafers. Harold was willow-thin and neat; when he crossed his legs, the crease stayed in his pants and his lower legs were pressed together to the feet. Even now he wasn't disarranged, but his eyes were red-rimmed and bloodshot, and the flesh of his face sagged.

"Yes?" he said, showing no recognition or interest in why they were there. He knew them, and they knew it, but Polly put out her hand anyway, saying, "I'm Polly Crother."

When he neither took her hand nor opened the door farther, she added, "We're in Ginger's group—the Monday group. The women."

"I know," said Harold, blinking. It may have been a wince.

"We wanted to know if we could do anything, if there's something we can do," said Polly. Behind Harold, barely visible through the ten-inch opening he allowed, she saw a girl, Ginger's stepdaughter, slight and taking up as little space as possible, her arms wrapped around her chest. She had a pinched and pointed face. She stood in the dark, in dark clothes, but the pale face floated forward in the hallway beyond Harold's shoulder.

"Thank you no, everything's taken care of," said Harold. He withdrew slightly, keeping his body across the narrow opening.

Kat pushed forward past Polly and put her hand against the door. "What happened, Harold?" she burst out. "How did Ginger die?"

She was as tall as Harold, and he drew back farther, though her gesture was hardly threatening. "It was on a trip to the mountains," he said, a toneless recitation he'd apparently made a number of times already. "They don't know; it was a sudden seizure of some kind."

"Was she ill?" Kat pressed on. "We knew her pretty well—we're all friends—but she never mentioned anything."

"No, nothing," he said. "They just don't know what it was."

"Will there be a service, and can we come?" asked Polly. "Could we help with that at least? One or two of us saying something about her as our friend?"

Harold was surprised. Blinking a few times, he said, "No, no service. I can't—not right now."

The face behind his shoulder floated farther back and away.

"Thank you for coming," said Harold, closing the door. Kat took her hand away just in time.

Shoulder to shoulder, facing the door, the two women didn't move for a few minutes. Polly wondered if Harold was watching them through the peephole, savoring the little triumph of giving them nothing. He might also be regretting that he hadn't reached out to them for comfort. Sure, said her mother, blood from a stone.

"Well, whatever happened to Ginger, she finally got his attention," said Kat as they started down the path.

"Hardly seems worth the price, does it?" said Polly. Kat was angrily kicking chunks of redwood bark that spilled over from the flower beds. The end of the path was marked by two clumps of epidendrum, their orange flowers shooting over the sidewalk on long stalks. Kat reached out and snapped off two of them.

"Oh, good," said Polly. "Probably the kind that blooms once every hundred years."

Light footsteps ran down the driveway, and the girl with the pale face appeared where the hedge met the sidewalk. The face was thin, like Harold's, above the pointed chin, and her hair, a puff of fine curls, was partly orange and partly a deep purple. The orange might have been the natural color. Though neither dirty nor disheveled, she was in rags—faded jeans with wide tears and threads hanging at the knees, thighs, and ankles, a

T-shirt with the ribbing stripped from the neck so it hung off one shoulder. She had a black book under one arm, tucked up into her armpit.

"I know about you," she said, panting. "You're her women's group."

"You must be her stepdaughter, Nina," said Polly, putting a hand on the girl's forearm. "She loved you a lot." She wouldn't have revealed Ginger so blatantly if she were alive, but it didn't matter now.

Tears flooded the girl's eyes, and her face reddened. She began to gnaw on the inside of one cheek. "Listen," she said in a rush, "Ginger was a good person. Something happened to her. Maybe you can find out."

"What do you think?" asked Polly.

"I saw how Dad was with you. He didn't mean anything." Unable to chew on the inside of her mouth while talking, she pulled her fingers until the knuckles cracked. "He just can't put it together, you know? And it's been hard on him, like, he had to identify the body—Ginger—Ginger's body."

She made a sound, a sharp intake of breath, that she quickly turned into a cough, and Kat put an arm around her shoulders while the girl gathered herself together.

"Do they know anything?" prompted Polly.

"That seizure business—the police here don't think it was a seizure," said the girl. "They were going to do an autopsy."

"What did they say it was?"

"They don't say a thing," said the girl. "They ask you." She paused, putting a hand on the book under her arm. "I think she had a boyfriend," she said. "My dad's away a lot, and she'd go out all made up. Like, Ginger always wore makeup, good makeup, but this was special. Like, if you could find out if she had someone, we might learn what happened."

Kat and Polly said nothing, stood motionless.

The girl looked for a hangnail and came a step closer, putting the three of them into a huddle. "The thing is, I don't think she was sick. I think something happened to her." She looked for a reaction, but since both women had had the same thought many times in the past days, they said nothing.

"Can you find out?" asked the girl. "Ginger and I talked a lot. I know you guys were really important to her."

The skin on her bare shoulder and her arms broke out in goose bumps. Maybe she feared they'd turn her down.

"We'll try," said Polly gently. "We had already decided we'd try."

The girl's sudden smile was wide, with a dimple, and they had a vision of how she could look in a decade. "I have something that might help," she said with more confidence, and brought forth the black book under her arm. It was not a book at all but an electronic personal organizer in a leatherette case.

"She had everything in here," said the girl. "Like, her appointments, address book, money stuff. She told me. But I think it has some kind of password. You can get that, can't you?"

"We can get it," said Kat.

"We can definitely get that," said Polly, not at all sure they could. "We'll get it."

She should never have made such a promise, she fretted later, particularly to someone Nina's age, who thought perhaps Ginger had a boyfriend and didn't judge her harshly for it. She was barely beyond the age of believing the promises in toy ads on TV, never mind the happy endings of fairy tales.

Angry at herself, Polly turned to her computer and drafted a letter to American Airlines, whose newspaper ads for fall fares had caught her attention and then, as always, failed to deliver on the offer. She followed her standard format for complaint letters: short lead, one or two paragraphs on the situation/problem, a paragraph of comment and/or demand.

Dear Sirs:

We were excited by your recent ad for super one-way fares of $179 (with round-trip purchase) from L.A. to thirty-nine eastern cities, particularly the 50 percent off for every child accompanied by an adult. We were quite ready to "just buy tickets by August 30."

Then we saw the mouse print lower down. Subject to change. Limited availability. Seven days' advance purchase. Travel Monday noon to Thursday noon. Stay over Saturday. One child per adult. What big print giveth, small print taketh away.

What's more, no such tickets were available on any of the sixteen flights we wanted, the very first day the ad ran. I know you say discount seats are limited. I even know you adjust their "availability" up to time of departure, depending on how well a flight has sold.

But this is wrong. What food chain could advertise prime rib at $6 a pound, limited to 12 roasts per store and only when bought in pairs between Sunday and Monday noon? What bank could offer mortgages at 7 percent interest, only for customers who take another loan as well, close escrow on Monday, and call on a day that starts with *T*?

If not deceptive, these ads are tricky. The gap between the offer and the limitations is the same as between bait and switch. We'd still like our three fares to Boston for $716.

Sincerely yours . . .

Polly turned off the computer. Then she walked her house, up, down, picking up papers and food, checking and rechecking the locks on doors and windows in an obsessive routine meant to keep her family secure and intact.

There would be a way to get into the organizer, she was thinking. A promise is a promise. Besides, they needed it themselves.

6

At Charlotte's request, Lotte left the conference room open for them the hour before their next Monday meeting. It was clear to all, Lotte included, that Ginger's death was a very different matter to the therapist than to the women in the group. For her, death might be sad but it was also an end to therapeutic interest. For them, something was beginning. The sudden mystery of Ginger's death opened a crack in their lives, with a new and unknown darkness beyond. Pain they all knew—disappointment, despair, sickness, even death—but violence was rare, and murder unimaginable.

"I just can't believe Harold isn't doing anything," said Kat, trying to adjust the blinds to put light in the room but not in their eyes. As always they faced a sun that was starting its descent. They had spoken several times by phone, but this was their first group gathering since Polly and Kat had called on Harold.

Everyone had left work early to get there at five, and they came in their usual work clothes, from Kat's neon exercise tights and T-shirt to Justine's flowered dress and linen jacket. They took their usual places— Dinah in the far corner of the room against an end wall of chalkboards, Charlotte and Justine and Kat against the long inside wall. Polly, on the near end just inside the door because she was usually last to come, sat on one leg, holding Ginger's appointment book. Lotte's chair, alone on the window side, wasn't yet occupied, and Ginger's customary seat, next to Dinah, was empty.

"Nobody's having any kind of service for her?" asked Dinah.

"Apparently not," said Polly. "Nobody's looking into it either. Certainly not Harold. He was embarrassed by her death."

"Well, somebody looked into it," said Dinah. "The daughter said there was an autopsy. Anything an autopsy comes up with is public information, like a death certificate, I believe."

"But you have to ask," said Charlotte. "And the people who usually ask are the family or their doctors or, if there's some question about the death, the police, the D.A., some sort of law enforcement. And if they did ask, none of those parties are broadcasting their findings."

They fell silent for a while, watching the setting sun. Then Polly said, "There's always this thing," and held up the electronic organizer.

"Ironic, isn't it?" murmured Dinah, "that of all of us, Ginger was the most computerized in her work."

Silently, they passed the device around the circle, each in turn pressing the on button. "You can calculate," said Polly when it ended with Justine, "but you can't get into any of the memo functions like calendar or phone book. That takes a password."

"Many of them do," said Justine, "but I think it's optional, for people who want to protect those functions. Unfortunately, the password could be anything," she added, passing it back to Polly. "Anything at all. So how do we get it?"

"Didn't you collect passwords once, Dinah?" asked Polly, rewarded with an immediate gust of laughter.

"I have a few, but it's not one of my bigger collections," said Dinah amiably.

Dinah Milanskaya was an obsessive collector, although the focus of her pursuit kept changing—Indian baskets, Persian rugs, glass paperweights, ceramic teapots, twentieth-century ceramic teapots, Early American samplers. She built each collection over a period of years, and when she was expert in the category and her collection was reasonably complete and even well known, she turned to something else with equal zeal. The paperweights were gone now, sold as an intact group, as were the samplers. So were the teapots, all sixty donated to a craft museum.

She bored easily, perhaps a habit engendered by her boredom in her chosen career. She had decided to specialize in dermatology because, as doctors liked to say, dermatologists keep regular hours, there are no night calls, nobody ever dies and nobody gets well. It was a good field for a wife and mother, she thought, but then she became neither.

Assuming that family would be the primary interest in her life, she had given up what drew her to medicine since childhood—emergency work, where you helped everyone brought to you as fast as you could, often against a background of sirens and flashing lights. As a child she ran after fire trucks, crashed her toy cars, mended her battered dolls. As a medical student and resident, she hung around the emergency room, galvanized by trauma, a volunteer for every disaster alert. Even now she jumped at each passing siren as she jumped whenever the building shook. The emotions behind the two responses were different, of course, but Polly liked to say that she couldn't decide whether Dinah feared earthquakes or yearned for one so she could resuscitate all of them.

Still, she was good at dermatology, had established a thriving practice, and made so much money that she couldn't easily give it up, in spite of being bored. She was oddly timid about making a change, admitting that she had joined this group in the hope that others could help her talk out her dilemma coldly and clearly. And they did, but her choice seemed so clear that they were sometimes impatient with her inertia.

"Just do it," Polly would say.

"Be decisive," said Charlotte, "like you are with artworks, not to speak of men."

Dinah was short and full-bodied, with green eyes, a cleft in her chin, and soft, shoulder-length brown hair, and there was no dearth of men who found her attractive—"the triumph of raw sex over mere prettiness," she said mockingly. Ever the collector, she chose among them often but not well, drawn to the odd and inappropriate: a pop record executive who spent his working hours in a white stretch limo, a radical lawyer who defended the constitutional rights of drug dealers, a rancher who bred elk and spit a lot. Each (in the group's analysis) dangled before Dinah some imagined excitement, even danger. Dinah took up with them, took off with them, even eloped with one, but woke characteristically sensible again the next morning.

"Sorry," she told the group now. "I have passwords for quite a few databases at the office, but they're not personal. And for my personal files, I use my mother's name, which is pretty standard." She was playing with the functions on Ginger's little terminal. "Well, Ginger didn't use her name or initials as her password," she said.

"There must be some way of cracking one of these electronic codes," said Polly, "and it should be relatively easy. It's just a piece of machinery with programmed responses. It's not the Rosetta stone, for God's sake."

But even Dinah, who was a computer buff, couldn't get them into Ginger's little machine without more information. For all they knew, a private electronic organizer had the same status as a safe-deposit box, requiring a court order to open it without the owner.

Finding the cause of Ginger's death almost seemed easier, but not fast. A death certificate was a public document, Justine explained, but it might not be recorded until a month after death.

"But it's there," said Polly. "It is there somewhere, isn't it?"

Justine studied her rings—a big pearl, a jade cabochon. Watching her, they were all thinking that the certificate was in county hands, she was a county official, and with her pull she could get it, and she knew they were thinking it. "It's not that easy," she said tentatively.

Pick up the phone, they said. Say you need it. Don't say why. Don't say too much. Justine didn't respond.

You can help us, they said. Just walk over and get it. Send someone over with a form. Requisition it.

"I can't do something like that," said Justine unhappily. "It's just not my way."

Nobody spoke.

"Well, what *is* your way?" cried Kat, jumping up to walk the room again. "We've been here over a year and I still don't really know."

Justine offered her characteristic response—none. She sat in her dark suit and her flowered blouse—always a flowered blouse—and showed no reaction. The group was tolerant, understanding that what they saw as a liability was for Justine a political asset. She had worked under four elected county assessors as their chief deputy, always responsible, efficient, and strictly background. Basically, she ran the assessor's office, doing whatever needed doing, and the assessor talked about what was done. She could have run for the assessor's office herself, with a fair chance of winning as a well-connected Japanese-American, but she didn't want to rock anyone's boat, particularly her own. "Safe as a bridesmaid, never a bride," said Kat.

What Justine couldn't make them understand was that this job wasn't her only work, so it wasn't that important. Nights and weekends she worked for her family. As the eldest daughter and first daughter-in-law of two Japanese-American families, she was enmeshed in family arrangements and activities. She was bookkeeper for her parents' import business, bookkeeper and financial officer for her husband's garden and landscape supply company, and personal accountant for any relative who needed her. Justine could do anything, they said admiringly, and gave her more to do.

Justine was a chump, said Charlotte, not unsympathetically. "You worked under what? Four assessors?" she'd needle. "For your husband at night? Your parents on weekends? I'm amazed you could get yourself here—or even realized you needed to come."

In fact, Justine didn't mind working in her husband's business. What she minded was not being at the center of it. She was out in the counting house, counting out the money, an officer, not a partner. She wrote financial statements and checks, but her husband had to sign them—a line of command that spilled over into their home, where he kept the checkbook and gave her a household allowance.

In fact, she loved the business. She wanted to travel, buy rootstock, move them beyond wholesale landscaping and into retail, maybe even growing. She wanted to get into the garden, but the business needed an accountant, not a botanist. So while her husband, Robby, flew around the world, visiting fields and showrooms, entertained by suppliers and maybe even women more ornamental than Justine, she took their young sons on garden tours, to garden clubs, to nurseries. With one she planted a vegetable garden; with the other she built a small orchid greenhouse. Had anyone asked her what she wanted, she'd have said partnership, choice, more time in the dirt. Instead she had the four successive assessors, a stable, prosperous family, and yearnings.

"All I'm asking is whether you want to help," said Kat, tight-lipped.

"The question is what exactly we're doing," said Justine in a measured tone, "and whether it's intrusive."

"Justine," said Charlotte, as if addressing a child or an addled elderly client, "nothing is exact right now, and we're not doing anything yet, but the rest of us have no question that someone should know why Ginger is dead."

"I just can't believe Harold won't help," said Kat again as she walked back and forth, flexing her fingers in and out of fists. Her hands wouldn't have made the cut in a fashion shoot. They were long and wide, with prominent tendons, though she kept them well-manicured, the short nails glossed, and she had a circle of diamonds on one hand and a big solitaire on the other.

"Kat," said Charlotte wearily, "you need to understand that everyone doesn't get the same amount of love in their lives. You have a husband who loves you and shows it. We don't know what Harold felt about Ginger, though this might be a good time to find out."

"Well, he felt something for her, or he wouldn't have married her," said Kat. "And he must still feel something; we saw how upset he was."

"Maybe he was just inconvenienced," said Dinah.

It wasn't that Kat was naive. She was simply an unregenerate believer, in spite of having lived a life in which she had had to plan well ahead where she would go and then do all the work to get there. Nothing unusual there. What was unusual was that her work and her belief had always been rewarded.

"It's not fair you're the one who's happy when you're so beautiful," said Charlotte with a stage sigh, a heave of the shoulders, a quick ruffling of her short hair with open fingers.

"It's not fair you're so smart," Kat answered, absolutely sincere.

"You missed the point," said Charlotte, but there was a point there, too. For Charlotte one result of being so smart was a life that felt stilted and chilly. Even though she herself had helped make it that way, she felt keenly the deepening cold.

She had married well and for love, but sometimes felt she hated her husband, Avery, a man so unsentimental, so uninvolved in the life of the family that once when he couldn't find a blank videotape to record a movie, he taped over the video of their daughter's birthday parties and the family Christmases. Avery Feinman hadn't always been that way, or if he had been, it was covered by the warmth of his wit. It was only as they got further into their life together that coldness and criticism filled the little spaces left after careers, home, family obligations. She then discovered that humor was Avery's only warmth, or what passed for warmth, and when he wasn't amused, he was remote. And the more remote he became, the more she took over the business of home and family, until he was barely a participant.

They were to some extent in the same field, tax law—he as a corporate accountant, she as a corporate lawyer. They used to talk philosophy while potatoes burned and ice cream melted, comparing notes on work, refining each other's jokes in delighted crescendos of wordplay. Now they corrected each other, letting no statement pass unexamined or unchallenged. They were in constant battle, one finding errors in the other's handling of the check register or the dry cleaning or the loading of the dishwasher and the other seizing on the partner's similar errors the next day. Once comrades, they were now at war, a life of skirmishes in which each jockeyed for the more righteous position.

In the hours just before dawn, Charlotte often woke and wept because she didn't even want to be right. She wanted them both to behave quite differently but was unable to work the transformation alone.

Given the enmity at home, Charlotte almost welcomed the disasters that got her out of corporate work and into estate planning. First her father died, not just slowly but intestate. A lawyer himself, he was surely conversant with the basics of estate law but apparently never considered the possibility of his own death. Having provided no directive to physicians, he was resuscitated after a cardiac arrest and kept on life support for five weeks. When he finally expired, the lack of either a trust or a will plunged Charlotte into a legal nightmare that left her exhausted but wealthy, if less wealthy than she'd have been if her father had organized his estate.

Then her mother's widowed, childless sister died after an auto accident that unfortunately didn't kill her outright. Her death was equally slow, if well anticipated in legal documents. But she had a doctor and a hospital who challenged her directives, claiming she might someday live without either brain waves or a life-support system. It took Charlotte four months to get a court order to unplug the system, and within thirty minutes her aunt died without waking or seeing her favorite niece. Charlotte was left even richer, more exhausted, and permanently scarred by the battles over lives that were dear to her.

At that point, philosophically dedicated and financially free to do as she liked, Charlotte went into her own practice, handling wills and trusts and estate planning, family and corporate foundations. She had a gift for organizing death that she'd never had for organizing life, and, having once billed twenty-five hundred hours a year in corporate law practice, she now took pride in billing fifteen hundred and working almost three thousand, gladly spending over half her working life gratis in the great beyond.

Much of that time was on evenings and weekends. She made a point of getting home by six-thirty, serving dinner, then making herself available for a precociously resourceful daughter who by the age of ten didn't need her and a husband who didn't want her. She was free to do whatever she wanted—casework, laundry, mending, paying bills, bookkeeping on their computer. Avery took care of himself. She took care of everything else, partly because she was more willing, partly because she was more able. Whichever, she was stuck with it.

"Smart's okay," she said now, "but you know it hasn't worked for me. Next time around I'll take beauty, Kat. Your only problem is they made the boobs too big."

Good-humored as always, Kat laughed along with everyone else.

Then the laughter petered out, and they just sat quietly as the pink of the sky turned to pewter and the building's outlines softened, and they had reached no conclusion.

"Maybe I can lean on Harold a little," offered Charlotte. "I'm good at leaning on people, though not everyone yields."

Suddenly they all thought of someone they could talk to. Kat remembered that two of her club's trainers worked dinner hours at the Palatine Club and served as stewards every summer at the High Camp. Polly could call an old friend of Dan's who wrote insurance for several of the largest private clubs in the state and see what he had heard. A friend of Justine's was a deputy D.A.; she'd call to see if the woman had heard anything, at the same time asking if there was any legitimate way to get a death certificate.

"I'll take the organizer, too," said Justine, eager to make amends, but safely. She'd present the problem to one of her sons, who was a computer nut and could call the company for technical information on passwords.

"I'll do Ginger," said Dinah.

"She should be a big help," said Charlotte dryly.

"Cut it out, Char," said Kat. She turned to Dinah. "What about Ginger?"

"The body," said Dinah, with no sign of impatience. "I'll visit the coroner. Haven't been down there in years, but at least I know where it is."

"Can I come?" asked Polly. "He's a civil servant—he works for me, too. I can ask stupid, naive questions, and you can understand any answers we get."

Lotte's arrival cut off discussion but not thought. They did manage to get through forty-five minutes of therapeutic exchange, struggling to eke out of their past week some slightly interesting, slightly provocative incidents to present, but all the while they were reviewing what they knew of Ginger's life and how they might learn more. Except for Charlotte, each was making a mental list of her own tasks; Charlotte, oblivious to being watched, made notes in her unique shorthand on an index card.

When Lotte finally put away her yellow pad, they rose and left abruptly. Nor did they linger outside, saying quick farewells as they went to their cars.

Fools rush in, Polly's mother warned her, but it seemed perfunctory.

7

Unspeaking, Polly and her children took their accustomed places in the car and drove down the hill. In the rearview mirror, her daughter's face was set and grim. Andrea had eaten bell peppers and kale for breakfast, and her hair had come out of its night braid uncombed, unparted, and unkempt. Her reddish eye shadow added a ghoulish cast.

Jeremy was hardly visible. He was so slumped down that the shoulder strap of the seat belt crossed his face. Under the visor of his baseball cap, his eyes were closed, but Polly could hear the toes of his Nikes tapping the back of the seat in front of him.

"Gorgeous day!" she said. "Just beautiful. You could see to Catalina if there were no trees or buildings in the way."

There was no response. People treated their chauffeurs better, but then, chauffeurs kept quiet. I'm not a chauffeur, she thought. It's a phase, said her mother, unusually indulgent; they'll grow out of it.

Jeremy's feet beat a faster rhythm.

"I'm going downtown with Dinah today," said Polly. "I should probably check the traffic before I go. It can be odd in the mornings." There
was an accident at Franklin where she came off Beachwood. "Anyone
care what they eat tonight? I defrosted chicken breasts. White meat,
Andrea. But I was going to make a yogurt-Parmesan sauce. You probably
don't mix milk and meat."

She regretted the gibe instantly, but Andrea's face didn't change.
Jeremy got out at the corner near his school, and she watched him plod
over to stand with several other boys before she pulled away. Their lips
didn't move in any apparent verbal greeting, but they punched at one
another's upper arms.

Andrea's school was a little farther on. As she opened the car door,
she said, "For God's sake, don't get out of the car and start talking people
up in the parking lot. Everyone thinks it's weird." She walked off, dragging her backpack and the big, loose cuffs of her jeans, which either were
cut huge by design or were several sizes too big.

Polly, clinging to the wheel, knuckles shining, watched her go, wanting to call her back. Don't react, her mother said as always, as if she had
followed the dictum herself.

Dinah's office was in an architectural showplace on Third Street,
in the neighborhood of Cedars-Sinai Medical Center, the County Art
Museum, and the Beverly Center, an upscale enclosed shopping mall.
It was perfect, Charlotte once said, because these were the anchors of
Dinah's life, symbols of how she made her money, invested her money,
and wasted her money.

The medical building, of which Dinah was a one-third owner, was a
high-tech triplex of glass and colored steel tubing that housed four doctors' suites. Dinah and her partner shared the top floor, a two-thousand-
square-foot area of skylights and marble that artfully displayed whatever
had been her last year's obsession. At the moment it was Indian baskets

and Pueblo pottery, two collections she wanted to sell off, preferably intact, although they'd net more piecemeal.

Her partner was amiable about the constantly shifting decor. He'd have been as happy with bare walls, as long as neither effort nor opinion was asked from him. This approach had served him well at home for almost twenty-five years, since his wife liked her walls painted faux marble (with faux cracks), leather window seats, hunting scenes, and pitted fruitwood wainscoting. He and Dinah had been partners for ten years, and the only objects that ever raised his eyebrows were the earthquake kits she insisted on placing everywhere.

Polly took the stairs, which had a blue trash barrel full of emergency supplies and rations at the street-floor entrance, and copper pots filled with flashlights and hard hats on each landing. Just inside the office door at the top was another of Dinah's homemade earthquake kits, a huge, urn-shaped basket filled with dried food and bottled water and batteries and space blankets. The room beyond, still empty of patients, was divided into waiting areas by floor-to-ceiling glass display cases. The nearest held four Paiute baskets on staggered pedestals, and through it she saw Dinah coming through the inner door.

"Excess becomes you," said Polly, sweeping the room with a hand. (If you can't say anything nice, her mother admonished her, don't say anything at all.) "I like the big greenish one," she added quickly, pointing to one of the four baskets.

"I do, too," said Dinah, "but I may have a buyer for all of the baskets." She paused, peering fondly into the glass case. "You have an eye," she said. "I bought that one for twenty-three thousand dollars, and it could sell now for enough to support a family of five a whole year in relative luxury. Unfortunately, I don't have a family of five, so I'll probably just buy more stuff."

"Good things come to those who wait," said Polly, turning back down the stairs.

They emerged into the garage as a truck rolled by on the avenue, shaking the building and rattling the garage gate. Dinah stopped, stiffened, and caught her breath.

"Truck," said Polly. Dinah nodded and moved forward.

There was no traffic, and Polly drove swiftly up the freeway ramp and out over one, two, three freeway lanes, savoring the illusion of flowing onto a moving belt. She enjoyed the freeways, prided herself on driving them well, and was critical of people who treated freeway driving like a Nintendo game, speeding up to pass now on the right, now on the left. Freeway traffic was more like the movement of a school of fish. It was pointless to shoot ahead a length or two whenever you saw the chance; the whole school would still arrive at about the same time.

During the twenty-minute drive to the county coroner's office, Dinah explained the gambit she'd devised. Several years ago she had attended an open house sponsored by the Los Angeles Police Department to interest medical students and house staff at local hospitals in careers associated with law enforcement. They were introduced to jail doctors, district attorneys, and the coroner's staff, who showed them the labs, the morgue, the file rooms, and the autopsy theaters.

"I'll just ask if they plan another open house sometime soon and, if not, whether I could help arrange it this year," said Dinah. "I could get both the regular and the clinical faculty at the med school to support it."

The county hospital and associated buildings took up a whole hill overlooking the downtown area. On a smaller hill, slightly behind the medical facilities, were the coroner's offices. The front building was old and venerable, beige stucco and roofed in red tile like the hospital itself. Trumpet vine wound up and over the entrance; bougainvillea frothed over the masonry wall bordering the parking lot.

Immediately inside the big front doors, Dinah and Polly faced a door with PUBLIC RECORDS etched large in its glass. Under it, cardboard signs affixed to the glass said "Death Certificates, Recent Year" and "Death Archives."

"Some detectives we are," said Polly. "Couldn't be easier."

As it turned out, Ginger's name and date of death were noted, and the certificate might well have been a public document, but it was checked out to the coroner's office. This could mean a number of things, said the desk clerk languidly; they'd have to ask at the coroner's office.

"Right," said Dinah.

At one side of the records room was a hall to the coroner's office. At the other side was a door marked GIFT SHOP, with a window in it. They could see shelves piled with goods and across the back wall a banner saying DEM BONES: SOUVENIRS OF THE L.A. COUNTY CORONER'S DEP'T.

"Tasteful," said Dinah.

"Just good marketing," said Polly.

"The coroner's the other way," said Dinah, moving off.

The anteroom to the coroner's office was big and dark, rimmed by old wall-to-wall oak file cases six drawers high. Behind a long counter, an obese woman in an orange nylon running suit and unlaced sneakers was taking files out of a cardboard box.

"Is the coroner in his office?" asked Dinah, and as the woman jerked her head toward the far corner, a man perched on a stool there looked over his open file drawer.

He was long, almost graceful, with auburn hair combed thick and straight. He wore white socks and desert boots and, under his white coat, a striped shirt and bow tie; he had a manila file in one hand and a sandwich in the other.

"Dr. Vere?" said Dinah.

He came forward, shifting the file to the sandwich hand and extending the other. "Wait a minute," he said. "It's Dr. Milanskaya, isn't it?"

"How do you remember?" asked Dinah. "I was here three years ago."

"You're memorable," he said, smiling. "And frankly, so few women pass through here with clothes on that those few stand out."

Graham Vere had a slight gap between his front two teeth—in Chaucerian days sign of a passionate and sensual personality, Polly suddenly recalled. She was as embarrassed as if she'd spoken the thought aloud. Then again, maybe it just applied to women; she had read it in a description of the Wife of Bath.

His hands were freckled; maybe under the white crew socks his feet were also. She looked at his feet, vaguely aware of Dinah explaining her visit, of Dr. Vere eliciting the information that Dinah was in dermatology and active on the clinical faculty at the university hospital. Now he was telling her about an interesting postmortem going on right now—something about some odd skin lesions and scarring as indication of where the person lived, how he died, and where he'd been taken after death.

"Would you like to observe, as long as you're here?" he asked Dinah, and within minutes Dinah was gone to view the procedure and Polly was following Vere to his office at the back of the building. "Come in." He held open another glass-paned door. "Attractive female company is as rare in my office as clothed bodies."

"I don't want to take your time," she began.

"It's perfect timing. There's a lull between corpses."

His office had a small sitting area, a massive wood desk facing the door, and, like the outer office, file cabinets and shelving all around. Books filled the shelves and cabinet tops, interspersed with an odd assortment of specimens and artifacts—antique microscopes and measuring devices, a 3-D phrenology map of the skull. Above the cabinets on the wall to Polly's left was a long framed needlepoint sign reading HIC LOCUS EST UBI MORS GAUDET SUCCURRERE VITAE.

"'This place is where . . .' No, 'This is the place,'" said Polly, "'where death is glad to help lives.' No, 'the living,' right?"

"Right. It's inscribed on the wall at the New York Medical Examiner's office, and a lot of other autopsy sites. My older son had mono last year, and the housekeeper taught him needlepoint to pass the time. The younger son had his own preference for a coroner's motto." He pointed to a black frame with diploma lettering that read OBESA CANTAVIT.

"Meaning?" Polly picked up a skeleton hand and gently flexed the fingers.

"'The fat lady has sung,' or literally, I guess, 'The fat lady sang.' I actually found a school that gives the boys Latin. That's not easy here. I'm divorced," he added, watching her. "My wife didn't want custody, joint or otherwise. Just didn't have a feeling for guy stuff, she said."

"Neither do I, I'm afraid," said Polly with a sigh, "but I don't do much better with my daughter these days."

"What do you do? For a living, I mean. Are you a colleague of Dinah's?"

"I'm a financial analyst—personal, not professional," she quickly added, never having come up with a good short statement of what she did. "I manage a family portfolio, actually my own and my children's funds. It's our living, and it is all finance, and it does involve analysis, so that's what I say, but it doesn't make for very interesting conversation."

"I'd like to hear about it."

Ask about the other person and he'll always find you interesting, warned her mother. He asked about me, retorted Polly.

"Well," she said, "I read annual reports, stock issues, and company papers, I look at sales and earnings, ask about their gifts, their lawsuits, what they pay their officers. I get marketing data—both their own and outside reports—and any pertinent articles and news stories, and I think about what they're selling and whether people want it."

"Everyone forgets that's the crux of it all, don't they?"

"I try not to. In fact, sometimes it comes down to whether the product is something I myself want—which has occasionally worked quite well for me and at least once almost ruined me. In any case, it doesn't make the best dinner-table entertainment."

"Beats my field," said Vere. "At least it's clean and dry. Here I am, a single father of teenagers, supposed to have a grown-up dating life, and who wants to hear about my afternoon autopsies? Anybody who had me coming home to her at the end of my day would want to hose me down on the front stoop. What would we discuss over dinner? Gangrene? And my association with death doesn't help."

"That's odd," said Polly. "In my case it seems to be a real turn-on."

"How so?"

"You know, poor young widow and all that. I couldn't handle any more popularity if I were really popular, and a lot of it is sight-unseen referrals."

"I wish I'd known of that. I'd have murdered my wife instead of divorcing her."

"I don't think it works for murder. Undercuts the sympathy factor. I thought every single girl alive was supposed to want a doctor, whatever his specialty."

"Well, there are many people these days who don't mind blood—the movies have done that for us—but body parts gross them out."

"Why do you keep so many body parts around?" Polly gestured at the cabinets.

"I find it instructive," said Vere. "Bearing in mind that this is what's left after death, and in many cases is what caused the death, each specimen speaks of ultimate consequences. Like that lump of coal in the bell jar. It's a piece of lung, a smoker's lung. The photo behind it is a cross section of the whole lung—almost an undifferentiated mass. The other bell jar with the pink, spongelike lump is a healthy lung—same-age guy, forties, but a garroting case, I think. And the picture behind that one is its cross section, but this one's filled with little lines of veins and deltas of oxygen-carrying alveoli."

He raised his palms apologetically. "The dead do teach the living, not just how they died but how to live."

Polly held very still, wanting him to keep talking.

"A lot of it is truly inspirational," he continued. "Coroners—maybe all pathologists—are notorious ghouls, you know, and some of their collections of horrors are quite famous. Hands with seven fingers, horns that grew from human heads, skeletons of Siamese-twin babies. I was never excited by the aberrations, although nature can't help but amaze. It's the ordinary that knocks me over. Normal is the miracle."

He picked up a small, straight bone. "This is one of the twenty-seven separate bones in a hand, the most perfect manipulative machine ever made. There they are all together." He pointed to the hand she'd set back down on the desk in front of her. "I love hands. Also eyes, the inner ear, the amnion, glomerular membranes. Other stuff that makes no better dinner-table conversation than stock reports."

I love this man, Polly thought.

"Now," said the coroner, clasping his hands on the desk, "what did you really come here for?"

"You mean aside from Dinah looking into another open house for students?"

"That's what I mean." But he was smiling.

"Is there some way I—we can find out how someone died?"

"It's not entirely regular, but if you know the coroner, you just ask."

"You don't have to answer," said Polly.

"Yes I do," he said, "if I want to see you again."

Polly heard the hands of the wall clock move, the rattle of gurneys along a hall somewhere below, a file drawer bang shut. She was aware of breathing in, then breathing out.

"Her name is Ginger Pass, probably Virginia Pass," she said. "She was a friend of ours who died up at Poderoso Pines two weeks ago. Under mysterious circumstances. Isn't that the usual saying?"

"I know the case," he said. "Let me get the file."

He leaned forward to press the button on his intercom. "Patty?" No response. "Patty? LaDonna? You there?"

A voice: "Yes, Dr. Vere."

"Could somebody give me a hand here?"

Polly pushed the skeleton hand over to him. He looked delighted.

"Sorry," she said. "It was irresistible."

"I know the feeling," he said as the door opened and the clerk in the unlaced sneakers scuffed in. "Patty, could you please get me Pass, Virginia? It's still in Investigation."

She shuffled out. They waited. "Your friend sustained a blunt-force trauma," he said. "She got a terrific blow to the head."

Polly felt tears come to her eyes. "Why would somebody do that?"

"We don't answer whys here," he said gently, "just how and when. It's not even necessarily a somebody. Such a trauma would also be consistent with a fall or even a flying wedge of concrete."

Patty, fairly spry in spite of her weight and flopping footwear, had the folder in Vere's hands in a couple of minutes. He skimmed it, reading parts as he went.

"'Cause of death—blunt trauma to the left posterior of the skull, causing fracture, cranial bleed, and large hematoma' . . . 'expired within twelve hours, more likely about eight. When found at seven A.M. was dead about two hours, putting event possibly between eight and ten P.M. Probably outdoors and immobile much of the time since then. . . .'"

He skimmed ahead. "'No peripheral signs of violent struggle. Some further body bruises, but consistent with a fall to the dirt path on which she was found. Stomach contents'—I don't know that we need this—'orange juice, pretzels, peanuts, white wine, some peppermint substance, maybe breath mints.'"

In the end you can't even keep your stomach contents private, thought Polly. Maybe all prostitutes work on a fairly empty stomach, like prizefighters before a big bout.

"There was sexual intercourse within the twelve-hour parameter, some rug burns, adhering carpet fluff, but rather standard stuff, nothing really kinky. At least one partner was a little rough; some oral . . . activity . . ."

"'At least one'?"

"Yes." He looked up. "We found two different semen types, neither a DNA match with a third sample—saliva—also found on the victim . . . your friend."

"'Victim.'"

"I'm afraid so," said Vere. "Under 'manner of death' it's coded for accident or homicide."

"You said it could have been a fall."

"It could still have been a fall." He nodded, then slowly, reluctantly, said, "You know, I'm not a cop, Polly—Polly? is that okay?—we just define and describe death and prepare to testify. . . ."

He hesitated, something held back.

She waited.

"Your friend's underpants were put on inside out."

She heard the words from a distance, clearly but without meaning, like the literal translation of an idiom, senseless. Then suddenly the meaning was there and overwhelming. Polly felt herself struggling to think of Ginger, all blond and beige and Armani-clad, covered with dirt and rug lint, her pants put on—by somebody—inside out, all alone. She must have sensed the coming day, the sunrise, even through closed eyelids, no longer able to hope for rescue, knowing only vague yearning for light and warmth.

"Are you all right?" Graham Vere stood up behind the desk.

"She was really a very nice person," said Polly. "Whatever she did, it wasn't fair that she ended so alone." A line of tears etched the length of her cheek, leaving a wound.

"I believe it." He was standing by her chair. His hand appeared, offering a blue-bordered handkerchief. She didn't remember men's handkerchiefs as so large and soft.

"I'm all right," she said, getting out of the chair. "Thank you. I need to find Dinah," and she moved on trembling legs toward the door.

On the way home, she and Dinah talked about Ginger and then spoke not at all for some time. Finally, almost reluctant to move on, they discussed the coroner and Polly's assumption that he'd call Dinah soon for Polly's phone number. It seemed like the kind of thing he would do rather than ask as she was leaving, especially given her mood when she left.

"Fine with me," said Dinah. "I give it to him, right?"

"Fine," said Polly.

Don't count your chickens, said her mother.

8

The coroner's information was passed around the same evening. It was conclusive for murder, said Kat immediately. Not necessarily murder, said Charlotte: Accident wasn't totally ruled out. Justine said she would report on Ginger's organizer on Monday, though the task of cracking the code seemed hopeless even as it became more important.

All five were slightly shocked that their suspicions had been borne out, and it made the conversations subdued. They took Dinah and Polly's information quietly and without further question. Suddenly, said Kat, I'm afraid.

For the next several days, Polly exercised one ruse after another to keep her children close to her. On Friday morning she let herself be drawn into one of Andrea's endless and ultimately acrimonious clothes debates: hat or no hat, lacy camisole over or under the T-shirt, shopping bag or laundry bag. She made Jeremy French toast and unwisely urged him many times to eat it. She rested her hand on his shoulder, ruffled Andrea's hair. She thought of Ginger, alone in the dark, and of the girl with the pale face floating out from the hall.

Jeremy made vomiting noises over the toast and drank his milk. Andrea, seeing a raw hamburger patty thawing on the counter for Polly's lunch, had to leave the kitchen.

"I have to get to school today," she called, moving down the hall. "That's today. As in Friday."

As she came back up the hill after driving the children to school, Polly tried to guess what was on Ginger's electronic organizer. Maybe it was a diary, itemizing the services provided each client. Maybe she noted down personal characteristics and sexual preferences. Maybe there were financial records, private phone numbers. Then again, maybe they'd never get into it at all, and it would remain forever a calculator, a fancy adding machine that revealed nothing.

So many of today's tools were inaccessible, even to the primary user. With that in mind, she spent the rest of the morning on a letter she'd started the month before to the Sony Corporation.

Dear Sirs:

I recently bought one of your VCRs—a machine almost as ubiquitous as the TV itself. Indeed, the VCR is so widely mass-marketed that people think it's like a toaster and they'll just plug it in and have it work.

Not so. The majority of buyers can work it only minimally. For starters, we all get someone else to connect the thing—someone who can understand the instructions or doesn't need them. If VCRs were really mass-market machines, they would be immediately un-derstandable to housewives and kids.

Using the machine is no easier. I once read that most VCR owners use it only to play rented tapes and never learn to record off the air, never mind "timer recording." When you make machines multifaceted and sophisticated, they become complicated. At least some of them should be simple enough to program by intuition.

As for the manual, it's obvious that millions are spent on packaging and marketing, nothing on the instructions. We get unreadable stuff translated from the Japanese: "To record from a source connected to the LINE-1 IN or LINE-2 IN jacks, turn DIAL TIMER or press INPUT SELECT on the remote commander to display 'L1' or 'L2.'" Huh?

How about color-coded diagrams and connectors? Instructions right on the machine? Quick-read cards for common procedures? How about some brand-new ideas for easy programming?

If you have any simpler instructions, or simpler machines, please let me know. Otherwise just register my distress.

Sincerely,

It was a voice-in-the-wilderness complaint. At best it might catch an alert manager who'd seek a way to revise instructional materials and make them into a marketing tool. In fact, that would be better than good enough, she thought, looking down the canyon while the printer ticked out the copy.

Once an upstairs porch, her little office had three walls of windows and extended out from the house. She was in effect projected into the foothills as if she sat on a camera boom. It was not a fast printer, and she had time, daydreaming, to float off down the hillside to the notch where the canyon met the city streets. She pictured herself above at her window, looking out year after year until her house was truly empty, no one was expected home at day's end, and she was alone. At least now there were days when she was too busy with family chores even to wish she could still call her mother.

She was late to the next Monday group, but Charlotte came later still, and angry after a frustrating afternoon in court. It was a propitious diversion, given that the rest of the women sat silent and preoccupied, wondering how they could pass the next hour with Ginger's death report on their minds and the organizer waiting in Justine's leather carryall right by her feet.

They managed to wring a half hour's desultory conversation out of the vagaries of the law and humanity in general. A little more on adolescents. Then even Lotte became distant and inattentive and, to everyone's relief, ended the session early and faded down the stairs.

"So," Charlotte leaped in, "how'd you do with the little black box?" Nodding at Ginger's organizer, which Justine now held on her lap.

"Well," said Justine, "my son the junior mathematician said that when anything allows for passwords of more than four characters, the possibilities run into the millions. This one takes up to six characters, including any combination of letters and numbers. So we have 1,838,265,625 possibilities. According to my son."

She looked around the circle of blank but expectant faces. "Thirty-five to the sixth power. Because each of the six spaces can be filled with any of thirty-five possibilities—twenty-six letters, nine digits."

"We all knew that," scoffed Polly.

Justine smiled, unruffled. It wasn't impossible, she said. Her son had learned on a computer-talk network that he could send the organizer to someone at Berkeley who could connect it to a mainframe computer and scroll through all the possibilities. But it would take six to eight weeks.

"We don't have that kind of time," said Kat.

Justine nodded. Alternatively, she said, the manufacturer could bypass the software that controls the password, "so you can get to the information without it. But you have to send the company proof that you're the owner of the terminal and its password or have a right to access. And even then it could take them four to six weeks to process the request."

"Still too much time," said Dinah.

"They suggested trying to come up with the password ourselves before sending them anything," said Justine. "Sometimes it comes up fairly quickly, they said. People tend to pick words and numbers of particular meaning to them—obvious things, like birthdays and nicknames."

"Let's try," said Kat, immediately on her feet, shaking one leg, then the other, as if warming up to run a race. "What are our own passwords? We all have them."

"What's yours?"

"On the office system, 'PECS.'"

"'BOOBS' would be more appropriate," said Charlotte.

Kat shrieked. "I wish I'd thought of it! What's yours?"

"You could probably guess it," said Charlotte. "It's 'RIP' for Rest in Peace. I wanted 'DNR' for Do Not Resuscitate, but it seemed too negative."

Justine used her son's name, "MATTHEW." Dinah used her mother's name at home and nothing in the office, because her nurse, technician, and office manager all needed access to her notes and files. Polly used essentially the same one for her computer, ATM cards, savings accounts, combination locks, everything—a form of her mother's birthday, 2/23/33.

Finally they agreed to start with the obvious in Ginger's case and move on from there by free association. Kat began to walk the room's perimeter again, while Justine carefully positioned the organizer like a ouija board on her lap and pressed "on" and then "password," ready to fill in the line with each suggestion in turn.

They tried "Harold," "Virginia," "Ginger," and various forms of April 6, 1968, her birth date. They tried her street (Rexford), her car (Audi), her birthplace (Milwaukee).

"How about her mother's maiden name?" suggested Dinah.

"Do we even know Ginger's maiden name?" asked Polly.

"Gunneson," said Charlotte. Everyone looked at her. She shrugged.

They tried it. Also "callgirl" and "escort," a bit reluctantly.

"Deep Throat," said Polly.

"Cut it out," said Dinah. Justine, not even looking up, didn't type it in.

They ran through more place-names, as many family names as they could remember, all of Ginger's favorite restaurants, favorite stores. They tried her favorite designers (Armani, Jil Sander), favorite perfumes (White Linen, Amarige).

"Favorite makeup?"

"Who knows? Try all the big ones—Chanel, Clinique, Revlon, what else is there?"

Everyone shouted brand names. Justine was feeding in words like an adding-machine operator.

"Red Vamp," said Charlotte quietly, almost dreamily.

"What the hell is that?"

There was an electronic beep. "That's it," said Justine.

"What's it?" Dinah rose from her seat.

"RedVamp—it's the password."

"Who said RedVamp?"

Again they all looked at Charlotte, who looked back defensively. "It was her lipstick," said Charlotte.

"How do you know that?"

Charlotte's eyes glistened, and she flushed. "I borrowed it once, and we laughed about the name," she explained. "Ginger said it made her feel a little freer, like she'd loosened one bond."

The room was absolutely still, except for the insectlike chirping of the tiny terminal. They were shocked that they'd been successful, amazed by what had worked. The name was completely foreign to them.

"Charlotte, you're really some piece of work," said Kat, draped against the chalkboard, her hands on the trough of markers. "Did you actually wear the Red Vamp?"

Charlotte took it as an insult, although coming from Kat it wasn't even ironic. "I may have more miles on me than you," Charlotte snapped, "but I'm not dead yet."

Polly studied her, then asked gently, "How did you come to know Ginger in a way no one else did?"

"We were friendly," said Charlotte sadly. "We sometimes had supper together after group, or maybe a drink." She shrugged. "People become friends, who knows why?" Charlotte, who prided herself on a direct gaze, on absolute focus, was looking out the window, her eyes scanning back and forth, sightlessly, over the rooftops. "She had a mother who never liked her, and I'm just learning to live with the same thing, because in my mother's old age she doesn't like me anymore either."

No one spoke. Justine's hands remained poised over the little keyboard. Kat's feet were for once still. Ginger's death had made them a different group: They had tightened their circle, come together in the space she left. They each felt something of what Charlotte was feeling, although hers was a Ginger they didn't know and this was a Charlotte who was new to them.

Justine put her hand over Charlotte's. "Ginger would be proud of you for getting that one," she said in her soft, even voice.

"Nah," said Charlotte, brisk again, one hand stirring up her hair. "She'd have hooted. But now that we've got it, let's do something with it."

For the next hour, they trenched through Ginger's miniature files. They started with the appointment calendar, which displayed either a full month or a week at a time with the given month a tiny insert in one corner. August included the night at the Palatine Club's retreat, a two-day weekend in Palm Springs, four hotel dates, and three Wednesdays with the notation "Marina." Two hotel dates had "Tammi" in parentheses. The out-of-town dates were cross-referenced to entries in the "Notes" file, which gave driving directions and clothes choices.

There were periodic dates for "thtr" or "dinnr" with "H" (obviously

Harold) and weeks with "Nina," her stepdaughter, on Wednesday and "no Nina" Tuesday or Thursday. Monday meetings of their group were filled in for a month ahead. There were various notations to call a doctor, a tailor, a store, and many notes about individuals, including Charlotte, "Tammi," and, most often of all, "Sophia." In fact, Ginger had reminded herself to call Sophia every few days.

There was also a "business card" section, which Dinah was familiar with in a different format. Names, places, ideas, or any kind of information could be grouped under a chosen keyword. For Ginger the keyword was most commonly a first name (male) and initial, and under that heading were phone numbers, dates, and partly coded information, including color words (blue, rose, "all black"), asterisks, one or two X's or O's, and the numbers six and nine. Each listing was also assigned a number from four to twenty preceded by a dollar sign: The women assumed it was a fee but didn't know whether to add two zeros or even three.

Other "cards" were headed by company names, each with one to three men's names noted below it. There was a card for "Group," with their own names and numbers, two school cards with names of principals and teachers and a subsection of daily classes, and a card for the art museum, listing several different volunteer councils with officers' names.

The expense file was meticulous but unreadable; most people's log of expenses is meaningful only to them. It was clear, however, that Ginger was noting tax-deductible outlays—some business meetings, travel, gas, entertainment, clothing purchases and dry cleaning, even categories called "Research," which included database fees for articles from *Forbes* and *Fortune,* and "Education," which consisted of monthly fees for dance classes and yoga.

The phone book was straightforward and a familiar mix. O'Brian, her hairdresser. Her manicurist. Trainer. Jogging partner. Doctors. Airlines and limo service. Caterers. Banks. Ad agencies with "(H)" in parens.

Nina. Lotte. All of their names. Couples, neatly by last name: Cane, Phil & Bonnie. Fruchtman, Jules & Joanie. Robinson, Don & Sophia.

"There's Sophia again," said Charlotte.

"Sophia who?" said Kat. "Who is Sophia?"

"Must be the same Sophia she calls all the time," said Charlotte. "Not too many Sophias around. Now that I see the whole couple, I think I've heard the name."

It seemed a good time to sit back and consider what they had here, if anything. They felt full, pushing their chairs back from a nonstop feed of information, but what they were filled with was impressions of a life, many of which corroborated their assumptions. All the different details seemed to fit together, giving them a sense of neatness, but no single detail offered a clue to Ginger's ending. They simply didn't know what hints to pursue.

"We could try to figure out who the men are by calling the numbers," said Kat, "and when someone answers 'So-and-So residence' or 'Whatsis company,' we'd hang up."

"Right. And when we figure out who they are," said Polly, "we just call them one at a time and ask if they killed Ginger."

Figuring out which of these men were with Ginger on one particular night was what they needed, Charlotte pointed out, and someone intimate with Ginger was the best place to start. Tammi was an obvious source: She'd apparently gone on some outings with Ginger, and probably not as a mere driver. The jogging partner had less potential. Ginger had commented more than once that the only interesting thing about the woman was the way she set herself a pace.

Then there was Sophia Robinson. "She keeps coming up," said Justine. "Ginger sees or calls her regularly, so they must have been close friends. But I don't remember ever hearing about her here."

"We didn't, and Ginger's lack of close friends was a topic we discussed," said Dinah. "Maybe their husbands had a business relationship? Anyone know what this Robinson does?"

"If they're the blue-ribbon society couple I'm thinking of, he's a periodontist," said Charlotte, "and unlikely to be in the market for million-watt marquees. Besides, there's no indication their meetings included husbands."

"Maybe they had a business relationship of their own," offered Justine. "She could have been another one of the ladies, like Tammi."

Kat groaned. "Come on, Justine," she said.

Justine closed up the little machine. "Why assume that Sophia wouldn't do that just because she has a rich husband? Did that keep Ginger at home?"

"Maybe they worked together on that art council Harold made Ginger join, that costume group at the museum," said Dinah.

Whatever the connection, Sophia Robinson was clearly close to Ginger in some way, or at least in constant communication, and both she and Tammi were worth talking to. "I'll call both of them and see if we can get together," said Charlotte, and Polly, whose time was most elastic, agreed to join her.

Graham Vere called Polly that night, when the air had cooled and the breeze started up and the children had both withdrawn to a pointed privacy and then to sleep, or so Polly assumed when she saw dark under the doors to their rooms. Andrea had spent the evening on the kitchen phone, all in whispers, frequent titters, occasional gasps, and some long stretches of muted singing, apparently in duet with whoever was on the other end. She sat in the dark and, whenever Polly passed the door, in silence. Jeremy watched a TV show on which the host demonstrated a number of amazing kitchen aids, each one half utensil, half small appliance. He stayed fixated on the screen when she sat down on a nearby ottoman to watch with him, and finally he went to his room to play something called "Baby Oh, Baby Oh" over and over again.

Neither child spoke to Polly, not of the day past or the day ahead, or of their hopes, dreams, or ambitions. Neither had any preference as to what she should put in their lunches.

This is not good, said her mother. Polly turned out the living room lights, sat down at her desk, and in the light of the computer screen, let tears spill over her eyelids and track down her cheeks, turning only when the phone rang.

"I need to know more about how to pick stocks," said a voice that she knew immediately as his, the coroner's.

"Any particular kind?"

"NASDAQ," he said. "I've always heard that if you really hit it on a NASDAQ stock, you can make a fortune."

"Well," said Polly, putting her feet up on the desk, "you hold a pencil out in front of you, absolutely parallel to the stock table, close your eyes, and when the point dips down, go with the stock it lands on. Same as finding water."

"I don't know," he said. "I think I need a personal seminar. Maybe over dinner Wednesday night? If it's safe for two redheads to go out together."

"Do you know whether it's allowed on the NASDAQ system?" asked Polly. "It's okay on the New York."

"It's allowed. But we might fight."

"Oh, I do hope so."

"Me, too. Wednesday night possible for you?"

"Wednesday's fine," she said. "Did Dinah give you my address or just my number?"

"The number. I still need the address and maybe directions."

It turned out that he was familiar with all but the last couple of loops on the ridge, but he wrote down everything anyway, repeating it after her.

"So," said Polly, "do I really have to hose you down in the yard?"

"It depends what comes in tomorrow," he said.

"Like what? You mean the type of person or the type of death?"

"Well, either. Both. You don't really want to know."

"Actually," she said, "I find it interesting. At least usually. I mean, I would . . . ordinarily."

She faltered, wondering if she really wanted to hear more, if she could stand more details about people's skulls and body temps and the final arrangement of their limbs and clothing.

"I'm really sorry about your friend," said the coroner.

"I know," she said. "Thank you."

The night air turned warmer, softer. It was the season for mourning doves. She could hear one in the garden and one down in the canyon.

Don't get carried away, warned her mother.

Polly could certainly understand that point of view. But as feelings go, she told her mother, getting carried away beats any alternative.

9

Charlotte had left messages on everyone's phones by the next afternoon, asking only Polly to call her back. As usual, Charlotte enjoyed an office lunch hour, eating a carton of yogurt and a bag of salted Bavarian pretzels, making calls that required no answer or answered other people's earlier messages. For Charlotte voice mail was a great gift: In most cases she didn't want contact or company, just closure.

She had already called both Tammi and Sophia Robinson—two people who probably had nothing in common but Ginger Pass, whatever her relationship with each. Tammi's voice message, light and breathy with a little chirp on the upper notes, announced that she was out of town and real sorry to miss the call. Charlotte left an unrevealing message with her name and number. Sophia Robinson's phone was answered by another breathy little voice, but this one called her "Señora" and went to get Mrs. Robinson. The next voice was low and silky, as Sophia Robinson declared herself delighted to meet friends of Ginger's and invited Charlotte to come the next day.

When Polly called back, Charlotte said she'd had a postponement—typical of probate cases—and had accepted Sophia Robinson's invitation for coffee at ten-thirty the next morning. Polly should meet her there.

Fine, said Polly, but it wasn't necessary. Charlotte was already off the phone.

The Robinson house floated on its wooded lot like a lily pad on a pond. All glass and oiled cedar, it was set pavilion-style in the middle of a big rectangle of reflecting pools divided from each other by decorative concrete paths. The lot was secluded, a green field of quiet protected by high stands of bamboo, xylosma, and melaleuca.

It was one of the older tracts above Beverly Hills, its generous lots spaced up both sides of the foothill road like pinnate leaves along the main vein of a fern. Those who lived there were guaranteed privacy because the road dead-ended halfway to the Mulholland ridge: There was no through route to the San Fernando Valley on the other side, so residents were the only traffic, and their cars were large and quiet.

Polly arrived first, drove up the long driveway through the trees, and emerged into what seemed an institutional preserve. Sculptures dotted the perfect lawns around the parking area—a tall stone stele with well-defined glyphs, a domed Olmec head, several stone benches in forms half animal, half man, that were once probably sacrificial altars. Even in the pools, several geometric arrangements of colored metal rose from the water like birds poised on one leg.

Hesitant to cross over the front pool alone, Polly waited for Charlotte, and even when Charlotte joined her, they stepped across side by side like two children coming to an audience with the wizard. As they approached the oversize red double doors, one swung open and a well-burnished woman with a strong voice said, "I'm Sophia Robinson, please come in."

She looked tastefully rich, large tortoiseshell glasses pushing back her caramel-colored hair, her body compact in a caramel dress. Gold circles added the highlights—hammered gold earrings, buttons at the shoulders, buckles on her shoes, two wide bangles, a Rolex watch.

"I've been expecting you," she said, drawing them in, taking first Polly's, then Charlotte's hand in both of hers. Charlotte looked at her watch: They were actually a minute early.

A man, almost surely the periodontist, stood at the other side of the entrance hall. "My husband, Donald," the woman said, and he nodded, a background consort in a soft blue-gray sports jacket, bow tie under a surprisingly pink face. An obvious back brace propped him so straight that he bent slightly backward. Under his shirt it came around front as well, girdling in any errant flesh.

"Your house is just beautiful," said Charlotte. "We're obviously on the threshold of a serious art collection."

"More enthusiastic than expert," said Sophia Robinson with a deprecating gesture. "Come, I'll show you around."

It started in the entrance hall, with its walls of glass blocks, cut out here and there to display dozens of pre-Columbian statuettes and pottery. There was water and sky inside as well as out. Above their heads was a rectangular skylight of wavy glass, and two feet up each side wall mossy structures of branches drooped bromeliads almost to the water beds of floating plants at the base.

The consort retreated to the back of the house as the tour began, the three women moving from room to room at a museum pace. Pre-Columbian was clearly the specialty, with sprinklings of African, a bit of Northwest coast on shelves and tables. The walls, however, went modern—big canvases of Pollock-type paint swirls, several vast monochromes (*Untitled I, Untitled II,* and finally *Without Title*) with a few flecks of color, a slight slip of the brush.

They finished in the largest living room, a virtual gallery with four long end-to-end skylights above their heads. A coffee urn, cups, a plate of cookies waited on a low table, alongside a crystal vase of gardenias, a pre-Columbian whistle in the form of a frog, a short-handled carved wooden rattle. Sophia Robinson poured, a big yellow diamond on one hand throwing light onto her chin like a buttercup.

"I knew of Ginger's little group of friends," she said. "And you all knew of me?"

The woman was as unsure of them as they of her. Ginger must have represented them as friends rather than a help group.

"We didn't actually know you were friends until after she died," said Charlotte. Without at least partial honesty in negotiations, she found, one got nothing in return. Trained examiner that she was, Charlotte saw an immediate change in Sophia Robinson's pose: She had received a significant piece of information and visibly relaxed.

"Well, in a city so big," she said more airily, "we rarely know all our friends' friends, do we? And Ginger was active in so many different circles. I really had no idea whom to contact when I heard she'd died. I just waited, hoping to hear from someone, hoping one of her friends would call me."

"Did you know each other through the costume council?" If Sophia was through probing, Charlotte was not.

"That's how we met, yes." She spoke carefully, poured carefully, knees together, feet together.

Polly and Charlotte were careful, too, careful not to look at each other, but as they said later, they were both aware that Sophia wasn't just evasive. She was even less informed than they, and even more eager for information. She might have known Ginger very little for someone who was such a regular part of her life. As they sat and she hosted, Sophia

described Ginger as being from Chicago, referred to the pale stepdaughter as a lovely child, and finally, making a decisive plunge into the subject
that really interested her, turned the yellow diamond around and around
on her finger and murmured, "I just had no idea that Ginger had health
problems."

Charlotte (she said later) thought of leaving, convinced there was
nothing for them here. But Polly (she said later) "suddenly just had a feeling" and, leaning forward, said bluntly, almost harshly, "There were no
health problems. She was with a couple of men the night she died." And
when she saw Sophia Robinson's face tighten, added, "Three, actually."

The china cup began to rattle on its saucer in the woman's hand, and
Polly, watching closely, said, "People do it, you know."

Sophia Robinson closed her other hand on the cup and saucer, put
them down on the coffee table, and rose. Blotches of red appeared on her
face.

"Quite a lot of people do it," goaded Polly. She wasn't at all sure
where she was going but sensed that some advantage had opened up and
pushed forward.

"Not on my time, they don't," Sophia Robinson spat out. "She was
mine. It's my business."

She pulled the big glasses down over her eyes. Farsighted, she en-
gaged them with a fiercely magnified gaze, her eyes and upper face unnaturally large behind the lenses.

Water was dripping audibly from the walls all around them. Here
they sat, in an unbelievable art gallery, filled with flowers and ancient
icons, having coffee with a society matron in good standing, whose day
job was luncheons and museum tours and flower arrangements and
whose real business was prostitution.

"Ginger worked for you," said Charlotte.

Sophia Robinson half nodded assent, gave a half shrug, flipped her
diamond hand palm up.

"Don't worry," said Polly. "We knew about the work. Not about you personally, but about what Ginger did."

Water dripped. Her rage contained, the blotches fading from her face, the woman looked down at them. "What do you want of me?"

With Sophia Robinson in command again, they weren't in the best position, thought Charlotte, but there was still room for negotiation. "We want to know who the men were," she said. "We don't even know what happened."

"I'll take care of them."

"It's not your fault," said Polly, thinking: murder, hit men, a playing-out of guilt and revenge far beyond the little gestures of which they themselves were capable. "It's not your responsibility; you mustn't blame yourself."

Self-blame was so foreign to Sophia Robinson that the suggestion turned her almost merry. "My dear, I don't blame myself," she said, stepping out onto a sunny part of the white rug. "Ginger was a big girl. Who knows what happened?"

She turned the big yellow stone around and around her finger. "But there shouldn't have been three of them. The contract, and the fee, was for one. Only one. Nobody brings in buddies on me."

Charlotte and Polly sat like schoolgirls, quietly, poised at the front of the couch, looking up and waiting for the madam to decide what she might give them and when. They had nothing more for her: She had no interest in how Ginger had died, or how she'd lived, or the number of hours she was finally alone in the dark.

"You want his name?" offered Sophia, leaning over to pinch two yellowed leaves off the gardenia bouquet. "It's Milo Till, the developer, and I'm perfectly happy if he knows you got it from me. Years I've served him. You know him?"

In the archway to the hall, the consort, habitual lurker, cleared his throat. Periodontics must be a specialty that practitioners could schedule at will, like pool cleaning or garden maintenance. Maybe all periodontists took Wednesdays off for golf games or prostitution rings.

Polly and Charlotte stood, having gotten what they'd come for. Just to be sure, Charlotte said, "Always a surprise element, isn't there? But this is what we wanted—some idea who she was with. And you wanted some idea of the circumstances. Just to close the book on it, I assume."

The yellow diamond pushed the glasses back up. "I was also fond of her," said Sophia Robinson, walking them into the entrance hall, which was now empty. "Ginger was an original. Not in what she did, of course. Everyone's the same there. But in who she was when she wasn't doing it." She opened the big front doors.

"All heart," muttered Charlotte as the red door closed and they stepped out from under the cedar beams into the surrounding glare of the sun and reflecting pools. For a few minutes, they stood between their two cars, reviewing what they'd just heard and what they'd said and what it added to their understanding.

They had the name of one of Ginger's clients—the main one, obviously. It was all they'd hoped for, and it was enough, they told themselves, in spite of the disquiet that came with learning more.

Before parting, they agreed that Polly would make the calls to share with the group what they'd learned. Better that only one voice do the retelling, so that if there were any shading in their two perceptions, everyone would at least start with the same fundamentals. Polly, moreover, had more time and privacy, whereas telephone calling was for Charlotte a red flag in an already embattled home. "How can you spend so much time on the phone?" Avery would exclaim. "Charlotte spends her evenings talking on the phone," he'd tell dinner guests while Charlotte tried to smile and tears of anger burned behind her eyelids. "I talk to people all day: I can't bear any more talk at night," he'd say, laughing. Nevertheless, he wanted to know all the callers and the business of every call, and he would stand in the doorway of Charlotte's study hissing, "Who's that? Who *is* that?" while she was talking.

Now the group knew one of the men involved. They had two to go, Polly told each of the women when she called that evening. Maybe four in all, said Dinah, if two left semen and one left saliva and a fourth did nothing to women but crack their skulls. Fine, said Polly, consider that another lead.

Charlotte had already promised to work up what she called "general background" on Milo Till, including both professional and personal associations. "You can know a man by his lawyers," she liked to say. Also by his decorator, said Dinah, whose medical connections were useful only if Till had problems that were dermatologic or if he happened to be enrolled with a managed-care provider run by one of Dinah's friends. But her office decorator, an old friend, could put them vicariously into both his house and his pocketbook, and Dinah had in the past found her gossip unusually factual.

Kat would talk to her trainers, trying to find someone who had served this Milo Till as steward or anything else at the Palatine retreat. She might at least learn more about the scene and the time of Ginger's death, if not the people.

Justine, always initially reluctant, greeted the request according to type. She was working for her husband the next two days, then for her father; she wasn't comfortable prying into someone's personal life; the police should be given more time. Ginger's dead, said Polly. We want to know why. We cared about her. Are you in or out? So Justine offered to check city and county records for all of Milo Till's property holdings and partnerships.

The coroner came exactly at seven. Polly was waiting in the hall near the door when the bell rang. She was wearing the third outfit she'd tried on and a pair of earrings Andrea had brought her after passing her door several times and noticing Polly's unusual attention to her preparations.

For once Polly wasn't inclined to fill the silence, simply saying that her dinner date was with a doctor she'd met through Dinah. Andrea, as always, said nothing. She'd already agreed, by not refusing, to watch over Jeremy, and Polly expected nothing more, certainly not the earrings, which were big, red enamel disks swinging on silver wires and matched her red blouse.

Graham Vere's hair was wet and he smelled of soap. He wore a yellow plaid bow tie and was holding a bouquet of plate-size sunflowers—the biggest flowers in the biggest bouquet she'd ever seen. It looked like a vaudeville stage prop. She introduced the children, hovering at the back of the hall near the steps to the kitchen. Andrea said, "Hi," and Jeremy, who had a fork in his mouth like a cigar, jiggled it up and down.

"Mom," said Andrea just before the front door closed. Polly turned back. "Have a good time," said Andrea.

"Yeah," said Jeremy, tipping the fork.

For the first ten minutes, they sat in Graham's parked car three loops down the hill and Polly wept into a surgical towel he found in the backseat, trying to explain why she was so affected by her children's goodbyes. It's all right, he kept telling her. She told him why it wasn't all right, and they ultimately agreed that, eventually, it might be all right.

Perhaps a good date, like this one, was a gavotte, a smoothly programmed dance: He steps, she steps, they come together, repeat. With each turn they were a little better matched, and felt it, proceeding with more and more confidence.

She admired the tie; he liked her daughter's earrings. She fretted over the gulf between her and her children. He rejoiced that the gulf between him and his adolescent boys seemed to diminish as their lives slowly separated from his.

While the restaurant filled and emptied and waiters entered the room with laden trays held aloft and busboys scurried out with tubs of dirty dishes, Polly and Graham leaned toward each other in their dark

booth and made their exchanges. Ever since he stopped smoking some
years before, he had a tic: He held a utensil between thumb and index
finger and dipped it up and down, up and down. Polly offered up her
habit of holding a satiny-smooth beach stone in her palm and stroking it
with her thumb.

He was quite free of past loves. There was an ex-wife, but he tried
to approach her with humor instead of hatred. When they separated
six years ago, she'd made no claim on the boys, then five and eight, and
she saw them only a month in the summer, at her parents' house at the
shore, and a half week at Christmas. In a recent renegotiation of support,
she produced without apology financial statements indicating, among
other things, that she spent more on her dry cleaning than on her sons.

As for Polly, she had had a good marriage, she thought, but they were
young, she had been a widow almost as long as a wife, and though she
felt deeply disloyal to admit it, Dan was dimming in her mind. She
missed him, but now it was more a general loneliness than a specific
ache. Her mother, who'd died earlier, was clearer and closer, painfully so.

"I could offer you an equity interest in my mother," he said. "A tough
cookie, but very funny, intentionally so, and she'd like to know about
buying stocks, too. Oddly enough, she and my wife got along well, and
while there was never any question who got her allegiance after the divorce, I think she suffered a real loss."

"What did your mother like about her?"

"She said Angela was an excellent shopper. I was never quite sure
whether she was serious. My wife was certainly a full-time professional
in that activity, but what constitutes excellence?"

"Good taste, I think, and a quick eye for value at a price. I don't have
it; your mother would never like me."

She was embarrassed to have leaped so soon into the personal, but
Vere seemed not to notice. "She would too," he said.

The evening passed. They got silly, then serious. It wasn't just a first date or even just a date. Not wanting it to end, she told him about the group and about Ginger and her double life and the probable circumstances of her death.

"It figures," he said. "There was no other significant trauma beyond the skull fracture. What I mean is that sexually this woman was not forced."

"We just want to know what happened," she said, "particularly because no one else does."

"Someone will, even if the family doesn't pursue it. We did report it as a possible homicide."

"And you got the feeling that somebody official was just waiting for your office to report so they could investigate?"

"Well, Poderoso and San Bernardino County are technically in charge, but for all I know, they may have an arrangement with the L.A. police for investigation as well as for medical examination—at least when the needed resources and the interest are here."

By the time they finished eating, she had told him about the madam, but not her name, and about the client, but not his name. She told him that she and the other women in the group intended to do their own investigation. Then, instantly uneasy about revealing their plans, she purposely lightened her tone, adding, "And we won't stop till we identify everyone responsible."

"And then what will you do?" Copying her mood, he leaned across the table conspiratorially.

She leaned forward to meet him and whispered, "Shouldn't we murder them?"

"Good idea. Obvious thing to do." He raised his glass. "To revenge."

"And justice," she said, raising hers.

The house was quiet when they reached her door. Andrea had put on the front lantern and the living room lamps and the patio floodlights, just as Polly did when Andrea was out late.

"I'd take you dancing if tomorrow weren't a workday," said Graham softly, the lantern casting a coppery sheen on his thick red hair.

"I feel very well danced," said Polly. "Thank you."

"I'll be in Ojai at a conference the next four days, and I have a dinner meeting Monday night till eight or eight-thirty. Could we take a walk at nine? Dinah said I should ask you to show me the Hollywood sign."

She nodded. He put the palm of his hand to her cheek, lightly, briefly, and left.

Real manners come from the heart, said her mother approvingly. Some things you can't be taught.

10

The next Monday morning there were birds in the canyon again after a long period of silence, or so it seemed to Polly. She had always wanted to chart the seasons of the various resident birds. One January she even started it when she heard a mourning dove for the first time in months: Did they leave California for part of the year? But she'd kept the bird log less than a week.

She also wanted to chart the sunlight in various parts of the house over a year. At certain times she was struck by a sudden change—the few weeks in February, for example, when a burst of early-morning gold would turn her bedroom into a glowing jewel box for about an hour. She never even started that chart, which seemed much less informative than the one on birds.

Acutely aware of birds and sunlight, she started the day with such a soft edge that when she returned from her trip downhill with the children, she opened her file of "pending" complaints looking for something interesting—maybe a matter of mere irritation, requiring pointed phrasing rather than persuasive reasoning. She wanted to be sharp when she made an exploratory call to the developer's office.

Dear Sirs [she wrote to Disneyland]:

Out-of-towners always ask us how to get to Disneyland. From now on I'll just say, Don't go.

My family went this summer, as we have every year. But Disneyland is too crowded now for a pleasant visit, or even a visit in which we see the whole park.

Rides are short, lines long. Dulled employees lip-sync their spiels. In ten hours we managed five rides, three snacks, two fast-food meals, and a tram connection. More than six of those hours we spent waiting—up to an hour and a half for one ride. We even waited twenty minutes to buy a pair of mouse ears.

But you obviously know all this. You urge locals to go off-season. You hold special corporate evenings. You push season tickets, knowing it takes multiple visits to see much of the park.

Your famous "crowd control" makes it even worse—the tight parallel rope lines looping people one way, then another, an inch at a time. You need something else. Maybe a reservation system? Attendance limits? Re-engineering rides built for yesterday's crowds? Surely a company that came up with a talking Lincoln, instant rapids, and the very notion of selling ears can devise more innovative ways to move crowds.

Our Disneyland day cost $361 for five people. Even the children agreed to skip next year's visit. If we get more people to do that, it should thin out the crowds. That would certainly help.

Sincerely . . .

The voice of Milo Till's receptionist was light and British, which meant one of two things. She might actually be British, one of a horde of young and untalented English girls who were ambitious but unfocused and had neither higher schooling nor professional training. But America meant adventure, and they had the advantage of an accent that might reveal humble origins to other Brits but sounded "classy" to the big firms in Beverly Hills and Century City with polished granite floors, Miró prints, and a yearning for cachet.

If indeed British, all accent and dumb as a post, she'd be an easy encounter for Polly. She could, however, be an American of equally little intellect and less ambition but enough peasant cunning to affect the British accent. To her the front office was not so much an adventure as an achievement or—worse for Polly—an entrée, in which case she had enough neurons to be an obstacle.

"Hello," said Polly, talking boarding school, Junior League. "I'm putting together the sponsorship for this year's LACAT—the L.A. Corporate Art Tours—and I want to send Mr. Till his packet. . . ."

"Mr. Till is out of town," said the girl crisply, with less accent. "May I help you?"

"Oh, I do hope so," said Polly, thinking, Ah, American. Strappy little high heels. Flippy little skirt. But not thoughtless. "We work with the Palatine Club," she went on, "following the lists from the campout. Mr. Till wasn't with the B of A party as in the past. I'm pretty sure he should be in the B of A group, but. . . ."

"I'd have to check with him." Some hesitation: Doesn't want to make a choice but doesn't want to lose something important.

"Well, we just wondered why. . . ." Give her a faint tinge of negative.

"He had several guests of his own this year," said the girl, taking charge, saving Mr. Till from embarrassment.

"Ah, that explains it. We just wanted to be very careful. I mean, if there were any rift with the bankers."

"Hardly," said the girl. "He and Mr. Reinhart—from O'Doyle and Dirkson?—hosted Walker Cannon, the Senate candidate?"

"Oh, of course." Polly jumped up, could have shouted, but instead did a few tap steps and a shuffle beside her desk.

"It's no secret," said the girl, confident again. "They were all photographed leaving here."

"Oh, good," breathed Polly. "That's fine, then: I'll just go ahead and put his packet in the mail. It should be there by week's end."

Odd how jubilant one could feel about a minor triumph over such a negligible opponent, but it carried her lightly through the day to the group's regular Monday meeting. They spent the session discussing a problem Charlotte presented. She'd asked her husband for information from his office files—on Milo Till, as it happened, but she didn't mention the name. Avery had refused on ethical grounds.

Yes, it was confidential, and it was another partner's client. But there were other considerations: Shouldn't you trust your spouse not to misuse confidential information? Doesn't love assume unquestioning support? What is love, what is support?

Everyone but Lotte guessed what it was she'd asked him to get. All but Lotte shifted in their seats, discovered various itches, wished the meeting over.

"Too many philosophical absolutes for me," said Lotte calmly. "I'm a therapist, not a Talmudic scholar."

Obediently, they laughed. Lotte was a decent soul, a good facilitator. But they were impatient now. They were activists.

"The question is not so much why he refused," mused Lotte, pencil to lips, "as why you feel betrayed."

The therapeutic turnaround, an admirable tradition. They put pencils to their lips, affected concentration, did their best until finally, fifteen minutes early, Lotte rose, winked, and said "When you leave, pull the door after you."

In silence they heard her footsteps leave the door, walk around the balcony, start down the stairs. Polly quickly outlined her call to Milo Till's office. "Oh, boy," said Charlotte happily. "That's one little bimbo gonna be in big trouble!"

"She won't even mention it to him," said Polly. "It's big stuff to us. To her it's nothing."

"Why would she tell you the names?" asked Kat.

"She was boasting," explained Justine, to whom this girl and this exchange were nothing new. "Part of her job is to boast of connections, and no one told her this one wasn't for boasting."

"Besides," said Polly, "don't forget that no one knows of the other connection but us. Even Sophia Robinson doesn't know as much as we do now. Not that it's anywhere near enough."

Charlotte knew Reinhart. Everyone in the legal community knew Mitchell Reinhart, she said, and everyone at the courts and everyone who'd ever been divorced. Everyone, at least, who had significant assets and had been divorced—the men because Mitch Reinhart helped them get away with most of those assets intact, the women because Mitch Reinhart helped their husbands cut their hearts out, kick their teeth in, and leave them begging in the street. With full custody of the children, of course.

Reinhart was the marital-law version of a criminal defense lawyer, who justifies his work by the assertion that even vicious, violent, evil criminals deserve fair representation before God and the court, and someone has to do the dirty job. Reinhart specialized in selfish, obscenely successful men who had passed the midlife mark, located a trophy wife within their grasp, and wanted to undo twenty or thirty years of community property so they'd have a better chance at happiness in the few years they had left.

Reinhart had already represented Milo Till in divorce actions. He'd probably get this Cannon fellow someday as well.

"But let's get to Till," Charlotte interrupted herself. "He's the one we wanted to start with, and it's not hard. He's pretty visible, at least the one-eighth of him that's above the water."

Milo Till headed a corporation that served as holding company for myriad financial enterprises. The most public were real estate developments, some wholly his, some partnerships. The less public were venture-capital groups that financed mostly midsize companies around the Southwest, mostly with Milo Till's own money. And the totally private ones were trusts administered by Milo Till and involving none of his own money.

"And whose money is it, you may ask," Charlotte intoned, standing before them in full court mode, hands clasped behind her, gaze directly on each of them in turn. "Politicians, many of them. Politicians are required to put into blind trusts any holdings in possible conflict with the people's interests. Remember when Ronald Reagan put all his little investments into a blind trust administered by his friends in the entertainment industry, and when he could finally look at his money again, they had, mirabile dictu, turned it into a fortune?

"Well, Till's got political ambitions, or at least political connections, and he apparently runs some of these for pretty powerful guys—our lieutenant governor, for one, and Nevada's governor *and* lieutenant governor. Some, like those guys, are already in high office. Some are candidates, including L. Walker Cannon, current Republican front-runner for United States Senate. Scion of an old California family, big in land and agribusiness. *L* for Lewis. Nickname, even among family: 'Loose Cannon.'"

"Yes, Cannon is a Till client," Justine put in. She didn't move from her seat, but Charlotte immediately sat down, yielding to her. Justine had done a search of L.A. County's property records as well as several contiguous counties with whom L.A. exchanged database access. Till had come up as owner, partner, or principal on a dozen large tracts of raw land and as many subdivided communities. He was general partner in a number of real estate investment companies. And he was administrator or trustee of eight or ten blind trusts on behalf of elected politicians, including Cannon, or their wives.

"I've listed everything here," said Justine, and took from her briefcase a folder of listings for each of the women.

"So what does he get in return?" asked Kat.

"Unusually thoughtful consideration for his projects," said Charlotte wryly, looking at the sheets, which included brief descriptions. "Someone with all this land right near protected deserts and vanishing foothills might well need special consideration."

"More than that," said Dinah. "He wants an ambassadorship."

Everyone turned to her, and she gave them back a sheepish shrug. "I haven't got much yet. But my decorator did this chain of restaurants Till co-owns, and according to his restaurant partner, the guy really wants to be an ambassador some years down the line, maybe to Latin America. The chain is called Caliente."

Kat had started bouncing around her chair while Dinah was talking, and now she was on the edge of it. "My turn?"

"Your turn," said Polly.

Kat stood and faced them, show-and-tell style, and took a loud breath. "Okay. I talked to my trainers, remember? The two who work the Palatine retreat every summer? One also works for the club downtown during the year. They said that by the middle of that evening there was a rumor that someone had a woman in one of the cabins, and one of their friends who went up to change his loincloth or something after a skit said he saw two men carrying something through the woods.

"Next day the police came, and everyone heard there was a body found outside. They all thought they'd be called in to tell what they knew, but next thing they hear, this guy Till has gone down to town to talk with the cops and that's the end of it."

"The end?" Justine exclaimed. "A woman's dead, and it just ends there?"

"Wait a minute," said Kat. "Paco—that's my best trainer—said nobody cared as long as the body wasn't on the grounds."

"Because of the liability?" said Charlotte.

Kat frowned. "I don't think liability had anything to do with it. What everybody worries about is the club's absolute rule that no women are allowed. It would have been a really big problem if she'd been found on the grounds: They'd have to investigate."

For a minute nobody said anything; then they all had questions, none of which Kat could answer. When they were quiet again, she added that she hadn't just left it at that, of course. She'd pushed them, and it turned out that Paco had a buddy in Personnel who was willing to look up who'd been assigned to work Milo Till's cottage. As it happened, Paco knew one of the two stewards pretty well, and called him.

"He had actually talked with this Reinhart guy the day after the whole thing broke. Reinhart always had his breakfast in the cottage, and the business of the body came up, and Paco's friend commented that the woman must have been by herself and fallen, because if anyone had known she was hurt, they wouldn't just leave her like that. And apparently this Reinhart guy said, 'Unless they were through with her,' and laughed.

"When Paco told me that," said Kat, "I couldn't even speak for a minute, and he put his arm around me and said, 'Guess it's a guy thing.'" She looked around the group. "You have to remember where he's coming from."

"Where is he coming from?" Justine asked.

"The best of my trainers, and he's the very best, are gay. I think he was being critical."

"You think it's possible there are . . . people who wouldn't be critical?" Justine was stammering slightly.

"A lot of people, probably," Dinah said gently. "Isn't that why we got into this? Because no one was properly critical?"

Charlotte waved her hand, clearing the air of tangential matter. "Okay, listen, here's what we've got: We know how Ginger died, and where and when. We even know who did it. Well, we don't know exactly what they did—assuming the injury was partly their fault—but there's no doubt they let her die. Now what do we do?"

"I thought we just wanted to know," said Justine, her resolve slipping to its habitual low. "What can we do?"

"Probably quite a lot, actually," said Polly, cutting off a comment from Charlotte. She tilted herself against the wall on two legs of the chair, head back, eyes on the ceiling. They were not without resources, she pointed out, not even without power, but their power wasn't the visible sort. What they had, as they'd already demonstrated, was an ability to divide up and join together, sharing their separate contacts and information.

"Isn't that what networking is?" asked Polly. "Anyone can do it. Everyone does it to some extent. And people like us—women, in a word—can do it better, because they don't mind being just parts of a whole. Nobody's insistent on operating alone. Nobody thinks that if they do band together, someone has to be in charge."

"Polly, you spend too much time alone talking to yourself," said Dinah. "Never mind the dynamics. Let's just get to it."

Only Justine had stayed in her seat, ankles crossed, briefcase on her lap. Kat and Charlotte were leaning against the edge of the table. Dinah was at the window, tying slipknots in the cord that hung from the blinds. Polly started walking.

"We should kill one of them," said Kat. "An eye for an eye. There must be a way."

"I like it," said Dinah, thinking Kat was joking.

"Oh, for God's sake," said Polly, who knew she wasn't.

"They got away with it, didn't they?"

"Come on, Kat," said Charlotte. "This is real life, not a detective movie. You can't go around killing people."

They took a break to go to the bathroom, to get soft drinks from the first-floor machine, to take one turn around the balcony. Justine stayed in the room, by the window, frowning, until the others returned.

"Here's an idea, maybe a little stupid," said Dinah tentatively, "but if we work through the right people, we might be able to get their wives' decorators to churn their accounts. Or their favorite gallery. I know Till's gallery. His decorator, too, for that matter."

"Come on," said Polly. "This isn't a sitcom we're in. Remember: It's real life."

Huge footsteps ascended the stone stairs, shaking the balcony and wrought-iron balustrade like a prehistoric battleground and sending shock waves around the mezzanine. Dinah grabbed at the arms of her chair. "Is it . . . ?"

"One of the overeaters," said Charlotte soothingly. "Late for their meeting."

"Right," said Dinah.

"Here's how I see it," said Polly. "First, we obviously can't expect the law or any other official justice to go after them for Ginger's death. They're too powerful, too well-connected. For the same reason, we probably can't go after them openly for anything in their professional lives, though they probably do as much evil there as in their private lives. And get away with it.

"So in the open they're untouchable. We'd be wasting our time. But there must be some way we can get them on a private, domestic level—something we can expose, or destroy, or aggravate. We need to find some weakness, some flaw, something that gives us a way to get at them personally."

"Something that will ruin them," said Kat.

"Or something that will make them ruin themselves," said Dinah.

"So they'll never even know it was us behind it," said Polly.

From the desk loud clapping and Charlotte's crack of a laugh. "Like the witches in *Macbeth,* playing on his ambition until he must destroy himself."

"This could take years," said Dinah grimly.

"My mother used to say 'Revenge is a dish best served cold,'" said Polly. The adage drew not a single look of comprehension.

"What does that mean?" asked Kat.

"I have no idea," admitted Polly. "Well, not quite. I asked her, and she said it meant that if you wanted revenge, you shouldn't act in the heat of the moment, that the best revenges were carefully planned and carried out coolly and dispassionately." She looked around. "Even then the adage isn't real clear, but I get the idea."

"Me, too," said Dinah. "So who do we tackle first, and what exactly do we do?"

They laid out immediate tasks. They had to know where each of the men was now and what he was doing, who was in his family and where they were, anything about his current life and business that invited closer examination. Once again they divided the work, though everyone was free to follow whatever she turned up.

Charlotte was going to search court filings for all three names and prepare what she called "general biography" on Milo Till. Justine would do a canvass of city and county records—property, business license, voter registration—on all three, along with state vital statistics. Dinah would look for health information on all three through contacts at insurance companies and hospitals, explore political attachments and donations, work her art and decorating sources, and gather general biography on Walker Cannon.

Credit reports and bank verifications went to Kat, because her clubs ordered dozens every day. She also wanted to investigate social and sexual affairs—"the dirtbag detail," she called it—pointing out with glee that trainers knew even more personal stuff than decorators did. And she specially wanted to do Mitchell Reinhart. "I'm pretty up on the divorce and couple scene," she declared proudly, "and something sticks in my head about him—something about a wife or a girl."

Last, Polly would check street accounts, Dun & Bradstreet reports and corporate boards for all three names. And she would search the last several years of newspaper and magazine hits on each name via several of the computer databases to which she subscribed.

"Done, then," and Polly pushed off from her chair. "What's the matter, Justine?"

"Well, I'm okay with gathering information. . . ."

"That's a step forward," said Polly, but with a smile.

"But when it comes to actually doing something to them, I'm just concerned they may not all be equally guilty."

"That's true," Charlotte conceded, "but only of the killing, if that's what it was. There's no doubt Ginger was left untended, and there's no question her death is still unquestioned, unexplained, and uninvestigated, and for that they're all guilty."

Polly held the door open. "Besides," she said, "as we agreed, we're not actually executing them."

All day, while she did other things, Polly had thought of the coroner's visit the coming evening, and at nine he arrived. Even seen through the side window, waiting on the front steps, he seemed excited—gleeful, really—and pleased with himself.

"I've got something for you," he announced as she was opening the door. "There was an arrangement, a fix. It was a guy from the Palatine Club, named Milo Till, who seems to have stopped the investigation into your friend's death—starting up in Poderoso Pines and probably a lot further, since nothing's happened here either."

Polly stood silent, her face blank. Confirmation, she told herself. We have confirmation. But somehow this was not the way she wanted it. "How'd you get that?" she asked carefully.

"I called the Pines Police Department—maybe the only Pines policeman, actually," he answered proudly. "We talked, one law guy to another."

She knew she should focus on the information or on his getting it for her, but all she could think was that she had lost command. For hours she had tracked the financial connections of three well-guarded men. For days she and her friends had pieced together the circumstances of Ginger's death. And for years she had managed her life, her family, her home and business, alone.

She looked at his big smile. "Why did you do that?" she said harshly. "I didn't ask you to help."

Vere was stricken. He stepped back, retreating to the stoop. "I wanted to help you. As we agreed in the beginning, it's all in who you know."

"Don't you think we tried?" Be quiet, she told herself, don't do this. Don't do this, her mother warned her. She hurtled on. "You think we needed help?"

"No, hardly, not at all."

Polly started to cry.

He moved to the bench at the side of the patio and sat down. "I'm not good at this," he said. "I spend too much time with dead tissue."

Minutes passed in this tableau. Polly snuffled a little more, then tapered off. The background music took over, a virtual convention of calling doves, tree toads, crickets.

"I don't suppose," he said finally, patting the bench next to him, "that you'd like to tell me more about this?"

So they sat until the stars were sharp white points of light above the city's glow and the birds settled down to occasional soft calls. Polly told the coroner what they now knew about Ginger's death—but still not the names—and he asked questions.

It was almost like having her mother back. Like her mother, he questioned her information, refined her statements, tested her conclusions. She welcomed the challenge. At worst a conversation with her mother was a joust, a contest she was destined to lose simply because she was the child and instinctively held back when she had the advantage. At best it was a workout. She threw out her ideas, they came back over and again, as fast as she threw them, until she'd found the proper stance and rhythm and gotten it right.

On one question she was not able to satisfy him. "What," he kept asking, "are you planning to do when you know everybody and everything?"

"Nothing," she kept answering. "Nothing yet. We just want to know."

And he would smile and shake his head, and they both knew he was remembering that just last week she'd mentioned murder and he'd applauded the idea.

By the time they'd hiked to the Hollywood sign and back, she felt better focused, a new calm in her intentions. "That was good," she said. "You could be my mother."

"It wouldn't be my choice," he said, "but I'm flattered."

Boy, said her mother, talk about easy come, easy go. But she wasn't really angry, and Polly felt her watching, satisfied, as they said good night, and Polly went into the house and fell into sleep more quickly than she had in years.

11

The group had parted as before. Each was assigned certain tasks, and a master list was compiled of calls to be made and information gathered by the next meeting. All of them were habitual list-makers. Lists gave them a feeling of moving on and moving forward, even when the goal was indistinct. No one had an idea what might come next, just a sense of something coming.

In only her third phone call, Dinah learned of a fund-raiser scheduled that very night for L. Walker Cannon. By her sixth call, she had an invitation for the group, which she described as an investment club of professional women.

Dinah had at one time been passionately political. Though it now seemed odd and unfitting, she had even been a registered Republican. She couldn't remember why. She hadn't actually changed parties. Consumed by some new interest, she had simply stopped voting, but friends in the Republican state party gladly referred her now to Cannon's people.

They were immediately welcoming. Any savvy politico wanted access to women donors of a certain age. All the better if they were among the women who held two-thirds of the passive money in the nation, and better yet if it was held in administrative trust at a bank. While there was no guarantee that Dinah's club included the kind of rich women who found bankers trust-inspiring, it did include the word "investment," implying money, and was all women, implying impressionable. It certainly sounded worth wooing.

Dinah made the calls from her office phone. She often stayed late or returned to the office after an evening of volunteering at a free clinic, and she always took the night calls for the practice. Unfortunately, night calls in dermatology were almost nonexistent. She yearned for a call, any call, any demand for quick response. Medicine should be an athletic pursuit, even a battle; she was sedentary. Patients were brought in, patients were taken away. Perched on a stool, she put on her eye lamp and studied whatever was presented to her. Usually it was a rash whose Latin name translated to some variation on "itchy red bumps." She yearned for a desperate pumping of blood, clammy skin, gasping breath, and a race against the cooling of flesh.

She envied paramedics, firemen, trauma experts, even residents and interns their constant personal testing. She remembered from residency the triumph of snatching a life from its slide into death. It exercised all one had learned about circulation, about respiration, about the response of body systems to threat—very different from the fine dermatologic inspection of a limited area, a few inches of skin at a time. Here there was no hurry at all.

Dinah had known she was in the wrong field some years ago, even before she stopped assuming she'd marry. She thought then of changing to internal medicine, maybe even emergency medicine, but hesitated, given already established commitments. Now it seemed too late. Every year such specialties took in a new group of young and younger doctors, more athletic, more aggressive, more ambitious. She was a middle-aged woman with a specialty in skin; why would they break ranks and make room for her at the gurney?

Facing a desktop so clean one could eat off it, but in no rush to leave, she walked out into the reception room, lit now by the green glow of the display cases and the night sky beyond the skylights. She hadn't expected this life—not the specialty or the practice or the solitude, and certainly not the quiet, the awful calm. Her biggest mistake had been expecting more to happen to her. She didn't realize that when you wait for more to come to you, you yourself become less. She could still make a move, she thought, wandering her darkened office among the glass cases like a visitor in an aquarium. She could still make a move. Unlike Ginger.

The fund-raiser was at Walker Cannon's home in Hancock Park, on a block of baronial homes dating back to the twenties. The house was set on a slight rise of unblemished lawn, as flat and even as Astroturf. To someone standing at the big front door, the house loomed enormous. The ground-floor windows literally came down to the ground, the second-floor windows went up to the roof, and the camellia bushes flanking both were thirty feet high.

The same grand scale applied inside the house. The front foyer was big as a reception hall, and the actual reception hall beyond was like a well-appointed living room, with arches on three sides that led to other, even bigger rooms. Any one could have been the lobby of a large hotel. It was heavily beamed, with several Oriental rugs the size of Kazakhastani villages and multiple conversation groups—three chairs and a couple of tables, five chairs and a couch, two couches and a love seat. Though the high windows already started at the floor, the drapes hung two or three feet longer, the extra fabric dramatically swirled out on the parquet floor like a bride's train.

Family portraits lined the walls, all Renaissance reds and browns, their lacquered surfaces glowing under gallery lights above the frames. Down at the end of the room, a huge triptych of screens covered the far wall. Projected on the two side panels were photos of Cannon on the phone, sleeves rolled up, and Cannon walking a sandy beach. In the center was a family portrait, a blowup of Cannon, his wife, two boys, a girl, and above the whole collage was a red, white, and blue banner heralding A NEW DIRECTION.

The room easily held a large crowd. All the men were in dark suits, dress shirts, and serious ties, and all the women in cocktail dresses. The guests were working the room while they themselves were being worked by a dozen staff members, distinguished by burgundy sashes from right shoulder to left hip, anchored by large buttons announcing A NEW DIRECTION.

What Dinah's group might have missed, had Dinah not alerted them, was what these staff members were doing. Gliding among the guests, murmuring greetings, they were collecting envelopes and checks as openly as church deacons at Sunday service. Periodically they'd deposit a wad of these offerings in big bowls set out on a refectory table like the gift display at Italian and Jewish weddings.

In the center of the room, strategically placed under a ceiling spot, was L. Walker Cannon, surrounded by dark suits and burgundy sashes. Not far off, on a side wall hung with a medieval hunting tapestry, stood the five women of the Monday group, with Dinah pointing out campaign notables and providing further background on the candidate.

Cannon was really a Northern Californian, son of a timber family with holdings all over the Pacific Northwest. The family interests extended south into coastal resorts and wine country and had became more agricultural when Walker married the daughter of a citrus empire centered on Visalia. His own interest as a young man was skiing, almost exclusively, and he was as expert as thirty years of full-time practice could make a person. But that also made him available when the family decided it needed a voice in politics, so they took him out of Bogner and dressed him in Eddie Bauer, thus turning a figure of idle recreation into what looked like a rough-and-ready outdoorsman.

Unfortunately, the upper half of California above and beyond the San Francisco Bay Area was basically poor and rural and independent-minded, and Walker was no populist. So the Cannon machine moved him down to Newport Beach, gave him the management of some family holdings in tomatoes, grapefruits, and shopping malls, and ran him again. The result was that he got two terms as a state senator from Orange County and, when he seemed ready for statewide office, was moved up to Los Angeles, where the family would live after the election.

Walker Cannon had never talked much, an excellent characteristic for someone with little to say. He was neither quick nor witty, neither intelligent nor thoughtful. But he looked good—lean, long-legged, handsome as only people can be who've suffered no cares, no trials, no ideals. He looked confident, comfortable, and ever so slightly country, which was appealing to city people. And he was unexpectedly good at memorizing the speeches he was given.

The lights dimmed, Cannon stepped up onto a small platform at one side of the big family photo, someone put a spotlight on him, and a wave of shushing went around the room. He held up his hand, to cheers, modestly waved them away, and began to talk.

"It's wonderful to see you all here. I'm sorry my good wife isn't here—many of you have asked after her—but she's with the children visiting the grandparents up in our great Central Valley. Which is why there's dust on the tables when you run your finger over them." He paused for the polite laughter. "But they'll be here on the weekend."

He gestured at the big banner on the wall behind him and raised his voice. "We're here to move together in a new direction, away from the

Beltway and out into the country, where the real people are and the real power should be!"

Cheers, followed by several minutes in which Cannon worked at describing his new direction—"away from special privileges and toward a level playing field for all. No more special quotas. No more favored admissions." He squinted into the light and started the roll again. "Away from tokenism and welfare and single-parent poverty and toward family values!"

Cannon paused, drew some applause, drank a little water from a crystal tumbler. He put a hand in his pants pocket, Kennedy-style, and launched into the main part of his speech. "'Family values' means that everyone has a right to a mother and father, a nuclear family! It means everyone has a responsibility to marry and be faithful to that marriage and to take care of that family. We don't believe in government welfare for the American family, in supporting other people's children."

After some side trips into the values of both right-to-life and right-to-choose, health insurance, government funding, and unemployment, he was interrupted again by cheers and applause. Dinah and Polly looked at each other and quickly looked away. Charlotte bit her lower lip.

"We must unleash business to grow," he said, "give the homeless jobs! Cut welfare and cut taxes and ordinary people, good citizens, will be able to keep more of what they earn, and they'll give more to others: There'll be more philanthropy! People are basically selfless. Just give them the chance and they'll do good!"

He held off the applause with a hand, leaning into his serious message, his face projecting concern. "Everything is interrelated," he said thoughtfully, tutorially, "and I believe in people," and he opened his arms to embrace all. "Sometimes I'm criticized for spending too much time with visitors up at the capital, but I do it because I believe in reaching out to people, because then they will go and reach out to someone else, and that's what this country is all about!"

There were shouts, cheers, more shouts, whistles. Someone blew on a kazoo. Charlotte had both hands clasped at her mouth, pressed against her lips. "I don't get it," whispered Kat.

Afterward there was a question period, brief and friendly. Someone asked Cannon about his recent votes against conservation, against preservation of wilderness areas and coastline, and he explained that he'd voted against the proposals because they "didn't go far enough." A burgundy-sashed worker asked if Cannon would release his income-tax forms as the opposition demanded, and, as obviously planned ahead, he said with a smile, "People don't care about my taxes; they care about theirs. But to settle this question now, I want to announce that this week I arranged to have all our assets, Melissa's and mine, put into a blind trust. So that no one, not in the campaign and not in the years I am senator, will be able to say I know anything at all about my finances!"

With that, Cannon stepped down from the platform amid cheers and inched through the crowd, grabbing hands. The burgundy sashes moved out from their wall positions, and the crowd began to break up. There was a sudden sense of motion, as if music had started again and dancers, poised, were taking their places for another round.

The women stayed another half hour while Dinah, Charlotte, Justine, and Kat greeted a few acquaintances. Polly drank mineral water, made no effort to mix, and periodically urged that they leave.

"Well," said Polly when they'd been seated in a back booth at a nearby Italian restaurant and placed their orders.

"He's rich and stupid," said Charlotte. "I like that in a man."

"He had no discernible platform at all, beyond hypocrisy," said Dinah. "What's he running on?"

"Borrowed time," said Polly.

"Rented time," said Charlotte. "Just think how many people own a piece of him. Some of them bought in right before our eyes tonight."

"I have to tell you," said Dinah, "that I feel really good about fixing this guy. Now, how do we do it?"

"Are we sure we shouldn't confront him first?" asked Justine. "It doesn't seem fair when we don't really know him or how he felt about what happened."

"Justine," said Charlotte, with the kind of studied patience they'd all begun using with Justine, "we know enough. We know he wasn't very concerned whether Ginger lived through the night. And when she didn't, he didn't show any concern then either."

She reached across the table to put a hand on Justine's arm. "Do we need to go around about this again? You can still opt out, Justine," she added softly. "We know you'd keep our confidence."

Justine looked at Charlotte's hand on her blue gabardine sleeve with its gold buttons, her flowered cuff sticking out, at Robert's ring of imperial jade in a circle of diamonds. "No, I'm with you," she said. "I'm sorry. I'm just not a very good terminator."

"It's not a field in which any of us have experience," said Polly. "But given the fact that we've agreed to get this guy, how do we get him?"

They worked on it as they ate. Clearly the ideal would be to make Cannon lose his Senate race and thus all hopes of further political career. Throwing their political strength into his opponent's campaign was useless, since none of them had any political strength. Nor could they finance a new challenge, let alone dream one up.

"His support is big money," said Polly. "We can't fight with big money. Or big anything. We have to work with little stuff, and in almost no time."

"We have to beat him out before the election," said Dinah, "and it has to be decisive—one of those twists of public image that defeat a candidate in midcampaign." She leaned her head against the back of the booth, contemplating the Chianti bottles suspended above their heads. "We could use one of those dirty-trick specialists, though with this guy who needs innuendo? The truth should be enough."

Expose him as a murderer, suggested Kat, but everyone pointed out that this was a case that couldn't even get the attention of the police, and that if they tried to demand attention, they'd have to fight some fairly powerful opponents. Expose him as a philanderer, said Justine. But they couldn't point to a sexual partner. The one they knew was dead, and they didn't know any others.

"We could give him a partner," said Polly, and everyone laughed and began to throw out suggestions. Sophia Robinson, but he'd have to promise not to share. Michael Jackson, if Mrs. Cannon permitted him to go on sleepovers.

Charlotte sat frowning, her hands holding fork and knife just above her plate. "Wait," she said. "I'm getting an idea. Remember Donna Rice, who ended Gary Hart's career?" She was thinking aloud. "It's a little un-derhanded, but well-deserved. Hit him right in the family values."

"Not Donna Rice herself, of course?" said Polly. Charlotte smiled, shook her head.

Kat bounced on the booth bench, suddenly animated. "It's good!" she said. "But who'll play the Donna Rice part?"

Slowly and deliberately, Charlotte turned to face Kat. In the heavy pause, so did the others.

"Wait a minute," said Kat.

"You don't have to actually be a girlfriend," said Charlotte. "You just have to look like it. Appearance, not reality: That's what politics is all about."

Kat, on the end of the bench, came partly out of her seat. "Why me?" she exclaimed. "Why pick me?"

"It's the price you pay, finally, for never having to hold in your stom-ach in a bathing suit," said Polly.

Charlotte was more specific. "In the first place," she said, "you're ours. We have to work with what we have. In the second place, you're blond and beautiful and have a body that could have been made in a lab—those parts that weren't made in a lab, that is."

Kat beat at her with a napkin, laughing now. "All right. It seems kind of tacky," she said, "but I like it."

"Our slogan is 'We Do What We Can,'" said Polly. "It's no worse than 'A New Direction.'"

Gleeful that they had an idea, they began to plan. In a few days, it would be the beginning of October, with the election a month later. Best to move on it in the next couple of weeks, on the chance he might gather so many adherents and so much momentum that they would have to upset a juggernaut, not a bandwagon.

They needed the layout of his Hancock Park lot and recent plans of the house and outlying buildings. Justine would get what she could from property-tax records and the Department of Building and Safety, and two of them would make an evening excursion to confirm the details. Several excursions.

Once they knew the setting, they could figure out what to stage: They liked the idea of some kind of confrontation at Cannon's mansion, perhaps with him there. And they needed press coverage of whatever they staged. That was Polly's task: She had an old friend at the *Los Angeles Times*.

"And I need to get in shape," said Kat, extending her legs out into the aisle, flexing her knees, rotating her feet at the ankles. Everyone looked at her. "In case I have to make a run for it."

"Good idea," said Polly. "Go train."

12

When Justine got home Monday night, it was midevening and the house was empty. Although her husband and sons had probably passed the hall table several times, coming and going, the day's mail sat there unopened. Justine skimmed through it, purse and carryall hanging from her shoulder. Several bills, a half-dozen magazines and catalogs, two invitations, some bulk-mail ads, and a bank envelope containing a deposit confirmation.

Every other Friday, when Robby stopped at the bank to deposit business checks and cash payments into their main checking account, he put eighteen hundred dollars into Justine's personal account to pay the monthly mortgage on their house and for the boys' after-school activities. That account was otherwise funded by her own county paycheck. Out of it she paid "her" household costs, including food, clothes, housekeeper, cars, and utilities.

Justine couldn't remember when this financial arrangement had begun, or when it had begun to irritate her. It wasn't that she ever lacked for money. When she needed more money, for tax payments or major purchases, she just told Robby and he deposited more. What bothered her was that she had to ask, though this was money drawn from a family business in which she was nominally co-owner and for which she served as accountant. She even prepared most of the checks on that account for his signature, including those meant for deposit into "her" account. But she wasn't a cosigner.

It didn't mean anything, Robby would say whenever Justine questioned what seemed to her an inefficient and inequitable arrangement. This was what he was used to, he'd say. His mother had always worked in the family business, but when it came to finances, his father handled the money and his mother took care of the household. No one drew a salary. When business flourished, the whole family benefited.

Justine certainly wanted the good of the family, but she wanted some other things besides. She wanted one joint family account with two names on it as signatories. She wanted to be a partner. She wanted to work there, to help steer the business, to change it, to move it beyond garden supplies and common landscape plants and into specialty plants and horticulture.

"Of course it's our business. I couldn't do it without you," Robby would say, looking perplexed and usually in retreat, halfway through a doorway. "The bank stuff is just mechanics. It works fine the way it is."

So it did, practically speaking. But every time she got a bank slip showing he'd deposited "their" money into "her" account, she thought of rows of greenhouses, long sheds of seed flats and bedding plants, roomfuls of files and records, and just behind the buildings acres of plants and bushes and trees in green tubs. And herself as head of the nursery, with all of her stock, production and experimental, labeled and documented, and much of it admired, and maybe some of it, someday, well known.

She had talked to Robby of this dream, which had been in her head from the day they married, when her career was less demanding and she was free to help him. But Robby, who as eldest son in his family and first college graduate had a voice that was usually heeded, said, "It's fine this way. This will work best."

It was this confidence and command that originally drew her to him, as did his devotion to his parents, his grandparents, her parents, her siblings. The solidarity of family was important to her. He worked hard. And he loved her, dedicating all family dinners and holiday celebrations to his wife in long, flowery toasts. He bought her presents, returning from every trip with clothes for her, and jewelry. Everything always fit, and he had good taste, if somewhat rigid. When Justine wanted to pierce her ears, he said, "I don't like that," and the question of her ears was settled.

Holding the mail, Justine sighed in the darkening hall. She put down her briefcase in front of the shoes lined up at the baseboard under the hall tree. Robby liked wall-to-wall deep white carpeting, and all who entered removed their shoes in the front hall and walked around in stocking feet. Most people would be grateful for a life as well ordered as hers.

Nevertheless, she didn't remove her shoes but walked across the hall and up the carpeted stairs in her high heels. They left little half-circle indentations in the deep pile.

She had told the women to come around the back of the house so they could meet in the privacy of Justine's potting shed. It was actually the old garage behind their Cheviot Hills house, an eyesore to Robby but a refuge for Justine, who'd insisted, for once, that it be left standing when Robby had a new, semi-underground garage built at the front of the house.

Within a month she had replaced the walls and roof of the two-car section with glass greenhouse panes. The room at the back—part office, part storage for the previous owners—she had gutted and insulated, then put in a big oval track of ceiling lights and potting counters all along the walls, each with shelving and hose bibs at the back and an open trough in front. In the center of the room, she put a long wooden worktable with a half-dozen stools tucked under it.

While she waited, with the door open and a breeze ruffling the papery leaves of the melaleucas outside, Justine listed the cymbidium plants she had repotted over the weekend. She'd broken apart several old yellows and a couple labeled as greens that she'd bought out-of-season at a garage sale. Each orchid was already numbered and newly labeled by type, color, and date of acquisition, but she kept summary lists as well. It wasn't scientific, but it gave her a quick sense of her whole collection, which she rearranged, as they bloomed, in a changing display of color.

The women arrived, their shoes crunching the redwood chips on the backyard path—Dinah, Polly, then Kat and Charlotte together. They moved the stools so they clustered at one end of the table, waiting quietly while Justine spread out the maps and building plans she'd gathered together.

"It's like a war room," said Polly, cracking her knuckles in the silence. Polly could also belch at will—long, rising cadenzas of sound that had been much admired in school dormitories and roundly applauded by Kat and Dinah and, unexpectedly, Ginger.

"It is a war room," said Charlotte. "A little respect, please."

Kat gestured with one arm around the group, all of whom wore gray, black, and navy. "Everyone's in skulker colors!" she hooted.

Justine ignored the comments. "This is the tract that includes Cannon's lot," she said, laying out a copy of a rectangular map-book page. In some parts of L.A., one such page might include up to thirty residential lots, but in Cannon's area there were only fourteen to a page, each about a sixth of an acre and somewhat irregular. The usual residential tract was an extended oval, or sometimes banana-shaped, with lots cut in from the perimeter like seating sections in a stadium. In Cannon's tract they were staggered like musical chairs, with the longer half of each lot extended another third of the way through to the next street on the other side of the oval.

"Now," said Justine, "our particular interest is not so much the streets as the alley." And she drew a yellow highlighter over the wavy line down the middle of the oval—the alley separating the lots on one residential street from those on the next and ending at a short cross alley one house in from the end.

All over L.A. such alleys were like a system of country roads laced through the urban grid. They were unpaved, lined with weeds and brush and old back fences. Deceptively rural, they seemed in another time, another place, behind the scrim of the city, attracting evening walkers, abandoned furniture and appliances, sometimes the campfires of the homeless. They bisected both residential and commercial blocks, even where they no longer served their original purpose, which was to hide everyone's garage and keep city services like electrical conduits, phone lines, and garbage cans out of sight. Many were unnecessary now, given buried cables, automated curbside trash collection, and people like Robby who preferred driving their cars into garages in front of their houses.

Kat pushed back a long panel of hair and bent over the plan. "Which is this guy's house?" she asked. "And what's the alley like?"

Justine laid out a series of house plans, and they all leaned into the light to look. The most recent were reductions of blueprints filed several years ago when the Cannon house was extensively remodeled. At one end a second story had been added to a wing that was itself a previous addition, and a wall was built around the property, along with an attached garden shed and a pool dressing room.

"Oh, God, look at the walls!" exclaimed Kat, pulling close the sheet with the elevations. "Is this six feet? Do I read this right?"

Polly bent nearer. "Six feet," she confirmed. "Two locked gates."

"Great," said Kat. "Probably topped with glass or barbed wire."

"It seems to be a clean top," said Justine. Everyone turned to her, surprised. "Well, I thought of that, too," she explained, sitting back on her stool, hands on her knees. "I mean, I don't know our plan yet, but assuming a need for escape routes, I drove by on the way home."

It was more than Justine's usual involvement, and she knew that's what everyone was thinking. "I went down the alley," she continued, a bit defensively. "Kat and whoever else goes will have to see it for themselves, of course, but it looks like height's the only problem."

"Not for me," said Kat blithely. "I can get over anything up to seven feet." She jumped up to stretch her length up the doorjamb. "You can count on pulling yourself up a wall a few inches less than your reach—higher if there's a good handhold and you take a little jump. So six feet should be okay."

She looked around, sensing some question, or maybe just their ignorance of such maneuvers. "Anyway, I only have to do it once."

"The bigger question," said Polly, "is, once over, can you outrun a pack?"

"I'll be running from a pack?" Kat came back to the edge of the table and supporting herself on her long arms, loomed over them. "Maybe we could talk about what we're actually doing? What I'm doing, that is?"

"All you'll have to do is look like a babe and be sure you escape," said Polly.

"You're on your own with the first," added Charlotte. "We'll help with the second."

Putting aside the maps and building plans, they began to consider possibilities, agreeing that above all the plan should be kept simple. There should be just the appearance of an assignation. There should also be just one news source involved, preferably an influential one, though Charlotte pointed out that today's pack journalism guaranteed that everyone would swarm on such a story no matter who got it first.

"No TV," said Kat. "Someone would recognize me on TV."

Just the *Times,* they agreed, not just because it was the biggest paper in town but because Polly's editor friend there was likely to leap on a story like this. It wasn't hard to decide the timing, either. In Dinah's earlier call to Cannon's campaign office, she had suggested ingenuously that Cannon meet sometime with a group of women she and her investment colleagues could gather together, and she'd gone over possible dates with a scheduler.

"This week was impossible," Dinah said, consulting the notepad she took from her jacket pocket. "He's on a fact-finding mission in Washington all this week. Next week he'll fly to San Francisco on Monday night for Tuesday meetings, has to leave Wednesday evening free to hole up at the L.A. house and work on an important speech for Thursday night, and he'll join his wife and kids in Newport Beach for the weekend."

She looked up from her notes. "Sure sounds to me like that Wednesday is our only possibility, right?"

"What if he's not there the exact time we set it up for?"

"Maybe it doesn't matter if he's there or not," said Dinah slowly, considering. "In one case, when the bell rings, he opens the front door and Kat runs out the back gate. In the other, no one opens the front door and she still runs out the back."

"Where are the *Times* guys going to be?" asked Kat.

"Both places, I assume."

"If he is there, he'll just deny it," said Justine.

"They always deny it," said Charlotte. "And with each further revelation, they still deny it, hoping to avert the next one. That's politics. Remember, it's how it looks that counts."

"Actually," said Polly, "it doesn't matter what he says or what happens at the front door. It's what happens at the back that counts."

"All of life is like that," Charlotte muttered.

By midnight they had made lists and sketched out a schedule. For starters Kat and Dinah would check out the house, street, and alley, and Polly would pitch the story to her friend at the *Times*.

Polly met her old friend Tess at a dark downtown restaurant named Dunlap's but known as "The DUI" because of its popularity with the highway and patrol cops who picked up all the drunk drivers. It had a low ceiling, a bar that ran the length of the room on one side, and on the other, high-backed booths covered in leather that would have been red in better lighting.

Tess was scrappy and hard-nosed, her hair a little too blond, her suits a little too dark. She had been an assistant metropolitan editor for almost a decade and was now the metro editor. It was a good position—good "for a woman" particularly—but Tess was quietly bitter about being passed over for deputy managing editor, a recent opening that went to a man who was younger and less experienced.

Her bitterness wasn't just feminism, because she was dealt another insult at the same time: Her second-in-command, a younger, less experienced woman, was made assistant to the publisher. That one was more complicated. The girl looked like Miss Teen America but bristled with purpose and efficiency and toiled long hours, broken only by a daily workout at the athletic club where she'd sought out and made friends with the publisher.

"So here's the question," said Polly after a few minutes of pleasantries and the ordering of lunch. They had met this way several times, usually at Polly's suggestion when she'd noticed something odd or interesting in a business she was examining—a labor violation, perhaps, or an unexpected connection with another company. "Who's the biggest drumbeater for family values this election?"

"Come on, Polly," said Tess wearily. "No quizzes today."

"Okay. L. Walker Cannon. Upright, pious, preaches nuclear families, no fooling around. I understand he has a girlfriend, and his wife and family are away right now, and she's spending time at his house. Any interest?"

"You kidding?" said Tess, instantly alert. "I hate the sanctimonious bastard. More important, Lurch would drool. Lurch, my managing editor. He of the quick-and-dirty school of newswriting, came from broadcast journalism, an oxymoron if ever there was one. How'd you get this?"

"Source, Tess," said Polly, shaking her head. "Source. Very close."

"This is for real, Polly?"

"You mean not a setup? Does it matter?" She saw the righteous look on Tess's face. "Just kidding! Putting you on!"

Too late. Tess set down her French-dip sandwich, a two-handed mass. "Polly," she said, senior figure to young upstart, "we're not in show-biz here. There's such a thing as integrity. We can't just let ourselves be used by every little starlet in town."

"Tess, she's not his first. One ended up dead."

"So give me that one. I like that one better."

"We can't prove that one. He's had others, but in the past; at this point they're just someone's say-so. This one is now."

"Dirty goat," said Tess. She licked meat juice from her lower lip. "You sure?"

"Trust me," said Polly. "There is a girl. If you get her, you've got him. Trust me."

"Trust has nothing to do with it," said Tess, folding her hands, visibly weighing ethics with a frown of consternation. "I have to think about whether we should be stalking some guy in his private life, sneaking around his house when it's his public office that's our concern. There's some question how far our public franchise can take us into someone's private life."

Polly waited her out. It didn't take long.

"We'll take the story," said Tess, picking up her sandwich. "Lurch will love it."

Wednesday night, Polly promised her. According to her source, Wednesday night for sure. Exact time still to come; they'd talk again.

Finishing their lunch, they spoke of the mutual friend through whom they'd met, of Tess's unattached brother—whom Polly was always, but tactfully, turning down—and of several local companies currently issuing layoff notices. Then they walked out into a downtown sun so bright they had to pause in the doorway to adjust before they parted.

For Kat time hurtled toward the next week in a frenzy of exercise. Everything she had: sit-ups, push-ups, curls, extensions, pulls, presses. Repetitions with free weights. Repetitions on the Nautilus machines. She spent her days at the headquarters club, where she had her offices. At home her equipment was limited to a LifeCycle and a Soloflex—a kind of giant Tinkertoy only good for late-night touch-ups after an evening out.

She had one of the weights rooms to herself when Barnaby came back in midafternoon on Friday. The club building was huge, almost filling a city block, with an Olympic-size pool, a hardwood track laid out around the mezzanine, and various exercise rooms, plus showers, steam room, locker rooms, restaurants, and several boutiques. But it was relatively empty between two and four, between the lunch crowd and the after-work crowd, except for the professionals and the competitive body-builders, who basically spent all their time there.

She was on her back on a bench, barbell against her chest, when Barnaby came in, singing as he crossed the room to stand a few feet from her head. He stood quietly, his muscular arms hanging comfortably at his sides, his partly shaved head shining under the fluorescent ceiling panels. Whenever she had no mirror view and was working with free weights or a barbell, he was careful not to startle her.

She grunted. "I feel like a damn racehorse."

"If the shoe fits," he said fondly, stepping closer. He smoothed her sweaty hair back from her forehead. "Besides, lovey, you are one. Thoroughbred, of course."

Everyone envied Kat her husband's doting. She liked it herself. As she told Charlotte, who asked if it ever got irritating, the words didn't matter when the meaning was that he liked her, cared about her, was proud even when pride wasn't called for. Barnaby had used bodybuilding as a way out of a poor neighborhood and then his work as a trainer as a way out of bodybuilding, and when Kat advertised for a club manager years ago, he had made the business his way out of being a trainer, just as he'd always dreamed.

He wasn't using Kat as a way out of anything, however. He married her because they fell in love, and he remained the general manager of the clubs, managing a larger and larger organization and more and more clubs. In fact, he was particularly proud that she was the head of it, the CEO, and he, though her equal partner, was chief operations officer. The third partner, a lawyer, was chief financial officer.

She sat up, let Barnaby take the barbell, and confronted him and dozens of images of herself in the mirrored walls. "Barnaby," she said, biting on the inside of one cheek, "do you remember the videos of my last hurdle meets? You think I could still do it?"

What was most rare about Barnaby was that he took all her fears and frets seriously. "You did two marathons this past spring," he pointed out.

"That's endurance. Hurdles involve agility, too."

"I don't know," he said. "You do some hurdles here from time to time. But a long series? A whole race? I don't know."

He wrapped a big towel around her, rubbing her hair with the end of it. "The nice thing is, you don't have to," he said. "You're thirty-six. A marathon's enough if you have to prove something."

Kat watched drops of sweat run down her shins in the mirror, caught a drop off her nose.

"All this week you've been driving yourself," said Barnaby, "more than usual, that is. Want to tell me why?"

She took his hand and wiped her wet cheek against it. Meeting his eyes in the mirror, she said, "Maybe not right now. But soon."

Wrapped in her towel, sitting under a vent that blew down a light stream of cool air, she stayed on the bench, alone in the room after Barnaby went to the office. She had never worried about her physical strength, had never really thought about it because strength was something she assumed. Her concerns had always been training, practice, rest—at least until she began to care how her body looked more than how it ran, worrying about later years when the strength would be much diminished.

The breast implants had been a turning point both physically and symbolically, an insight that had come to her in Monday group. Although it gave her some distress, she felt calmed by the understanding. She realized that the modeling and the fitness, however successful, gave her none of the feelings of triumph she'd had in actual sport. There was some triumph in her business success, but it was lessened by the fact that she was selling a concern with body over ability.

She had the weekend, then a couple more days. It didn't seem like much, and she had no real idea what would be asked of her next Wednesday night. Taking a long, pointed look in the mirror before going out to do an hour on the track, she remembered something from her school days about ancient athletes dedicating their efforts to their king, and she liked it. Feeling a bit embarrassed even though she was alone, she gave her mirror image a little salute and dedicated Wednesday night's run to Ginger.

13

It was a pretty simple plan. Kat would hide in the yard. Someone on the news team would knock at the front door while someone else watched the back. Kat would come over the wall and, keeping her head down and her dress open, would sprint down the alley to the waiting car.

Four times they'd been to the house, the street, the alley, by day and night, and Dinah would give it a final check late Wednesday afternoon. There were no dogs, no floodlights, no regular patrol. A big old magnolia tree at the back corner of the lot gave Kat a place to wait. She had already tested it, climbing over from the avocado in the next yard while they watched from the shadows. "Catwoman!" she stage-whispered, and took a deep bow.

Dinah and Polly would be on the next street where the short cross-alley came out. Charlotte and Justine would come down the boulevard at the north end of the tract and would set off their car alarm at 11:10. "It's called a diversionary tactic," said Charlotte. Both cars had gotten tune-ups, and their gas tanks were full: They had all seen movies in which plans failed because a getaway car didn't start. As beginners they were more than willing to take instruction wherever they found it.

When they were absolutely sure of the plan, Polly called Tess to have a news team there at eleven sharp. Lurch was pleased, said Tess, but her ass was really on the line.

On Wednesday everyone arrived at Polly's house while it was still light. They were all quiet and tense, hugging each other more than once, even repetitively, like a nervous gesture. Polly had set out food on her dining room table and told them to help themselves. "No," said Kat, walking past the dining room archway. "I don't eat before an event."

Andrea hovered for a few minutes, aware only that this was not a normal visit. Jeremy was in his room; they could hear his music. Kat was going to do an exercise demo tape, Polly had told her children, and her friends were helping her.

The group gathered around Kat in Polly's room, up a half level in the back. Sitting on the bed, in a corner armchair, on a chaise, they watched Kat strip to lace bikini underpants and a scarlet bra from Victoria's Secret, which drew immediate hoots and catcalls. She changed into a button-front dress and her Keds, brushed her heavy blond hair, put on earrings, and carefully applied makeup—foundation, blusher, eyeliner.

"What a waste," said Dinah. "You didn't get this gig for your pretty face, babe," and suddenly they were all blithe and joking.

"It's like a wedding!"

"More like a sacrifice," said Kat.

"Like a lark," said Charlotte. "Bunch of stupid women hoping to change things."

"You don't think it'll work, Char?" asked Polly.

"I don't know," said Charlotte, "but it doesn't matter. I think it's worth doing. If you couldn't avert a disaster, at least there's something in being able to pay it back."

"It's not much of a payback."

"There's not much available to us. But maybe we can make him one sorry dude. He probably won't even be sorry for the right thing, but that's okay. We only want him sorry."

"It's even simpler than that," added Polly. "Even if he's too dumb to be sorry, it'll make us feel better. Like we did something."

They reviewed the plan, called the phone company's number for the exact time, and set their watches. Then, picking up their flashlights, their keys, Kat's change of clothes, and the car-alarm tripper, they filed out through the front hall and into the evening.

On the stoop Charlotte stopped, offering each in turn a formal handshake. "Break a leg," she said. "It's going to be great."

"It's going to be fun," said Polly.

"We'll be with you, Kat," said Justine.

The best-laid plans, warned Polly's mother. Schemes, said Polly. It's best-laid "schemes." Same thing, said her mother.

By the time they left, it was nine-fifteen. They got into the cars grim and silent. It was night now, and the dark and gauzy sky was starless. The city's glow was reflected by the clouds, a low canopy that gave them a sense of cover and confinement. Each withdrew to her own thoughts.

Dinah drove wordlessly, hands parallel and firmly on the wheel, feeling like the driver in a bank robbery or a Secret Service convoy. Periodically reviewing the route in her head, she was glad to be moving, gladder yet to be moving swiftly but carefully controlled, as she did when she'd chased an ambulance or fire truck as a teenager. The trick was to keep back, drawing no attention. She could hear Kat's measured breathing.

Alone in the backseat, Kat was doing yoga-like exercises that worked one muscle at a time. This was, after all, a race, even if one involving some nonstandard factors. With the usual course, timing and direction were set; what was unpredictable was the other racers and one's own physical changes. This short, solitary run should be more straightforward, pure exercise, except for the fact that it was run on a public path of unfamiliar obstacles.

Already, thinking ahead, she started a mantra she'd chanted for years. It was a foolish little thing—she didn't even know what a mantra was, strictly speaking—that came from the ending of a book she'd once read and forgotten. What had stayed with her was the last line, as the main character, a regular jogger, runs off and the book ends. "Ah: runs," it said. "Runs." She liked that, and it worked for her. Runs ah runs (inhale); runs ah runs (exhale).

Up front Polly felt Kat pushing her feet against the frame of the passenger seat and wondered what the phrase "riding shotgun" meant. Maybe it just meant her hands were free to warn off all pursuers, or to shoot them. Maybe to yell "Turn here!" as the car sped past a promising alley or roadhead. For now her hands were in her lap, holding Kat's clothes, neatly folded, and Kat's sandals, while streetlamps moved by in regular cadence outside, their light briefly arching toward the car, and behind her, Kat was inhaling, exhaling, all in little controlled puffs to match her working of this or that muscle, sometimes against the back of Polly's seat.

They were really doing it, Polly thought. But she was also thinking, Are we making too much of a lark out of it?

No, not a lark, but a maneuver. Relishing the idea and enjoying the action didn't make it a lark. It was an attack, the only method of attack possible. It was guerrilla warfare, unexpected and opportunistic, using the only weapons they had and leaving no clue as to how, where from, by whom. When opponents are so much more powerful, any action against them has to be covert and anonymous, though it was a pity they couldn't do public battle. It would be a signal pleasure to make these men realize that this was being done in the name of Ginger Pass.

Baloney, said her mother. A real accomplishment stands without credit. But her mother didn't understand that revenge was a special category.

Down Cannon's street, at Cannon's house, two cars sat in the driveway and there were lights on outside and in the big living room. Dinah drove slowly past, then to the main boulevard at the south end, where they sat for a while in their parked car.

Somewhere nearby Charlotte and Justine sat in theirs. Both cars had phones, but they couldn't use them for fear of being overheard. Odd, thought Polly: The greater the array of private communications devices, the less the privacy. One heard neighbors, police cruisers, even passing strangers on cellular phones. Apparently even baby monitors sometimes transmitted household sounds. The airwaves were thick with overheard voices.

At 10:10 they dropped Kat where the alley came out at the north end of the street behind Cannon's. In a second she had disappeared behind the houses, and they drove off, just to drive around. They'd wait for her later at the other end of the street.

Particularly at night the alley was a country road, a long, winding strand splashed with occasional brightness from backyard spotlights. The limbs of fruit trees, bougainvillea, and trumpet vine drooped untrimmed over the alley side of the back walls.

With the merest stirring of branches, Kat swung up into the avocado tree and across the neighbor's wall onto the magnolia in Cannon's yard. There she calmed herself, retying the scarf on her head, relieved to be up and off the dirt road where she had to worry about her footfalls.

She'd spent her childhood in trees—small-town trees, which were sycamores, chestnuts, and beeches. No avocados, no fancy vines. Running was something you did to get somewhere, and you were always running. Trees were where you dreamed. Now you went running to dream.

Still dreaming, she heard them come shortly after 10:30, softly crunching loose leaves on the alley below. Two guys with flashlights and equipment, whispering. From then on she was alert. Together, she and the newsmen, they heard phones ring, often from a great distance away. They heard canned laughter on television shows, tree toads, sometimes a dog. There was a hissing skirmish between two cats. They heard toilets flush and a heavy door slam. A radio played "Nessun dorma" from *Turandot*.

Twice someone came around to the alley to hold a whispered conference with the two men. A breeze came up just before eleven o'clock, allowing Kat to stretch and flex her limbs. She'd unbuttoned her dress now and loosened the scarf that covered her bright hair, keeping her head back in the thickest place among the leafy branches.

Eleven, exactly eleven, and the door chimes sounded; they must ring in the back of the house. There was a stir of activity from the newsmen, hushing each other, rattling metal (a tripod?), swearing. Kat dropped gently to the ground on the house side of the wall, well hidden by foliage, and let her scarf fall.

She could actually hear voices in front. All that money, all this space, this big house, and the front and backyards were barely separated. The backyard might as well be on the street for all the privacy. She heard a voice say firmly, "Nonsense," and a door closed. The chimes rang again immediately.

Though quite ready to pull herself up and over, she carefully tried the door in the back wall. It opened easily from inside. She poised herself, took several full breaths, and, flinging it open, burst out, head down, face hidden behind the great fall of hair, dress unbuttoned now and gaping open to show the scarlet lace bra.

"There she is!" she heard as she turned hard right and out into the dirt alley toward the south end. She saw camera flashes, heard running behind her, more flashes, quite safely behind her. She put on speed once she knew they had gotten their photographs.

The lightweight Keds were an unaccustomed feeling, as was the bumpy and uneven dirt alley. Nevertheless, she ran light as Atalanta, effortlessly outstripping Hippomenes. Her short dress flapped around her thighs as she ran. She set her breathing: Runs ah runs, runs ah runs, she said to herself.

One back wall, another, then another—two masonry, one wood—could have been a blur of spectators. The only light was the glow from the back rooms of houses, mostly kitchens. There were sounds of a party. She was aware of the rubber breasts, *whumping* up and down with each jolt. Usually contained by a sports bra, they were on their own in this lacy thing: Victoria's real secret was that her underwear provided no control at all.

The alley wasn't a straight strand but a series of gentle bends because of the irregular backyards. She approached the final bend at the end of the long section, heard "Wait! We won't hurt you," and suddenly, lifting her eyes, she saw fifty yards ahead a huge bulk parked at the end of the alley, blocking her passage and cutting off access to the cross-alley just beyond.

It was a big RV, as wide as a road and twice as long, obviously driven in after Dinah's afternoon check. The alleys of Los Angeles drew not only the homeless but the mobile-homed, who could park and sleep the night unchallenged and undisturbed and pull out before the neighborhood woke the next day. This one almost filled Kat's alley, its nose jutting out into the cross-alley, ready to roll at dawn's first light, assuming it could turn the corner.

Running, feeling panic start in her chest, Kat took in the fact that she couldn't get to the end of the road as planned. There was some clearance on the driver's side, but lights were on inside and someone might hear her and step out into her path. At the same time, she saw that the last lot, a construction site for a new home, had no back wall but was open to the alley, if partly blocked by equipment and building materials. Still aware of camera flashes well behind her, she reached the lot, saw an opening, and veered off left onto the site, cutting between a parked Bobcat and a side wall.

Cleared of trees and structures, it was open to the sky. Between her and the front of the lot almost three hundred feet away, she could see a wide aisle, lined by piles of rubble and building materials. And in the aisle were three wooden sawhorses spaced as neatly as on a formal course of hurdles, maybe twenty feet apart, and off at the far end some fencing, barely visible, and some trees left standing in a bunch at the south corner.

She covered the first hundred feet or so and approached the first sawhorse. There was a series of flashes behind her; they'd caught up, they were at the back of the lot. Piece of cake. She felt a surge of excitement and leaned forward, her eyes swiftly and instinctively assessing the distance, already calculating that the trough between hurdles was shorter than her usual four strides.

She dug in the Keds and came up to the first sawhorse, arms outstretched. She placed one foot firmly and, as it took her weight, thrust the other leg out, up, and ahead and rose with it, up and over, tucking up the takeoff foot as she rose. The leg motion was instinctive, moving as smoothly as an exercise machine. But the rubber breasts, the damn breasts, rose a fraction of a second after the rest of her body. She felt the twin drag on her chest, and when she landed, they came down, after the same slight lag, with a *whump*.

As she landed, she automatically gauged the next distance. Three long strides. She took them. She opened her arms to the breeze, to fly. Plant, forward, up, tuck, over and down, with a *whump*. One more. She could have gone a full course. She could have gone all night, acutely aware of her rhythm, of easily clearing the tops of the sawhorses, of breathing deep and taking off, her long arms like wings.

Then, in the second trough, looking ahead to the third sawhorse and beyond it, she saw trouble. Across the front of the lot, where she was headed, a grape-stake wood fence stretched unbroken, seven, maybe eight feet tall. She'd assumed some opening, as in back. Actually, she didn't know what she'd assumed, but wood stakes meant no toeholds, no flat top where she could put down her hand and scramble over.

In three seconds—no, two seconds at most—she saw a mass of poles leaning against a sawhorse at the side, perpendicular to her path. She rose for her third and final hurdle, and as she came down, and as the rubber breasts came down, and almost without breaking her stride, she bent slightly at the waist, reached out, and seized a pole. With no more conscious thought or analysis, she was prepared for what she was going to do.

Later, when she told the other women about it, Kat did recall something—an image more than a thought. It was a memory really, one of those sudden, crystalline recollections of childhood ritual. They had run a lot. They had leaped. Surrounded by woodpiles and farm fences, pens and corrals, they had jumped and hurdled whatever presented itself.

And sometimes the boys, including Kat, had picked a fence or a wall, or built one, and ceremoniously chosen some kind of available pole. Then, running up from a way off, they planted their pole firmly and projected themselves toward the wide blue sky of Illinois, up and over, arms flailing, legs madly bicycling, to land on the soft pasture or path beyond. The poles they chose often snapped midflight, or bent too far, or bent not at all, and they just laughed and, laughing, did it again. They were ten or twelve, maybe thirteen, and the days were full of wild endeavor; a fall was nothing.

In the given millisecond, Kat added to that childhood memory some bits of knowledge later absorbed at her years of track meets—though she never competed in pole vault—about the size and the nature of vault poles, the technique of planting poles, the presentation to the bar. So, somehow, she had confidence in the feel of this particular stick—a little thinner than a closet pole, a little shorter than a fruit picker—and that confidence carried her the last hundred feet to the grape-stake fence.

A few yards off it, she planted her pole. Behind her, she heard, "My God, look!" And as in her memory, as in her lifelong dreams, up she went, loosed the pole, twisted her body, cleared the fence by a couple of feet, and fell to the lawn on the other side.

So she was not afraid, she told them later. She was aware of the heaviness of the breasts and the lightness of her feet in the minimal sneakers, but she felt no fear or even hesitation.

On her feet again, she ran down the slight slope to the sidewalk. A few steps to the right and she was at the car, idling where the short alley opened to the street.

"Move," she gasped, wrenching open the back door. "Move!" And Dinah, startled, said, "Jesus Christ," thrust the car into gear, and leaped forward down the street.

All of the women escorted Kat home, one car following the other. They had agreed to meet there anyway—Kat, having come with Charlotte, had no car of her own at Polly's—but triumph made the trip back almost ceremonial. In another day, in a different contest, they'd have carried her on their shoulders.

Behind the tinted windows of Dinah's car and her purposely restrained driving, there was locker-room jubilation. When she'd stopped panting, Kat laughed, cried, slapped club soda all over herself, and tried to answer questions. Polly, who'd been watching the corner where the front wall met the alley at the moment Kat flew over, had climbed into the backseat and was plying Kat with towels and clothing. "Keep it down," Dinah warned, alternated with "I just don't believe it!"

Charlotte's Lexus was already waiting in front, and the five women jostled each other amid stifled exclamations toward the family room at the back of the house. The family was asleep—Barnaby, their little girl, and the nanny. Kat, now in shorts and a shirt, toweled her hair, and everyone settled down to exchange the details of their evening, always returning to its high point—Kat's run.

According to Charlotte and Justine, who were parked at the corner of the nearest cross street, it was probably Polly's friend Tess (given Polly's description) and another reporter who went to the front door and rang the bell about the time Kat was dropping from her tree. A houseman came to the door, then Cannon himself, holding a newspaper. There had been rising murmurs of conversation, Cannon trying to close the door, and then finally, abruptly, he did so.

It might have been about the time Kat was approaching the sawhorse hurdles that their car alarm went off at the diagonally opposite corner of the tract. The two women, seemingly unable to turn it off and visibly distraught, accepted the help of a passing security guard, who found an "off" switch under the left front fender. This stage business was watched by the two newspeople and several homeowners, drawn from their houses by the din, and when it was over, Charlotte and Justine pulled out onto the boulevard and headed west.

It felt good. They all felt good, and as they made much of Kat for her successful run, they drank Cokes and hiccuped, ate pretzels and sagged against one another, helpless with laughter and drunk with success.

In the midst of it, they knew, of course, that only the maneuver had been successful. What it would actually accomplish was unknown. "So much for the cause," said Charlotte at one point. "We have to see the effect."

Eager to hold their circle and the feeling within it, they were reluctant to part. But midnight became one and almost two in the morning, and finally they hugged and left.

Alone again, Kat carefully examined her breasts in the shower and decided to consult a plastic surgeon about removing the implants. Then she hung the red Victoria's Secret bra over her dresser mirror and went to bed.

Charlotte drove Justine to her car at Polly's, then went home herself, and when her husband muttered from his pillow, "How can you stay out so late?" she was able to ignore him and avoid a fight. Justine spent a half hour in her white living room, feet up on the coffee table, leafing through a new horticulture magazine. Then she fluffed the sofa cushions and went to bed.

Dinah and Polly had a cup of tea together, after which Dinah went home and immediately to sleep. Polly listened at her children's rooms, checked all the outside doors, but only once, and then, looking down the ravine toward the carpet of lights, turned as always to her mother.

It's sinful how good I feel, she said happily. I shouldn't get cocky, right?

Ah, sweetie, treat yourself for once, said her mother. Predictably, she was always good for a surprise.

14

Shortly after eight the next morning, the morning paper thudded against Polly's door—unusually late and, more unusual, a direct hit. Even a quarter flight down and in the back of the house, Polly heard it. Her dormant mind registered body, accident, child, and she was out of bed and in the foyer before the delivery truck was more than one house farther along.

It was the lead story: "Late-Night Visitor No Tryst, Says Family-Values Candidate Walker Cannon." Flanking it were two sidebars, one on Cannon's family life and conservative stances, the other on past candidates who'd been toppled by such dalliances.

Flapping barefoot down the hall in her untied bathrobe, Polly skimmed the front page, chortling. She tried to open to an inside page for the continuation and dropped the sports and classified sections. The kitchen radio was on, connected to the same timer as the coffeemaker.

Official comment would be "forthcoming at the end of the day," someone at Cannon's campaign headquarters was saying. For now there was "no comment."

"We understand that Mrs. Cannon is on her way to Los Angeles," prodded the reporter.

"No comment just now."

Spilling newspaper pages, Polly careened into the living room, turned on the TV, and gave each station a few seconds. Still no comment, but one channel had pictures. A long shot of the front of Cannon's house. A few seconds of him and his family walking on the beach. A still photo of Kat, caught in the light of a flashbulb, running deeper into the dark alley—just her back, dress flying, hair flying thick as a scarf. Above it a big question mark: "Who Is This Woman?"

"Oh, boy! Oh, boy! Oh, boy!" Polly was switching channels, clapping her hands. She was hopping up and down. Another channel. An eyewitness, a man who saw Kat's final leap as he walked his dog at the other end of the block.

"Sir, did it look to you like a man?"

Man? Polly stopped, frozen. The phone rang.

"Are you watching? Did you read it?" It was Dinah.

"What man? What's the man?"

"Kat's on the line. She's hysterical."

"What's the man, Dinah? The man!"

"For God's sake, read the damn story," said Dinah. "Just read it!"

Polly took the phone and the paper to the big leather chair and sat down heavily on the ottoman. The story was straightforward, moving chronologically from the unattributed tip to the ringing of the doorbell to the action in the alley, observed by two *Times* staffers.

There was a photo sequence of Kat, face hidden, caught like a nocturnal yeti in flight—the start, the straightaway, a hurdle, the last leap. And near the story's end, some descriptive matter on the athleticism of the subject, the height, the powerful legs, the obvious ease with which she vaulted sawhorses and fences. And the hair, "unnaturally" long and golden, possibly a wig. Finally, given the appearance and the extraordinary feat, "some surmised" that the night visitor was not a woman at all but a male. A male in woman's wig and clothing, including a red lace bra.

Polly shrieked. "Patch her in!," she said to Dinah, and immediately heard Kat's voice. It was definitely hysterical but not distinctly all sobs or all laughter.

"Kat," she said, cutting into the noise, "Kat, this is not a bad thing."

"It is!" But she was laughing.

"It isn't. You've gone as high as a woman can go: People think you're a man."

Over the weekend the stories became a swirl. It was classic swarm journalism. A single event raised questions, and whole newsrooms were sent out for answers. Each answer was instantly aired or written up, however close to conjecture, however far from fact.

Rumors about the woman's identity precipitated stories about other women linked to Cannon, each carefully matched with a denial story. The suspicion that "she" was actually male soon overwhelmed the stories of women, and then denial stories overwhelmed suspicion stories.

Cannon's campaign manager called a press conference on the gender question alone. L. Walker Cannon was not gay, he declared, passing out press releases that put the denial in hard print. He had never been gay. He was the furthest thing from gay: He was not just a family man but a churchgoer, a decorated navy officer.

That statement offended decorated, churchgoing gay men, and, shortly thereafter, nonmilitary, atheistic gays. Cannon's campaign manager called another press conference to take a safer stance of heterosexual, God-loving tolerance, emphasizing family values again and avoiding any mention of sexual preferences.

That Saturday night, over dinner, Polly and Graham Vere spoke of the Cannon affair, like everyone else. But it was a distraction, a short break from their main focus, which was themselves, their similar interests, their different lives, how they met, and what they'd first said to each other. Ahead was discovery: All they needed to move forward was background, some pertinent history. They wanted to do it right, to start off right.

Vere was neither a conservative nor an admirer of Walker Cannon, and he admitted he was enjoying every minute of the roiling coverage. "I can't believe he's hoist on the petard of family values," he said, "and that he was caught. In fact, his being caught is more unbelievable. I figured he was sharper than that, or his campaign people were, or at least the people that own him."

"Maybe they all cheat on their wives," said Polly.

"They don't get caught. They certainly don't get caught if it's with a man—can you believe it might be a man? Boy, those reporters were sure lucky in the way things went down."

Looking into his suddenly, surprisingly dear face, and suffused with pride at what she and her friends had pulled off, Polly wanted to tell him it wasn't just luck. Three seconds passed at most. In that time she weighed the obvious reasons for secrecy, her loyalty to the group of women, including Ginger, and her feelings for this man she had known only a couple of weeks, and she knew absolutely that she should say nothing.

Maybe it was four seconds. "We did that," she said.

"Did what?" he asked, dipping a piece of bread in olive oil.

"Set it up for him to get caught."

The bread hand stopped in midair. "Polly . . ."

"That was Kat Hurley. One of the women in our group. The fitness one."

"What for?" he asked, trying to put it all together, frowning. But it wasn't criticism, because he laid his fingers lightly over the back of her hand.

"He was one of the men who let Ginger die, maybe killed her."

"And what's going to happen to him?" he asked, sitting back in his chair.

She took the words as patronizing and the motion as a kind of withdrawal. "He's going to be embarrassed," she said curtly. "He's already embarrassed. Maybe he'll lose the election."

He said nothing. She had made a terrible mistake. "We had to use the only weapons we had," she said defensively. "They have money, power, and connections, and we don't. But we weren't totally unarmed."

After what seemed a long time, when he just looked at her, he leaned forward. "What the hell," he said, reaching for her other hand as well. "Bastard got what he deserved. I love it."

On Monday, Walker Cannon called his own press conference for noon, returning to Los Angeles that morning from Newport Beach. All weekend, television stations and newspapers had staff positioned outside the Newport house, his campaign headquarters, and his Los Angeles home, pressing everyone who came or went for a comment. When Cannon announced that he would come back to L.A., they began bringing in camera trucks and laying cable. And while everyone waited, and their editors and anchors kept pushing them for updates, the field reporters and photographers covered every minute of his drive north.

Some drew alongside his black Town Car, photographing the tinted side windows. Some sent helicopters to circle over the freeway and beam home footage of the cavalcade making its way slowly north, while faster cars passed on both sides like racers in a computer game. None could give more than a location ("Cannon's car, on its way to a noon press conference, is now passing the Harbor Freeway exit"). Many kept summing up the events that had led to all this.

The street was packed with people, trucks, mobile TV units, and police cars, as were the cross streets. At noon someone raised his light pole, all the other light poles went up, and an expectant silence spread through the crowd. At five minutes past noon, Walker Cannon opened his front door and walked down the steps, followed a few paces behind by his wife, daughter, and two sons. At the bottom he waited while his family arranged itself behind his left shoulder.

He stepped up to an array of microphones in as many sizes and heights as a bank of altar candles. His wife, a bony society woman in a tailored white suit and dark hair pulled back by a gold barrette, drew the youngest child against her. The elder boy rested his hand on her shoulder.

"This is a time of many important issues," Cannon began. Camera shutters clicked. "This is a race involving many issues, and I have tried to run a campaign focused on issues."

Somebody in the crowd clapped twice and stopped.

"In such times the candidate himself cannot be the issue. I cannot be the issue." He looked around. "What I do as your representative, yes. What I believe, yes. But not me personally. If I myself am going to be made the issue, the campaign and its goals have no chance. It is for this reason that I'm bowing out of the race—but not, I assure you, out of politics."

There were bursts of applause, and a lighting pole collapsed with a clang. Several reporters edged to the side, already poised to break away. There were sounds of movement in the crowd.

"Mr. Cannon!" came from the crowd. Everyone stood still. "There are reports that the person seen leaving your house was male. Would you comment on that, sir?"

Cannon reddened, his jaw tightened, and veins puffed out at the sides of his forehead. "I have said this before and will say it again: No one was with me in my house."

His family huddled closer. The wife, whose face had been carefully set, looked frightened. The child in front of her turned his back to the crowd, put his arms around his mother's waist, and pressed his face into her bosom.

"The person seen leaving at the back fence," called another voice. "Could she have been a neighbor? Is she an athlete?"

"I have no idea who you saw." Cannon raised his voice, his hands clenched around a microphone tripod.

"Is she a Republican?" came another voice, drawing laughter and a little clapping.

"Is she a he?" A new voice.

Two of Cannon's managers stepped to his side. A third drew the wife and children back and into the house. One of the men leaned into the microphones. "No more questions."

Cannon seemed to remonstrate with them, dipping his head to listen, and, still holding a mike with both hands, glanced yearningly at the crowd now drifting off. Finally he turned to go up the steps.

"Thank you, Mr. Cannon," called out a young reporter, taking it upon herself to close the press conference. She sounded quite earnest. Not a hint of sarcasm.

By the time of their Monday meeting, the women had talked out their elation and were quiet, even muted, when they came through the door. Lotte was already seated, wearing her Birkenstocks, a pleated gauzy skirt, and a long tunic. Her yellow legal pad sat on the table.

Everyone greeted her, but they offered each other more physical gestures—a squeeze of the shoulder, a hand on the arm, full embraces for Kat. Given the unusual demonstrations and the mood, Lotte watched closely. In the last few meetings, she had sensed a tremor of excitement but asked no questions, believing that information and attendant emotions surfaced in their own time. Even now she only asked mildly, "Is everything well? All are in good spirits?"

Polly answered. "I think we're all a little shocked, if that's the right word, by this Walker Cannon business. We've kind of been following it."

"Yes?" said Lotte. "Shall we talk about it? What is disturbing?"

It wasn't personal, they hastened to say. Cannon was just another political hack. Still, the story was titillating, and they'd followed the coverage, even joked about it. But now, said Charlotte, there was something disquieting about the swarm of media. "You can almost feel the rush of air as everyone hurries to the town square, and then you watch the end, and you suddenly think how easily someone is brought down."

"And it's sad," murmured Justine, "that no one ever goes down alone."

"Yes?" prodded Lotte. "Sad how?"

Justine was looking not at her but at the others. "I kept watching his family. This was rolling over them, and they were so powerless, just people attached to him like cars on a runaway train."

Charlotte shrugged it off. "The guy probably got what he deserved," she said. "There's always collateral damage."

"I think it's sadder to have power and not use it, or to misuse it," said Kat.

"As in what?" asked Charlotte.

Lotte leaned closer, registered the interesting turn in the discussion, but held back. She seemed unsure what they were talking about or where they were going with it.

"As in me," said Kat. "Look at me. I used to be a powerhouse, literally, and I lost it. Or maybe I let it go." She said it airily, but the rims of her eyes reddened and she blinked several times.

"It's not that bad," said Polly. "You just chose beauty over speed."

"Pretty useless, beauty," said Kat. "It fades fast."

"So do speed and strength," said Dinah.

"Wait," Charlotte cut in. "How did we get on this?"

Lotte's head was turning from side to side as if she were at a tennis match.

"Who cares?" said Polly. "Kat's right: This is what we're here for." She paused, apparently weighing whether to continue. "It's Charlotte, too, with power over everyone's affairs even beyond the grave and a power struggle at home. And Dinah, given powers over life and death but still stuck with scars and rashes. And Justine . . . Justine, you won't even rock the boat, never mind grab the helm."

Everyone was taken aback. Lotte scribbled on her yellow pad.

Charlotte inspected her hands, momentarily wordless, then said, "Yes, that does kind of sum it up."

"So," said Polly, oddly nervous, "what's *my* problem?"

"Ah," said Dinah gently, "yours is more complicated. No one has power over misfortune. But you've done just fine with plain fortune."

"Small comfort," said Polly. "I need a worthier goal."

"Goalwise, we're doing pretty well for beginners," said Kat. "We could probably do anything if we really tried. You get what you put in, as we say at the gym."

"Not just the gym," said Charlotte. "That really covers everything."

She looked pointedly from one to another. Every face but Lotte's indicated that they'd gotten the reference immediately. Lotte, frowning slightly, was gathering together her papers.

"What goes around comes around," said Polly, as a kind of closing.

"You sound like your mother," said Kat.

Polly nodded. "I come by it honestly," she said.

15

The women met for lunch the following Thursday at Kat's sports complex a few miles south of Beverly Hills. Excited by their success with Walker Cannon, they wanted to move on to their next revenge and couldn't wait until the following Monday. Kat, moreover, was insistent they meet at her club, because she had something important to show them.

In fact, it was convenient for all of them. Charlotte would run over from her Century City office, Dinah was volunteering at a free clinic near the beach, and Justine could finish the day at the assessor's west-side office. As for Polly, she said it was both a good thing about her life and a bad thing that she was free to go almost anywhere at almost any time and had no preference.

The flagship location of Kat's club, the Sport Scene, was in an area of new "office parks" filling a half-dozen city blocks. These were just groups of buildings unified by attractive landscaping and walkways, but to disguise the fact that "office park" was an oxymoron, developers gave them evocative names like Birnam Woods or Sycamore Suites or—this was Kat's location—The Gardens. Sometimes the name was no mere stretch of imagination but a bold stroke: One office park in the Valley was called Forty Oaks for the forty aged oak trees that had been cut down for its development.

The Sport Scene was an impressive complex in itself, three stories with roof gardens, all gleaming white stone, standing back from the boulevard on a rise of several hundred feet and visible from some distance away. To anyone approaching from either direction, it stood out like Mount Olympus, complete with godlike creatures, fit and muscular, ascending the wide front steps and passing through the oversize doors at the top.

Parking attendants in white suits and red ties and belts stood along the curved driveway, darting out to open the driver's door. It was a swift and orderly procession, only a minute elapsing between the arrival of a car, the emerging of the owner with briefcase and gym bag, and the car's removal.

"It's like orderlies lined up at a really swell mental facility," said Dinah, who drew up just ahead of Polly and was waiting for her on the curb. "New patients think they've come to a resort, when actually they're being committed."

"I was thinking of Oompa-Loompas myself," murmured Polly, moving up the stairs. She and Dinah, both in street clothes, with no gym bags or purpose in their step, were recognizably visitors, and it ran across Polly's mind as she looked at the young women hurrying past her that she would always be just a visitor to such places. She was out of their weight class, out of their age class, and, compared to them, definitely out of shape. Most of the women looked like what the fashion world called Young Career or Young Attitude—two age levels that Polly must have skipped over entirely.

It was as light inside as outdoors, because the entrance wall was all glass bricks, and it took Polly and Dinah a moment to adjust to the size and shine of the lobby and the gleaming expanse of its red-and-gray granite floor. Kat was coming forward from the concierge counter along the back wall, glad to see them and gorgeous in a tan tank top over white trousers, a matching jacket tossed on her shoulders.

"You don't look like a man anymore," said Polly.

When Charlotte and Justine arrived, Kat gave them a quick descriptive tour of the club from the center of the busy lobby. Around them were shops and offices; below were the swimming pools, whirlpools, steam and locker rooms, plus squash and racquetball courts. Above them was a vast central room of weight-training and bodybuilding equipment overlooked by a balcony track, with side rooms for classes in aerobics, yoga, and kickboxing. In a separate wing were the beauty and massage salons. And throughout there were places to eat—a salad bar called Savannah because it was all grasses, a juice bar (The Juice), an ice cream stand (The Ice), and an outdoor patio grill named The Brazier, but unfortunately known, said Kat, as The Bra.

She guided them to a door marked "Stairs" but stopped as she reached out to open it. "Sorry," she said, turning. "Pure habit. The elevator's this way."

Charlotte leaned past her and yanked open the door. "We can make it," she said. "Worst that happens is you have to carry me up the last flight." And she gestured them all through, then followed.

Kat's office was on the top floor, light and spacious. Half of it was a work area, dominated by a long, white-lacquered table with her computer on it, two phones, and several piles of paper weighted down by one-pound barbells. There were two pairs of track shoes underneath. The rest of the room was a conference area, with couch and chairs and a glass table set for five, with bowls of gazpacho, tall glasses of iced tea, bread plates—each with its little puddle of seasoned olive oil—and in the middle a big bowl of Chinese chop salad and bread.

Kat went right to the end of the table, looked it over to be sure every-thing she'd ordered was there, and gestured the others to sit down. "Good," she said. "We have everything we need, so no one will disturb us."

"It's great," said Charlotte, reaching for bread. "Is this how manage-ment eats?"

"It's how everybody here can eat," said Kat, dropping her jacket over the back of her chair. "It's all from our restaurants, and I think they're pretty good."

"Wherever it's from," said Justine quickly, "we're assuming we split lunch, as always."

Kat waved away the offer. "This one's on me," she said. "It's the price I pay for having no stomach. Or too much chest. I forget which deserved the punishment."

"The stomach," said Polly. "It's the stomach that offends other people. The breasts are your private hell."

"Okay," said Charlotte, tapping her watch. "With Cannon done we're one down, two to go. Let's get moving."

"I feel like we're moving a little fast as it is," said Justine, eyes on her soup.

"Good," said Charlotte. "Justice should be swift."

"The question is, who we do next?" said Polly. "We started with the weakest, so logic says we move up, building to the toughest, which I figure is Milo Till."

"Actually," said Charlotte, contentious even in agreement, "it was pure serendipity that we started with Cannon. We split up the investiga-tions, and it just happened that Dinah heard about the fund-raiser right away." She looked at Polly, who shrugged. "Not that I disagree about doing Reinhart next," added Charlotte.

"Till does seem to be the one pulling all the strings, so—" said Kat, but Charlotte interrupted her.

"It's not that Till is more important but that Reinhart would probably be easier for us. He's less hidden. Or at least more obvious in the ways he's hidden."

"What's that mean?" said Kat, reaching for a bread loaf and a serrated knife.

"I can only talk about Reinhart professionally," began Charlotte, "but it's a start."

She rose to stand behind her chair, the lawyer ready to outline the case. "Mitchell Reinhart is a creation of no-fault divorce," she said, "a concept that sprang from good intentions, like telephone deregulation or no-fault auto insurance, but brought in a whole new set of complications."

Before no-fault, she explained, divorce in California was all about casting blame, trying to label the "guiltier" spouse, with photos of trysts in motel rooms, tawdry tales of abuse or alcoholism. By contrast, said Charlotte, no-fault divorce "was based on the theory that both parties bore some responsibility in a failed marriage, and if you eliminate blame, you eliminate acrimony, and the whole business can be done with dispatch."

It didn't work that way, of course. The actual divorce, or "dissolution of marriage," became almost automatic, but the acrimony just transferred to the custody fight, with both parties yelling "unfit parent" at each other, or to the property settlement, which divided up all their assets.

In a community-property state like California, the rule was now a strict fifty-fifty division, which established the axiom that even a non-working wife deserved half the couple's assets, because her help contributed to the husband's ability to earn. But with no-fault divorce, said Charlotte, "all the hate and bitterness on both sides went into finding every last penny of assets and getting their fair share. I've heard of couples each taking four place settings of china and flatware, and in one case they literally halved the *Encyclopaedia Britannica*. He got volumes A through K, she got L through Z."

Now divorce became a game of misrepresenting assets rather than virtue and was a field for a very different kind of lawyer. He wasn't all dirty photos and finger-pointing, but there was still, said Charlotte, "an element of sleaze, if a better class of sleaze." He dealt in "valuations," not moral grievances, with tax codes and pensions, stocks and estate planning. He knew good accountants and good appraisers for both real and personal property, and he himself was never without his calculator.

It was perfect for Mitchell Reinhart. The son of two movie producers, he grew up in Pasadena and went to Stanford and UCLA Law, planning a career in corporate law. "I think he also got an MBA," said Charlotte. "You can't call Mitchell Reinhart a slacker."

But on his first job, he got caught up in two high-profile divorce cases and found that he enjoyed the open combat. He also liked the visibility. A celebrity divorce drew reporters to the courtroom, making the lawyer a star. And given his knowledge of business and finance, Reinhart was soon a master at dividing and often hiding assets.

"Which I don't hold against him," said Charlotte, circling the table for the third or fourth time. "He's brilliant at putting funds where they can't be found or stating them as a fraction of their value. But he only represents men, either because he likes men better or because he likes playing dirty with big bucks—or both. I have a bias toward the wife's side myself. It tends to be cleaner, if only because most wives have less money to lie about. The spouse who wants to misrepresent income is the one who has it. That's who gets Mitchell Reinhart, and he is a shark."

"So how do you embarrass a shark?" said Kat, tipping back on two legs of her chair.

"We don't have to do Reinhart the same way we did Cannon," said Dinah. "The goal doesn't have to be embarrassment. It's figuring out where they're vulnerable and then using that."

"In Cannon's case," added Polly, "he was so stupid and empty and pious about family values that any challenge was bound to embarrass him."

"All I know about Reinhart's personal life," said Charlotte, "is that he has two ex-wives and one now who's a real trophy. She had to sign a stringent prenuptial contract that's a model for family lawyers everywhere. And something sticks in my head about his ex-wives hauling him into court over money."

Kat's chair legs hit the floor. "I may be able to get us something," she said happily, but nobody seemed to hear her.

"I think I knew one of the ex-wives from PTA," said Polly, "probably the second, because her kids were young and this was just a few years ago. I know that her name was Reinhart and her ex-husband was a lawyer and she had a big house. Nobody knew much more about her, because conversationally it was hard to get by the fact that her children were named Madison, Wellesley, and Dallas. That you never forgot."

In the outburst of laughter, Charlotte took her seat, saying, "I knew the first wife, but it was some time ago. She was the one who helped him through law school."

"I've got something better," said Kat, bouncing impatiently on her chair.

"Hey," Dinah cut in, "I know his dermatologist."

"How come you know that?" Polly asked.

"He's a friend of mine," said Dinah. "Reinhart did his divorce."

"Great," said Polly. "But is it useful?"

"You bet," said Dinah. "I can find out if he has psoriasis."

Kat slammed both hands down on the table, pushed back her chair, and stood up. "When you're all finished, I can do better," she said.

Finally everyone looked at her. After a dramatic pause, she said, "I've got the wife."

It drew a satisfying flurry of response: "Meaning what?" "Where?" "The trophy wife?"

"You've got us now," said Dinah. "Go on."

"Remember way back when we first divided up assignments, I said

I thought one of our members was his wife or maybe his girlfriend? Remember?"

Everyone nodded.

"Well, it's the wife. The current wife. The trophy. She's here."

"Where is she?" asked Justine, putting her napkin on the table, ready to get up.

"Justine, 'here' doesn't mean literally," said Charlotte pedantically. "It's not like she lives here. It just means here sometimes, not necessarily right now."

"As a matter of fact, it *does* mean right now," said Kat, practically dancing in front of them, one hand lightly on the back of her chair, doing leg stretches, one side and then the other. She was enjoying the exchange. "She *is* here. Literally. And she practically *does* live here."

She straightened up, reached across the corner of the table, and took Justine by the elbow. "And Justine and I are going to go look at her," she declared. "Anyone want to join us?"

The corridor outside Kat's office opened onto the jogging track, which was blond wood nicely polished by running feet, wide enough for four people and slightly banked to within a yard of the inside barrier. It was chest-high, with a broad wood rail that people could lean on while watching the weight trainers and bodybuilders below.

The big room was organized by body part: one quadrant for leg exercise machines, one for arms, one for torso and full body, the fourth for rowing and pulling machines. Against the walls, under the balcony track, were racks of free weights and benches and rows of NordicTracks, stair-steppers and stationary bikes.

At a break between joggers, the five women quickly crossed the track and looked down. The separate noises rose with remarkable clarity—the clanking weights, the grinding of the NordicTracks and the bike pedals, even the grunts and exhalations of the weight lifters. It was all activity, a constant shifting of place and position as people finished their prescribed repetitions on one machine and moved to another. From above, it looked like a large and fairly organized square dance. Few faces were visible, just arms and legs flexing rhythmically, most in standard gray sweat clothes, with moving spots of color here and there or the occasional flash of shiny spandex leggings.

"It's like looking down on a kids' playground," said Polly.

"More like that incredible scene with Olivia de Havilland in *The Snake Pit*," said Charlotte. "Or maybe Dante's fourth circle of hell."

"Ah, Charlotte, ever the ray of sunshine," said Dinah.

"There she is," said Kat, and they drew closer to follow her gaze.

Reinhart's wife was working one of the full-body exercisers, a mini–torture chamber requiring users to pull down a padded bar with their hands and push up another bar with their thighs so their bodies jack-knifed open and closed, open and closed. It didn't look easy, and even from well above, the group could see the sheen of sweat on the woman's arms and the dark wet patch on her back.

She was a strawberry blonde, her hair caught at the back of her head in a butterfly clip, and she was in very good shape. Lean and leggy, she wore a pink sleeveless leotard over silver-gray leggings that ended midcalf. As they watched, she finished, extricated herself limb by limb from the contraption, and stretched several times to her full height. Then she picked up her water bottle and towel and wove her way among the machines to a stair-stepper on the opposite wall. As she shook out her hair, rewound it, and clipped it up again, she punched in a sequence of numbers on the display, then stood for a while before starting, sipping at her bottled water.

Kat looked at her friends, lined up on her left like a tour group, riveted. "She'll work this one for a good thirty or forty minutes," she said. "Had enough?"

Back in Kat's office, the table had been cleared. They sat down in the couch area.

"Well." Charlotte looked at Kat. "What do we know about her?"

"Must be a runner," said Polly. "She's pretty flat-chested. Aren't runners usually flat-chested?"

"I'll ignore that," said Kat. "Besides, in top social circles thin and flat-chested is in." She turned to Charlotte. "All we know so far is that she's here, is Mitchell Reinhart's wife, and has her bills sent to a West L.A. address. But that means we can find out quite a bit. She's a regular with one of my best trainers and with a facialist as well."

"But what can we do to him by focusing on her?" asked Justine. "Do we want to break up their marriage?"

"Not necessarily," said Polly. "It's just information. We need all we can get." She leaned forward, hands on her knees. "Let's lay this out and divide it up," she said. "Who's doing what?"

It took only a few more minutes. Charlotte would call up the court filings associated with both of his divorces and try to get more information on his current prenuptial agreement. Justine would check for all real property under his name. Polly would research his business connections and the press coverage of his high-profile divorce cases and his own marital history.

Kat would pull credit reports on both Reinhart and his wife and would talk to the wife's trainer and anyone else who dealt with her at the club. "Hell," she said, "I'll talk to her myself. It's my club, and she's been a valued member for over a year, right?"

"I'll do what I can with his political connections," said Dinah, "and any dealings he's had with decorators or the art world. I'm meeting with my decorator anyway to pick a sales agent. Did I tell you I'm selling most of my Southwest baskets and pottery?"

"You might have," said Polly. "You're always selling something. Unless, of course, you're buying."

"And I'll check his health records," Dinah added. "Maybe he does have psoriasis. And I'll wear the red bra and do the run this time. It could scare him to death, which leaves no marks."

_____

Justine's Ford was the first car brought when they lined up at the valet parking curb. She was almost reluctant to leave, moving slowly down the driveway and out onto the boulevard, thinking of Dinah's crack about the red bra. It made her feel, as usual, imprisoned in her own seriousness, lacking the antic impulse of the others, even Charlotte. Inevitably, she was the straight man of the group.

She had always considered her composure an asset. It wasn't that she was incapable of joy or excitement. She loved her family, loved playing with her boys and working in her garden, took great pleasure in running an efficient office, and was virtually transported by horticultural magazines. But in comparison with Kat's constant motion, Polly's gaiety, Charlotte's conviction, and Dinah's surety, Justine felt gray and boring. Who could know that her secret life was a canvas of colors, that she dreamed herself barefoot, wrapped in silks of wine and crimson and lemon yellow, with citrines or peridots in her ears instead of Robby's diamonds? Who knew that she wasn't just the perfect bureaucrat? She herself wasn't really sure.

The state and local government offices were clustered in a six-block area near the Sport Scene, and in minutes Justine pulled in to a reserved space behind the county building. Usually she went in the rear door and up the back stairs to the assessor's satellite offices, but now, feeling contrary, she walked around to the front and the public elevator. This way she entered the suite and got the same greeting as the general public at the front counter.

She was ignored. Three heads were partly visible at cubicles just beyond the counter, and the doors made a loud noise both opening and closing, but no one looked up. Justine waited, hands clasped on the countertop. Still no movement. She felt a prick of shame and a little mean pleasure. A minute passed. She thought of Polly, whose letters to businesses and government bureaus often focused on their poor service. "Nobody wants to work," Polly would say, shaking her head. Justine never argued, but she had dismissed it as hyperbole.

Eventually one woman's gaze slid sideways and her face appeared over the low partition. "Oh, my God," she mouthed.

Another face came up, and then the third, which immediately flushed red. "Ah," said the man, "Mrs. Teyama."

Justine nodded at them. "Perhaps we need some kind of buzzer when the door is opened?" she said in a neutral voice.

"Good idea!" said the man, with toady enthusiasm, coming forward. Without further comment Justine gave him Reinhart's name and suggested a Beverly Hills or Century City or West L.A. location. Then she walked around the counter and down the back hall to her small office. Since she was there every two weeks, the in-box wasn't full, and she could sort through the mail while the deputy found Reinhart's property records.

His residence was a large double lot in an upscale enclave just south of Century City. On one lot was a house built in 1988, and a building permit had been issued a few years ago to remodel and extend it over into the second. The assessor's office had sent out a standard request for further information and plans, but there was no record of an answer. On the chance that Reinhart had gone ahead with construction anyway, Justine decided to check with the county building department.

Strangely, the same contrary impulse that had sent her to the front counter in her own department made her pick up her phone now and dial the department's public number. For the next eleven minutes, she was bounced from menu to menu—six sets of options, with frequent waits. She chose a language (English) and an area of the city. She selected a division (permits, inspections, codes, etc.), building type (commercial, residential), building size (multiple, duplex, single family) and permit status (sought, filed, or expired). She was then put on hold, with frequent assurances that her call was important. Then she was cut off. Twice.

Justine thought again of Polly's drive to change whatever didn't work right. It had probably helped Polly through years of pain and loss, giving her a forward outlook that propelled her out of misery. Justine was the opposite, a tacit defender of the status quo. She had kept her position through four administrations by accepting the system, working within and sometimes around it. She had the loyalty of her employees because she trusted them to do their jobs on their own and systematically rewarded those who rewarded that trust. Like Polly, she survived, but instead of feeling like a survivor, she felt trapped, no longer in command of her life.

Impatiently seizing the phone again, she punched in the direct number of a department deputy and had her answer in thirty seconds. After Reinhart's permit was filed, there had been no further filings—no request for inspections, no amendments. New-construction permits were valid for two years while work proceeded but expired in six months if there was "no action," which didn't necessarily mean no action at the site. It meant the building department hadn't been told of any or asked to inspect, and it had no authority to go out and check.

But the tax assessor could, so Justine called her own department to order a site check. Decidedly testy now, she used a public number again, and again she ran the gauntlet of options. Language. Location. Type of information sought. Address, parcel number, map-book page. And finally: a recorded voice saying that all service reps were busy helping other valued citizens and that she should leave a message or call back later.

Shaking, she called an inspector's direct number and asked him to visit Reinhart's property to see if there was any new construction. Then she thought some more about the need for everyone to right a few wrongs, decided it was about time, and sent an e-mail message to her whole staff telling them to call the general number a few times themselves before the next staff meeting. And to come up with several ideas each for improving the bureau's phone system.

Justine got home with less than an hour to prepare dinner for Robby's family, who always came on Thursday or Friday night for what Justine, uncharacteristically snide, called "the weekly genuflection." Slightly more social than a weekly staff meeting, the gathering always included his parents, Sammy and Reiko, his brother, James, and his family, and when she was in town, his sister and her new husband, both graduate students. James, a dentist, wasn't actually in the garden-supply company with Robby and his father, but he grew up in it and owned a portion, so it was fitting that he should be party to the business discussions.

At first Justine had cooked fairly elaborate meals on these occasions, spending much of the previous evening on preparations. When that became burdensome, she quietly changed her approach, following a mundane but lifesaving principle she'd learned from the mother of one of her son's kindergarten friends. A busy cardiologist, this woman would pause before responding to any demands on her time and ask herself, "Is this a problem I can buy my way out of?" Usually she could. She sent store-bought brownies to the school bake sale. She contributed a thousand dollars to the school Booster Club and skipped the meetings. She hired a college student to drive her boys to midweek soccer practice, saving herself for the Saturday games.

It worked just as well for Justine, particularly for the weekly dinner. She started picking up boxes of food from a Japanese restaurant on Wilshire, an upscale place where Robby's family went for birthday and anniversary celebrations. Initially they all protested, with their characteristic tinge of criticism, that it was unnecessary and extravagant to buy such food for an ordinary weekday supper, but they enjoyed the treat and came to look forward to it.

With the help of James's wife, Akemi, Justine opened the boxes in the kitchen and set out everything on the table as the family was sitting down. The seating plan was as predictable as the meal. Robby's parents sat at the head of the table, side by side like Emperor Akihito and Empress Michiko. Robby sat at his father's corner and James at their mother's. Next to each was his wife, with the four children—Robby and Justine's two boys and James's son and daughter—at the other end of the table.

As always, the two men talked with their father about garden supplies and equipment, occasionally asking their mother, "What do you think, Oba-chan?" while Justine and her sister-in-law went back and forth from table to kitchen, kitchen to table. Justine always pushed her boys to help, and once or twice, early in the meal, Justine's mother-in-law would rise to clear plates or help in the kitchen. But Justine would always say, "No, Oba-chan," using the form of traditional address that was both fond and deferential. "You sit."

This Thursday they were discussing the idea of offering on-site consulting services to the landscape and garden contractors who were their customers. Strictly wholesale now, they hoped eventually to establish a retail arm, selling directly to consumers, and this might be a good transition. But at the moment even their informal recommendations to contractors resulted in many returns and rejections. They'd stocked a lot of rose standards, for example, and sold them vigorously, but they were not as universally appealing as bush roses, many were coming back, and contractors were irritated by the inconvenience.

"There may be a better bridge to retail," Justine said, leaning forward so she could address her father-in-law. "Why not have contractors bring the clients in to help pick out their plants?"

Given no response, she continued, "It would probably mean fewer returns and less trouble. After all, those clients are ultimately the people you have to make happy."

"Very few would be knowledgeable," said Robby. "We don't have time now to deal with their questions and criticisms."

"It would be good to hear their criticisms," insisted Justine. "It could guide us toward what we really should be stocking."

"Maybe so," said Robby dismissively, turning back toward his father. "The bigger problem is all the thirty-six-inch boxes that come back. These people know ahead what they're getting. They approved a thirty-six-inch box, but when the guy brings it out, they make him take it away."

Justine couldn't hold back. "The problem is when you say thirty-six inches, it sounds small," she said, "and the ordinary homeowner isn't prepared for how big it actually is when it's delivered and there's an eight- or ten-foot tree in it."

"Okay, okay," said Robby with an admonitory tap on the back of her hand.

There was an embarrassed silence, broken by Robby's mother. "I'd never have picked rose standards," she declared. "Too formal for today's gardens. Too much like lollipops."

She sat motionless, her hands in her lap, her voice soft but firm. "And the way they come, so stiff and compact, they're easy to return even if you already planted them and have to dig them up."

"Why didn't you say something before?" asked James.

"Maybe I did," she said calmly. "But before, you wouldn't have heard."

She spoke without blame, with no intonation at all, as was her style. What was unusual was the context, and the clear correction, although she was, as always, composed. This was a characteristic often attributed to Justine, but her mother-in-law's composure was easy, almost gentle, and Justine's seemed rigid.

When Justine and Akemi got up to clear the dishes for dessert, their mother-in-law rose with them. Again they said, "Sit, Oba-chan," but this time she said, "I'll come."

Together the three of them opened the dessert boxes, laid the little Japanese pastries on plates, and scooped green-tea ice cream into bowls. When Akemi had taken her seat again and Justine was about to carry in the last dessert dishes, her mother-in-law stopped her just inside the swinging door. Reaching up, she laid three fingers against Justine's face, soft and light as silk, and said, "Your ideas are good. They need your ideas."

"I think they do, Oba-chan," Justine managed to say, taken aback. How long had her mother-in-law been aware of Justine's yearning? The older woman herself had always shown an interest in the details of the business, had never hesitated to speak, and had been heard. For all her quietness, she was confident, even assertive. Perhaps, Justine thought, she had made a conscious decision to comment from the sidelines, uninvolved in the daily activities, believing that this was the best exercise of her considerable power.

Even so, such an arrangement was not for Justine, and she wouldn't ask when or why Robby's mother had made that choice. At least she now knew that she could go to her mother-in-law when she was ready to change her own position, that she had someone to help her.

She put down a bowl and took her mother-in-law's hand. "Thank you, Reiko," she said.

16

Mitchell Reinhart's wife didn't come into the Sport Scene that weekend, so Kat spent some time instead reviewing her account. As it turned out, Suzanne Weil Reinhart never came in on weekends, unlike most club members. Instead she'd come four out of five weekdays for several hours at a time, a schedule she had followed religiously since joining up two years earlier.

In Kat's experience the typical club member visited two or three times a week, stayed about an hour and a quarter, and devoted half that time to changing clothes, showering, and getting refreshments. More often than not, the person stopped coming entirely after several months, which was why health clubs always discouraged month-to-month memberships. Given dropout rates of over 50 percent, they wanted long-term contracts and as much money as possible up front.

The Reinhart woman was both unusually dedicated and a good customer. During her lengthy visits, she bought a lot of services and a fair number of goods. She worked with a trainer and made regular appointments for massages and facials, had her hair done and her nails manicured. She bought sneakers, leggings, and spandex sports tops.

Maintaining and improving her looks was apparently her main occupation, and a pretty successful enterprise. She was medium tall and fashionably thin, with prominent cheekbones, prominent hip bones, and a prominent collarbone. Hers was a thinness made for high fashion, not strength or agility, and forged by a lot of aerobic exercise that reduced the flesh without building ugly muscles. She was also handsome, with dark blue eyes, the strawberry blond hair twisted up on her head in a tortoiseshell barrette, and nicely tanned skin.

The following Tuesday she was there again, in navy blue spandex leggings and a navy tank top. Even from a distance, she was almost luminous, the leggings and top tight and shiny, and her skin wet with sweat. She did thirty-five minutes on the stair-step machine, gazing at the TV on a nearby wall and sometimes at the wall itself, and she didn't turn her head when Kat started working a machine next to her, even though it was two in the afternoon, the midday crowd had departed, and they had the section to themselves. When Mrs. Reinhart moved to the upper-body exercisers, Kat switched to a NordicTrack and stayed there while Suzanne Reinhart moved on to the abdominals and then the various leg exercisers.

At three-fifteen she seemed ready to quit. She had toweled off each time she switched sequences, but this time she went to a wall bench and sat down, mopping her face and neck. In a few minutes she gathered up her things and walked through the arch into the juice bar, and shortly thereafter Kat stopped her machine and followed. Mrs. Reinhart sat alone at a table near the terrace exit, and after picking a bottle of seltzer out of the ice trough, Kat went over and stood by her table.

"That's some pace you set," said Kat, resting her hand on an empty chair. "I told myself I'd stop when you did, and I was about to give up or just fall over. You always do a full sequence right after the stair-step?"

"Usually," said Mrs. Reinhart, wiping the side of her face. She was still flushed and slick with perspiration. "If I don't do them one after another, I'm tempted to quit."

"Most people have that problem," said Kat, "and most do quit. They call it 'taking a break' and just don't go back." She draped her sweatshirt over her shoulders. "People's exercise habits are pretty funny."

"That's for sure," said Suzanne Reinhart. "My husband doesn't exercise at all. He golfs and pretends that's exercise. But then he works hard. Or at least late," she said, twisting down the corners of her mouth. "It must be a pretty good workout at that: When he finally comes home, he's good for nothing but a glass of wine and a sauna."

Kat laughed, and when she did, Suzanne Reinhart smiled slightly.

"Okay if I sit?" asked Kat, and she put out her hand. "I'm Kat Hurley, the owner of the club. Or part owner. Me and my partners and the bank."

"Sure," said the woman, shaking the hand. "Suzanne Reinhart." She moved her towel and carryall from the other chair at the table. In front of her was an empty glass and an almost-empty bottle, a membership card in a windowed leather case, a small purse on a skinny shoulder strap, and a little brown suede drawstring pouch. The pouch probably held jewelry; she wore only a watch and two big sapphire studs in her ears. Indeed, as Kat sat down, Mrs. Reinhart began to remove one of the earrings, maybe in preparation for taking a shower. The stone was a deep cobalt blue and at least three carats. Kat had once seen a stone like that in a *National Geographic* article and never forgot it. Mrs. Reinhart's eyes were the same blue; Kat had never seen eyes of that color either.

Kat waved at the man behind the bar, held up her bottle and Mrs. Reinhart's, and gestured for refills. "What beautiful stones!" she said. "They're sapphires, aren't they?"

"Yes," said Mrs. Reinhart, holding the earring in midair over the little pouch. She turned the stone back and forth in the light. "They're Burmese. The setting's new, but the stones are old. It's almost impossible to find sapphires that color anymore. I think I've worn them every day since I got them."

"Gift for a big round birthday?" asked Kat.

Mrs. Reinhart dropped the earring into the pouch. "Not a gift," she said curtly. "I bought them for myself."

Kat nodded. The woman looked at her intently, tilting her head slightly as she worked to remove the other earring. "It's not so remarkable," she said, although Kat had made no comment. "You know, I used to have my own business, like you. I was pretty successful."

"Did you just give it up?" asked Kat. "Or sell it to some big conglomerate?"

"Come, now," said the woman, pushing the little pouch into her purse. "I'm sure you've heard of me—Mitchell Reinhart's trophy wife?"

Kat shook her head and shrugged, hoping the effect was noncommittal.

Suzanne Reinhart snorted. "Come on," she said again, studying Kat's face, "you probably know a lot about everyone who comes here. Don't worry: I may be bitter, but I'm not sensitive."

"Bitter? Why?" Kat was truly surprised.

"Lemme tell you about trophy wives," said Suzanne Reinhart, snapping the cap off her second bottle of seltzer and then quickly checking her perfect mauve nails for damage. "I don't mind telling you. I don't tell everyone. I don't hang around the ladies' locker room chatting, and I usually eat my lunch alone. But you're safe. What you know about everybody who comes here is probably very helpful, but it's good business only if it stops there."

She took a long drink from her seltzer and leaned slightly toward Kat. "I figure given your ownership and my membership, our talk is protected by something like an attorney-client trust, right? Like, if you told anyone else all the stuff you know about your members, you and your club would be dead in the water."

She smiled, and Kat thought, This is scary. "Pretty scary," she said out loud, and they laughed together, but Kat knew she had been served warning.

Suzanne Reinhart sat back. If she'd been smoking, she would have taken a long drag. "It's hard work being a trophy," she said, as if musing aloud. "As work it ain't bad, but it is definitely work. Look at me." She swept a hand from head to waist. "I'm . . . what? Thirty-eight? Close enough—and I'm here every day, doing the StairMaster and the step aerobics and the Pilates. I've got a trainer and a manicurist and a facialist and a masseuse, and I've got a personal shopper who has me on call—I'm on call to her, you get that?—for whenever she has something she wants me to see. Something she knows is perfect for me, so she calls me to come and get it."

She looked intently at Kat, who was somewhat taken aback by the turn of the conversation, and went on. "Oh, I know what 'trophy' means. It means somebody won you and now they've got you. But the thing about trophy wives is they had to be somebody themselves. They had to be a catch.

"Mitch liked me because I was a somebody. I had something of my own, and it was good. My business was called Gala. Still is, though I don't own it anymore. We did event planning—all the arrangements, all the setting up and decorating, putting on everything from big charity benefits to weddings, press conferences, award ceremonies. We even did all the promotion and the PR. And we had just started a subsidiary company in partnership with a caterer, so we wouldn't even have to contract out the food. That one we called Dish."

"Great name," said Kat.

"It is a great name," she said wistfully. "I love it. I loved every minute. People knew my name, my picture was in all the columns. I miss it."

"Why'd you give it up?" asked Kat. "Didn't your husband like what you did?"

"Yes and no," said Suzanne Reinhart. "It's certainly what attracted him. He liked that I had all that but not that I did it. Once I was in his life, it got harder. How could I do the St. Luke's benefit when he wanted us to go to London that week? How do I do the *Vanity Fair* Oscar party when it's the same time as the Family Lawyers Convention in Vegas? Or the big June weddings when that's his time to go fishing in Cabo?"

She looked down at her hands, folded in her lap, turned them over, smoothed the skin over her knuckles. "I'll tell you how. I gave it all up." She paused but didn't look up. "That's the thing about trophy wives. They have to give up whatever made them a big catch, because to the man it's no good having someone who's somebody in her own right unless he can say, 'Hey, she was a big cheese, but she gave it up because all she wants now is to make me happy.'

"I did keep my connections, as many as I could," she continued, more briskly. "I'm like a consultant to the corporation that bought me out, and I do an occasional party for special people. I guess the consultant thing is kind of an insurance policy. It means I could go back to it all someday if I had to."

"That's true," said Kat. "Meantime, isn't it kind of a trade-off? For right now, for at least this period of your life, you're doing something else, something satisfying in other ways?"

"Satisfying? Well, let's see, what do I get for giving it all up?" Suzanne Reinhart's voice took on a definite edge. "Money, for one thing. Money, ease, clothes, trips, all the extras. I drop a lot of money right here, for instance, just in this one little place. Not that I didn't earn plenty on my own. I made enough money to buy most of it myself, but it left me no time. I worked too hard to spend hours here every day."

She sighed. "I guess you can earn it or you can spend it, but you can't do both. Actually," she added, "you can't always spend it either. Like I love entertaining, and we do entertain, but never at home. We were going to remodel, to make the place great for entertaining, but now Mitch says he wants to wait a while."

A look of irritation came over her face, and Kat felt the mood go sour. "I'm sure you'll get to it," she said in her most comforting voice. "And if you get tired of waiting or bored, as you say, you can always go back to your business and build your own house."

It was meant lightly, even comfortingly, but Suzanne Reinhart waved it away. "Sure I could, and I might yet, but this trophy-wife stuff is not pension work, you know. I'd be leaving almost bare, with no more than I came with, and I wouldn't like that."

"What do you mean?"

"Well, the other thing everyone knows about me is this famous pre-nuptial agreement of ours." The blue eyes fixed on Kat questioningly, but Kat shook her head.

"Okay," said Suzanne Reinhart. "He made this big deal about a prenup when we got married. Said he was burned once, twice, and three times would be incredible stupidity on his part. Everyone feels sorry for his first wives. Everyone says they did the work and I get the gravy." She poured more seltzer, and the bottle shook in her hand. "Gravy, my ass. I get to spend a little money here and there, but I also get a prenup that says what's his is his and what's mine is mine, period, and nothing more."

"Meaning?" asked Kat.

"Meaning what exactly *is* mine? Nothing. According to this famous piece of paper, if I walk, I get nothing for the years I put in. In other words, I can't ever walk." She drank down the seltzer in her glass. "Isn't that the meaning of 'trapped'?"

Kat couldn't think how to respond, and Suzanne Reinhart, appar-ently talked out, began to gather together her things. They exchanged some pleasantries about how much they enjoyed meeting, spoke briefly of getting together another day after working out, and parted cordially.

Feeling both touched and offended by the business bases of Suzanne Reinhart's life, Kat went looking for Barnaby in his office, then in the trainers' room, then on every floor of the building. As she went up and down the stairs, she tried to define what most disturbed her. She was hardly surprised that a marriage wasn't founded totally on love, but she'd assumed that where love was lacking, there might be affection, and if there wasn't affection, there was at least faith and some community of interest. She had no idea what the Reinharts had, but it obviously wasn't enough to create a close and trusting alliance.

Unable to find Barnaby, Kat shut herself in her office and called Polly, who was about to leave, late as usual, to pick up Jeremy at school. So all Kat said was that she'd had a long talk with Mitch Reinhart's wife, and all Polly said was, "Good for you! What's she like?"

"Well," said Kat, "I don't think life with him is so good, but she's a survivor."

That's what people called me, Polly thought as she got ready to leave. They meant it as a compliment, impressed that after Dan's death she'd made her way through months of legal, practical, and administrative chores without collapsing in grief or publicly snuffling into her hand-kerchief. She took it as a compliment, too, although it seemed to her that survival was not an achievement or even a choice. It was a necessity, and therefore just assumed, like life, and children's needs, and occasional food preparation. Sometimes late at night, she found herself saying over and over, piteously, "Everyone's dead now, and I'm totally alone," but it was really just a reminder of her survival, now that there was no one to help her define her situation.

It's not hard, her mother used to say. Just put one foot in front of the other and you'll move forward.

Polly had absorbed the rubric well and followed it willingly. But now a little tremor of excitement pricked at her life, and she sensed the pos-sibility of something a step above survival.

An hour later she was on her way to the Valley with two silent children, because Graham Vere thought it would be nice if everyone met. Polly had protested that they themselves had just met, that she couldn't count on her children to be friendly and outgoing in a social situation, and that it was likely to be an awkward evening at best. But it was his view that when two people had known each other only six weeks and were already talking on the phone every night and getting together several times a week, it was a good idea to bring the children into it.

Andrea had rolled her eyes and said, "Oh, man." Jeremy had made kissing noises accompanied by some sort of shuffling motion of his feet that was suggestive only to him. Nevertheless, they rode with her now in unprotesting silence.

"Shall I tell you a little about the Veres?" asked Polly.

"We've met him," said Andrea from the passenger seat next to her.

"Meeting someone isn't quite the same as having dinner with them," said Polly.

"What's the big deal?" Andrea lifted her shoulders in an exaggerated shrug.

I don't know that it's a big deal, thought Polly. It's probably no deal at all, and I'm beginning to act very silly about Graham Vere.

"It's no big deal," she conceded.

Perhaps Andrea heard something in the way she said it, or in the long silence that preceded it. In any case she made an uncharacteristic effort at conversation. "I don't eat meat," she said, "remember?"

"It's an Italian restaurant," said Polly. "There's a wide choice, lots of it not involving meat."

In the backseat Jeremy played on his GameBoy, the little melody that accompanied the particular game playing over and over like a tinny nickelodeon. They spoke no more.

At the restaurant they were placed with other families in the Siberia of a big back room. The decor was the same as in the front—open rafters, hanging Chianti bottles and green plastic plants, and murals of grape arbors and distant hills meant to create the illusion of sitting on the patio of a Tuscan villa. But as at many restaurants, the clientele was segregated. Couples and parties of adults got the front room. Anyone with children was sent to the back. As she followed the waiter, it occurred to Polly that she'd married so young and passed so quickly from childhood to parenthood that she hadn't had much of a turn in the front room with the grown-ups.

They sat down stiffly at a round table. Polly and Graham sat next to each other, Polly's children on her right, Vere's on his left. Polly's two were the more casual. Andrea was a fifteen-year-old bohemian in her black-eyed, black-lipped makeup, dangling jewelry, and floor-length green gauze wraparound. Jeremy, at twelve, in his precious Nirvana T-shirt and khakis, was barely there, his eyes focused, or rather unfocused, somewhere above their heads. The Vere boys—Michael, fourteen, and like Andrea, in the tenth grade, and Duncan, eleven—were dressed for presentation, in collared shirts and twill pants, their faces scrubbed to a high flush and their hair neatly combed back.

None of them spoke. There had been a brief flurry of negotiation at the outset. Jeremy had refused to come in without his GameBoy, although he was willing to turn it off, and Duncan immediately insisted on getting his own GameBoy from the car. A deal was struck: They could have the GameBoys but couldn't play them until after dinner. As a result the gadgets sat by their plates and the boys sat quietly, not playing but poised to play.

Over pizzas (kids) and pastas (grown-ups), the parents spoke haltingly, with occasional insertions from their children. Vere told Polly a few stories of office politics. They discussed Dinah's program for students and house staff. Then Vere said, "We got another one from San Bernardino today."

"Dad," said Michael immediately, "no cases."

"Not dinner-table conversation, I guess," said Vere, and then he

2 SUSAN DIAMOND

asked Polly. "When you were growing up, did you have topics that were prohibited as dinner-table conversation?"

"NDT," said Polly. "Not Dinner Talk. There was also FHB. Did you have that one?"

"I don't think so," said Vere. "What was FHB?"

"Family Hold Back. When the supply of some food looks like it's coming up short and you have to make sure the company is taken care of first."

"Didn't have that," he said. "But if we didn't eat everything, we heard about how people in India or some neighboring country were starving. My brother and I always offered to send them our food, which we thought hysterically funny."

Michael and Duncan were twisting straws into finger rings. Jeremy studied the ceiling fan.

Finally Polly and Graham Vere gave up and decided to please themselves. Ignoring the stony faces of their offspring, they discussed the menu selections, a topic they'd enjoyed in previous dinners. When they moved on to specific components of the food, the stony faces showed some reaction. It wasn't positive.

"Which part of the calamari is made into the little rings?" wondered Polly. "Was it the main body and the rings are crosswise cuts?"

Vere clicked on his pocket pen and began to draw on the sheet of Thursday specials. "This long tube's the body of the squid," he said, "and the legs all hang down at one end."

Andrea, across from Michael, saw him roll his eyes. He caught her looking at him, she rolled her own eyes, more broadly, and he responded with a delighted smile. Some unspoken accord was struck between them, and almost simultaneously they asked if they could be excused to play pinball games at the back of the room. Then they were gone. Immediately, and more noisily, Jeremy and Duncan asked to leave, and then they, too, were gone.

"Tell me again why we did this," said Polly wearily.

"So they could meet and start getting to know each other," he said, putting his arm across the back of her chair. He was in gray, mostly—gray slacks, light gray crew sweater, gray-and-red-striped shirt showing at the collar. She thought him handsome, but he certainly wasn't flashy or even colorful. This close she could even see gray sprinkled through his hair.

"You and I barely know each other," she reminded him.

"That's not so," he answered patiently. "We're already sure we will know each other, which is the same thing. And they need to absorb the idea so it doesn't hit them as unexpected."

What a nice man, she thought, looking into his face.

"To them our meetings are rare. This is only our fourth dinner. They're not in on all the phone calls, the e-mails, the walks, and even if your kids are there when I arrive, they don't go out with us."

"This is true," she said, and didn't think of the children again until it was time to pull them away from the pinball games and go home.

As soon as Polly opened the front door of their house, the children squeezed past her and headed down the hall to their rooms. Just before they were out of sight, Polly called out, "Thank you for coming and for being good company."

To her amazement Andrea stopped, although she didn't turn around. Picking up a corner of her long skirt that apparently required some inspection, she said softly, "It was cool, Mom."

Startled, Polly couldn't respond, and when she finally thought of some responses, all questions, Andrea was gone. On balance, she supposed, it had indeed been cool, if "cool" could mean not just fine but also okay. Everyone had gotten along. The children had found their own meeting ground, essentially wordless but comfortable for them.

Alone in her room over the canyon, she thought of a letter that had been sitting in her file for some time. In the eight years since her husband's death, the Los Angeles County court system had sent him several questionnaires for jury duty and even two summonses. At first she'd wept, pained by what she assumed was only a mistake, and sent back the forms with a notation that the addressee was deceased. The next couple of notices she ignored, in spite of the threat of a fifteen-hundred-dollar fine, but by the second summons she was irate, the more so because they demanded his death certificate as proof.

To the Clerk of the Superior Court:

You just summoned my dead husband to jury duty for the fifth time.

I've heard the court is desperate for jurors. Now I believe it. This is someone who will have to decide right and wrong, and he can't even hear the evidence. Justice is traditionally blind; in Los Angeles she can also be dead.

Much has been written about scofflaws who refuse to do their civic duty, but nobody points out that many of your mailings go to people who have indicated that they're poor prospects. My husband is a good example, since I responded and your reaction was distrust. The registrar of voters believed me, deleting his name. The DMV stopped sending renewals. The tax assessor changed our property title. (Come to think of it, if someone isn't a registered voter and has no driver's license or property, where do you get the name? Mail-order catalogs? Reader's Digest sweepstakes?)

What seems distrust may just be incompetence, but it's endemic. When an elderly friend of ours got your inquiry, she wrote that she was "ninety years old, blind, frail, and housebound." When she got another the next year, she wrote, "Last year I told you I was ninety, blind, frail, and housebound. I'm ninety-one now and not improved."

A twenty-year-old college student I know received three juror inquiries in a year. Each time she checked off the applicable excuses. Each time they were ignored. She's not a citizen, doesn't have permanent-resident status, and doesn't drive. (Did you get her name from a Macy's charge card?)

One can't discuss this problem, because the phone number given prospective jurors allows only recorded requests for a different date or venue. There is no public number for the clerk's office.

Then I noticed that if someone writes, "Moved—not at this address," no proof is required—no deed, no new lease, no postal affidavit. So I circled my husband's name and wrote, "Dead. Left no forwarding address."

Can it rest at that?

Sincerely . . .

Only when Polly had pruned it and patched it and marked it "Final Draft" was she suddenly disturbed by the fact that she had chosen to write this letter now and particularly this night. The symbolism seemed blatant: She needed to lay Dan to rest because now she had a replacement for him. Or, allowing a more sympathetic interpretation, she herself needed to recognize that he was beyond summoning. Either way, she told her mother, it was time both she and the county accepted his death.

Death is pretty final, her mother agreed. Few come back.

Polly's throat filled, and her eyes spilled over. The stars and the lights in the canyon became obscured. She was overwhelmed by the feeling that she had some choice to make. Blinded by her tears, she wavered.

Her mother softened. We all want you to live, she said, Dan included.

17

On Wednesday, Charlotte cleared her schedule so she could spend most of the day on Mitchell Reinhart, and by late morning she was at the downtown courthouse. Just skimming through some of his biggest cases would give her a sense of his professional principles and methods. Better yet, she might glean some useful personal details from lawsuits in which he was himself a party—fee disputes perhaps, malpractice claims, certainly his own divorce filings.

Unlike most attorneys, she enjoyed searching through old case files, a category of scut work generally assigned to junior associates. To Charlotte it was like archaeological trenching, digging back down the years for bits and pieces of people's lives. She even liked the site. The superior court's archives were in the depths of the courthouse, and Charlotte eagerly took the marble staircase, winding down two, three, four flights, resting one hand lightly on the banister and looking over the edge. Fortunately, she wore low heels, because over the years thousands of feet had worn dangerous depressions in the steps. The stairwell narrowed in descent, spiraling down like a whirlpool—perfect, thought Charlotte, for a system that sucked people up, whirled them around, did terrible, irreparable damage to them, then buried their stories far underground.

From above, the bottom of the spiral looked like the floor of a well, dark and doorless, but there were actually several recessed corridors, and Charlotte took the one to the family law archives. On the computer there, she quickly found Reinhart's two divorces and two property settlements, plus several later orders to show cause, an action that usually meant that a husband wasn't paying the agreed amounts or the wife wanted more. One of the orders was pending, and the file was in another office.

To find Reinhart's professional cases, she needed help, not knowing the filing customs in family law. To some extent each department followed its own procedures, and an attorney who crossed into an unfamiliar field without guidance did so at considerable risk. The forms, the filing system, even the presiding judge's personal habits could be quite different from one specialty to another and even from court to court.

There were two clerks behind the main counter. One had her back to Charlotte, facing a computer screen. She didn't move, and nothing on the screen was moving either, so Charlotte concluded that she was asleep. The other was sitting sideways at the counter, wearing khaki twills and hiking boots, with her shirtsleeves rolled up. Obviously a law student, she was taking notes from a big brown textbook labeled *Torts III* and was so absorbed that she didn't look up until Charlotte asked how one could search a particular attorney's cases.

"Sure, who do you want?" the girl asked, rising immediately.

"Mitchell Reinhart?"

"Ah, Mr. Divorce," said the girl pleasantly. "I can print you out a list. It'll be pretty extensive. Do you want to limit it by date or anything?"

"How about the last ten years, just case cites, dates, and filings?" said

Charlotte. She figured she'd look only for recognizable names, but there should still be a lot. "That too much? I want to get a sense of what he takes."

"No, that's fine," said the girl, who looked barely twenty, with a braided ponytail and little gold balls in her ears. "I'll run it off, and you can check what looks interesting."

"That would be great," said Charlotte. "Can I get these as well?" and she held out her list of Reinhart's own divorce filings.

The girl took it. "You know, he's got a big one upstairs today—Rick Lorus, the guy who produces all those explosion films. Wife of thirty years. I'll drop in myself if I can get away later."

"Personal interest or academic?" asked Charlotte, appreciating now the instant accord possible between women, however far apart in age and position.

"Both, really," said the girl. "I want to go into family law. Not to level the playing field, because it's sort of level now, but to make sure it doesn't start tilting again."

"I'll go now and fill you in on what you miss," said Charlotte. "Many thanks."

She ran up the stairs and found the courtroom, where a notice on the door said the morning session had adjourned early and would reconvene at one-thirty. Pressing herself into a niche on the central hall to use her cell phone, she called Polly to come downtown so they could study Mitchell Reinhart together. Polly was easy to persuade: She did her trading early in the morning and her research whenever it was quiet, often late at night. With two hours to wait, Charlotte went back downstairs, found that the young clerk had already pulled the files on Reinhart's personal squabbles, and started reading.

When Charlotte emerged from the snack stand with a bottle of Snapple and a Balance Bar at half past one, Polly was waiting in the main lobby. She was all in white—cotton drawstring pants, white T top, loose white overshirt.

"Come straight from the yacht?" asked Charlotte.

"For me this is dressed up," said Polly, following Charlotte into the elevator and watching her peel back the paper and take a bite of the Balance Bar. "Don't you sometimes wonder what food group you're eating?"

"It's dead. And it's fast," said Charlotte. "For me that's all that counts."

The courtroom was nearly full. Rick Lorus was a draw and Mitch Reinhart even more so, and the autopsy on a thirty-year Hollywood marriage with $300 million worth of vital parts was sure to be entertaining. Charlotte and Polly found seats halfway to the front behind the wife's legal team, with a good view of Reinhart at the husband's table across the way. He was on the aisle, with three other lawyers on his left— one Reinhart's age and two young associates. Rick Lorus sat farthest in from Reinhart.

Lorus could have been typecast as a successful movie executive. He looked rich, Hollywood style, with his dark hair curling over the collar of a soft olive blazer, gray slacks, and a cream-colored shirt. Since he was leaning his elbows on the table, his Rolex watch was visible on one wrist, a heavy gold cuff on the other. His wife seemed a suitable match for him, but she wore her wealth more quietly. She sat on the aisle directly across from Mitchell Reinhart, her hands in her lap, back straight, eyes front. Her sun-streaked brown hair was tucked into a French twist, her suede skirt was topped by a plain beige sweater set, and her only jewelry was the pearl studs in her ears.

Reinhart was "of counsel," not lead attorney but clearly in command of the defense. The other lawyers leaned over to confer with him. Files and exhibits were placed in front of him. Notes were passed up from the audience and put under his eye.

Mitchell Reinhart wasn't handsome, but he looked forceful. He was tanned, with graying hair and the high cheek color and pinpoints of broken blood vessels that indicated a drinking habit. It was a fleshy face, and his shoulders were bulky enough for a taller man, but the rest of him seemed fit, his navy pinstriped suit flat and smooth to his body. His posture was almost military: He faced front, feet planted on the floor, the fingertips of both hands poised on the edge of the table. Even when he inclined his head to take an inquiry from a colleague, he watched the bench over his reading glasses.

There was a lot of conferring among the professionals. The judge was already in place, peering over his own glasses at the recording secretary, who was unwinding a long strip of white tape from her machine to show him something. Mrs. Lorus's lawyers stood by their chairs, one listening with his eyes closed, reading glasses pushed up on his head, while the other talked, gesturing with the hand that held his glasses.

"What's with all the half glasses?" whispered Polly.

"Vanity," Charlotte whispered back. "Glasses look old, contacts are sissy, so if you're in court and have to see something, half glasses are the answer. Plus, you look smart and incisive peering out over specs."

The husband's team was about to present its main arguments after a morning spent questioning witnesses and displaying a lot of financial and chronological data. Blowups of several years' calendars stood on big easels, outlining Lorus's production schedules. When the judge called the session to order, Reinhart rose and stepped out into the aisle, and though he addressed the judge, his back to the courtroom, his voice carried easily.

His legal stance immediately struck Polly as pretty radical, although she knew little of family law. In an even voice, uninflected but not monotonous, Reinhart summed up his morning presentation. "The law says that all earnings in a marriage must be divided fifty-fifty, a split recognizing that when only one spouse works to generate income, the other spouse's unpaid work, usually running the home, contributes equally to the communal gain.

"But there are situations that demand some adjustment. A non-working spouse is sometimes not a helpmeet at all but an obstruction to that communal gain. Mr. Lorus rejected some productions at his wife's insistence and had to back out of others because she wouldn't join him or let his family join him on location—*The Big Bang,* for example, and *Fission,* which were kazillion-dollar hits for his replacements."

During the responsive ripple of amusement, Reinhart paused, removed his reading glasses, and rubbed the bridge of his nose. He continued, expressing not blame but simple logic. "Mrs. Lorus's obstruction dangerously compromised the earnings of other productions. Remember *Scorched,* which Mr. Lorus shot in Nevada instead of North Africa at her insistence—a change of locale that added seventeen million dollars to the movie's cost, with a commensurate loss in profit. In a strict accounting, that should be debited from her share."

There was a rising murmur in the courtroom, but Reinhart cut it off. Arms at his sides, he faced front—for most people a rather stiff pose, but Reinhart appeared utterly relaxed. "Similarly," he continued, "let's consider the films he made against his wife's wishes, well documented by both parties. They were some of his biggest movies, his biggest moneymakers, done without her help, without that fifty-fifty contribution. She didn't join him on location the seven months on *Blown Apart,* the four months on *Tsunami.* Her own brief describes those months as 'tantamount to a separation' and elsewhere as a 'separation she considered legalizing.'

"We believe," he said quietly, almost regretfully, "that she should not share in the revenues on those thirteen movies—three hundred forty million dollars over thirty years or, if annualized, eleven million dollars a year. Those sums should be subtracted from the community assets in the property settlement and from all calculations of his earning power."

The murmur increased, and one of Mrs. Lorus's lawyers noisily pushed back his chair. Reinhart didn't turn. "Peripherally," he went on, "we note that in several of those periods Mrs. Lorus's expenditures during Mr. Lorus's absence exceeded their normal household expenditures by a factor of four, even six, and involved not just living expenses but extraordinary purchases. Some large pieces of jewelry, a late-model BMW, and most extraordinary"—he pronounced it "extra-ordinary"—"a second home in the desert. If we're talking equal work and fair share, it's clear that Mrs. Lorus was significantly overpaid while contributing not at all to the communal income."

The murmur broke into a collective gasp. Mrs. Lorus's shoulders began to shake, and her lawyer sprang up. Although younger than Reinhart, he had obviously studied the master's technique and outdid Reinhart in sounding calm and reasonable as he said, "We appreciate our esteemed opponent's creativity, but expenditures have always been irrelevant, admissible only as indications of income. That income is well documented and beyond dispute."

"No matter," said Reinhart, conceding the point with a flick of his hand. Mrs. Lorus put her head down and her hands up to cover her face, and the elder of her two lawyers draped his arm across her shoulders.

For all his reasoned tones, Mitchell Reinhart was known as a man who liked testing legal limits with daring and even outrageous ideas. He was willing to lose some skirmishes as long as his overall battle plan advanced. No one, therefore, was surprised when, after further analyses of Rick Lorus's earnings and acquisitions in various years of the marriage, Reinhart stepped into the center aisle and dropped another live bomb.

One of the documents in evidence, he pointed out, was a marital agreement written in the twelfth year of the marriage. Mrs. Lorus had initiated divorce proceedings at the start of that year, but after some months of living in separate households the Loruses had reconciled. This contract was one of several conciliatory arrangements at that time, and in the current proceedings both sides had accepted it without comment or question.

This important document must now be recognized, said Reinhart, as a watershed in the couple's marital history. Given the duration of the rift, and the legal action taken to dissolve the union, the contract was hardly a minor occurrence in the continuum, but the mark of a decisive divide. It demonstrated, he said, "the clear belief on both sides that they were entering into a wholly new partnership. That partnership," he said, "is the one that concerns us here—an eighteen-year partnership, not one of thirty years."

There was no murmur this time, no gasp, just a charged silence. Mitchell Reinhart stood and looked at the judge. The judge stared down at Reinhart. All of the lawyers, on both sides, held a single breath. Everyone knew this couldn't float, at least not for long. There was certainly an answer to this wild assertion, and probably a simple one, but it would take many long days of billable hours to put it together.

The court adjourned shortly thereafter, and Reinhart, with no papers to gather and no briefcase to carry, was first to leave. He walked down the center aisle, and as he passed, seats emptied and people, Charlotte and Polly included, fell in behind him like the closing of the Red Sea after the little band of Israelites. Out in the hall, he was confronted by a dozen photographers and reporters, all pushing microphones and cameras and questions at him. Some were general, such as "How do you feel it's going?" and "How long do you expect this trial will take?" but a few questioned the final stunning demand that the very length of the marriage be restated.

"The point," said Reinhart again, "is that this is not really a thirty-year partnership, as it was called. Nor are we looking at a partnership, whatever its duration, that deserves the fifty-fifty division we would apply to a true community."

"What else do you call it?" asked one bearded middle-aged reporter.

The corners of Reinhart's mouth curved minutely. "The desperate claim of a sixty-year-old woman looking at an uncertain future?"

"Isn't Mr. Lorus also sixty?" asked a young woman.

"That's different," said Reinhart. "He has years of productivity ahead of him and should be allowed to live them fully." And he moved forward, breaking through the circle of reporters.

"What a shithead," muttered the girl. Reinhart showed no indication that he'd heard, but continued down the hall, trailed by several legal associates. Charlotte and Polly, who had stood at the back of the gathering, were now ahead of him as he approached the elevator.

"Well, hello there," he said softly as he passed close to Polly, veering slightly in her direction. Without glasses now, he looked at her, sideways and upward, because Polly, at five foot ten, had a couple of inches over him. Startled, she stepped back into Charlotte, and Reinhart swept on into the elevator.

"Sorry," she said, grabbing at Charlotte's arm to steady them both. "What was that all about?"

"Guess he likes skinny redheads," said Charlotte. "Want some coffee?"

Late that night Charlotte sat down at her kitchen table with the morning's notes spread before her and thought about Mitchell Reinhart. Working in the kitchen was an old habit, a carryover from her childhood when she did homework while her mother read magazines and smoked in the pantry, and from her graduate-student days, when her apartments had a single table and she ate at it, studied on it, sometimes fell asleep slumped over it.

This table, and the room around it, bore no resemblance to those others. The kitchen was huge and stark and extremely bright, with big ceiling lights, white walls, white cabinets with black glass doors, and black granite counters. Avery had Bauhaus taste, preferring his surroundings bare and geometric. Small appliances were tucked away in "appliance garages" at the backs of counters; pots and kitchen utensils were hidden on roll-out drawers. It was what realtors called a "chef's kitchen," including the latest in stainless steel equipment—Sub-Zero refrigerator, lava-rock stovetop grill, and thermal, convection, and microwave ovens.

To be fair, Avery did a good share of the cooking, whatever cooking was done, and he had a right to the kitchen of his dreams. Charlotte handled more law than food in the kitchen, and while she preferred the painted, flyspecked tables of her youth, she ended up working here night after night, instead of in her home office, with its angled desk, ergonomic chair, and built-in files. She liked the hard kitchen chairs, the decisive tick of her father's old wall clock, the periodic hum of the refrigerator, and the memory of other kitchens and other, warmer days.

Thinking about Mitchell Reinhart and how much she disliked him, she thought also of her father, whom she had loved and revered. A labor lawyer, he had no patience with Reinhart's ilk, and only scorn for that kind of nerve. He agreed that everyone should have representation, but he believed that there was always a third party to be served—justice, and justice required some judgment of right and wrong. His kind of lawyer would voice clear, comprehensible concepts of right and wrong, then apply them.

He might have accepted Reinhart's bias toward rich men in marital cases if it were tempered by a sense of their obligation. With all the formulas for dividing property, none could adequately weigh what one person owed another morally. And he'd have had no doubt that a rich moviemaker who was free to fly around doing what he wanted owed a lot to the sixty-year-old woman who had guaranteed a home and family waiting for him when he returned.

He was a very sure man, Charlotte's father, unlike Charlotte, who for all her authority was so full of doubts that she often made the same decision several times over before it was set. Even in his final illness, he was often disoriented but never unsure. Or so it seemed at the time. And because he'd had the foresight to give Charlotte power of attorney over much of his property during his life, she assumed he had prepared as well for his death, filing all the applicable documents with his other papers. Exercising an incredibly foolish but loving tact, she never asked, and was stunned by the mess he left.

Charlotte felt very alone. She wished she could talk to her mother, even though she and her mother hadn't really talked in years. When they did, the talk was superficial and very careful. Her mother lived in San Francisco on her own family money, which was considerable, took good care of herself, dressed well, and spent much of her time handling her investments. Charlotte also wished she could talk to her daughter, who was studying for an MBA in New York and was, in character and intellect, a cross between Charlotte's mother and Avery. She already dressed well, took good care of herself, and spent her time preparing to handle other people's money.

Most of all, as Charlotte thought about her father's death, and about Ginger's, and about Mitchell Reinhart, she wished she could talk to Avery. Overcome by her loneliness, she didn't hear him drive in, open the front door, or come down the hall, and she didn't know he was there until he spoke. "Dissecting a particularly wealthy corpus tonight?"

He leaned against the doorjamb, the jacket of his suit slung over one shoulder, tie loosened, collar open on his pinstriped shirt. Almost Edwardian, Avery was slim, even bony, with dark eyes and fine straight gray hair that he wore long off the part. He was also lithe, with the swing in his walk of a habitual runner, hardly the stereotype of a neurasthenic green-eyeshaded CPA, though he had spent his entire career in a big accounting firm. She had married a very handsome man, as much so now as twenty-six years ago, thought Charlotte.

"I was thinking about Mitchell Reinhart," she said. "Mr. Divorce."

Avery lifted his eyebrows inquiringly.

"I saw him argue a case today," she said. "What a depressing view of men and marriage."

"All men and all marriages don't fit his mold," said Avery. "You rather load the cards by focusing on scum. Why are you following Mitchell Reinhart's career?"

Charlotte was tired, and her tea was cold. She touched the cup with the back of her hand and considered heating it up. "He had something to do with Ginger Pass's death," she said.

"Tell me about it," said Avery, leaning over to pick up her tea. "I always liked her."

In the days when they used to stay at the dinner table and talk for hours, Avery would finish his dessert and reach for hers without thinking. When Charlotte talked, she stopped eating and paid no attention to the food in front of her. When Avery talked, he ate more, paying no attention to whose food it was. He'd finish his tea, and instead of refilling his cup he'd drain hers.

She watched him do it now, thinking, He's very welcome to it, and she let down and told him a little about how Ginger died. Avery knew that Ginger wasn't faithful—it was his opinion that Harold deserved it—but he didn't know that her faithlessness was professional. So Charlotte just implied that a nightclub evening had gotten out of hand and Ginger had been injured and then abandoned. "I can't tell you too much about it yet," she said, "but Reinhart was probably one of the men involved."

Avery nodded. "I never liked him," he said. His jacket still hanging over his shoulder, he opened the refrigerator and took out a bowl of black grapes. Avery had a way of spitting grape pits into the top of his fist that made eating grapes not just neat but attractive. "Even less now that we're supposed to believe he's given up a practice worth a few million a year to go on a ridiculous salary at his firm, doing mostly client divorce work. Cutting down to spend more time at home—yada, yada, yada."

"Or maybe trying to trick an ex-wife out of some support," said Charlotte disingenuously. She wanted to ask his help. She was afraid she was about to ask his help.

"That's usually part of it," said Avery. "What's your interest? Not his estate planning, I hope. This man may actually find a way to take it with him."

"It's not just me. It's my women's group. Our interest is Ginger," said Charlotte. I will ask, she thought. Maybe he'll help us.

"Probably shouldn't go where it's not your business," said Avery, inspecting his fistful of grape seeds. Then, looking over his fist, he saw Charlotte's mouth set and her face tighten as she looked down again at her papers. He quickly amended his remark. "Be very careful of Reinhart," he said. "You wouldn't want to cross him in any way."

Charlotte said nothing, eyes down.

"Why do you feel you have to do something?" asked Avery gently.

"Things are not going well," said Charlotte softly, suddenly unguarded. "Everyone dies on me. My marriage is dying on me. My daughter's gone."

"Hard to fix our own lives, isn't it?" said Avery, sardonic again. "Easier to take on someone else's life. Or death."

Charlotte didn't bother to rise to the challenge. "That may be my unconscious motivation," she said, "but it's not important. The conscious feeling is motivating enough. Ginger just didn't deserve it—not death, and certainly not an unexplained death."

Tears burned her eyes, spilled over, ran down her face. "I can't let her just fade off into darkness," she said. "I want to light her way."

She heard Avery breathing deeply, felt him come around the table to stand by her chair. Neither of them spoke for a few minutes. Her father's clock was very loud.

"I know you think I loved you for your steel-trap mind," he finally said, "but it's not so. I fell in love with your soft heart."

And he put his hand along her wet cheek, and after a while they put the dishes in the sink, turned out the laboratory-bright ceiling lights, and went upstairs.

18

The women next met as a group on their regular Monday. It was sometimes hard now to get through the meetings. Whatever they discussed seemed less pressing than their campaign to avenge Ginger, although it did remind them that what they were doing was hardly a normal activity for people like them. They were becoming adept at switching focus, however, and today they rolled through several mundane topics without impatience, and even with interest.

Kat led off with an announcement: She had definitely decided to have her breast implants removed. "It's not scheduled yet," she said, "but I've been thinking about it for several weeks, and I'm going to do it."

Everyone was congratulatory, and without apparent irony. It seemed a reasonable choice, said Dinah, all things considered. It was a novel experience, said Charlotte, to be congratulating someone on the decision to remove her fake breasts, but they were glad for her. It wasn't totally unexpected, said Polly.

Lotte was looking from one to the other, trying to understand their lack of surprise. Finally she turned back to Kat. "What's behind this decision?" she asked.

Kat had risen from her chair, as always, to stand at the window. Giving the group a quick warning look, she said to Lotte, "Well, I had to do a kind of exhibition race and had to get in shape fast, and all that running wasn't easy with these things."

She put her hands on her breasts. Lotte nodded encouragement.

"I was getting away from where I started and who I was," Kat continued, "doing all this PR stuff for the club when I should be serving as an athletic example. Which I can't be if I don't exercise properly. These things aren't the right example of what you should be anyway."

"We never know what will precipitate a decision, do we?" said Lotte. "One event leads to another, one feeling engenders another, and suddenly we are in the middle of a life change."

"I don't know about the life change," said Kat. "So far it's just the boobs."

"If nothing else, you'll think more clearly without all that drag," said Charlotte.

Most of the hour went to Justine, who had sat through the first quarter with a remote expression, thinking about what had happened at her family's dinner. She wanted now to ask the group how she could demand to be made a principal in the business without seeming demanding. It wasn't just a matter of wanting, she said. She needed a change in what she did—not merely accounting but marketing and product development.

"That doesn't seem like such a dramatic leap," said Charlotte.

"In my family it is," said Justine sadly.

To Kat it was simple: Justine should simply present the idea to Robby outright and enlist his aid. But as everyone pointed out, Robby wasn't Barnaby. In fact, Robby was probably Justine's biggest problem. Charlotte suggested a process something like negotiating with a board of directors, approaching not only Robby but Robby's father and brother and maybe his brother's wife and his younger sister as well. Dinah said Justine should make it a direct request when all three of the men were together, figuring that no one would want to be the naysayer. It was Polly's view that Justine should just quit and make them beg her to come back.

Through it all, Justine sat composed and attentive as always, but not really drawn to any of the ideas. Lotte, on the other hand, seemed pleased by the whole discussion, exhibiting a high degree of alertness and greeting each suggestion as "very interesting" in her therapist's murmur. She had been concerned about the increasing air of distraction in the group and was delighted to return to one of the group's stated goals—that each should make some significant but as yet undefined change in her life. So this meeting seemed to her a definite step forward.

When she left, she forgot her usual admonition about listening for the click of the door lock. In the silence that followed her departure, moreover, her descending footsteps sounded almost trippingly light.

"Okay, you first," said Polly, turning to Kat. "You're the only one with any human interest. The rest of us, it was all digging through papers and files."

"Not quite," said Justine. "I can always offer a description of raw land."

"Hold that thought," said Kat. "I have to get Mrs. Reinhart out of my system."

She began her characteristic walk-around, circling the table with her arms raised to the ceiling in a sinuous stretch, rotating her head on her neck so her long ponytail was whipped from shoulder to shoulder. "This Reinhart woman is one bitter lady," she began, "but it's sort of sad. There's probably a fairly good brain in there, but it's not getting much exercise now."

She described Suzanne Reinhart—her unexpected candor, the

successful business that had made her a trophy in the first place, her regrets about giving it up. She quoted her comments on the hard work of being a trophy wife.

Dinah snorted. "Oh, please," she said. "She chose it. Anyone with half a brain could see what was ahead."

"Maybe she thought she could have it all," said Kat, halted behind her empty chair. "She found his power attractive, and forgot that trophies are basically possessions."

"More important, she forgot she was marrying a real pro in the marriage business, in more ways than one," said Charlotte. "Did she mention the famous prenuptial agreement? That could give us some idea of his finances."

"Yes," said Kat, "and it was obviously a sore point. She said he had been burned before and wasn't about to be burned again, and that if this marriage ends, she gets nothing from it."

Charlotte nodded approvingly. "Exactly what a prenup's supposed to do."

"I guess he's the expert," said Polly. "I found one interview in which he said that marrying without a prenup gives the woman a license to steal as her wedding present."

Kat was walking again, hair swinging. "Mrs. Reinhart also said—and this was another sore point—that they had planned to make their house a showplace, but then he suddenly told her it would have to wait and dropped the plans. So they don't entertain much. I guess in their circles you can't entertain unless you have a showplace. It sounded as if a big evening at home right now means they have a sauna and a glass of wine and turn in."

"At least they own a sauna," said Polly.

"They don't," said Dinah. "The sauna's communal. Justine gave me the address, and I dropped by last week pretending to be in the market. They showed me a bunch of maps and listings, and every section has a minimal gym, sauna, and tennis court. And I saw Reinhart's empty lot on the map and asked about it, but they said it's not for sale."

She turned to Justine. "What did you find? Any plans filed for the second lot?"

"There were some plans for a remodel," said Justine, "but no record of any work done. I've got some maps and things to show you, but first I'd like to hear what Charlotte found on his assets. If that's okay."

It was fine with Charlotte, who had several legal pads of notes to summarize. She started with the two most interesting legal actions she'd found pending against Reinhart. One was an order to show cause filed by his second wife—the most recent of several she had filed against him in the last half dozen years. "It isn't unusual that a divorce agreement is challenged later," Charlotte explained. "It can take years before an ex-wife realizes how badly she's being treated, particularly if the husband leads a quiet life. Mr. Divorce's high profile made him a sitting duck."

The second was a breach-of-contract suit filed by his twenty-five-year-old daughter from his first marriage, asking for seventy thousand dollars to cover her last two years of medical school. Reinhart had married for the first time when he was only twenty-two, and this union, "which Reinhart kept referring to as a 'student marriage,'" sneered Charlotte, lasted seven years and produced one child. While surely painful for the young wife who put him through school by working as a secretary, the divorce had faded into a distant amicability. He saw his daughter regularly and, when she graduated from high school, offered, in writing, to subsidize both college and graduate school, if she decided to go that far. But two years ago, at the end of her second year in medical school, he stopped paying.

His second wife, whom he married a year after divorcing the first, ran his home while he built up his practice and had three children, now almost seventeen, fifteen, and ten. When he divorced her six years ago to marry Suzanne Weil, she got the house, five years' spousal support, and annual child support of fifty thousand dollars a child—not unreasonable for a man making a couple of million a year—plus an insurance policy with the kids as beneficiaries and a calculated interest in his future pension. Remarkably trusting for a woman scorned, she accepted all his financial representations and his offered terms and moved quickly to return to school and become a social worker.

"But after several years," said Charlotte, "I guess she got tired of seeing Reinhart and the Trophy in *Vanity Fair* and the newspaper's style section, of reading about his flashy cases, his celebrity clients, his purchase of a pricey town house and his plans to put up a mansion. She must have started thinking he had hidden a lot of assets, which had multiplied further, and she wanted some adjustment in her family's share. So she got herself one mean mother of a lawyer this time around, and they went after him."

Reinhart's first response was to delay, then release some sparse and insignificant income figures, then delay some more, all the while, said Charlotte, reducing his known assets and diminishing his discernible income. He dissolved his practice and joined a large entertainment-law firm, taking a straight salary of $350,000 as an in-house attorney handling divorce actions for the partners and their clients. This seemed an unusual step for someone whose retainers alone had run into six figures, said Charlotte, "but he said he was ill and exhausted, running a big office was draining, his debts were mounting, and he was filled with self-doubt."

Charlotte put down the notes from which she was reading. "I suppose it's possible," she said, "except for the self-doubt."

"You think he really had health problems? " asked Justine.

"I checked his available medical records," said Dinah. "Nothing exciting. Maybe a drinking problem. He saw a cardiologist half a year ago and not long after that spent a week at a Napa Valley facility known for drug and alcohol rehab. All covered by insurance, of course."

"You just have to look at him," said Polly. "He's got that flush and the beginnings of the broken blood vessels."

"Let's not forget the little nightcaps in the sauna," said Kat.

"Look, I'm only telling you what he claims," said Charlotte, "not necessarily the truth. As I said before, lots of men hide assets in divorce actions. Some start with the first separation, some even while it's still a happy marriage. And we're dealing with a master here. His whole career is helping rich men hide their riches."

The idea was to turn both assets and earnings into something hard to see, something no opposing lawyer would even think to look at. "Maybe he takes some salary in cash. Maybe it's paid to another name that's hard to trace to him. Maybe he postpones a large chunk of pay, and in a few years, when the heat is off, he'll call in the money or take control of that unknown bank account or sell off those hidden assets."

"Why would any company help him do that?" asked Justine.

"Why not?" said Charlotte. "It costs them the same however it's paid. If he says pay it to this business name or that account, that's his choice, not their affair."

Polly, who was foraging in her manila folders while Charlotte talked, held up her own sheet of notes. "In one search I did, he turned up as part owner of a San Diego company called Jarndyce Legal Research Service, which is hired by law firms to do the kind of basic research normally done by associates and paralegals. A lawyer friend of mine says the customers are mostly small firms and sole practitioners, and the service may also write their briefs. Even big firms may use them, because their own associates cost them more by the hour than these outsiders charge."

"And of course those big firms are scrupulously honest," grumbled Charlotte, "and don't turn around and bill their client for those hours at their usual rates."

"They probably do, but don't get distracted," said Polly. She waved her papers in the air. "Is this a hidden asset? A place to put hidden income?"

"Maybe," said Charlotte. "I guess a Reinhart client could pay his legal fees directly to the research company, or to Reinhart's employer for 'research services.' So it would go to this San Diego group, and Reinhart could draw it out in some form or leave it there until he's free to collect it. But it's hard to prove without some inside help."

"We'll also have to figure out where he hides the money after he gets it," said Polly. "We're absolutely sure that three hundred fifty thousand isn't all he earns?"

"Not if he's been paying a hundred fifty thousand in child support and the trophy's spending twenty thousand just at her health club," said Kat.

"We have to work like the IRS," said Polly, "and look into what they call the 'economic realities' of his lifestyle. Not his declared income but his expenditures. All I have so far is DMV records, which show a three-year-old Mercedes sedan in his name, a smallish BMW in both names, and a nonoperating Porsche Carrera somewhere in a garage. A nice collection, but not overwhelming."

She turned to Justine. "So what did you get?" she said.

Justine was ready, her hands already resting on an oversize leather folder. "Well," she began, "as an asset the house is neither hidden nor huge, but it's a good parcel in a prime development."

Reinhart had bought a three-bedroom, three-thousand-square-foot "villa" four years ago for $900,000, plus $325,000 for the adjacent lot, another five thousand square feet. Justine had a copy of his plans to build over into the second lot, the building permit, and the assessor's inquiry—unanswered—about the additional footage. There was nothing further recorded.

"If we get nothing back, we assume nothing was built," said Justine. "But we can go out and examine the property if we suspect that the work was bootlegged and our inquiry just ignored—an offense against both us and the building department.

"After our meeting last week, I sent someone out to look," she said.

"He came back with nothing—nothing for the assessor anyway, and probably nothing for us."

Admitted by the maintenance manager, Justine's deputy had found the house just as it looked on the original plans and the empty lot still empty, except for a lot of "stuff" so uninteresting that he'd made no notes or drawings. Trained as a real estate appraiser, he saw nothing appraisable and obviously wondered why he'd been sent. He stood before Justine's desk in his shirtsleeves and corduroys, pens in their plastic pocket guard, big tape measure clipped to his belt, and had to be prodded for information.

There was a rough storage structure there, he said. It was about six feet wide, ten feet long, and basically just wood framing with a corrugated-plastic roof and heavy plastic sheeting on the sides—more like a greenhouse than a shed. There was a long table, some benches, and open shelving made from boards and concrete blocks. And lots of plants.

"He said it wasn't a real garden," said Justine, "just bunches of plants in tubs and pots, some on the ground, some on the shelves, some labeled and some not. It was more like the makings for a garden." She looked around the table. "You don't suppose he's given up on the house expansion and is just going to landscape the second lot, do you?"

"Mrs. R. doesn't seem like the type for trowel and clippers," said Kat, "though you never know. But what you say sure fits the credit information I called up. His highest expenditures seem to be on food—mostly restaurant charges—and building supplies, going by all the purchases at hardware stores, lumberyards, garden centers."

"I couldn't find anything on house decoration," Dinah inserted. "He could have worked with someone out of the area, I suppose, but nobody around here knows of anything he's doing, and they certainly would know if he was spending big. Big is what we're looking for, right?"

Charlotte, looking puzzled, was shaking her head. "A garden just doesn't seem like Mitch Reinhart," she said. "Not his kind of dirt."

"He's not in any of the garden societies," said Justine seriously. "I checked."

"Justine, you're so thorough," said Charlotte, laughing, but fondly.

"What does all this mean for us?" asked Polly. "Even if he's bootlegging some construction, how do we embarrass him with that? Is there a really big fine?"

Justine started to answer, but Kat cut in. "What's so embarrassing?" she said. "Everyone bootlegs."

"In any case, his condo is the biggest asset we have so far. He may be putting money into it, and we should see how he lives," said Polly definitively, pushing back her chair.

"It shouldn't be hard," said Justine. "There's no perimeter alarm."

They all turned to look at her. She flushed. "Well, considering last time, I thought you might ask, so I checked. And the wall is only six feet."

"Oh, God," said Kat, "this whole business is getting to be like a stealth tour of L.A. by night, all back alleys and back walls."

"That's L.A.," said Dinah. "For the very rich, America is like living in a Third World city, all walled in. It's the poor and the middle class who live free."

"Well, it has to be the back way again, and definitely after dark," said Polly. "So when do we go, and who's going this time? Besides me, of course, because I'm always available."

Given all the garden stuff, it was agreed that Justine should go with Polly. Charlotte said it wouldn't be a good career move if she got caught breaking and entering another lawyer's property, and Kat didn't want to chance a meeting with Suzanne Reinhart. Dinah would go along, but in a second vehicle, in case they needed backup.

They decided on that Thursday evening. Polly would drive. They'd wear dark colors and carry cell phones with mute controls so they could talk with Dinah. In the meantime Charlotte would go over Reinhart's big cases of the past half-dozen years and estimate their billing value.

Later, during what had become a nightly telephone call, Polly told Graham Vere about both Kat's news and Justine's quandary; he had met neither, but he knew enough about them from Polly to appreciate their situations. Since her triumphant outburst after their first revenge, Polly had managed to keep the group's plans to herself, although Vere seemed aware that avenging Ginger was an ongoing project. Indeed, he was both sympathetic and entertained, occasionally referring to their "unsettled score" and gleefully suggesting ways to settle it.

Now, however, Polly felt in need of a listener, and she did tell Vere that they were following another lead—Mitch Reinhart. He knew neither the name nor the reputation but was immediately enthusiastic.

"Good," he said. "Going to get him, too? Another midnight ride in a high-rent district?"

"Sort of," said Polly, adding that it was purely exploratory at this point, just a preliminary look at the condo complex where he lived.

"I'll lend you a pair of night goggles," said Vere. "I have some from a stakeout I was once invited to join."

"It's not necessary," said Polly, although she found the idea appealing. She was sitting with her feet up on her computer table, looking out over the canyon at the dots of house lights and streetlamps and the blurred line where the dark hillside met an equally dark night sky.

"I insist," he said. "If you're caught this time, the photos will be really fetching. They look like those Halloween glasses you wear with the big bug eyes that pop out on springs in front of your face. What else? Pitons? Crampons? How high up is his condo?"

"Very funny," said Polly.

It is funny, said her mother.

19

For some weeks in the hot late autumn, the sky over Los Angeles becomes a stage set of sunsets so dramatic that traffic moving west on the city's freeways slows to ten or fifteen miles an hour. It's a side effect of the local Santa Ana winds, blowing in desert air so hot and dry that one cigarette carelessly dropped on a sere hillside may take out a thousand acres of chaparral. The hot air and smog become trapped under the cool ocean air along the coast, forming an inversion layer between the sweltering city and the atmosphere above, but at the end of an unpleasant day, out of that dust and soot and ashes comes astonishing beauty.

Behind the thick veil, the sun begins to sink, transforming all those hydrocarbons, those motes of dust, into the pinks and purples and blues, the oranges and tangerines of a fiery end-of-the-world panorama. The world doesn't end, of course. For an hour or so, the city's commuters drive slowly, awestruck, straight into that incredible sky; then the hues fade and the edges blur and the billows and streaks of color recede to the horizon and darken into twilight.

It was the beginning of November, and the show was briefer, the colors less vibrant as Justine drove west that Thursday, but she was still enthralled. Having told her family she was staying late for a meeting, she was going to Polly's house directly from work. Justine's house was closer to Reinhart's, but if she'd gone home first, or they had met there, there would have been many questions and few good answers.

Although nervous, she was confident that she'd packed everything they needed in her leather sling bag, briefcase, and map carrier. She had a tract map, plot maps, and building plans for Reinhart's house, all reduced to page size, and she'd brought her laptop so she could sign on to her office database system if more was needed. Finally, following Polly's instructions for night reconnaissance, she had dressed in black, from her sneakers to her long-sleeved turtleneck.

The sky overhead was turning to pewter as Justine tamped down her fear, telling herself that she had organized well, her research was thorough, and besides, it was only research. They wouldn't actually do anything until they knew a lot more about Reinhart. Moreover, it wasn't as if they'd be breaking and entering. Her inspector said the backyard was open, so security was neither a concern nor an obstacle.

When Justine arrived at Polly's house, it was half past six, and all that was left of the sunset was a reef of dusty rose on the horizon. Standing on the stoop, briefcase and map carrier in her arms, purse and carryall hung over a shoulder, Justine pushed the bell and heard it sound deep in the house. There were no footsteps, no responsive noise behind the door, and she looked down to put away her car keys before ringing again. When she looked up, the door was open, and there stood a tall figure in black, with Polly's red hair and the face of an alien trooper—bug eyes coming out of a metal box below a metal shield that covered the forehead, heavy straps around the sides and over the top of the head.

Justine screamed, dropping both keys and purse.

"It's okay, it's just me!" said Polly, stepping out from the doorway and extending one hand to Justine while with the other she pulled off the headgear.

Justine stumbled backward off the stoop, gasping. "I know," she said, "I know," but her throat constricted, and the words were indistinct.

"I'm really sorry," Polly said, grasping Justine's upper arm. Then, seeing the sky beyond her, she exclaimed, "Jeez, look at that sunset. And I probably missed the best part of the show."

"Okay," said Justine. Managing a cracked smile, she stooped to pick up her things. "I knew it was you, but it's still frightening. What are those things? Where did you get them?"

Polly led the way into the house, moving ahead of Justine and down the hallway to the kitchen. "They're night-vision goggles," she said. "When I went out for the paper, they were in a mailing bag in the big ceramic pot. I told Graham I had a nighttime field trip, and he must have left them late last night or early this morning."

Gesturing for Justine to put down her things, she began taking plastic containers of leftover roast chicken, fettuccine Alfredo, and peas out of the refrigerator. Jeremy and Andrea had shut themselves in their rooms with their homework and their big-beat, tuneless music, so she and Justine could eat and talk freely. Polly always suspected that as soon as she left, the doors would open and the children would move back and forth between the rooms—less with any specific purpose than because they really wanted the comfort of company, unobserved by their common enemy.

"Do we really need those things?" asked Justine. "We want to *see* his place, not raid it."

"I know," said Polly. "I'll probably leave them in the car. On the other hand, what if it's black as pitch and we keep tripping over bags of money in his yard?"

For the next hour and a half, they went over the maps and building plans, familiarizing themselves with Reinhart's lots and his neighbor-hood and discussing what exactly they should look for. Given the goal—some indication of assets or expenditure beyond what he declared—and the fact that there was no obvious construction on the extra lot, they'd look first for changes in the house itself. At least they might get a better sense of what he was spending.

The development was a mix of apartment buildings, town houses, and separate villas like Reinhart's. According to Justine's maps, the villas were in the northernmost section, grouped in ovals of eight to twelve lots that shared green space, parking and communal garages, gyms, pools, tennis courts, party rooms. They had marked several access roads and gateways but weren't sure how to get into his particular oval or his lot. "My inspector said Reinhart's lot was 'open,'" said Justine, "but I didn't want to quiz him on it or he'd have known something was up."

She suggested parking just up from the villas in the lot behind a shop-ping mall with a five-screen movie complex. The border landscaping was tall and dense, so they could park at the back and leave the car almost hidden. Then they could walk to the development, and, if stopped, they could say they were just strolling the neighborhood.

At eight they called Dinah, who was going to leave in a half hour, planning to sit in her own car in the parking lot until they returned. If challenged, she also could say she was waiting for friends who had gone for a walk and she was just too tired to join them. Polly called out final instructions and good-byes to Andrea and Jeremy, and they left the house at a quarter to nine.

After the drama of sunset, the night was very dark, moon and stars obscured by the haze over the city. As Polly negotiated the winding streets down to the city floor, she'd glance now and then at Justine, who was organizing her leather sling bag. First she put in the plot map and Reinhart's building plans, accordion-folded for easy access, then a tape measure, a miniflashlight with extra batteries, and a mirror gadget for looking over walls. Then she hitched herself upward and put a little spiral notebook and pen in her pants pocket, hooked another miniflashlight to her belt, and was about to add a Swiss Army knife when Polly said, "What's with the knife?"

Justine looked at it uncertainly under the dash lights. "I saw it on the kitchen counter on my way out," she said.

"Do we need it?" asked Polly. "We can't take samples of everything, and we're not likely to be attacked. Arrested, maybe, even embarrassed, but not attacked."

Justine put it back in the briefcase on the floor behind her. "I don't really know what-all we need," she said. "Probably just our good eyes."

Dinah's compact Mercedes wagon was parked at the back of the lot, its nose thrust into the oleanders. Once she chose a car model—small enough to park easily, big enough to move art objects, and always black—Dinah rarely thought about what she drove or whether it got dusty or scratched. Behind its tinted windows, Polly and Justine could see the glow of a reading light, and as they drew alongside, the window rolled down and Dinah watched them get out.

"All ready?" she asked.

"Yes," said Polly. "Pretty quiet here."

The lot was less than a quarter filled. Shops were closed, and only the movie theaters and restaurants still had patrons, most of whom had parked close to the buildings.

"Your cell phone on?" asked Polly, putting hers into its waistband case and her car keys into the pocket of her windbreaker. Justine had put on a hooded sweatshirt and was arranging her leather bag to hang at her back with its long strap diagonally across her body.

"Yeah," said Dinah. "Don't forget to set the thing on vibrate."

"Right," said Polly. "You okay for a couple of hours?"

"Don't worry about me," said Dinah. "I have to catalog and price the Southwest pieces that I want to sell. And I can always sleep. Haven't done that in a while." She tapped Polly's hand, which was resting on her window. "Break a leg," she added.

"I don't think that's the right send-off here," said Polly, and she and Justine turned away.

Reinhart's development was just on the other side of the oleanders, set apart from the surrounding neighborhood by the perimeter walls and the controlled architecture. It was Pueblo style—an odd choice, since nothing was less like the rich west side of Los Angeles than the arid, wind-strafed deserts and desolate buttes of Indian country. Still, it had an odd credibility en masse, with town houses, villas, and apartment buildings all showing the basic Pueblo silhouette of successively smaller stories above a broad, low base and all brown stucco with wood beams jutting out at the roofline. Irrepressible, the developer even recessed the windows, painted kachinas and dancing stick figures on the doors and added luminaria lights on the balconies and some rough-hewn ladders leaning against the walls.

The motif was less successful in the landscaping. There should have been no landscaping at all—just the dry and sandy earth, a cactus here, an agave there, some tumbleweed in between. Instead there were neat rows of cactus plants and creosote bushes and beds of succulents in redwood chips. The streets were softly lit by ground-level luminarias and rather dim streetlights shaped like mission bells and equipped with coiled bulbs that emitted a continuous hissing.

About a block from Reinhart's oval, they backed into the bushes to consult the map by flashlight. Most gardens were at the rear of the lots, so they wanted to turn into the alley that ran behind his house and count four lots in to his property. They could already see that these were no mere alleys. They were fully landscaped, with their own mission-bell streetlamps and, every few lots, a passageway running up from the alley. Some were broad enough to park cars; some were just walkways, with planters and benches under the streetlights.

"Here it is," said Justine, looking up a walkway with a tennis court behind a chain-link fence on the right and the stucco wall of Reinhart's empty lot on the left. Farther up was a bench under one of the mission lights and, beyond that, according to the map, the entrance to the gym building and tennis court.

It was too dark to see much, although the sky had taken on a lighter sepia tinge, an indication of fire in the far-off hills. Removed from the noise of traffic, they could hear the low hissing of the streetlights, voices and taped laughter from a nearby television, and the faraway beat of "La Bamba." Over it all, and eerily, came the sporadic cascade of an operatic laugh several houses away, sudden and startling.

Reinhart's gate was a big, heavy thing made of vertical boards about three inches wide. There was a brass-tongued latch at the top with a lock below it.

"What did the guy mean, 'It's open'?" whispered Justine.

Polly reached up and pressed the latch tab. "It's open," she said, as the gate swung inward. She leaned in, looked around, and pushed it further. The yard beyond seemed totally black. Holding the gate, Polly saw Justine hesitate; then she gave her shoulder bag a decisive tug, said "Let's go," and stepped past Polly through the opening.

They couldn't go far. They were immediately blocked by a charcoal jungle of potted shrubs and bushes, some taller than they. Beyond it they could see the taller silhouettes of a dozen sapling-size trees that divided the two lots. Some light came down from the house on the main lot, and they saw, beyond the saplings, the glow of lamps in an upstairs room and the latticed roof of a back patio. The patio itself and the ground floor of the house were obscured from their view.

"It is a garden," said Polly, but it wasn't. It was more like a nursery, but in such disarray it could have been the back lot of a grower. The plants in front of them were crammed so close together that there was no path between. Against the wall farther up were some bulky structures, and in the middle of the lot, barely visible through the leaves, were what looked like long, flat tables or platforms. They couldn't see well because this lot was unlit, but the row of saplings ran only partway down, and they could tell that the lower part of the main lot held more plants and, at the far wall, a massive tree with multiple trunks and branches.

"What is all this?" whispered Polly, but Justine merely shook her head and squeezed her way in among the planters. From the house came the sounds of television—an announcer's voice, some music, audience laughter—but it was otherwise dark and quiet, and they felt well hidden. Justine turned her flashlight onto the nearest plant, shielding the beam with her other hand. She bent over, inspected it, moved to another plant, then another, trying not to jostle the leaves as she moved, bending, inspecting. Camellias, she was thinking, and mostly *Camellia japonica*, but until she saw flowers, she couldn't be sure. She moved on while Polly stood, arms folded, watching her but keeping an eye on the house.

Then Justine stopped, drew in her breath, and held it. The little beam faltered, tracing a zigzag of light on the massed plants, and came back to a yellow flower among the leaves.

"What?" whispered Polly, pushing through behind her as Justine moved to another plant. "What is it?"

"That's funny," Justine said softly, pushing aside branches, scrabbling around the base of the plant. "It's not possible."

Tugging gently, she pulled up a metal tag, looked at it, then held it out to Polly, turning the beam on it. The tag said "*C. sasanqua* 'Little Buttercup.'" She felt around in another pot, a round one, and came up with another tag. This one said "*C. japonica* 'Mme. Buttercup.'"

"Look," she urged. "Look!" and when Polly looked, but blankly, she said, "These are camellias that don't exist—yellow camellias. No one has ever bred a yellow camellia before, at least not this kind."

She thrust the tags into Polly's hand. "Take them," she said, turning to thread her way through the plants toward the center of the lot.

Clutching the camellia tags, Polly watched her go from inside the dense thicket of plants. Mostly her eyes were following the intermittent beam from Justine's flashlight. Everything was black, Justine herself was quick and thin and all in black, and Polly caught only parts of her as she turned and ducked and bent, occasionally visible through the silhouetted leaves and branches like a Kokopelli dancing from one place to another in the dark.

The long tables in the middle were wide and waist-high, with a series of poles extending up from the far end, each hung with several dark cloth bags. Once there, Justine could see that they weren't tables but metal planting trays filled with flowering plants. "Yellow impatiens," she murmured, puzzled: Yellow impatiens wasn't new, like the yellow camellia. It was, however, very big news when it was introduced a few years ago, because until then impatiens, arguably the most popular shade plant in America, had been all pinks, purples, and whites, and yellow was a significant advance.

Justine reached up to give one of the cloth bags a little shake. It made a dry, swishing sound. She shook a few more bags, very gently.

Seeds. Seeds were the big advance. The yellow impatiens, though heralded in the industry, was sterile. It produced no seeds and had to be grown from cuttings, which was expensive. Seeds made the growth easy, the packaging minimal, and the market limitless. The yellows could now be sold in millions of nurseries and stores to millions of customers, all looking to buy a little extra "curb appeal," a bit of color for a window box.

"I get it," she said, more to herself. "This is amazing."

"Get what?" Polly asked, coming up behind her, clutching the camellia tags. "Are they all rare plants? What's he doing?"

Justine didn't answer, turning this way and that, debating what to look at next. She saw now that one of the structures was an enclosed shed with sheet-plastic walls, the other just a series of open shelves under a lattice roof. Leaving them for last, she moved toward the big boxes of sapling-size trees. Polly came behind her, keeping an eye and ear on the house. The TV was still going over the sound of running water upstairs. She was pretty sure that they themselves were almost noiseless, and Justine was careful to block the beam of her flashlight.

Suddenly Justine was gasping, swaying back from the little trees and groping for Polly, who was knocked off balance. At that moment the water was shut off and the television went silent, and they heard voices in the house, which grew louder and closer, coming down to the patio. Bracing herself, Polly put her arms around Justine and dragged her back past the tables of impatiens and deep into the camellias, almost to the gate, both of them scraping and bumping against plants and planters like animals crashing through underbrush.

Holding Justine, feeling her tremble and trying to keep her leather bag from dropping to the ground, Polly looked through the camellias toward the front of the lot. A spotlight went on over the patio, then a series of small track lights high on the stucco wall illuminated a walkway leading across the top of the lot to the upper gate, out to the gym and the sauna. With the house looming at back left and the high walls as backdrop, with the dark sky and the dark yards, the lights made the lot a theater, with Justine and Polly the secret audience.

As if from the wings, now came Reinhart and his wife in procession, both in white robes. He led, holding a bottle of wine by the neck and obviously unsteady on his feet, taking exaggerated care to stay in the middle of the walk. His wife followed by a few paces, her backless mules clacking on the hard surface. In her outstretched arms, she bore folded towels and two glasses, upside down, by the stems.

Through the foliage Polly and Justine watched them cross under the lights, heard the upper gate open and close, then the door of the gym. A short wait, holding very still. Then, confident that they were out of sight and close enough to the back gate to escape quickly, and sure that the Reinharts would be occupied for a while, they could talk, if still in whispers.

Justine swallowed, made a few starts, and finally said, "The saplings are American chestnuts—*Castanea dentata*—which are virtually extinct, wiped out by blight almost a century ago. I've never seen one. Few people have. And these say 'sine pest.', meaning *sine pestilentiae*, I'm assuming, or pest-free. I just can't believe it."

At that she put down the leather bag and, pushing through the camellias in a crouch, went back to the saplings. She ran her fingers up and down a trunk, leaned forward to smell the leaves. So must a monk have felt before the Shroud of Turin, or an archaeologist when the first Inca mummies emerged from the Andean ice—each looking at something they'd heard about or imagined but never thought they'd see. Justine carefully freed a tag from one of the chestnuts and very gently clipped off a leaf with the edge of her fingernail. The leaf was long and slender, with sharp-toothed edges, just as it was in books. She would press it. She could tell her children about it. She might never see one again.

Remembering why they were there, she returned to Polly's side. "You want hidden assets?" she asked. "There's millions here, millions."

"You're kidding," said Polly. "Millions?"

Justine didn't hear. The thought of money had been fleeting and irrelevant. How could a person who helps bring back the American chestnut have caused someone's death? she wondered. She bent to pick up her bag, saying, "I have to see the rest. How long you think they'll be gone?"

"Well," said Polly, "a sauna runs about two hundred degrees Fahrenheit, I think. You can't be in it more than fifteen minutes, I'd guess, allowing ten or fifteen for it to heat up. So maybe twenty-five minutes? Thirty?"

Justine nodded and moved off into the adjacent lot, playing her flashlight over dozens of potted rosebushes, many in bloom. Wanting to give them more time, she went straight to the huge multitrunked tree in the back corner. She studied it from every angle, keeping low and close, because more light reached the back of this lot and she might be visible from the house. She broke off a leaf, a flower, inspected the enormous wooden planting box, shone her light behind it, then said, "Of course," under her breath and turned back to the roses.

On first glance, and in the limited light, they had appeared purple. But she saw now that they weren't purple, or burgundy, or deep red, or any other known rose color. They were blue, clearly, amazingly blue. She was looking at the long-sought, never-achieved deep blue rose.

She felt like an intruder, an industrial spy come upon this hidden hybrid, stealthily bending over one and then another, touching them carefully. Finally she extracted an identifying disk. In the little circle from her penlight she read: "*Rosa reinhartii* 'Lapis.'" The name of the new rose, obviously financed and therefore named for Reinhart, and then its parentage—"*R.Gallica Malmaison* 'Mon Secret' x *R. Persica* 'Indigo.'"

Like many modern hybrid tea roses, they had no scent, being bred more for color and shape. They were also beautifully pruned and well cared for, and Justine was briefly envious of the expert who got to be steward of this living treasure. But then, the thrill for him was probably the achievement rather than the flower's beauty, and Reinhart's interest was purely monetary. Justine might get as much or more pleasure when she managed against all odds to grow an eastern lily of the valley in her western garden.

From the other yard, Polly watched Justine clicking the penlight on and off and muttering a little, apparently making notes. Suddenly, to her horror, she heard the gym door open and footsteps; then the latch rattled on the upper gate and the hinges scraped. Too late to signal Justine: Polly pressed herself back into the camellias, as low as she could in the tight space. But Justine had also heard, and, without turning her head, she threw herself prone on the ground between the rows of roses.

They were both out of sight when Mrs. Reinhart, and only Mrs. Reinhart, came back, heels clacking on the walkway. Leaning forward, straining to find gaps in the screen of leaves, Polly saw Suzanne Reinhart pause halfway across, directly under one of the lights, wiping her forehead with the back of her hand, then wiping the hand on her white terry robe. Then she was still, caught like an actor in a single spot on a small stage. Her face was turned away, but her whole body spoke of indecision. With a shift of weight, the scuff of a foot, the smallest of shoulder movements, she leaned slightly back toward the gym.

It was hard to say how long she stood there or whether she was really so still: Polly's view of her shifted with every stirring of the leaves. But in a minute, maybe two, Suzanne Reinhart walked back to the gate and out, and they heard the door of the gym. Another minute and the sequence sounded in reverse—the door, the gate, the heels on the walkway, coming back. This time she didn't pause. Polly tipped her head left, right, around branches, but saw only movement as Mrs. Reinhart marched, heels clacking, across her patio and into the house.

The closing of the back door was followed by a quiet so intense that Polly was acutely aware again of her own breathing, careful as it was, the hissing of the streetlamps outside, and the faraway continuum of moving traffic. Then, as if on cue, the woman with the operatic laugh let out a volley that cut through the night like the cry of a loon.

Justine must have started back across the yard when the door closed, and so soundlessly that Polly's first warning was a rustling only a few feet away. Then Justine was right next to her.

"They're back already?" she asked Polly.

"Just her," said Polly.

Justine nodded. "It was a blue rose," she said softly, matter-of-factly, well past astonishment. "Another horticultural dream."

"And the big blobby tree?" asked Polly.

"I think that one's hot." Justine smiled, her teeth briefly catching the light. "I mean, it was stolen. I read about it a few years ago. It's called a desert orchid—a collector's piece, a hundred-year-old bush orchid with over eighty separate blooms, weighed half a ton, worth three-quarters of a million dollars. Disappeared from a Pasadena botanical garden where it was on loan for a show."

"Is it a big deal?" asked Polly.

"To some people, definitely," said Justine, "but not to me," and she turned away. "I'm hitting the greenhouses," she said.

Polly grabbed at her sleeve. "You can't," she said. "He'll be done any minute."

But Justine was already inching through the camellias toward the sheds, so Polly followed. There were sounds of activity inside the house— doors closing, heels crossing various surfaces. Polly couldn't recall such constant motion in her own house, ever. There were the unmistakable sounds of a shower running full force in an upstairs bathroom. Justine paused only briefly to look up from the greenhouse before stepping through the wood-and-plastic door. Polly hunkered down outside, holding the door slightly ajar with one outstretched hand.

Justine's feet crunched lightly on the pebbles of the greenhouse floor, and through the dirty plastic Polly could make out the spot of illumination cast by her penlight. Listening nervously to the audible scratch of pen on paper, Polly fretted about the amount of time they were spending.

"We have to leave it," she whispered, leaning around the door frame. "He'll be done soon, too," and as she got to her feet, Justine wriggled out past her.

Polly gently pulled the rickety door closed and backed out. She was looking up at the house, basically feeling her way by trailing her fingers along the side of the greenhouse, when she bumped into Justine, who had paused at the end of the structure and, cutting her beam to a pinprick, was looking at the pots lined up on the open shelves.

"Come on," urged Polly. "We've got enough," and they made their way back through the camellias to the gate in the wall. While Justine shifted the strap of her leather bag over her head, Polly reached up and felt for the latch pin. "Wait," she said, letting it go. "We can't leave now. He'll be coming across the path any minute."

"Okay," said Justine, opening her notebook to jot down some more names before she forgot them. Then, under cover of the running water, Justine gave Polly a quick rundown. "I'm not good at orchids," she said, "but I recognized some names in there. Most are collector's items. There are some black pansy orchids in bloom, and a black phalaenopsis, a moth orchid, all probably rare or new to their species. Also a lot of exotic lady's slippers with tags from places like New Guinea, Borneo, Brazil, probably smuggled in illegally."

The water went off. Justine looked toward the house. "Shouldn't he be done by now?" she asked.

"You'd think so," said Polly. "What time is it?"

Justine pushed the illumination button on her watch, and the faint glow lit her face from below. "Eleven-thirty," she said. "He must be okay. They do this all the time."

"You think it's okay to stay in a sauna for an hour?" replied Polly.

"I don't know. Maybe it's not as hot as we think," said Justine.

"She was out in a half hour," said Polly.

"You think we can go now?" asked Justine.

"Better wait till they're both back in the house for good," said Polly.

Justine slid down the wall until she was sitting on the ground. Polly followed, trying to picture the inside of the sauna and Reinhart's position in it. She couldn't imagine that a dry heat and a headful of alcohol would make for a pleasant experience, but she didn't like a lot of things that other people found sybaritic. Polly would have liked to call Dinah, but the buttons on her cell phone made little musical tones that she had never been able to shut off, and with cell phones one always had to talk louder than normal. It was absolutely quiet now. No shower, no footsteps, no voices. Faint, far music, just a beat, really. The hissing of the streetlamps.

They sat, not uncomfortable in the dark, but the ground was cold and seemed to be getting colder. "So what he's doing is stockpiling valuable plants?" Polly whispered.

"Priceless, some of them," Justine whispered back.

"What kind of money are we talking here?" asked Polly. "Roughly speaking."

"Well, I'll estimate and you keep track," said Justine. "The yellow camellia: It might sell a quarter million pieces a year at fifty dollars each retail, or over twelve million dollars and be worth half that, say, six million dollars, to a big grower, so he'd probably pay two or three million for the stock. The yellow impatiens seeds: That's big, worth a million or more to some grower, who'd own the market for a while. The blue rose, maybe a couple of million, plus a million in prize money for developing it. Okay so far?"

"Six or seven million," said Polly. "Go on."

"The desert orchid was worth three-quarters of a million, maybe a million when it was stolen. The various orchids, I don't know. Orchid collectors are fanatics. Three million? Five? And the American chestnut? Well, if it's really pest-free, it's worth billions to the timber industry, but it'll take another decade to be sure. For years fallen chestnut trees were putting out shoots that everyone hailed with great optimism, but the blight was inherited, and when they reached a certain height, every one of them sickened and died."

Justine's voice trailed off as she gazed at the line of saplings, but she caught herself and continued, more briskly, "My guess is that even at this stage it could be sold to the federal government or the timber people or both. So I'd say twenty million over a couple of decades if he gets some sort of patent on it." She paused. "Where are we?"

"Over thirty million," Polly whispered. "You sure?"

"Maybe not that much," said Justine, "but it's up there. At least twenty, no?"

Polly nodded assent, needing her own desk, her calculator, wanting to factor in costs, wholesale and retail, and time. "What time is it now?" she asked Justine. "You think he's okay?"

"After midnight," said Justine. "Shouldn't we call someone?"

"Who?" said Polly. "Call 911? And give them our location? Do we care if Mitchell Reinhart overcooks himself?"

They sat, and then Polly said, "If it's all worth that much, how come it's not better guarded? Anyone could walk in."

"The house probably has an alarm," said Justine, "but this is just a backyard. If you wandered in here and saw a tag that said 'C. dent.,' would you know it was an extinct chestnut? Would you see the 'Lapis' rose and connect it to a million-dollar prize? Would a burglar? A maintenance manager? Would Reinhart's friend Till? Only one in ten thousand people would know what they were looking at here."

"In other words, you," said Polly as a window was closed, an internal door slammed, and Polly and Justine hunkered lower behind millions of dollars in horticultural wonders.

"What do you think she's doing?" said Justine.

"I don't know," said Polly, once again picturing Reinhart in the sauna, in suffocating heat, slumped over. "I'm calling Dinah."

During the few rings it took Dinah to answer, Polly's hands started shaking. "What are you doing?" she asked, close into the phone.

"Sleeping, like I said. What's up?" said Dinah's voice.

"How long can you stay in a sauna?" asked Polly.

If Dinah found the question odd or inappropriate, she gave no indication. Very little startled Dinah, with the exception of earth tremors. "A half hour, maybe? I'm not sure of the temperature they reach, but the real problem is dehydration."

"Something's going on," said Polly. "He's been in the sauna almost two hours."

"You sure enough to call for help?" asked Dinah.

"I don't know," said Polly. She was very cold.

"Can you get out of there?"

"Don't know."

"Try to get out of there," said Dinah, and hung up.

Polly eased onto her knees and, pushing her way between camellia pots, crawled the few feet to the corner of the open shelves. At this level her view of the yard and the walkway was totally obstructed, but she couldn't stand or move any farther out because Mrs. Reinhart could be heard coming downstairs again. She was out the patio door, she was across the walkway, with a purposeful gait, but different shoes—softer this time, probably a lower heel and leather. Once again she was out the yard gate, and the gym door opened and closed.

It was followed by a burst of noises—the heavy slam of an internal door, a clattering, something dropping, and over it all was Suzanne Reinhart shouting, the words mostly indistinct except for "Mitch!" and "Get up, Mitchie!" Then the outside door banged open against the gym wall and she was running through the gate of her own yard. Through a gap Polly saw her rush past under the lights.

Behind Polly, Justine whispered, "Do you think he's okay?" but there was no need to ask, because now they heard Suzanne Reinhart's voice clear and shrill, obviously on the phone. She was giving her address, several times, and urging whatever authority she'd called to "Come quickly, quickly! Hurry!"

"We have to get out of here. Now!" said Polly, backing up, pot by pot, still on her hands and knees. Justine was on her feet, fumbling for the latch on the garden door. Lights were going on all over the house. The gate's hinges squawked against the wood as Justine tugged it open a foot. Both women squeezed through just as high floodlights lit up the patio, casting their intense beams over into the empty lot, and as the gate latch clicked behind them, they were already moving swiftly down the path toward the back road and down the back road to the street beyond.

Not wanting to break into a telltale run, they walked rapidly up the street, moving from streetlamp to streetlamp, in and out of the greenish light. A siren was wailing, coming closer.

Dinah got out of her car as they came around the oleander hedge. They were breathless, and she grasped at their shoulders, saying, "Slow down, slow down."

"She must have called 911," panted Polly. "We have to go there and say what happened."

"What happened?"

"She put him in the sauna, and he never came out."

"On purpose?"

"She checked on him before she left, so she obviously knew he was there."

The siren was very close, a few streets away. Then it stopped.

"Do you know where they'll take him?" asked Polly.

"I can find out," said Dinah. "Probably the university hospital."

"Go," said Polly. "Please go!"

"Can you get in there?" asked Justine.

Dinah smiled. "They're used to me in the ER," she said calmly, moving Polly gently away from her car door and getting into the driver's seat. "I do a night a week there, or more. They know I'm an ambulance chaser. Never can tell when there'll be an emergency acne case."

"Tell them what happened," urged Justine.

Dinah looked at Justine, then at Polly, an odd expression on her face—no expression, really. "I don't think so," she said, then rolled up her window, put the car in gear, and backed out.

20

They were working on him when Dinah got to the emergency room. She had followed the paramedics until she was sure they were heading for the university hospital; then she slowed down and took her time. If the sequence of events was accurate as reported by Polly and Justine, she couldn't imagine what anyone could do for him. She tried to guess at the physiological effects of two hours in a sauna, calculating the possible heat levels, his body temperature, and the rate of dehydration. The same amount of time in a steam room might be worse, she thought, because sweat can't evaporate in that kind of moisture. Still, rapid dehydration in a dry, intense heat was bad enough, and if it was true, as Kat had said, that the Reinharts usually drank before and during their sauna, the alcohol intake had sped up Mr. Divorce's dehydration.

Her thoughts drifted, as they often did, from the medical to the moral. Arranging a long sojourn in a hot sauna did seem a perfect way to kill someone without laying a hand on him. It wasn't murder to have a few drinks together and relax in a sauna. It probably wasn't even murder to leave him there alone. What was definitely murder was knowing he was in there, passed out and in danger of dying, and letting him die. But whether it could be proved or prosecuted was another matter.

It was not unlike what happened to Ginger, she thought, and thinking of Ginger, Dinah wondered whether Polly and Justine should have called for help and whether she herself would have done so. But she couldn't really put herself in their place or even judge them, because, given her expertise, she would have known that his life was in danger and, given her training, she would have moved to save his life without questioning whether he deserved it.

The hospital always seemed to Dinah another world at night—an underworld, actually, in the mythical sense. Every time she put her key card into the slot at the parking entrance and began to descend the long ramp down to the emergency level, she felt she was about to enter Erebus, the land of the shades.

Dinah had been steeped in myth by her mother, a gentle woman whose three sons, two brothers, husband, and brother-in-law were all firemen, policemen, or paramedics in the Boston area and who was determined that her only daughter have art and poetry in her life. So she read her myths and fairy tales from an early age, and when Dinah, already both a reader and a romantic, also exhibited an inquiring and logical turn of mind, her mother sent her to Catholic school for the discipline, the Latin, the art, and the music associated with the church. The discipline was good, but Latin had been removed from the curriculum when church services converted to English, Dinah turned out to be tone-deaf, and she found the religious art of the Middle Ages and Renaissance stiff and unappealing. She stayed a few years, accepting her mother's argument that, if nothing else, Catholic education offered the rare opportunity to study a living mythology in the company of people who actually believed it. Then she switched to a tough and crowded public high school and began to excel in chemistry, biology, and math.

The myths, however, stayed deep within her, and as she parked her car in a dark corner of the underground garage and headed for the automatic double doors, she half expected to find them guarded by Cerberus, the watchdog of hell, with the Fates doing triage in a cavern off the staging area beyond. The illusion held even as an ambulance drove up, red lights flashing, and the paramedics pulled out a gurney that was quickly seized by ER attendants and rushed through the automatic doors, which closed after them.

The doors burst inward again at Dinah's approach, and she moved briskly through the waiting room. For her it was a brief stop. For the people sitting around the room, it was a night's stay in purgatory. Most were quiet, overcome by fear or discomfort, and their eyes followed Dinah, probably because she wore the white coat and identification badge that she kept in her car. As always, these got her immediate access: The clerk, phone at her ear, gestured Dinah on, buzzed open the internal doors, and Dinah passed through to the emergency arena. Brighter than daylight, it hummed with the noise of continuous machines, accented by the blips of heart and oxygen monitors, the snap of scissors cutting gauze and clothing, the scrape and clang of metal instruments picked up and thrown back into surgical trays. Talk was minimal; the work of a trauma center was not discursive but manual, fast, and desperate.

The examining rooms were wide and doorless, the privacy curtains rarely drawn, and finding Reinhart was easy. He was in the second room, surrounded by ER personnel in white coats and surgical scrubs. Standing in the doorway, Dinah caught the eye of one of the attending men, who nodded at her and held up a tense hand to bar interruption.

For the next forty-five minutes, Dinah wandered the hospital's lower floors. The medical center was huge. It was said to be second only to the Pentagon in size, but at least the Pentagon was built on a five-sided organizing principle, while this complex had expanded, year by year, one building and one wing at a time. It was now as labyrinthine as the underworld: One often heard stories of people found weeping at the intersections of major corridors, lost for hours and unable to find their way forward or back.

The hospital was strangely peaceful in the night hours, the dimness and quiet taking the edge off sickness and pain. Dinah walked, calmed by the slowing down of time. Lights were turned low or off; the temperature was set on chilly. Rounding a corner, she'd see a long corridor stretch empty into the distance, until a gurney would glide into view, guided by spectral figures in surgical drapes, masks on their faces or hanging below the jaw. The gurneys passed almost inaudibly, the attendants acknowledging her presence with a nod, then moving on to some distant cavern behind her. At night even the patients—those who sat waiting and those who walked the dim halls—were pale and toneless, as unreactive as shades, unlike in the daytime, when everyone projected an air of anxiety and sometimes hysteria.

Almost reluctantly, Dinah returned to the ER desk and learned that Reinhart had been transferred to the fifth-floor intensive-care unit. The clerk, whom she knew, gave her a long and loaded look, warning her what to expect, and Dinah, aware of people in the waiting area, nodded and left.

The atmosphere on the fifth floor was less muted. It was also warmer, though the ceiling lights here, too, were dimmed, and only pale fluorescents shone in each cubicle. Few words were exchanged and those few in low voices, but the place was hardly silent, given the rhythmic puffing of ventilators and the little bleeps of the various monitors. Two nurses manned the nurses' station, both known to Dinah, and when Dinah asked about Reinhart, one of them pointed to a cubicle with its side curtains drawn and two people working on the unconscious patient in the bed.

"Chart?" the nurse offered, pushing a loose-leaf notebook across the counter toward Dinah. Dinah started with the vital signs—body temp of 107 degrees, blood pressure of 60 over 40, heart rate 170, and a blood alcohol of .19, which at almost twice the legal limit meant fairly drunk. The attending she'd seen earlier, a middle-aged professor who was often called into the ER for iffy cases, came up beside her, looked over her shoulder companionably, and said, "This one's pretty sour. You know him?"

"No, but he's interesting," Dinah replied.

"Not much chance," said the man. "Two hours in a hundred-and-eighty- or two-hundred-degree sauna. Just going through the motions here." He dipped his head toward a small waiting room on the perpendicular corridor behind them. "Wife's in there."

Dinah skimmed the rest of Reinhart's statistics, none encouraging, and turned for a look at Suzanne Reinhart. Though some distance away, she was visible through the open door, and more clearly when Dinah moved to the corridor intersection to study the notices on the bulletin board. Mrs. Reinhart wasn't alone, having apparently summoned a friend to keep her company, and she was not downcast. Dressed in leggings and a long silk shirt, she had crossed one leg over the other and was resting one hand, palm down, on her upper knee, working on her nails. Her friend, a blond woman in a lavender running suit, was smoking, despite the No Smoking sign at her elbow on a side table. From where Dinah stood, their words were inaudible but not their laughter. Suzanne Reinhart's mood was quite cheerful, considering.

When Dinah got home, it was past three in the morning, but there was a message from Polly to call, whatever the time, so she did. Justine had left a short time before, realizing it could well be morning before they found out if Mitchell Reinhart was all right.

"Well, no, I wouldn't say he's all right," said Dinah, unable at that hour to keep some irritation out of her voice. "They've got him in an ICU, because technically, I suppose, he's not yet dead in every particular. But I'd call him pretty dead."

"Why an ICU?" asked Polly.

"As opposed to what?" retorted Dinah. "They have a burn unit, but this is way beyond burn."

"He was burned?" Her voice quavered.

Dinah sat down on the edge of her bed. "How can I explain this?" she said, almost to herself. She sighed. "He was roasted," she said. "His skin still looks like skin—darker, maybe, and somewhat reddened—but the flesh inside is cooked. . . ."

"Cooked?" Polly was horrified.

"The tissue cells are breaking down. The organs are hardening. The brain is probably fairly liquefied already." Dinah ticked off the indications. "They have him on life support, but it's meaningless. His lungs are barely inflatable. His circulation is essentially nonexistent."

She paused. "Roasted," she said finally. "'Roasted' is still the best word," and she signed off to go to bed.

Polly sat in her sleeping porch office staring out over the dark city for another half hour, then went to the medicine chest and found some Valium left over from when Dan died. Early morning was not the best time to think anything through, even when thoughts came quickly and with so little transition that one had the illusion of clarity, of connections being made.

A man had died almost under her eyes—not by her hand but on her watch, literally. She and Justine weren't mere witnesses to an accident, helpless to stop its course. They'd had time and opportunity to intervene, but they hadn't. Like Dinah, she was struck by the scenario: Reinhart, Till, and Cannon had let Ginger die. They might not have killed her, but they had let her die. What was the difference between what they'd done to Ginger and what she and Justine had done to Reinhart?

She tried to remember what she was thinking at the time, why she and Justine had done nothing to save Mitch Reinhart's life. Obviously they hadn't wanted to reveal their presence there. Probably they couldn't comprehend the seriousness of his plight, of his wife's intentions. Maybe they just didn't want to help Reinhart; the whole excursion, after all, was predicated on the wish to harm him.

How easy it was to let someone die! Polly, of all people, for whom death was as much an expertise as it was for Charlotte, should have responded instinctively, particularly since Reinhart's was a slow death and there was time to fend it off. So often death happened in an instant. One second alive, breathing, animated, the next second still, a shell.

At what point was Mitch Reinhart dead? When his body temperature passed some critical point beyond which he couldn't recover? When he sank into shock? Did he actually die on their watch, with their acquiescence, and not in the hospital the next dawn, and was there indeed a point at which they could have saved him?

She couldn't summon her mother, nor did her mother come unbidden as usual. "I helped kill someone," she whispered, and when the idea just hung there unanswered, she said instead, "Did I really help kill someone?" Even that brought no answer.

Don't leave me, Mummy, she pleaded, though of course she knew that her mother had been gone for years. That was when she took a pill and went to bed.

She got three hours' sleep before the alarm woke her to drive the children to school. An hour later she was home, feeling as if her head were stuffed with cotton and her eyes were barely focused, and fell into bed for another couple of hours. When she woke, all of the distinctions between Ginger's death and Reinhart's, between Suzanne Reinhart's actions and hers and Justine's, were in the front of her mind and seemed remarkably clear. She and Justine were observers—unable or unwilling to recognize what was happening, but still just observers. At the same time, she knew that finding Suzanne Reinhart guilty didn't leave her and Justine guilt-free. She felt better, but not blameless.

After many calls back and forth that morning, the women agreed they'd all leave work early and meet at Dinah's office, which closed at three on Friday afternoons. Dinah was alone in the suite when Polly, Justine, and Charlotte arrived about four-thirty, but they nevertheless gathered extra chairs to crowd into Dinah's private office, and when Kat came, they closed the door.

Dinah, still in her white coat over a silk blouse and dark slacks, sat behind the desk, one leg tucked under her, hands professionally folded on her pages of notes. "Well," she said, "as we all expected, I learned an hour ago that he's dead. He died early in the morning."

She paused, looking from one to another for reaction. There was none.

"Let me run through the medical history," she continued, "and then we'll back up and Polly and Justine can tell us what happened in more detail." And she explained what she had seen at the hospital and what she had learned about what happens to the human body in a sauna.

"Do you have to keep saying 'roasted'?" muttered Kat. Dinah ignored the inquiry.

"Did you see the wife?" asked Charlotte.

"I saw the wife."

"What was she like? What was she doing?"

"She was buffing her nails," said Dinah, and when they looked blank, she said, "Buffing her nails. You know, with one of those little silver things with chamois on one side. Little antique thing. Satin case."

"Jesus," said Kat, wincing in disgust.

Dinah took it personally. "What's the matter?" she said, looking from one to another. "Is something wrong? I thought everyone agreed he was a real shit."

Justine sat forward. "Dear God," she said, "she has that garden now. That unbelievable collection is all hers."

"Well, that might be a comfort, I suppose," said Dinah. "Is she known to like flowers?"

Their laughter changed the mood to some degree. Reinhart's death was put aside for a full account of the evening in the garden, including Justine's description of the extraordinary plants Reinhart had assembled in his empty lot. Again she estimated that he might get twenty-five million dollars for everything, adding that it was only an estimate, and probably low. For a little while, the women gave way to a triumphal giddiness: They had found Reinhart's well-hidden assets, and those assets were substantial.

But they came back to Reinhart's death and Polly and Justine's distress at their part in it. Polly laid out her careful distinctions between Ginger's death and Reinhart's, his actions, their actions, his wife's actions, her undoubtable intentions. Everyone nodded and agreed: It was exactly as she said it. But like Polly, they could make no definitive separation between being witnesses and being accessories.

"We all understand why you held back," said Charlotte. "You didn't know he was dying in there. Who could? Such things are inconceivable."

"Why keep going over it?" said Kat, who could waver as well as anyone but was quicker to let go of what couldn't be changed. "Personally, I'm glad he got his without us doing a thing."

Charlotte put her fingertips together and studied the ceiling. "Technically," she said, "we did do something, if only by omission. There was probably a point when he could have been saved."

"Don't be so prissy, Charlotte," said Kat. "Never mind whether they could have saved him. Why should they?"

"In fact, maybe they couldn't have," Dinah cut in. "Polly and Justine did wonder why he was taking so long, but by the time they really understood, it was much too long and probably too late."

"I understand that," said Charlotte crisply. "I'm just saying that technically—or legally, if you like—they could well have contributed to his death by doing nothing, whatever their reasons." Looking at Justine, she softened her tone. "That said, if I had been there, I would have done the same thing."

"I've gone over it and over it in my mind," said Justine wearily. "It just never occurred to me that anything could be done. It was like I was watching a movie."

"I think I was aware he could be saved by a call," said Polly slowly. "It just didn't occur to me that I should be the one to make it." When this wasn't questioned, she added, in a low voice, "It's just so surprising how easy it is to let someone die."

Kat, right next to her, reached out to take her hand, then said, with a firm pragmatism, "In any case, we have one less revenge to work out. She did it for us."

"I'll hold that thought," said Polly.

By the time Polly got home, it was almost dark—not yet the black of night, but the dusky purple that followed the sunsets. Graham Vere's car was parked in front of her house, and she pulled up behind it, wondering why no one had put on the outside light. For some reason she didn't feel the usual pulse of anticipation, but an unmistakable trepidation as she opened her car door and eased out of the seat. And yet they hadn't spoken for a couple of days, and she wasn't aware of any bad words or feelings lingering between them.

As she came around the bushes to the front path, she saw him on the stoop, sitting in shadow on the rim of the big ceramic pot beside the door. He didn't look comfortable, he didn't rise, and, worst of all, he didn't offer any greeting.

"How long have you been here?" she asked, halfway up the walk.

"A while. The children said you'd be back before eight." His voice was toneless. "I told them I'd wait out here."

She moved forward, but he waved her off. "Just what is going on?"

he said, and she realized that his voice was not calm but taut with anger.

"What do you mean?"

"Your friend Reinhart," he said, standing up. "Monday night you tell me you're all going to get the guy, and Friday noon he's on my table. What kind of people are you?"

She put her hand on his forearm, but he shook her off. Now she was calm and he was becoming more agitated.

"At least come around back," she said, and led the way around the side of the house and down the steep stairs to the terraced backyard. She sensed him behind her, but neither spoke, and when they came out onto the narrow patio behind the house, she moved aside so he could pass her and take one of the chairs. Instead he went on down the steps to the next level, walked across it, and at the end went one lower yet and back toward her. When he came up the steps again and started another rotation, she realized he was going to keep pacing her terraces, so she started to talk. The levels were so close together she didn't even have to raise her voice.

"We did go to his house, just to look, but he died," she said, and she told him what they'd hoped to learn, how they'd gone in through the gate, and what they'd found. She couldn't see his face or expression as he paced—sometimes down a level and then up, sometimes back and forth on the level just below her, like an animal in a zoo enclosure. Sometimes she paused, hoping he'd speak, but he kept moving, silent.

"We didn't know it could kill him in there," she said, after describing their examination of the plants and their hiding, huddled at the wall, sure that any minute he'd come out of the sauna. "And now," she finished, "neither of us knows how to handle the fact that he died."

"I already know that he died. I don't need you to tell me that," he said curtly, coming to a stop just below her and looking up, so she could see his features. "The paramedics called in with a heads-up. They thought he was about to die in the van." He said that the next day the hospital had called him about the death, and that was when he learned the name of the victim. "The coroner hears first," he said. "Unexplained death is our job."

"There is an explanation," said Polly. "Dinah said he was roasted, in the sauna."

"Come on, come on," said Vere, "I know that. That only answers the medical question." He kneaded his forehead with his hands, rubbed his eyes. "I'd be satisfied with that myself if I hadn't known your plans."

"We didn't mean it to happen," said Polly. "We just went to look at his yard and his buildings. He didn't even know we were there."

"Oh, good, that answers one question," he said. "So you didn't shove him in there like Hansel and Gretel and close the door. But it does raise another question: Why didn't you do something to get him out?"

Polly sat down at the foot of an outdoor lounge chair and put her head in her hands. "We don't know," she said faintly. "We keep going over it and over it, and we don't know. Maybe he wasn't really a person to us. Maybe we couldn't really believe what was happening." She was almost inaudible. "Maybe we didn't really care."

He was suddenly sitting beside her, or behind her, on the upper half of the chaise, but he didn't touch her. "And later, when you had time to reflect, why didn't you tell anyone what happened?"

"I don't know," she said. "And why tell? What difference would it make? Maybe we're coming to think of it as justice."

"Kind of a free and loose view of justice," said Vere, stern again.

"You knew what happened," she said, "or at least you thought you knew somebody involved. And you didn't tell, even when you thought we'd caused his death."

"That's different," he said, "because I love you."

"Believe me," Polly implored, turning to put both hands on his arms. "Justine and I can't stop thinking we could have done something, that we should have saved him." Then she registered his words. She was close enough to see his gray eyes clearly now, looking at her, no light needed to illuminate the tenderness. "You love me?"

He put his arms around her. "It's complicated," he said, holding her closely and smoothing back her curly hair.

I guess that's what passes for profundity in the new millennium, her mother commented, not unamiably. But it must have been Polly who said it, because Graham answered.

"It beats Kahlil Gibran," he said.

He's good, said her mother. He's very good. It was her standard accolade for anyone who came out ahead in an argument.

21

The women were all subdued at Monday's meeting, having spent much of the weekend talking about Reinhart's death. Dinah was the least affected by the way he died. To her, death was simply cessation of life, and once it happened, one death was the same as another. Kat found it startling but not disturbing. She didn't know Reinhart, didn't like the sound of him, and although she had a sentimental streak and wept at newsreels of Jesse Owens and Paavo Nurmi and Barnaby's occasional recitation of Housman's "To an Athlete Dying Young," Reinhart was hardly known for a physique worth mourning. Mostly she was impressed that Suzanne Reinhart had "the balls to do it."

Justine's distress was unabated, as she reviewed over and again their hours in the garden, how they should have realized Reinhart was in danger, how they might have intervened and with what results. Polly had gone beyond that, worrying about how Reinhart's death, and their part in it, could affect the progress of their plan. As for Charlotte, she thought only about Milo Till, and Monday noon she made a quick trip to the courthouse to see what was filed under his name.

When Lotte was late, they were actually relieved, and they spent the time in silence, listening for her steps on the stairs and watching the sky change color as the sun slipped down. Even when she arrived, apologetic, they were quiet, unable to come up with a topic that didn't involve Reinhart or Ginger or what they now thought of as their other life. Lotte, however, had scheduling questions, some general inquiries into their moods and general health, and finally, a specific topic to explore—Kat's upcoming surgery.

"I thought we might share in any fears you have about the surgery and your expectations for its outcome," she said, directly addressing Kat. It was a cool day, and Lotte was clothed in heath-tone wools—a long brown skirt with teal flecks, a sage wool vest fastened with little chains, a muslin blouse with a stand-up collar and long sleeves.

"I'll be a lot flatter," said Kat, literal as always. "Which is just what I want. And the scars are underneath, so they won't show."

Lottle put the tips of her fingers together. "Self-image is so interesting," she said. "We become used to our appearance, invested in it, really, and any change forces an adjustment which can be quite traumatic. You are one person; suddenly you are another person." She looked around the circle, saw no one prepared to comment, and continued.

"For therapists," she said, "an alarm goes off when clients make a significant change in appearance. They become very literally 'not themselves,' not so much a different person as the same personality inhabiting a different form. Whenever I read a news story about some public figure who has lost a huge amount of weight, I think, Uh-oh, this person is going to be crazy for a while, and I wouldn't trust their reactions."

Kat nodded. "I can understand that," she said, "especially if their only goal was the weight loss, or if they thought it was their only goal. But

I've thought a lot about why I got these boobs in the first place and why I want to get rid of them now. In other words"—she leaned forward, a flush of earnestness on her cheeks—"I've thought about the connection between my appearance and my goals and what I'm changing in my life," and she sat back in her chair and looked around for approbation.

"You go, girl," said Charlotte.

"Of course, you're of less use to us now," said Polly.

Kat was unruffled. "Nah," she said, "you need my fleet foot, not my big boobs."

Lotte leaned forward, looking confused, but before she could speak, Justine said softly, "I think it's a wonderful thing that you defined a goal, and that you're doing something about it."

"Ginger would be pleased," added Charlotte.

"We're all pleased," said Lotte, "of course," and after a pause she recovered to take up what was obviously the second part of her two-part topic. "And the surgery itself?" she asked. "Are you at all fearful?"

"No," said Kat slowly, unsure what Lotte was after. "If you mean afraid of dying under the knife, not at all. I've been there before. Two knee operations, a pin in one forearm, a C-section, and of course the implants themselves. I'm still here."

"Maybe Lotte's getting at the whole idea of elective surgery, something you don't have to have," suggested Dinah. "Kat's original implant surgery was truly elective, purely cosmetic. A reversal is more of a necessity if it corrects a bad choice, though it may take years before you understand that something *was* a bad choice."

"At least cosmetic surgery's safe now," said Charlotte. "Almost everyone I know has had 'a little work done.'"

"Not that safe," said Dinah. "Even with the best conditions, the incidence of infection isn't insignificant. I've seen people badly defaced—and I mean literally de-faced—by cosmetic surgery. I can't imagine taking such a risk."

"Don't worry, I won't," said Kat. "The face stays."

"Actually," said Dinah, "this brings up something interesting. As you know, I've talked quite a bit recently with my favorite attending in ER, and I got a call today inviting me to take part regularly in their trauma conferences. I said yes, of course."

"And who knows what this might lead to?" said Polly. "Speaking of revising goals."

There was a wave of congratulations, even from Lotte, who had enjoyed the last fifteen minutes of discussion immensely, turning to one or another as each spoke, now smiling, now nodding encouragement. Lotte was always pleased when a discussion took off, moving from one idea to another, one insight to another. Understandably, she took it as partly her achievement, although she described herself as only a facilitator, precipitating discussions but providing no conclusions. She obviously felt good now as she gathered her papers, packed her carryall, folded today's shawl over her arm.

"Next week, then," she said, moving toward the door. "You'll put the cat out as usual?"

They laughed obediently, though it was hardly a new joke, and sat listening as her footsteps made a quarter round of the balcony and clumped down the stairs. Even after the gate settled back into its latch, they hesitated. Either they were talked out after their weekend calls or they had left so much unsaid that they were reluctant to start in again.

"Does it sometimes seem," mused Polly, "that there's a huge split between the Lotte part of our meetings and the part that's just us? Sometimes I'm actively waiting for her to go, and I wonder if maybe we started discussing revenge because we got bored with discussing ourselves. Unless we're bored with ourselves now because revenge is so much more interesting. I mean, should we worry about our motives for what we're doing?"

"No," said Charlotte. "I remember our motives, and they're fine."

"Does it matter?" asked Dinah. "Even if we decide that our motives were suspect, we're in it now, and I for one need closure, as they say."

"So do I," said Kat, feeling around under her chair for a shoe, "so can we move on to Milo Till, even if I'm limited in what I can do on this one?"

Charlotte moved her chair closer to the table, where she'd piled up several folders, but didn't open them. "This one's not going to be easy," she said, "because this guy's entire modus operandi is to keep his plans, his dealings, his whole life fairly well hidden. I know we've all done a little on him—Polly actually got more biography than I did, though it was my assignment—so we must all have a feeling for what we're up against."

"Which is . . . ?" Dinah cut in.

"Which is, how do you get someone who survives every challenge? This man can play any system. What he doesn't win in civil court, he settles. When regulators go after him, they back down. Even in tax court he prevails, citing their own codes. Hell, we've seen this ourselves: Look how he finessed Ginger's death."

What they had on Milo Till's personal life was scant and sketchy, perhaps, said Polly, because he had little life outside his work. He was born in western Massachusetts in an old mill town, the son of Greek immigrants, graduated from Northeastern University as an economics major, and went on to Wharton for an MBA. At some point in these school years, he married a hometown girl, because about twenty-five years later, after what one write-up called "two decades of marriage," they divorced, and his wife went back east and married the owner of several Italian restaurants on Long Island.

"If he's that good a fixer, he probably arranged it," said Polly, who'd been searching past news stories, "because there was no bad blood over the breakup, no contest, no acrimony, and if there were children, they quietly disappeared."

Milo Till's business life was more visible, but so complex that it would probably prove even more opaque. Till Properties & Development was active throughout California, and signs heralding ANOTHER TILL DEVELOPMENT! were not uncommon in Arizona and Nevada. His specialty was turning raw land into suburbs or vacation communities. He'd unerringly home in on land that was not just raw but pristine, prize it out of the hands of family foundations, historic land grants, or government protectors, and by the exercise of one legal stratagem or another convert it to residential use that was previously prohibited.

He was helped by batteries of lawyers and accountants, including the firm in which Charlotte's husband, Avery, was a partner, but his greatest asset was what Charlotte called "peasant cunning." He had an instinct for finding lax and lazy trust managers, government bureaucrats asleep at the switch, regulators more interested in personal aggrandizement than in their sacred trust. It was only later, after he'd skirted some law or regulation and taken over, that someone might notice and issue a late challenge, and by then Till would be bolstered by friendly trustees, administrators, and officials and backed by his lawyers and accountants. "And he always wins," said Charlotte, "or if it's a real firebomb of a case and nobody really wins, he's at least left intact and standing."

Certainly he was sued, and often, over his properties—over the price he paid or refused to pay, even the loans he took out. One case currently pending against him had been filed by a lender who foreclosed on a construction loan only to find that the value of the land and improvements was nowhere near what Till had claimed. "Justine recognized the gambit right away," said Charlotte, looking to Justine for help.

"It's crooked but not uncommon," said Justine. "A developer will get an unrealistically high appraisal on some land, then pad his stated construction costs to get a much bigger loan than he really needs. He pockets the difference, which works fine unless the project is a bust. Then the lender has to take over the property, finds it's not worth anything near the appraisal, and is left holding the stick."

"Even if they go after Till, he'll probably beat it down," said Charlotte. "He's really crafty."

"Or else he has a guardian angel," said Polly, who had turned up an old criminal-fraud action against Till Properties for selling lots in a desert community where it turned out there was no way to pipe in water. "Till's company was trucking in water so that something would come out of the taps at the model homes, and his sales force went on right on selling. Fortunately, when it hit the news, a religious group that didn't want any utilities or public services came forward and bought the whole parcel, and the AG's office backed off." She did a little drumroll on the table. "How's that for luck?"

"I don't believe in luck," said Charlotte. "He probably bought it himself in the name of some fake church. Certainly luck doesn't cut it in tax court, and he usually prevails there, too. At worst he pays some additional tax but no penalties or interest."

Some of his "luck" was good connections. His real estate partnerships included some of the biggest names in California business, and Till was on the board of directors of many California corporations. Some big names were politicians as well: Till was in charge of several blind trusts formed when those politicians won elections and had to separate themselves temporarily from their assets, and one of them had even short-listed him for an ambassadorship, "which, thank God," said Polly, "he didn't get. But it did get him some news coverage, or I wouldn't have anything personal on him at all. He doesn't like interviews, and the critical exposure he got as a potential ambassador is probably one reason he didn't pursue that ambition."

Apparently Till was a Republican at the time, a temporary commitment, and had been virtually tithing to the party for several years. Ambassadorial appointments had been a spoils system for over a century, rewarding a ruling party's friends and donors. The establishment of a career foreign service in the 1920s opened the competition somewhat, but it still favored rich people with no foreign service, no foreign experience, and no experience, period. Till had both money and brains, but not in the preferred order. He was beaten out by a tycoon who publicly thanked Switzerland, an aggressively neutral country, for fighting on our side during the war, referred to Nova Scotia as a country, said that the dropping of the atom bomb on Tokyo was Eisenhower's only mistake, and expressed his concern that if we relaxed our vigilance and cut defense funding, the Russians might once again cross the land bridge into Alaska.

"Except for that one futile foray into politics, Milo Till doesn't seem very partisan," said Polly. "He's just drawn to power, whatever the party. I can't tell you how many photos I saw of big gatherings, political and governmental, with Milo Till just behind the shoulder of the principal figure. But there's so little personal stuff on him that I don't even know where he lives."

"I do," said Justine, "and his political affiliation, too." And she laughed out loud at the surprised faces.

"He's on the voter rolls as 'declined to state' a party," she said, "which is hardly evidence of political interests. And he lives in a Wilshire Boulevard high-rise near Westwood Village. In the penthouse."

"I knew that," said Kat, jumping to her feet. "I play racquetball with our grill chef, who works with a caterer and has been to Till's apartment. He says it's all black and white with a stainless steel kitchen and a good-size gym." She was circling the table, tapping the backs of chairs like a child playing Duck, Duck, Goose.

"Also," said Justine, "the DMV has him driving a BMW and a Porsche. The BMW's registered to his company."

"My guess," said Charlotte, "is that his sympathies as a Greek immigrant kid were probably Democratic, but land and banking are Republican, so out go the sympathies."

"As I said, he's equal opportunity," said Polly. "Those blind trusts? One is for a two-term California state senator, a Democrat, and another's for the Republican governor of Arizona."

Abruptly she stopped curling her hair around her finger and sat forward. "Hey," she said, "maybe there's something there. According to this one business journal—a long, boring, technical thing, by the way—these guys started out with modest assets. Till began investing in land for them, and by the time they left office, they were millionaires."

"Can we find out exactly how these work?" asked Charlotte, looking up from the notes she'd made on her yellow legal pad.

"If it's land, it's traceable, even in a trust," said Justine. Once they'd identified the original parcels, they could track when they were bought, sold, combined with other land, renamed, developed, or reassessed. Then they'd know how Till had increased the value.

Justine was talking with enthusiasm, even relish. To her this was an appealing exercise, but when no one showed any interest, she shrugged and said, "I'll do it."

"Good. So what else do we have?" asked Kat, bending one arm after the other at the elbow and stretching it behind her head and as far down her back as she could.

Not a lot, they agreed, mostly possibilities. They had the construction loans and the tax cases and the blind trusts. What they needed was something more personal, something on how Till conducted his private business or his private life—the kind of stuff, said Polly, that only his hairdresser knows for sure.

"I looked specifically for personal stuff," said Dinah, "but haven't come up with much yet. Medically, he's clean, by which I mean uninteresting. He's on my health network, on a special executive plan, but there's nothing there beyond an annual physical, which he passed with flying colors. He gives five or ten thousand a year to the art museum and is on the acquisitions committee but rarely shows up. And he's interested in pre-Columbian art, which tends to be a dirty, underhanded, often criminal field of collecting. Probably just his cup of tea."

"And ours," said Polly, "if we could get him on it."

"If we're lucky," said Dinah, "he's smuggling, although that's so standard in pre-Columbian that catching him at it would be only a minor embarrassment."

"All I could find out," said Kat, "is he's a competition-caliber squash player and a competitive-caliber heterosexual. And his credit reports are clean. He has a Platinum American Express and one MasterCard, both with high credit limits, always paid off in full. Biggest recurring expenditures are airline tickets, restaurants, limousine companies, and a Porsche service garage. Standard stuff, but I'll keep plugging."

"I'll pull the tax cases," said Charlotte. "I don't know what we could get on him that the IRS can't, but sometimes their focus suggests something else, like when they have some gangster in for income tax evasion because no one can nail him on his narcotics business and prostitution ring. At least you get a look at some of his tax filings, otherwise known only to his accountants."

"So," said Kat brightly, "anyone know his accountant?" And she looked at Charlotte, who put her hands up defensively.

"Try not to ask me to get Avery to help," she said.

"No one mentioned Avery," said Polly.

"He'd refuse?" asked Kat, immediately intrigued. "Would he turn us in?"

"I don't know what he'd do," said Charlotte, staring at the papers in front of her. When she looked up, her face was unhappy. "I should know what he'd do, shouldn't I?"

"Charlotte," said Polly, "no apology is necessary. We're not in this to make our husbands and boyfriends do the work."

"I know," said Charlotte, "but if we're going to be looking at tax dodges and creative accounting, we should be able to draw on an expert close to home. Avery doesn't handle Till himself, but I'll see if I can get some general background from him."

"If Till's such a manipulator, there must be a lot to look at," said

Justine. "And it fits our idea of exploiting some central weakness in these men, like Cannon's family values or Reinhart's hiding assets."

Maybe they could find some financial deception that had escaped more professional investigators. What gave them their edge was that the pros would want to get him legally, and they only wanted to embarrass him. It was not a negligible goal: A man who hobnobbed with politicians and tycoons, who aspired to an ambassadorship, wouldn't want to be embarrassed. Better a fine or a penalty or even a legal judgment, which could be shrugged off as "just business."

Charlotte, as always, would cover the courts. Justine would explore the blind trusts, with Polly's help. Kat and Dinah would keep calling friends in banking, construction, and art circles.

"If only we knew what to look for," said Justine. "You know, I do have a friend—a former colleague, actually—in the fraud division of the IRS, who might give us some guidance on typical tax dodges."

"Can you go see him?" said Polly eagerly. "And can I come?"

"We'll go together," said Justine. "Maybe we can redeem ourselves."

They broke up so late that Polly drove home into foothills almost entirely in shadow, their outline softened against the darkening sky. She felt her usual anxiety about Andrea and Jeremy but didn't call on her cell phone because they rarely answered, which made her even more nervous. Both came home with other parents on Mondays and by now had either finished their homework and were wasting time or had already wasted the afternoon and were just starting their homework.

Mulling over the discussion, Polly kept returning to Kat's summaries of Till's and Reinhart's credit purchases, struck by the ease with which one could learn such intimate facts as the number of times someone had his car serviced. Maybe it was easier to uncover details of a private life because the public persona was carefully arranged to be opaque. It hadn't occurred to Reinhart to hide his purchases of building materials. Milo Till took his car to the Porsche mechanic without a thought that anyone might inspect the charges. And wasn't there a Supreme Court candidate some years back whose credit-card history included porn movies checked out of his local video store?

Halfway up the canyon, Polly stopped for Chinese takeout. Jeremy would eat anything, but not Andrea, whose vegetarianism was more principle than practice, and therefore unpredictable. Polly sometimes brought her mixed vegetables and chow mein only to have them turned down as boring, and sometimes vegetables with shrimp or scallops, but Andrea would sigh dramatically and with a face of sour concentration, pick out every trace of fish before eating.

The outside light was on at the door, but the front rooms were dark. The mail, still in the carrier's rubber band, was on the floor, and Polly picked it up, turning on lights as she passed. Andrea was in the kitchen, drinking Dr Pepper from the can, painting her nails gunmetal gray, and reading *The Great Gatsby*. Polly couldn't worry too much about a child who read *The Great Gatsby* on her own time.

"Hey," said Polly, putting the bag of aromatic Chinese food on the counter and her mail and purse on the table.

"Hey," said Andrea, not looking up.

Polly took her liter bottle of everyday wine from the refrigerator door and poured herself a glass. Then she took a seat across from Andrea, who had removed the rubber band and was opening what looked to Polly like a piece of junk mail. "This one's for me! They sent me a credit card," said Andrea, who sometimes went shopping with Polly's Nordstrom card and a note saying she could sign for purchases. "In my own name, free!" and she turned it over and back.

Her face, within its close frame of long corkscrew curls, was bright and animated. Polly recognized instantly that for a parent this "gift" was quicksand.

"It's not really 'free,' Andrea," she said, trying not to sound tutorial. "It just records your purchases and bills you at the end of the month, just like when you take my card shopping."

"This would be mine," said Andrea defensively, sensing refusal. "It says I can't spend over five hundred dollars and have to give them my bank-account number, and there's more than five hundred dollars in there."

"So why not just take the money from the bank when you want something?"

"This is easier," muttered Andrea. "And it says I'll be establishing a credit history. Isn't that good?"

Polly straightened in her seat. This was like a first talk about sex. She wondered briefly how much she should go into credit principles and practices, then plunged in with tentative remarks about credit as a convenient payment method for people who earn money and expect to make regular purchases. "A good credit history establishes that people are responsible about paying for what they buy. For someone your age, responsibility means saving money ahead for things you want."

Andrea's eyes were on her, suspiciously fixed, but she wasn't listening.

"It doesn't let me spend more than five hundred dollars," said Andrea.

"Not exactly," said Polly. "You have to keep track yourself, and if you go over, they charge you very high interest and a big penalty."

"I'd keep track," said Andrea sullenly.

Polly looked at the letter and switched tactics. "I have to sign as your guarantor. Do you know what a guarantor is?"

"You promise I'll pay?"

"No," said Polly, "I have to pay if you don't."

"You don't trust me," said Andrea bitterly, gathering up her drink, her book, and her nail polishes. The discussion was over, and Polly knew that its potential could not be salvaged.

After Andrea left the room, Polly picked up the offer—from a Delaware corporation, as always. They must have gotten Andrea's name from her savings bank, or school roster, or maybe her subscription to *Rolling Stone*. Polly inspected the small print with growing irritation. There was a lot about the benefits of credit and nothing about the responsibility, more about "purchasing power" and nothing about paying. And there was no real explanation of terms, just a note that minimum payment was one-twenty-sixth of the total due, and the interest rate of 21.5 percent was somehow calculated on the unpaid balance, or "average daily balance" of new purchases, or perhaps, for all one could tell, the square root of the days in the month or the distance to Delaware, whichever was greater.

Dear Sirs [Polly wrote]:

My fifteen-year-old daughter was thrilled when you sent her a credit card. I was not: I cut it up immediately.

I understand a kid's eagerness. Kids are big spenders and want a lot of stuff. They've also heard it's good to "have credit in your name," so you have access to even more stuff.

I also understand your eagerness. You want a piece of what they spend and hope to be the first card in their pocket, because that's the one people tend to use the most.

But somebody there should address the question of *money*. Should a kid get her own credit, and credit history, before she has her own income? Should you get money from people who have none? Are you thinking that I as a parent will cover her debt?

If you want my children, you must help educate them. Tell them about "benefits" and "purchasing power" but also about responsibility. Don't advertise the "ease" of putting off payment. Tell them to put aside money for what they want before buying it, however they plan to pay. Explain how credit works and what it costs: If you could invent your inscrutable system of tabulating daily balances and interest on "revolving" amounts, you can find a way to explain it.

That would be marketing. This is just exploitation.

Sincerely . . .

Polly printed out the letter, clipped it to the post-paid return envelope, and, as usual, put it aside to age for a while. At this point she usually felt a little stir of satisfaction, but tonight the ritual was flat, with no sense of accomplishment or hope. It was just another note that she had written essentially to herself in a kind of creative onanism. If there were in fact live readers on the other end, they'd know it needed no answer.

Complaint, like revenge, should be public. She was wasting her time.

You have to try, said her mother. Nothing ventured . . .

Nothing's ever gained, Polly cut in. I have to try something different.

22

The day after the meeting, Dinah's decorator called to say that her collection of Southwest baskets and pottery might have sold, "and not piecemeal, darling, but intact." When she was selling art for a client, Bonnie usually worked through a gallery in Beverly Hills, and the previous weekend, as Dinah was reviewing her catalog notes and tentative prices, Bonnie had trucked everything to the gallery, which had lined up a prospective buyer on the description alone. Now this buyer had seen the collection, made his offer, and was ready to take ownership: Bonnie was therefore informing Dinah of the sale and at the same time telling her to go in and sign an agreement for the gallery to represent her.

So at ten-thirty on Saturday morning, Dinah sat in her car outside the Wilshire Boulevard building, a huge stainless steel cube with recessed window displays under a big copper sign that spelled out "Auralia" in cursive script. The look was stark but not unattractive, and a minimal outside was always good warning that inside, things would be expensive. As to what was inside, two of the window displays featured stark and steely sculptures on bare pedestals, but one had a large still-life on a standing easel and the other a painting on a table easel surrounded by brushes, palette, and rags, as if the artist had just left the nineteenth century to go out for coffee.

The store was closed and the street quiet, except for an occasional long luxury sedan gliding by. Gallery hours were twelve to eight, even on Saturdays; apparently the people who participated in the art market were not early to bed and early to rise. Indeed, all of Beverly Hills kept hours from twelve to eight, with a late dinner. Dinah was always early, because, like most dermatologists, she got a full night's sleep, unless she was volunteering in the emergency room.

On the passenger seat beside her were a last few pages of notes on her Southwest pieces. They were probably unnecessary, since the lot had sold without them, but she'd done them and perhaps this Auralia would like to pass them on. Dinah had long ago gotten over her amazement that she, Mrs. Milanskaya's little girl, inhabited a world in which her agent had an agent. She discussed the height of display stands and the angle of indirect lighting with someone who took 15 percent whenever Dinah sold off things she had bought one by one—some for pennies at roadside trading posts, some for hundreds and even thousands of dollars at galleries like this one. And now someone who went by the single name of Auralia waited inside her eponymous establishment to earn her own share of Bonnie's 15 percent, plus whatever the buyer paid her.

Obviously Auralia was well worth it. She had taken a quick, calculating look at the pieces, done no advertising, mailed no flyers. Acting "on a hunch," she had made a single call to a regular customer, who came through. Indeed, Bonnie had told Dinah to get over to the gallery as quickly as possible, having understood from Auralia that there was some hurry about completing the sale.

"What hurry?" Dinah had asked. "Is something perishable?"

"Darling, don't be silly," Bonnie had said. "It's some financial consideration. As always."

At ten-thirty Dinah got out of her car and fed four quarters into the parking meter. She didn't expect to stay an hour, but Beverly Hills was famous for its vigilant meter maids and Draconian parking fines, and she didn't take chances. It was said that the city supported its entire municipal infrastructure on parking fees and fines. Most meters allowed only one hour, and the surrounding residential streets allowed only permit parking for residents and were well policed, with fines over a hundred dollars for each infraction.

The doorbell was silent, and Dinah wondered for a minute if it had rung at all, but the big metal door eventually opened, and a girl as thin as a stick figure beckoned her in. She wore skintight pants and a skintight sweater, and her hair was cut skintight like a boy's, but she gave Dinah an unexpectedly warm welcoming smile, invited her to look around until Auralia could join her, and offered her coffee.

Dinah declined, and the girl retreated, leaving her alone in a big, open foyer with archways into galleries on both sides. Just over her head hung a large banner announcing THE NEW NOW: A FORWARD MARKET, and beyond that, on the back wall, was a spiral stairway of metal steps going up to the mezzanine. According to a standing sign at the bottom, that was where private collections were displayed for sale, including Dinah's "Southwest Ceramics and Basketry," a collection of export porcelain, and a group of Australian bark paintings.

But Dinah wanted to educate herself on forward markets, so she moved into the right-hand gallery, picking up a brochure at the entrance. A "forward market," not surprisingly, was just an opportunity to buy into a trend about to take off, to get in on the ground floor of a developing market. As for the "new now," said the brochure, it was "not just new, and not just now, but the next now, which will make the now now passé."

The first gallery had a display of "New Now Colors," described in the brochure as "color in its presence and color in its absence, so absent that the absence becomes a presence. It is the essence of color, in which the hues are a distillation of color."

She stopped first at a big canvas called *One Color*, a six-by-eight-foot rectangle of solid blue, undifferentiated in any way. It was paired with another, even larger canvas called *No Color*, which appeared to be an unpainted muslin canvas. A sign between the two directed the viewer's attention to the "absolute honesty of presentation, the noncommittal surfaces all the more compelling for their refusal to define themselves." There were a half dozen more in this series, but Dinah moved briskly, stopping only at *Two Colors* ("Between the yellow and the blue is great drama, a contrapuntal intensity") and *Dirt Color* ("A poetry of garden innocence, even primordial ooze").

Fascinated, Dinah moved eagerly into the next room, where the second exhibit of this forward market was titled "New Now Media." It was totally different. The room was filled with representational art, mostly portraits and sacred scenes, much of it as dark and crowded as Renaissance church art. Some were, in fact, copies of old paintings—a Last Supper, a Madonna and child that looked familiar to Dinah, a Henry VIII.

The difference was in the paint, literally. An explanatory placard heralded the "wholly realized integrity of a full commitment to the medium." The familiar figures at the long table in *The Last Supper* were done in chocolate syrup, all shades of tan and beige with heavy brown outlines. An Annunciation, although somewhat monochrome, was done in linseed oil and beeswax, slightly tinted. *The Washing of Christ* was almost luminous in creosote, a stunning Madonna was done in a combination of carrot and celeriac puree, and a rather out-of-place night sky reminiscent of van Gogh arched across a canvas done in mustard, eye shadow, and Pennzoil—"an intentional evocation of the tools and materials of other arts."

Dinah was standing five feet back from a large canvas slathered with Vaseline of a fairly even thickness, trying to see its "undisturbed serenity," when she felt a stir of motion and turned to see a figure taking a pose at the arch behind her. This was surely Auralia, draped in gray, a full-length swirl of several materials including floor-length satin and floating tulle. She had a cap of short, sleek hair and black-lined eyes in an otherwise pale complexion. Once seen, she glided forward on the hem of her dress and, drawing up next to Dinah, said of the artwork, "It's called *Nothingness.*"

"The artist's self-portrait, perhaps," Dinah murmured.

Auralia gave her a sharp look and a tight but not unfriendly smile. "*Doctora,*" she said, extending a long slim hand. "A pleasure."

Auralia had a distinct look of the exotic, but she was homegrown, an L.A. girl who had known Bonnie at Hamilton High School. From there Auralia had launched herself into a world beyond Bonnie, beyond Los Angeles, beyond the Mississippi, then the Atlantic, returning two decades later in an impermeable mantle of sophistication. She had made several marriages, each a little rise upward, and finally the jackpot—a Catalonian of vaguely noble birth, good connections to high society, an intact family fortune providing an adequate income, and great taste in art. He had died or disappeared in some other accommodating fashion, but not before Auralia had put on his knowledge with his power, coming home with the taste, the connections, and a fair chunk of the family fortune.

"Forgive the rush," Auralia said, gently taking Dinah's arm to guide her to a table and chairs behind the staircase. She didn't actually take Dinah's arm: She put her hand under Dinah's elbow, lightly touching it with her open palm, all the while speaking in a low voice, faintly accented by her precise way of sounding every letter.

She gestured Dinah into a leather-and-steel director's chair beside an old wood refectory table and seated herself in the armless chair behind it. "As soon as I saw your wonderful things," she said, drawing Dinah's folder out of a neat pile, "I had the perfect customer. I just knew he would like the collection. It goes with the rugs we bought him and the baskets he already has."

She took several printed contracts from the folder and spread them on the table facing Dinah. "He has a beautiful place," she went on, "exquisite taste. And I was right: He loved everything! But he's in a bit of a hurry . . ."

She picked up a pen and held it in the air over the papers. "I know this was done backward"—she smiled conspiratorially—"since you hadn't yet signed our agency agreement. But after checking with Bonnie, I went ahead, and we've already moved most of the collection." She handed Dinah the pen. "It's being installed as we speak, though technically, of course, it's still 'on approval.'"

"That's not a little irregular?" asked Dinah, holding the pen.

"What? The hurry?"

Dinah nodded.

"Not at all, *Doctora*," Auralia said soothingly. "We do a lot of business this way. It's coming up on the end of the fiscal year."

"What difference does that make?" asked Dinah, who knew about fiscal years and even predated contracts and art purchases but had no idea how it all tied together here.

Auralia shrugged elegantly and raised her hands in a gesture of *Who knows?*

"Conceivably, he could be slow to pay now," said Dinah more forcibly, "since he already has the goods, or he could skip out on paying entirely."

Auralia threw back her head and laughed merrily. "Hardly!" she said. "I do a lot of business with him and know him well. I know his business intimately." (Was there a wink?) "If I wanted, I could ruin him!"

She laughed again, cutting it off when she saw that Dinah was not laughing. "*Doctora*," she said, "I'm joking. Please don't concern yourself.

This is a very good customer. He never quibbles about price, and he always pays promptly."

She moved the papers infinitesimally closer to Dinah. "Now," she said, "to business. He will pay for everything in one single check. This is all right?"

"Of course," said Dinah, bending to the contract. "I assume you know his check is good?"

"My dear, it's drawn on his corporation. I'm not giving anything away—after all, you'll have the check—but it's Milo Till Properties & Development. Very big company, very solid."

Dinah's pulse skipped forward, her hand trembled, and she felt her heart beating in her throat. She kept her eyes on the pages before her.

"Ah," she said casually, still skimming the print, "so these works will be displayed publicly in his office?"

"His home, I believe," said Auralia. "But I don't get into that. I only arrange the sale."

Dinah looked up but said nothing. Auralia gazed back. A long silence. Finally Auralia said, quietly and with some care, "*Doctora.* Almost always we bill to the business. And we always deliver to the home. Any problem?"

Dinah signed the first page on the line marked. She turned over the page and moved on.

"No problem," she said, and signed the two remaining pages.

When Dinah stepped out of the gallery into the noon sun, there was more traffic on the street, and at the back bumper of her car there was a meter maid sitting on a three-wheeled motorcycle waiting for Dinah's meter to click into expiration. Quelling an instinctive twinge of anxiety, Dinah leaned over to check the meter. Four minutes left. She looked directly at the meter maid. The meter maid stared back.

Dinah got into the car and put her key in the ignition. In the rear-view mirror, she saw that the meter maid hadn't moved but sat like a vulture perched near its prey. Perversely, Dinah withdrew the key. She had a clear view of the meter and, with her watchbird watching her, watched it click down to three minutes, then two. Could the woman really think she'd let it expire before moving? When the readout changed to 1:00 and then 00:50 and 00:30 and 00:10, Dinah started the car, put on her turn signal, and pulled out. Feeling childish, she gave the meter maid a fingertip wave and drove off.

She had agreed to go back to the gallery after Thanksgiving to sign final papers. Till had requested a meeting with both buyer and seller present, because, said Auralia, he liked to get a look at the last owner involved. This was fine with Dinah, who was definitely curious, if not at all sure she could pull it off. Several times, as she drove through Beverly Hills and Westwood Village and up the canyon to Kat's house, she picked up her cell phone, wanting to call Polly, but each time she put it down. She would tell everyone at once about this unexpected development.

The women converged on Kat's house at one o'clock, bringing Kentucky Fried Chicken, extra crispy, Ben & Jerry's Cherry Garcia ice cream, and pecan sandies—all Kat's favorites. She had had her surgery early Thursday morning, was released to go home late that afternoon, and had been doing well ever since, according to Barnaby. Polly had spoken to Kat herself Friday evening, as had Dinah, and Kat had called Dinah twice more with questions about whether she could take an ibuprofen instead of the prescribed Vicodin and when she'd be able to wash her hair. Both times she was apologetic, but Dinah said, as always, that having a friend who was a doctor meant you never had to ask your dumb medical questions of people in authority.

Kat and Barnaby's high-tech contemporary house shone in the sun. It was several levels of glass brick and concrete with exposed steel beams, dramatically landscaped with plumes of pampas grass and purple-leaf smoke trees. It was on a precipitous lot, its only backyard a wide deck cantilevered over a lap pool dug into the hillside underneath.

A housekeeper let them in as they arrived and showed them upstairs to the master bedroom. Kat was stretched out on a chaise at the big wall of windows, Cleopatra on her barge with an ocean of sky beyond her. One by one they hugged her gingerly or patted her gently; bandaged on both sides, she couldn't lift her arms in response. She looked tired, her face gaunt, but kept assuring them she was in no pain.

"I don't sleep well, because every time I turn in my sleep," she explained, "I pull at something. I'm just so happy to see you all," and she smiled tremulously, which seemed unlike Kat. She turned to Dinah. "What's with you and the Armani?" she asked, leaning her head forward to eye Dinah's eggplant-colored pantsuit. "It's Saturday."

"Later," said Dinah. "I want to hear how you're feeling."

For the next half hour, they sat in a semicircle around Kat's chaise, eating messy food on big paper plates that Justine had brought with the bucket of chicken and talking about hospitals, doctors, and Kat's plans after recovery. She was very pleased with her surgeon—a woman in her thirties who was an associate in the particular practice and at the last moment had substituted for Kat's plastic surgeon.

"We didn't know until we got to the hospital," said Kat. "Apparently Dr. Terschel had an emergency: Somebody 'came apart,' they said, and I'm not making that up. That's what they said. We could have insisted on rescheduling, but I'd met Dr. Caen and liked her, and she asked if we were comfortable switching on a dime, and I said, 'Yes, this is an emergency now, too,' and she said she understood. That when you've made up your mind and you're ready to go, you don't want anything to stop you. Particularly with something like this, which is an emotional decision rather than a medical one."

While she was speaking, Barnaby came into the room with their daughter, T.J. Blond like Kat, she was two and a half, hid behind him while being introduced, and was happy to go off with the au pair girl after patting her mother a few times on the lower leg.

"You okay?" Barnaby asked Kat, and then turned to the other women. "I wasn't totally in favor of this, you know."

There was an uneasy silence. "You didn't want her to do it?" asked Polly.

"No, not that," said Barnaby. "It's just that any time you have an anesthetic, there's some danger involved. Isn't that right, Doctor?" he asked Dinah.

"Of course," said Dinah, visibly relieved. "For a minute I thought you meant you wanted her to keep the boobs."

Barnaby stood utterly relaxed at the side of the chaise, pleating the fabric of Kat's sleeve with his fingertips. "Well, she kept asking me, and I kept trying to remember if that had been something I noticed about her first off. In a way, yes," he said, watching their reaction, "but I was impressed by her pectorals, not her breasts."

Enjoying their laughter, he added, "Guess I'm a trainer to the core."

When Barnaby left them alone again, after cleaning up around Kat and taking away a bag of trash, Dinah said that she had visited the gallery that morning and it appeared that her whole collection was indeed sold. Humorously, and taking her time, she described the gallery and its current exhibitions, then Auralia and her handling of the sale. "She admitted it was kind of ass-backwards," said Dinah, "because the usual procedure is that seller and agent contract to work together and only then the agent puts the stuff up for sale."

Her friends were clearly waiting for her to finish or move on to something more interesting, but Dinah continued at the same leisurely pace. "She had a feeling this one customer would want it all, and she was right, and there was this big hurry because the guy buying it has to buy before the end of the fiscal year, or so she said."

Dinah smoothed her sleeve, inspecting an invisible spot at the wrist.

She sensed Charlotte shifting in her seat as she added, "Apparently that's what he always does."

"So?" Charlotte prodded. They were not used to such verbosity from Dinah. Polly was tapping a foot on the floor, and Kat's eyes were closed.

"It's very interesting," said Dinah. "She says the collection's going to his home, but his corporation pays for it, and it's probably taken as some kind of a business deduction. So—"

"Dinah," Polly cut in. "Why are you going on about this?"

"Because the guy is Milo Till," Dinah said.

There was a collective breath, and then Justine exhaled, "Oh, boy."

"My God," said Charlotte.

"No shit?" said Polly, grabbing at Dinah's upper arm.

Kat had flashed awake and was leaning forward as well as she could, holding her arms close to her sides, eyes dancing.

"This is interesting, right?" said Dinah, looking at them sideways and laughing.

"'Interesting' is not the word." Polly released Dinah's arm and threw herself back against her chair. "I smell blood. Remember Leona Helmsley?"

"She charged all her household linens to one of her hotels," said Kat.

"More than that," said Polly. "She went to jail for tax evasion because of all the personal stuff—art, clothes, home improvements—that their hotel business paid for. Sound familiar? Bill the corporation? Deliver to the house? Dinah, you're too much."

"This is good, really good," said Charlotte, and turned to Justine. "Can we talk to your tax guy? Soon?"

There was a final flurry of discussion and planning. They wanted to be careful not to spend all their time on a single lead, however promising, that could well fall apart. Charlotte said she'd continue plowing through court cases, particularly those in tax court. "But those," she said, "are so arcane—interpretations of capital gains and questions of tax-shelter status—and this . . . this . . ."—she stammered in her enthusiasm—"this is seminal."

"I'm not dropping the blind trusts either," said Justine, "and I still have calls in to some lenders about construction loans. But I must say I like tax fraud better."

"Ah," said Polly happily. "Who wouldn't?"

23

There was no meeting the next Monday, because Lotte was spending the Thanksgiving week with family in Canada. Everyone was just as glad, what with Kat out of commission and all with holiday plans of their own. Dinah was flying east on Wednesday. Polly spent Thanksgiving and most other holidays with Dan's family. Charlotte and Avery were going to her mother's in San Francisco. Kat expected Barnaby's family from Riverside, and Justine was having everyone at her house, including her own parents, who lived in Utah.

Justine, however, was imbued with a new purpose and energy since the night of Reinhart's death, and first thing Monday morning she called her source at the IRS. And that night she called Polly to see if they could visit him together that Tuesday.

At twenty minutes before seven on Tuesday morning, Polly opened her front door to pick up the newspaper and found Graham Vere sitting on her front step. Instinctively, she grabbed at the ties of her bathrobe, already laughing, because as the door opened he stuffed the folded paper in his mouth and lifted his chin to offer it to her.

"What are you doing here?" she said.

He handed up the newspaper, patting the step next to him. "I missed you," he said.

"We practically spent the weekend together." She made a clumsy attempt to gather the terry-cloth robe under her thighs and over her knees while lowering herself to ground level. "At least the evenings."

"I know," he said, "and it spoiled me for separation. Then I talked to you last night, and I realized that what with Thanksgiving and you going to Dan's family and my taking the boys to San Diego, I wouldn't be seeing you for most of this week. Esperanza took the boys to school this morning, so I got the good idea of stopping by on my way over the hill to work today." He took her hand from her lap. "Was it a good idea?"

"It was," she said. "I don't leave till twenty to eight, and the kids don't eat breakfast anyway. At least nothing of my fixing. Jeremy eats cereal, and Andrea drinks some veggie-fruit sludge the color of sinus drip."

"Nice," he said. "You do have a turn of phrase." He bent each of her fingers back and forth. "You sure you have time for me? It won't make you late?"

Polly readjusted the knot on her bathrobe ties. "I can go as I am. The only person I care about seeing me this way is you, and it's already too late."

For a quarter of an hour, they sat outside together. Mostly they just listened to the few birds still in the canyon and the increasing noise of the city and talked a bit about their plans for the weekend.

"I'd ask you in for coffee," said Polly, "but the kids would probably think you'd spent the night."

"Not a bad idea," he said. "Would they mind?"

"I don't know," said Polly. "Being kids, they probably don't think about us one way or the other. I suspect they'd be shocked. In any case, I'm not ready to handle that."

"Handle what? The staying over or the kids being shocked?"

"Either. Both," said Polly, and they sat another five minutes, fingers laced together.

"Well, time to go," said Vere, getting himself up and putting out a hand to help Polly. "Talk to you tonight," and he kissed her on the cheek, patted her head none too gently, and headed down the path to his parked car.

"Bye, Graham," came Andrea's voice from an upper window.

Vere waved his hand toward the voice and looked at Polly, who backed against the front door and covered her face with her hands. He took a step toward her. "Did that sound like shock?" he said.

"Oh, God, they probably think you did stay last night." Surprisingly, her face was suddenly hot, and she knew she was blushing.

"Might as well, then, next time," he said happily, clicked the remote opener at his car, and, with another wave, got in and drove off.

Polly drove downtown to Justine's office, but they took Justine's Taurus to their appointment with her friend at the IRS. He was a special agent in the elite division that investigated criminal fraud—an activity sensitive enough to be housed in a separate building out in Alhambra, ten miles east of the downtown headquarters and nowhere near any other IRS office. He had warned Justine that it was an unmarked building with tight security, that he'd leave her name at the guard station, and that both of them would be asked for a picture ID, home addresses, and telephone numbers.

It was a half-hour trip through continuous city, part freeway, part surface streets. Technically Alhambra was a suburb, but a suburb thick with factories and offices, many of them divisions of corporations and government bureaus that maintained downtown headquarters but moved their backroom work—accounting, technology, personnel—to low-rent places like Alhambra.

They drove in silence as Justine threaded her way through city streets to a chosen freeway on-ramp, then negotiated two freeway changes in quick succession. When they were finally on the one that would take them to Alhambra, Polly asked, "What did you tell this guy?"

"Nothing specific," said Justine. "Just that we needed information about tax fraud—what constitutes fraud, how they find it, how they prove it."

"Won't he suspect something?"

"Suspect what?" said Justine, giving Polly a quick sideways look. "That we're planning to commit a fraud? That I'm hoping he'll teach us how?"

"No, that we already have something."

"All the better," said Justine. "Listen, he's known me a long time. He's probably already preparing some clips and publications on tax fraud for us."

Justine was a surprisingly fast driver for a cautious person. She moved into the fast lanes swiftly, held her place, and didn't like being passed, but had a professional's grace about waving people in if they signaled a wish to change lanes in front of her.

"What do you expect here?" she asked Polly. "No, really," she pressed when Polly didn't answer right away. "How do you picture this man?"

Polly was startled; Justine was not normally playful. "Thin, not very tall. Unsmiling, wire-rimmed glasses," she said, watching Justine's reaction. "Vinyl sleeve guards. All business, maybe mean."

"Not mean," Justine said. "Everything else, but not mean. He's a sweet and very gentle person. Not a close friend, but we worked together for some years at the assessor's office, and I know him pretty well."

It was a warning, Polly thought, that she shouldn't be put off by how he presented himself. More important, she shouldn't say anything against him.

"Ray is quiet," said Justine, "but I always found him interesting." He was a math major in college, she explained, planning to be a teacher until he realized that he had no interest in students and didn't really like theoretical math. What he loved was arithmetic, basic calculating. He thought of becoming an accountant but instead, on impulse, took the civil-service exam and was hired by the assessor. There he worked in several areas—from reassessments to demographic statistics—until one day, again on impulse, he answered an H&R Block ad for seasonal tax workers and moonlighted in one of their branches for several months. "It was the perfect fit," said Justine, "so, with my blessing, he went to the IRS as an auditor. It's worked out very well, I think."

She smiled. "Ray's kind of IRS-y," she said, and when Polly just looked at her inquiringly, added, "You'll see what I mean."

They had left the freeway and were moving up through Alhambra on a central boulevard. In the distance they could see the rise of the foothills above Pasadena. Then Justine turned east onto a street that for blocks ahead was all low, spread-out office buildings, some identified by signs and many more unmarked. She swung left into one of the nameless gates and stopped at the guard station to identify herself. The building was undistinguished—three stories of flat gray siding and long windows with metal awnings, a parking lot in front and chain-link fencing all around the property.

There was no lobby to speak of, just a stretch of speckled linoleum with elevators on one wall and a single bulletin board of flyers, announcements, and official notices with a cartoon of Uncle Sam at the top. A long table served as another guard station, where Justine and Polly again showed their photo IDs and opened their purses and Justine's briefcase while the guard called Justine's friend Ray to come down and get them.

Ray was indeed thin and taller than most Asian men, but shorter than Polly. Behind his wire-rimmed glasses, his eyes were serious, but he greeted Justine warmly and gave her a one-armed hug as he guided them to the elevator. On the way up to the third floor, he asked after her two boys, told her about his wife's thriving College Board tutoring business and his daughter's computer-science courses at Cal Poly San Luis Obispo, and told Polly several times how glad he was to see Justine, whatever had brought them here.

The elevator opened on the long side of a huge room of work pods, each a circle with a column of conduits at its center and four wedge-shaped cubicles. Shoulder-high partitions separated the occupants, and glass offices lined all four sides, the light from the windows visible behind the vertical blinds.

Ray led them around the perimeter to one of these outside offices. Just as he was opening his office door for them, a man jumped up from behind a nearby partition, pumped the air with his fists, and over the noise of voices and keyboards, exclaimed, "Got one!"

"Awright!" "Yes!" and "Way to go!" came from other cubicles, but the jumper had caught sight of Ray's guests, reddened, and sat back down. Ray, equally embarrassed, pushed Justine and Polly through the door and closed it after them.

It was an extraordinary little office, a secret garden in a landscape of institutional drab. Ray's desk faced the door, and behind it three long shelves of plants crossed the broad window, set on brackets on the sides. There were ferns, flowery plants, plants with variegated leaves, plants with runners that dripped over their pots and down to the sill. Ficus plants five feet tall grew in wooden boxes at the corners of the room. Flanking the window were big ceramic pots of vines, staked to the sill, then anchored to the wall every foot up to the top of the window, where they turned in and met in the middle, the white blossoms of one twisting with the yellow of the other. Next to Ray's desk were more shelves, holding tiny bonsai—miniature pines and lacy cedars in stiff little poses.

Overcome, Polly and Justine sat in his two visitor chairs, looking from place to place and pot to pot. Ray turned up the cuffs of his plaid cotton shirt—one turn, very neat—and slightly loosened his knit tie.

"I hope you had no trouble finding the place," he said. "We don't invite many people to these offices, certainly not taxpayers. We prefer to go to them. Actually, most of our public contact—even audits—is by mail or phone, and this floor in particular stays fairly remote. It's all revenue officers, who pursue delinquent accounts, and special agents, like me, who investigate criminal fraud."

"What do you have against taxpayers?" asked Polly, not sure how light one could be with this man.

Ray put the tips of his fingers together. "The taxpayer is an unknown quantity," he said carefully, "and sometimes dangerous. They all know we're after their money." He made a tight little smile. "There've been a number of assaults—auditors getting punched out in office exams, even a couple of agents kidnapped. We understand that their beef is with the tax laws and not the employees, but we have to be careful."

"You just let me know any time you want to come back to the assessor," said Justine, getting up to go behind Ray's desk and examine the plants in the window.

"Actually," said Ray, "by the time Criminal Investigation gets a case, we're dealing with the taxpayer's lawyers and accountants. It's the most serious level."

Justine, who knew more about the dangers of government work than Polly, was absorbed in close inspection of the plants. She deadheaded some African violets on the lowest shelf, then tamped down the moss around an oncidium that was just opening its tiny burgundy blossoms.

Ray watched her, smiling, then turned to Polly. "Did you know that Justine is an expert on plants and gardening?" he asked.

"I did indeed," said Polly.

"I owe my job to Justine," he said. "Both jobs, actually—at the assessor's office and here with Uncle."

Justine was back in her seat and listening, one hand exploring the bonsai near her, turning the little plants from side to side to see their shapes. Occasionally she pinched off a minute bundle of needles or a leaf, turned the plant again and narrowed her eyes to check the barely discernible result.

Ray put his hands down flat on the desk. "Now," he said, "all I know is you're interested in how we recognize and prove tax cheating. Would a little background be helpful?"

They nodded.

"Okay," he said. "First, I assume we're not talking about a tax protester. You know what that is?"

"Sure," said Polly. "A nut who refuses to pay taxes because it's forbidden by the Constitution or by his church or by God Himself."

Ray's lips turned up at the corners. "Right. So we're talking about tax *cheats*. For starters, there are many degrees of malfeasance and many levels of punishment. Everyone cheats a little. Maybe people make some unreported cash sales or underestimate their tip income. More often, they overestimate their charitable donations or deduct a business dinner someone else paid for. They're not really criminals, just a bit 'aggressive,' shall we say, in their claims.

"Actually, unreported income is not an option for most people, whose salary information goes to the IRS on W-2s, or self-employed people whose nonwage earnings are reported on 1099s. Our job is to get the guys whose businesses can take in a lot below the radar and who are intent on not reporting it. We often find a telling gap between the income they report and the 'economic reality' of their lives—DMV records of fancy cars, expensive real estate, high interest reported on savings they should be unable to amass. Cheating on deductions is easier to police. We just ask for proof. No proof, no deduction."

The women nodded in unison. Ray was not at all boring, but he was so deliberate in his presentation that Polly kept thinking she was supposed to take notes.

"The really big deal is suspected fraud, on either income or deductions," Ray continued. "Unlike other audits, we have no time limit on investigating fraud, and there are big penalties—fines up to seventy-five percent of the tax due and maybe jail. We're not talking simple error here, or negligence, or even aggressive interpretation of the code. Criminal fraud involves a 'degree of bad purpose.'"

"Like prostitution rings and narcotics deals," said Justine.

"Yes, but not only those," said Ray. "It's also money laundering and fake tax shelters. It's the Maryland dentist who filed no returns on a million dollars earned over three years, which he spent on two boats and a plane. It's the fake religious order in New York whose members took vows of poverty but worked in outside jobs and turned their paychecks over to the order in return for cash 'living expenses.' It's the rich guy who claimed a big theft loss on a Picasso we proved had never existed."

He paused, saw both women looking at him intently, and went on. "What makes something fraud is the proof of intent. You see bank deposits way beyond reported income. You find two sets of books. You're not just looking at a five-thousand-dollar charitable deduction on a portrait worth only twenty-five hundred dollars. You see that the people actually got an appraisal of twenty-five hundred and they still declared a deduction of five thousand."

"And these are the cases you turn into headliners," said Polly, "like Leona Helmsley buying fancy linens for her home and deducting them as business expenses for her hotels?"

"That was a fraud case, yes," Ray said, rearranging the pencils on his desk, "and yes, we may publicize such celebrity contests, not just as an object lesson but to tell Joe Taxpayer that we're not only after the little guys but take on the big names as well."

Polly and Justine must have indicated heightened interest by breath or posture because Ray went on, "You want to go into Helmsley some more?"

"Please," said Justine. "We're particularly interested in things bought for personal use and charged to a business. Like the Helmsley case."

"Okay," said Ray, "but bear this in mind: We don't necessarily care if things are bought through a corporation for an executive's personal use. That's an offense to the stockholders, and the concern of the SEC. It's when the executive fails to report it as income that the IRS gets involved. Leona Helmsley charged several million dollars of goods and services to her hotels when she was decorating her own mansion—like a one-hundred-thirty-thousand-dollar indoor-outdoor stereo system, I recall, that they reported as security equipment for one of their hotels. The corporation got business deductions and the Helmsleys got the equivalent of undeclared income. So we went after her."

"She was convicted?" asked Justine.

He nodded. "She got four years for tax evasion, for paying no taxes on some four million dollars of income—the value of all the goods they'd put on the corporate books."

"How did they catch her?" asked Polly.

"An inside tip," he said. "Unless our people find something wrong in a return, it's almost always an inside tip, maybe a disgruntled employee or business associate. Sometimes it's just a tip for us to pursue. Sometimes the informant has done a lot of our work for us, but we still have to prove it."

Neither Polly nor Justine was sure how much to ask at this point. Justine looked at a plant on the desk in front of her. Polly looked at Ray, whose expression behind his glasses became expectant, even encouraging.

"So tell me," he said finally, fingertips together, "what are we looking for here? Or, more specifically, what are you already looking at?"

"It may be the same kind of fraud," said Polly slowly. "Where people buy things for themselves but their company pays, pretending it's for business."

"Okay," he said briskly, "here's what you need. Take Helmsley, where it had to be shown that the goods went into their personal residence but were specifically listed as business deductions on the corporate returns. You need both halves: first, that the corporation paid and deducted the items as business purchases and, second, that the use was actually personal."

"In either order?" asked Polly.

"Either way," he said. "But both demonstrable." He saw the women nodding—Justine slowly, thoughtfully, Polly more vigorously. "So is this what you wanted?"

"You've been wonderful," said Justine. "You're the clearest person I ever worked with, and you've been most generous with your time. But your African violets need some attention," and she rose to leave.

He came around his desk, shook Polly's hand, then took both of Justine's hands in his before moving to the door. "One more thing," he said, reaching for the door handle. "If you do have something, or someone, you'd like to bring to our attention, let me know and either I'll have someone contact you or I'll submit the tip myself. In any case, you will remain anonymous. We're extremely careful about that."

When Justine got home, Robby was already there, having picked up the boys and taken them to soccer practice. He was an active participant in the family schedule, readily stepping in when an activity was clearly in the fatherly sphere—the boys' sports, a home building project, or preparation for a trip. Justine couldn't hold it against him that he didn't count in grocery shopping, meal planning, or kitchen work; his mother had always accepted a "woman's role" quietly. Similarly, he was only emulating his father in keeping a firm grip on the checkbook and the banking and household finances, though Robby had a wife whose professional life suggested her own financial proficiency.

What's more, that wife at least superficially accepted this division of roles without question, and whose fault was that? Her own, she often told herself, even though she knew that both the question and the answer were overly simplistic.

The boys were upstairs, probably doing homework, and Robby, in stocking feet, came from his office at the back of the house. He was almost at the front door when she came in, struggling with her briefcase, her shoulder bag, and two sacks of groceries.

"How come so late?" Robby asked, but Justine barely heard him. All afternoon at her desk, elements of the IRS visit played in her head like background music. She took pleasure and some personal pride in the flourishing of both Ray's plants and Ray's professional life and, methodically, was already breaking down the investigation of Milo Till into workable parts. Given Ray's directive on the required two-sided proof of a tax fraud, she was reviewing what they had and what they needed and how to get it.

"Take these, please," she said, moving the arm with the grocery bags toward Robby. He reached instead for her briefcase, which she'd tucked under her other arm.

"No," she said sharply, "the bags," and as he relieved her of them, she marched past and through the dining room to the kitchen.

"Matt's in the starting lineup for Saturday's game," said Robby, leaning against the kitchen counter on which he'd set the bags.

"That's wonderful," said Justine. "He thought he didn't have a chance." Nudging Robby aside, she began to remove the plastic boxes of chicken enchiladas and the big quart container of Mexican rice from a bag. "Would you please break up the lettuce and slice tomatoes for a salad?" and she tipped the cutting board forward from its place at the back of the counter and reached up into the cabinet for the salad bowl.

Robby looked down at the cutting board and then at her. Justine tapped the board lightly, for emphasis, and turned away to get an oven dish for the enchiladas. When she looked back, Robby was gingerly taking items one by one from the second bag and, shortly thereafter, was holding the tomatoes and lettuce, both whole, under running water.

"How did Philip do in the practice?" she asked, working beside him companionably. They chatted. She arranged food in an oven dish; he sliced the tomatoes and then, after a brief consideration of its size and shape, the head of lettuce.

Justine, looking sideways, felt almost gleeful. Way to go, she thought, and then, oddly, flashed back to Ray's office, Ray's plants. All this time, she thought, she'd acquiesced to living with a bonsai husband, even maintaining him as a bonsai, when she should have been forcing some growth. She was very pleased with her little analogy.

They prepared the whole meal together, simple as it was, talking about family activities and plans, like every other couple, or at least the other couples in Justine's imagination. Robby was a beginner, of course, and his lettuce was poorly washed, his tomato pieces raggedy, but Justine let it pass.

"You know," she injected when they had everything ready and were setting the table, "I'd like to do more with the business, finding new products and new suppliers. I could help get us more into consulting with both contractors and their customers."

"We're doing pretty well," Robby said, without looking up.

"I know," she said. "You've done wonderfully since you took over the business. I'd just like to take more of a part in it."

At first she thought he wasn't going to answer. Then he said, "Would you want to give up doing the accounts?"

"Of course not," said Justine. "We wouldn't want to change that at this point. But I'd probably leave the tax assessor's office after a while."

"That's fine. We don't really need the extra money," said Robby, as if that was the crux of the matter, and he went to call the boys down for supper.

Standing at the table, salad bowl in her arms, Justine realized that Robby had never been one to examine life much, never wondered why people, himself included, behaved as they did. Oddly, it was one of the characteristics that had attracted her to him: She had seen it as decisiveness rather than rigidity, and even as she came to realize that he instinctively resisted change, she had never wondered why. Perhaps it involved his place in his family, she thought now, the need to explain everything he did, the risk of being called on the carpet like a child. The question could certainly use some probing, but it wasn't about her, and her own life was her immediate concern.

When dinner was over and the boys went upstairs, Robby returned to his desk in the den with Justine following behind him. "You know," she said from the doorway, "Ken Morrison's landscape company got the contract for that new town-house complex near the airport, and I thought I'd talk with him about providing the plantings."

Robby was facing her, tipped back in the big chair, but before he could answer, Justine hurried on. "And I'd like to go see that tree farm in Camarillo that has all the exotics and tropicals. We've never dealt with them, and their stuff is good. Can you take the time to come with me this week?"

Swiveling his chair back toward the desk, Robby reached for the computer keyboard. "It's in your hands," he said managerially.

Maybe it always was, thought Justine, but all she said was "Good," and returned to the kitchen happily.

24

Polly went to the next Monday's meeting late and morose, unaccountably depressed since the previous evening, when Graham Vere came back from San Diego and immediately drove over the hill to see her. At first she was pleased, having felt his absence more than she'd expected, although he'd called her on three of the four nights he was gone. And she was thrilled when he suggested that for the Christmas holiday they send the children to their respective grandparents a couple of days ahead and spend some time alone together before joining them.

Later, however, a wisp of self-contempt crept into her joy and grew into a full despair over the fact that she was so affected by his suggestion, his eagerness, his very presence. She picked at it, trying to understand her reaction, her feeling of being controlled. The more he was attentive, the more he took over, the more he made her dependent on him. But even as she inspected the thought, she knew there was something wrong with it.

The problem isn't him. The problem is you, her mother said, with unmistakable scorn, and left it at that.

As Polly told the group when she slouched in and was asked to explain her sour mien, the whole thing made her feel very shallow, "like all I needed was a good man."

"Well," said Lotte, "the premise of this group was that everyone felt a need for change. What did you think you needed?"

"I don't know," said Polly. "I was doing really well, but sometimes I just felt isolated, like everyone had died and left me alone."

"I hope you weren't thinking we'd bring them back," said Charlotte.

Dinah gave Charlotte a sharp look. "In fact," she said to Polly, "you were doing well, at least with the grief, and you were certainly independent and successful."

Lotte pushed slightly back from the table—a professional's "distancing" technique, no doubt—and was nodding proudly, as if she'd trained them in her methodology. From the outset this group had been more self-directed than most, and she had chosen to run it with a minimum of control, realizing that much of its success came from the participants' own growing strength. Still, she liked to think she had contributed.

"Well, okay," said Polly. "I just feel shallow. Maybe it's even simpler. Maybe I feel guilty about being in love. If that's what I am."

"It's not shallow," said Justine gently. "It's just that sometimes things get better unexpectedly, which makes us suspicious. You were so competent even in distress that you probably thought you weren't allowed to be lonely."

Everyone looked at Justine, who was normally not inclined to such analysis. They seemed to be waiting for her to continue, so she did. "Sometimes our problems are so entrenched that we assume the solution will be very complicated, when it may be quite simple."

"For instance?" prodded Lotte, understanding that Justine wasn't commenting only on Polly's situation.

So Justine told them about her Thanksgiving dinner. She described the company—Robby's whole family plus her visiting parents and her brother's family up from Orange County—and the meal, a combination of traditional Thanksgiving dishes and Japanese foods. And she told how everyone lingered, uncomfortably full, and how in a lull Robby slapped his hands on the table and announced, "I've been thinking about what Justine said, about providing consulting services for contractors and their customers together. I've wanted Justine to be more a part of the business for a long time, and this interests her, so I'd like her to come in and develop this for us."

Everyone was stunned, said Justine. Everyone but Robby's mother, who listened without reacting, then broke the silence. "Good move," she said firmly, which meant, said Justine, that the decision was final.

She couldn't tell them more, because nothing more had been discussed. She couldn't continue anyway, because just then there was a heavy clumping up the stairs, shaking the second floor even more than usual. With a quick intake of breath, Dinah grabbed the arms of her chair as Justine reached out to her across the end of the table. Everyone, Dinah included, knew immediately that it was only someone coming, and indeed the door opened and there was Kat, striking a pose in the door frame.

She looked big, freshly blond, and healthy, though she wore a loose T-shirt and kept her upper arms close to her sides. They all rose to greet her, and Lotte gave her a gentle embrace around the shoulders as Kat slid by to her window seat.

"It's like a triumphal return," she exclaimed. "You'd think I'd done something . . . besides survive and come out flatter."

"We can't really tell," said Charlotte, "until you go back to your usual revealing outfits."

Kat was good-natured under teasing, but obviously impatient. Tempering her upper-body movement, she was shifting her weight on the seat of the chair, and her answers were curt. "I don't want to talk about how I look. I need to discuss what I'm going to do with it, okay?"

"I thought you wanted to get back to running," said Polly, "now that you can run without the bounce."

"But not competitively," said Kat. "I'm too old for that."

What she did want, she continued, before anyone could jump in with a comment, was to explore a suggestion from the young doctor who'd operated on her. Dr. Caen had been intrigued to learn that Kat felt her implants had transformed a highly functional body into a pinup. She had seen the same dichotomy in her volunteer work with teenage girls at community centers and high schools. Whatever their socioeconomic background or athletic ability, all the girls were unhappy and obsessed with their looks.

"We both thought it's too bad," said Kat, "that their self-esteem depends on how they look rather than how their bodies work. Popularity gets less important, but your body has to carry you through life, and how you use it should determine how you feel about it."

The upshot was that Kat, whose body had literally been her life, was going to talk to these teens, she said. Her announcement drew immediate interest and encouragement, while Kat looked from one to the other, obviously pleased.

Soon after, Lotte rose to leave, and after the usual collective pause Polly said, "Okay, it's Milo Till time. Justine and I have quite a lot on tax cheating, so we should cover everything else first."

"That's mostly me," said Charlotte, "and what I have is a bunch of complex activities, which are either already public or so complex they'll never make a public stir, because nobody can understand them." She had first called up the lawsuits over Till's construction loans, one now winding its way through court dates, the other a "copycat filing" in its early stages. Both were filed by lenders who had taken over failed developments, only to find that Till's appraisals and estimated costs, and thus the amounts they'd lent him, were grossly inflated.

But those cases, she concluded, had already been reported, then neatly explained away by Till's lawyers and public relations people. There was nothing new to uncover.

As for the blind trusts that Till managed, Charlotte, working online with Justine's guidance, had followed several from the moment Milo Till took over the assets, converting everything that wasn't already land into land investments. She traced them from one title to another, sometimes through multiple transactions, moving through the records of several states and counties as the acreages were traded or annexed to others.

"Basically, he turns dirt into gold," said Charlotte. For one California senator, as an example, Till had taken over a six-hundred-acre parcel of undeveloped land worth only $180,000, or $300 an acre, divided it into thirty twenty-acre "ranchettes," put them on the market for $140,000 apiece, and quickly sold all of them to the man's friends and supporters, who had already donated the legal maximum to his campaigns. This gave him, legally, another $4 million.

"That was a typical arrangement," said Charlotte, sitting back and running both hands through her short hair. "He's really a genius." At that she noticed that not a single face in her audience showed any response. Indeed, they seemed unaware that she had reached a conclusion. "It's a little hard to explain," she conceded.

"It's a little boring," said Kat.

"We're not in this for our amusement," Charlotte snapped back.

"Children, children," Polly interjected in a soothing voice. "I get it now. The problem with the construction-loan gambit is that it's a scam that's already been outed."

"And the problem with the blind trusts," said Justine, with a smile to Charlotte, "is that it is very hard to follow. I've covered just a few of the same steps as Charlotte, and it's incredibly time-consuming."

"More important, it's probably not illegal," sighed Charlotte, "or someone would have jumped on it by now. It may be veiled, but it's not really hidden."

There was a lot of shifting in seats. Kat rose with some difficulty, gingerly pushing off against the chair arms, and began her usual table rounding. Charlotte closed her leather notebook.

"Now, then," said Polly. "Let's talk about the IRS."

There was a little stir, a rise in the flagging attention.

"If it turns out that Milo Till is buying Dinah's art for his personal digs but charging it to his corporation as a business deduction," said Polly, "we may have something to work with. You're sure that's the plan, Dinah?"

Dinah shrugged. "Aurora, or Auralia—whatever—definitely said that with Till, like many of her clients, the goods are paid for by the corporation but delivered to the individual. And he was so anxious to do it within the fiscal year ending November thirtieth that it must be a deduction."

"This is good!" exclaimed Polly. "And it might fit what Justine's tax guy told us."

Justine nodded, and Kat sat down again. "Remember at Kat's house when Dinah dropped her little bomb and someone mentioned the Leona Helmsley case?"

"That was you," Dinah said.

"Right. Well, according to Ray, what they did was criminal fraud—charging personal purchases to their hotel properties, then deducting them as business expenses." With some relish, Polly told the Helmsley story in greater detail—from the half million dollars they spent on jade objects for their mansion to the dinner dresses that Leona reported as hotel uniforms. And ended with the fact that in 1989 the Helmsleys were found guilty of tax evasion, were fined, and Leona "got four years in the slammer."

Her summary precipitated some exuberant comparisons to Milo Till, as the women realized what they might have. It was Justine who broke in. "We have to be very careful," she cautioned. "It's a simple idea but a difficult proof. Ray said two conditions must be satisfied conclusively. First, we have to be absolutely sure that Till is keeping Dinah's artworks for himself. He could be moving them into his office or some other property."

So not only did they have to know exactly where everything went, but they had to see it there themselves. Somebody had to get into his apartment, his personal office, his office suite, even his model homes, if necessary.

Second, Justine said, they had to know not only that the corporation paid the bill but that the expenditure became a corporate business deduction. Otherwise it was conceivable that Till made his corporation pay for his art but was properly reporting it as personal income.

"Sure, and I'll sell you a bridge *and* a sports club," scoffed Kat. "Once we know he's keeping it himself, why can't we just tip off the IRS and let them go see if the company's claimed it?"

"Because it's our project," said Polly. "We have to have everything, all the facts, before we turn it over to the government, or it's not ours. Isn't it the whole point that *we* get the guy?"

At this moment they didn't know quite how to manage either side of the proof. They already knew, through Charlotte, that Avery Feinman's accounting firm handled Till's corporation but maybe not Till himself. And Charlotte had already told them, mournfully, that Avery would be unlikely to give them any help, even if she asked. But there was a little current of excitement about this possibility. It seemed, in Polly's word, "do-able," and on their scale, involving as it did a personal, private, and petty kind of malfeasance.

The more they considered it, as the sky darkened outside the big window and the silhouettes of nearby trees melted into the background, the more it seemed philosophically right: If they took everything they'd done so far as a continuum, it fit. They had had a politician destroyed by public opinion. They'd had some hand, if unintentional, in the perfect murder of a husband-serving divorce lawyer by his trophy wife. They wanted very much to see a cunning and manipulative empire builder punished by a government bureau he'd made a career out of manipulating. Maybe the treasury codes he'd diddled with for so long could finally get him in return, thanks to a few baskets and figurines.

"Little stuff, but telling," said Polly with satisfaction. "Definitely do-able."

Charlotte's house looked dark from the street, but when she pulled up the driveway, she saw that the kitchen and back-door lights were on. As she walked in, she knew immediately that Avery was in the room behind his office, where he kept his wines. She could hear the opening and closing of the slanted drawers that held the smaller bottles and assumed that an order had just come in and he was cataloging the wines by name, vintage, origin, date of purchase, and price.

Avery was a serious foodie and a committed wine buff, the result, Charlotte surmised, of a background he described as limited—not poor, just "limited." His mother was an optician for one of the first discount-eyeglass stores. His father was a sales representative for a suit manufacturer. Neither was interested in food or wine or any nicety of life except education, and that they stressed vehemently, bringing up all three of their children under the dictum that school ended with a professional degree.

Charlotte herself had no great interest in what she ate but would eat almost anything. Food appealed to her only for the company that gathered to eat it. Wine appealed even less. At first she was tolerant when Avery started getting interested in wine. She made fun of it, but in a good-natured way, and Avery responded in kind. Back then—was it ten or fifteen years ago?—he used to say mildly, "A man needs a hobby," and, after a pause, added, "Beats chasing girls."

In time, however, she became less tolerant, and when she made fun of him, it was no longer funny. Fascination with food led to convivial dinners with friends, but wine had a solitary side. Avery organized his wine collection by country and type, keeping careful records—*F* for France, *G* for Germany, *US* for America, and so forth. He numbered the bottles as they were purchased, assigning odd numbers to the whites and evens to the reds, marking them by their age as well—not the age of the wine but the expected age of its readiness for drinking. For the first few years, Avery had also put a colored dot on the cork end, indicating when to open the bottle, but even he found the dot system impossible to keep up and abandoned it.

Now Charlotte went through the kitchen and his office, pausing to knock at the door of the wine room in case he had the refrigerator open: He was fussy about the temperature, keeping his reds at sixty degrees, the whites and champagnes at or below fifty.

"Come on in," he said, and looked up as she entered, the overhead track lights illuminating his face in sharp lines and hollows. "Hey," he greeted her. He was poised on a stool at the high worktable, a barlike expanse of wood framed in metal. Above his head dozens of glasses hung by their stems from a ceiling rack, and to the side was a row of old oak catalog drawers. Spread before him were several big ledgers in which he recorded first the details of his purchases and later his tasting notes, under the wine labels.

"I thought I heard you in here," said Charlotte, climbing onto the stool opposite him.

"A couple of orders came in," he said amiably, gesturing toward the cartons open at his feet. Behind him, in the refrigerator alcove, racks of wine were lined up like the stacks in a library, two sections of three shelves each, slightly tilted. It was glassed in, and the door was shut, but the workroom was always cold, and Avery wore a cardigan. Charlotte was glad she had on a jacket and a turtleneck.

They sat in silence. Occasionally Avery bent to pull a bottle up from one of the cartons. He's so serious, thought Charlotte, who liked seriousness for its own sake, whatever the focus.

"Shall I read off the labels while you write?" she finally asked.

Avery's eyebrows went up in surprise.

"Man needs a hobby," she said with self-conscious lightness. "Beats chasing girls."

Avery smiled, closed the ledger he was working in, and folded his hands. "Very true," he said. "You must want something, Char, buttering me up like this. Wine stuff drives you crazy."

"I do want to ask you something," she said, never very good at dissimulation, "but it's not only that. I want to take part. I don't care what it is we do."

But Avery had already put her offer aside. "Just ask me," he said.

"I need some information," she said slowly, "about the business deductions of Milo Till's corporation."

"What for?" asked Avery, his eyes fixed on hers.

"I can't tell you," she said.

"Does it have to do with Ginger again?"

Charlotte nodded.

"Dear God," said Avery. "Mitch Reinhart was dangerous enough, but he's a pussycat compared to Till." He looked at her inquiringly, but Charlotte made no answer.

"This is not a good thing to do," said Avery.

Charlotte said nothing.

"Till Properties isn't my client," said Avery. "Basically, I'd be going into someone else's work files, even though they're available to anyone in the firm. You understand the problem?"

"I do," said Charlotte.

"I feel the same way about the trust between accountants and clients as you do about the attorney-client trust," he said.

"I know that," said Charlotte.

They studied each other for some time, but it was not an uneasy exchange. Charlotte even had the eerie feeling that they were communicating, like a couple of followers of the paranormal.

Finally Avery spoke. "Anything you learned could only be background," he said. "How do I know it wouldn't be cited in any way?"

"You'd have to trust me," said Charlotte.

Avery put the two ledgers at the side of his worktable, picked up the cartons, put them in the aisle on the other side of the refrigerator, and pushed his stool neatly under the table. Then he came around the table and, with his hand on the light switch, held the outer door open for Charlotte. As she preceded him through it, he said very lightly, "I have to think about it."

The way he said it suggested that he wouldn't, thought Charlotte, sitting disheartened in the kitchen after he left. She was glad to have her thoughts interrupted by the phone.

"Dinah's going to sign the final papers with Till tomorrow," said Polly. "She's thinking she can be friendly, maybe get to see his place and learn more."

Her worried tone was unmistakable and, thought Charlotte, totally valid. "My instinctive feeling is Dinah should stay distant," she said. "On the other hand, maybe she really can learn something. Is she afraid of anything in particular?"

"Not afraid," said Polly. "More excited. But she has some of the same feeling about staying well behind the curtain. Myself, I don't like to see her have any dealings with him at all. Everything I've read stresses his power, his charm, his connections. She's no match for that."

Charlotte snorted. "Come on," she said. "This is Dinah. He's a man. Dinah takes men on, uses them up, casts them off, and somehow they still think of her fondly for the rest of their natural lives. What could happen?"

25

When Dinah got to Auralia's gallery fifteen minutes early on Wednesday afternoon, Milo Till was already there. The gallery was full, Dinah had never seen the man before, and his back was to the door, but the moment she entered, she knew who he was. He was of average height and build, dark-haired and dark-suited, but there was something in his carriage that so set him apart that her eyes went right to him: It was a surety, of stance and attitude, and it was unmistakable.

Instinctively, she adjusted her own mien. She had arrived irritable, having spent an unusual amount of time on her appearance even while feeling ashamed of the concern. She'd chosen a particularly good suit, particularly good jewelry, and was particularly annoyed with herself for letting her hair fall to her shoulders, loosely pulled back by a couple of old Indian silver combs.

She had barely a minute before Till turned and saw her and immediately came over.

"Dr. Milanskaya?" he said.

"How did you know?" asked Dinah, putting out her hand.

"Guessed," he said. "Actually, I didn't care. Whoever you were, I wanted to meet you."

He had taken her hand in both of his and drew her in toward the "New Now Colors" exhibit. "It was good of you to come and meet a fellow Southwest collector. Or maybe I should say a 'rival' Southwest collector, though I'm hardly in your class."

The voice was unexpectedly deep, with a remnant of accent, a slight eliding of vowels, a little extra clip on the consonants. Milo Till was not unattractive, given his aquiline features, a high forehead, and closely cropped wavy hair. But it wasn't the features. It was the set of the face, the lift of the chin, the carriage, that all said power, control, command.

"Come, let's look at what you and I will never want," he said, and they entered the exhibit gallery. For the next quarter hour, they moved from one New Now canvas to another, sharing amused comments and criticisms, occasionally speaking of themselves in the way of recent acquaintances who already know they have one thing in common and maybe more than one.

"You have a classic Greek face," he said, looking at her sideways when they'd paused in front of a two-color New Color canvas. Before she could answer, he added, "I'm Greek. I came here as Tomopoulos."

"How did you get from Tomopoulos to Till?" she asked.

"Process of elimination. I couldn't really use just the first piece of it, because you get 'Tom,' which isn't much of a last name. Go to the next consonant, you get 'Top'—not an improvement. Then you go to the *l,* and while 'Tol' doesn't work, Till's good and works with Milo. So I went with it."

He was watching her, enjoying her amusement, so she said, "I am partly Greek, but mixed up with some interlopers from farther north, as you can tell from my name."

By the time they got to the New Now Media, they were talking about the art that did interest them and the collection that was changing hands. "Do you have any more fabulous pieces of Southwest at home?" asked Till.

"Not much," said Dinah. "A few rugs that I'm actually using as rugs. On the floor."

"Refreshing," murmured Till.

"And I have a couple of Maria Martinez bowls that I'll never give up and quite a bit of silver jewelry. But basically I'm out of Southwest, so the field is clear for you."

"What are you collecting now?" asked Till, making an assumption reasonable only to another inveterate collector. He had a way of lightly touching the back of his hand to her elbow as they moved along. Thus he was, in essence, moving them along—a trick she found too purposeful but undeniably attractive. He was surprisingly likable.

"I've bought and sold three different collections by now," Dinah admitted. "I'm ready for a rest."

Till smiled, turning his hand so he was holding her elbow. "Why so fickle?" he asked.

"I seem to like the chase more than the possession."

"Ah," he said. "Me, I like possession. It gives the chase a point."

Dinah let a little silence pass, then asked, "Where are you putting all the new things? There are over forty pieces—do you have a big lobby?"

"I have a big home," he said. "Two homes, in fact. These things are for me, and I don't intend to share the pleasure."

Dinah would have asked him more about both the homes and the placement of his art, but at that moment there was a sudden quiet and a rustling as everyone turned toward the double doors at the back of the gallery. They were opening, together, and there was . . . Auralia. She was again wrapped in veils, but now they were in shades of russet, artfully graduated from light to dark.

She swept into the room and around it, graciously inclining her upper body toward one person after another, her palms pressed together. She worked the room masterfully and, in a coup de brilliance, somehow managed to end her circumnavigation with Dinah and Milo Till, who were at the back of the group, opposite where she'd started.

"Darling!" she said to Till, offering her cheek, and, "Come in, my dears," to both of them. Stepping between them, she linked one arm of hers through one of theirs and drew them through the double doors into her office.

It took little time to sign the formal purchase papers, and Dinah already had her check from Till Properties & Development. There were some last arrangements for delivery of the remaining pieces to Till's Wilshire Boulevard condominium—"the penthouse, yes, darling?"—and a final embrace. Then the anorexic assistant appeared, opened the big metal door, and Dinah and Till found themselves on the street.

They had met before five-thirty, and it was now a quarter of seven and almost dark. While they were inside Auralia's gallery, the lights of Beverly Hills had turned on, and they emerged into the middle of several blocks of art galleries, fine furniture stores, and Oriental rug dealers, all of whom lit their front windows for maximum display. It was briefly disorienting. Till paused, then confidently took Dinah's arm and began to walk around behind the building to the parking lot.

"I hope you can stay out just a little longer," he said. "There's an auction that includes some of your favorite pottery—your former favorite, that is—and I'll be lost without your help." He leaned his face closer to hers; they had rounded the corner and the side street was poorly lit. Still, Dinah had no trouble seeing that his upper lip was narrow and taut but he had a full lower lip. Dinah liked a full lower lip.

"You'll come?" he asked.

"Of course," said Dinah.

It was less than a mile away, in the mid-Wilshire district, and his directions were easy, but Dinah drove slowly to make sure he got there first. It was a large building with a lot of art and design tenants, going by the big glass display windows that occupied the first three floors. As she drove into the self-park garage entrance, Dinah passed under a banner that announced DECORATIVE ARTS TONIGHT!

When the elevator opened on the seventh-floor lobby, Milo Till was waiting near the long table but hadn't checked in yet, so Dinah caught the gust of recognition and welcome that he set off among the greeters. Two ingenues in tube tops and tight pants checked him in, gave him his regular number (seventeen, the age he came to this country, he told her later), a small notepad, and one of those stubby bridge-party pencils to keep track of whatever he wanted to keep track of.

One of the rooms off the lobby had food tables on three walls, offering white wine, soft drinks, platters of half-inch cheese cubes, and crackers much too big for them. There were also big bowls of what Dinah took to be potpourri but turned out to be fancy chips in different colors made from white potatoes, sweet potatoes, beets, taro root, and butternut squash.

"Eat," said Till, covering a plate with cheese squares and chips. "We need our strength," and he moved her forward to the room where the items to be sold were on display. There were just fifty or sixty lots, and they were already being removed, leaving empty spaces behind some lot numbers. Till's only interest was a suite of three pieces by Maria Martinez from the early 1930s, when she and her husband, Julian, were working together on the black-on-black polished ware that took the Southwest art market by storm a decade earlier. Two of the pieces were bowls, large and small, and the third was a round platter so deep it could serve as a bowl. All had the high glaze and matte black geometric designs for which Martinez was famous, and these were not just vintage Martinez but stunning. The suite bore an estimate of seventy-five hundred to twelve thousand dollars.

"What do you think?" asked Till, speaking low and very close to her. "Ten thousand dollars? Fifteen thousand? You think we can get it for that, or should we go higher?"

"It is wonderful," said Dinah, regretting briefly that she had stopped collecting Southwest pottery. "It might be worth more, but better wait and see who else thinks so."

The auction hall held more than three hundred chairs with the standard auction-house gold frames and yellow damask seats—twenty rows of them, eight on either side of an aisle. There were almost that many people as well, but quite a few chose to stand closer to the front, crowded together along the walls and leaving empty seats, even rows, at the back. Some of the people standing were girls who worked for the house, plugged in via their headsets to clients who couldn't attend but wanted to join in the bidding by proxy.

The auctioneer was already at the podium. He was tall and slim and well turned out in a very fitted brown three-piece suit, probably in his late thirties, with thinning reddish hair. A slight brogue was evident in his instructions to the workers bringing in the lots, and he nodded to a dozen people as they came in, including Till.

Dinah and Milo Till took seats two-thirds of the way back in the middle of an empty row. Till sat to Dinah's right, immediately inching his chair back so he was slightly behind her and could brace his little notepad against the back of her chair. Quietly they discussed how to proceed. Just a month ago, he'd seen a Martinez platter of the same size go for $9,000, all alone.

"You think," he asked again, from just behind Dinah's shoulder, "that I should go for fifteen thousand?"

"Your call," said Dinah. "Depends whether you want a bargain or an acquisition."

The bidding started. On the first dozen lots, which were mostly pottery, Till made some notes. For the second dozen, he'd stopped writing, and the hand that held the notepad was resting not on her chair but on her shoulder. He was close enough for his breathing to ruffle her hair, and when he whispered, she felt his breath near her ear.

The Martinez suite was greeted by a perceptible stir of heightened interest throughout the hall, and Dinah was very aware of Till behind her and alert. He had put down the notepad, and his hand held her shoulder now, but still lightly. His other hand gripped his number card in his lap.

The lot was introduced at $7,500 and moved quickly in increments of $500 to $12,000. Milo Till hadn't entered the bidding. The next bid was a $250 raise, and Till whispered very close to her ear, "Shall we go now?"

"We" again. Dinah looked back, but he was so close that she couldn't see his face or even his profile, just his mouth.

"Now?" he whispered again, more urgently but calm.

She nodded, and he raised his card just barely, a few inches at most. Her immediate thought was that no one would see it, but they must have assigned someone to watch him, because the auctioneer looked sideways at some signal and then directly at Till.

"Number seventeen," he said. "Same increment?"

Till nodded, and the bidding picked up—$12,500, $12,750, $13,000. Then someone signaled higher increments, and the bids went to $13,500, $14,000, then leaped to $15,000.

"Higher?" came Till's voice in her ear. She nodded again, and he took it to $15,500. It went immediately to $16,000, then $17,000, then $17,500.

"Higher?" came his voice. The room was uncomfortably warm. Till's fingertips were smoothing the silken edge of her collar against her neck.

"Higher?" The bidding was at $19,000, and his voice, his breath, his hand on her shoulder radiated heat. In spite of herself, she nodded.

"Higher?" he'd ask. "Higher?" And the bidding rose, and Dinah felt hot and very conscious of her own breathing. She felt his hand press on her shoulder, and she clasped her hands in her lap.

At $23,500, the bidding went back to increments of $250. Till was bidding against a single person. Dinah was dizzy, aware of the open room around and beyond them but focused on the circle of heat that held them close, of his voice asking her to go higher and the rhythm of his breath as it came and went in her ear. Finally he asked "Higher?" one last time, she managed one last nod, the auctioneer could get no more, and the gavel fell on $27,000.

"Sold to number seventeen," said the auctioneer, with no apparent sense of the drama in which he'd just taken part, and he gestured for the Maria Martinez suite to be removed. It was gone in a minute, replaced by a big piece of terra-cotta that could have been a sitz bath or a planter, while Milo Till's hand remained on Dinah's shoulder, two fingers stroking the green silk at her neck.

"Well, we got it," he said. He leaned forward, cocking his head so she could see his whole face. He was flushed, his forehead shining with perspiration, but his eyes laughed and the lower lip was smiling.

"Did we pay too much?" he whispered.

"Not if you wanted it," she said crisply. "And there's no 'we.' It's all yours," and she tapped his cheek and moved her chair off a little way.

They left immediately, stopping at the front desk for Till to arrange billing and delivery. Dinah, standing close to him because his hand encircled her upper arm, had no trouble overhearing the arrangements: This purchase was going to his home along with the bill, in his own name.

As they got into the elevator, he put his hand toward the panel of buttons and looked at her. "I'm on the third level," he said.

"I'm one level lower."

"I'll drive you to your car," he said, pushed three, and stepped back to her side. "That was wonderful," he said. "I felt like I had a guiding angel and wasn't competing alone."

He lifted her hand and turned the palm to his lips. "Did you enjoy it?"

"I did," said Dinah as the door opened.

"You'll have to help choose the best place in my apartment to display them."

"You're going to be pretty heavy on Southwest," said Dinah. "Isn't it going to be a bit crowded in there?"

"No," said Till. "Last year I bought the next-door apartment and cut through a wall, so I have extra rooms. Some of it is strictly gallery space."

He helped her into his car and went around to climb into the driver's side. Then he closed the door, leaned over, took Dinah's face in both his hands, and kissed her, first softly, tentatively, then very deliberately. He even does that well, Dinah thought. It was a kiss full of mastery, she was thinking, but it was an aimless analysis, given the feel under her hands of the line of his jaw, the muscles in his shoulders and neck. Then there was the feeling of his hands in her hair, on her neck, drawing languid circles around her breast.

Eventually her eyes fell on the windshield, which was steaming up. She put out a hand and made three X's in the vapor with her fingertip. Till laughed, reached for the hand, and drew the finger into his mouth.

"We chose such a romantic spot," he said.

"At least now we're four floors below a big audience," said Dinah. As they separated just enough for conversation, she noticed a placard on his dashboard, facing outward, that spelled out MILO TILL in block letters. Milo Till, thought Dinah, and her next thought was, What am I doing here? And before thinking again, before she could stop herself, she said out loud, "'Milo Till.' Didn't you know Ginger Pass?"

His face showed no recognition.

"I remember hearing your name somewhere." Did he not remember Ginger's name, or had he never known it?

He was expressionless, willing to wait for an explanation. "I don't know the name," he said. "Who is she?"

"A woman I met once," said Dinah, appalled that she'd opened the question, unsure how to close it. "I think she died recently."

"Doesn't sound familiar," said Till, this time after a slight pause. "Do you want to talk about her?" he said softly, his face in her hair.

No, thought Dinah. No. And she said, "Nothing to say."

It was impossible to judge whether he truly didn't remember or was dissembling, and which was worse. What Dinah did know, with overwhelming clarity, was that she had to let him go. No matter that he was the most attractive man she'd met in a long time. No matter that danger itself was attractive to her. This was not one she could pursue.

Dinah leaned into one long, last kiss. She moved her hand to his thigh, her wrist directly over his groin, so she felt him strain up against the silk material of his trousers. Then she turned away, opened her door, and put one leg out of the car.

Till seized the other wrist. "Shall I follow you home?"

She kissed him again, lightly this time. He took it as assent and reached for his keys on the dashboard. Dinah backed away, drawing her hand by degrees from his grasp.

He raised his eyebrows, surprised. "Not tonight? Tomorrow perhaps?"

Dinah slid her fingers away along his hand until he held only air. "I'll call you," she said.

"That's usually my line," he said. "This'll be a first for me."

"Not for me," said Dinah, and closed the door.

She walked down the ramp and around to her own level without looking back. Behind her she heard him rev the Porsche engine and drive up toward the exit, tires squealing around the turns. Then she got into her own car and sat, her hands on the wheel. She was neither glad that she'd walked away nor really sorry. She had only the quiet conviction that she'd followed the sole course possible.

She did feel very let down, which was hardly surprising considering the pitch of excitement over the past several hours, and she was puzzled, not for the first time, at what it was in her that drew her to the difficult, dangerous men. Had it always been her preference, or only now that she was older, and the easy, more amiable men had been taken out of the field? Why hadn't she connected with someone like Graham Vere? she asked herself, but right along with the question came an answer. Chance: Such a man hadn't presented himself when she was open and available. Or maybe it was her instinctive rejection, which was worse.

At that point she shrugged off the brooding and, on impulse, called Polly to ask if she could come over. Even as Polly said yes, with no questions, Dinah was backing her car out of the space and winding up the ramps to the exit.

It was an unusual impulse for Dinah, who had never had many close female friends and even now considered none a real confidante. From time to time, she felt the lack, usually after the breakup of an affair, but didn't know how to remedy it. She had grown directly from tomboy to "popular," so most of her life from age eight on had been spent with boys, although there was some overlap—years in which she was like a boy and the object of boys at the same time, playing lacrosse and field hockey by day and dancing and flirting the nights away.

Maybe one reason she was so committed to the Monday group was that it was the first time she'd had such good friends. She had so quickly felt close to all five of them—four now—that calling Polly in a moment of distress might have been unusual but not unexpected. It felt good.

At Polly's she led off with the confirmation that Milo Till's home galleries would soon include the pottery just purchased with corporate funds, but it didn't take long to move on to Till himself and the intensity of their meeting. Polly didn't disappoint her, being immediately understanding, properly commiserating, and, at the end, admiring of Dinah's decision.

"It's like something out of a romance novel," she said. "Most of us will never in our lives experience this kind of drama."

"The problem is," and Dinah, who had gotten through her narration of the evening's events in a fairly matter-of-fact way, felt tears blur her eyes, "I know it's all wrong, but I keep thinking maybe I could call him after all, even see him again." She looked at Polly expectantly, seeking some unlikely encouragement.

"I go with your instinct that it's a really dangerous dalliance," said Polly gently. "This isn't just another of your rich industrialists or well-placed lawyers or influential art patrons."

"I know, I know," said Dinah. "It just seems so ironic that the man we're gunning for is almost perfect for me."

Polly was taken aback. "Perfect?" she exclaimed. "Are you saying this is the man of your dreams? Your ideal mate? From all we know, and we know more than most people, this is a bad one—dishonest, manipulative, cold, even murderous. That's your type?"

"Maybe he'd be a different person with me, if I were someone he was in love with," said Dinah softly, looking down at her hands.

Polly studied her for a minute, then said, "Are you really thinking you could have a future with Milo Till?"

"He could change."

Polly's lips were a tight line.

"Anyone can change," said Dinah. "Why do you think he's beyond changing?"

"Two words," said Polly, with grim emphasis. "Ginger Pass."

Dinah nodded, then drew in a sudden sharp breath, horror sweeping across her face. "Oh, God," she said. "It's even worse. I mentioned her, asked if he knew her."

Polly stared, gripping the arms of her chair.

"I'd thought about her off and on all evening," said Dinah. "I think part of the excitement was the possibility that we could get more on him."

"Not this way," said Polly. "It could ruin our plans if you've tipped him off to your interest, our interest. You think he wouldn't guard himself against anything we might do? Or worse?"

"I know," said Dinah. "I knew it even then. All along, I've known that. And I did get out of the car, and I won't be calling him, and I hope he forgets me fast."

"And if he doesn't?" Polly asked dryly. "Considering that he does sound like your type in many ways, except for the evil part. What's going to keep you straight?"

Dinah sighed. "Two words. Ginger. Pass."

The response to Dinah's encounter took a harder edge by Friday. She was scheduled for Friday duty at the office, with a full day of examining lesions, cysts, and various eruptions, freezing warts and excising growths, and between patients she was taking or returning calls from one or another of the women.

"What were you thinking?" exclaimed Kat. "You may have blown our cover."

"This could be a significant problem," said Charlotte. "Tell me again exactly what you said and his response."

What was I thinking? brooded Dinah, over and over. What exactly did I say?

"I can't believe you and I were actually talking romance afterward," said Polly. "Romance is the least of it."

"What were you *doing*?" said Kat. "Were you thinking at all?"

"It's probably not that bad," said Justine evenly. "We have to wait and see."

"Thoughtless," said Charlotte, several times. "And dangerous. This is a really dangerous situation. Of all people, Milo Till."

I just asked if he knew her, Dinah kept thinking, and I said she was dead. That's definitely when I saw the recognition—not when I mentioned the name but when I said she was dead. Maybe he doesn't even know her name. Did she use her real name? But "dead" struck home:

He wouldn't remember all his lying and cheating, but he probably hasn't murdered that many women.

Her phone light was on when Dinah finished her last patient at six and sat down in her office to record her notes on the visit. She buzzed the front desk.

"I'm closing up," said Stacey, the receptionist. "There's a Mr. Till in the waiting room, no app," meaning no appointment.

"I'll be right out," said Dinah, because Stacey couldn't leave if anyone was waiting. Dinah clasped her hands, gripping and releasing, measuring out her breathing.

Milo Till was at the window, his back to the room when she came through the door, saying, "Thank you, Stacey. Sorry to keep you."

Till turned, his look of immediate pleasure at seeing her quickly covered by a wariness. He didn't move as Stacey gathered up her purse and her sweater or when Dinah crossed the room, but he took Dinah's outstretched hand in both of his.

"Am I in trouble because I didn't wait for your call?" he asked, but there was no humor in the eyes or around the mouth.

Dinah shook her head.

So they stood, as Stacey pushed in her chair and walked to the stairway door, carefully casting no glance in their direction. Then she left. They were alone, and Till released Dinah's hand and began moving around the room, circling around and between the mostly empty display cases. Dinah followed him, not closely. Sometimes their paths crossed, sometimes she'd be on one side of a case and he would appear on the other, his face magnified at the corners where the glass thickened, then its normal size, then magnified again at the next corner. The magnification of the display glass was a surprise to Dinah, and she was fascinated by Till's moving in and out of her vision, now bigger, now smaller, always watching her. Now cat. Now mouse.

"I'm a direct person," he said, still in motion. "I also know what I want."

She waited, following slowly, seeing him head-on every few display cases. She wondered where this was going, and then, suddenly, it was there.

"We were fine," he said, "until you asked if I knew someone. Who is this person, and what's the problem?"

The mouth smiled, the face was relaxed, but the eyes were on close watch.

"What person?" asked Dinah, buying time.

"The woman who knew me."

Dinah paused, as if struggling to call up all the inconsequential names and bits of conversation they had touched on Wednesday evening. Then—ah, sudden recall—she said as casually as she could, "Nobody. A woman at my hairdresser's."

An eyebrow lifted, but the eyes didn't move.

"I saw your name card in the car and flashed on these three or four women who were talking about you, sometime ago. This one didn't say much, but hers was the only name I knew, because her daughter's a patient."

He watched her.

Then she had it—the perfect answer. "In the car I suddenly thought of them and thought, I don't even know this man. And all these women did."

She lowered her eyes, standard preliminary to a sensitive point. "You have to understand," she said slowly, with seeming reluctance. "My business is lesions, all the usual transmitted diseases," and she looked up.

Till himself looked away. It was the word "lesions." Gets them every time, thought Dinah, with a resurgence of confidence.

"I avoid men of multiple contacts," she added quietly, though it was unnecessary.

Neither of them spoke while seconds, maybe minutes passed. As she studied his face, the wariness began to dissolve, and then, clearly and unmistakably, she saw relief.

"I don't believe in multiple alliances," he said. "And I'm very careful."

"Good," said Dinah.

He was not just relieved but visibly easy, even affable. He gestured at the glass cases. "It's very empty here," he said. "You need to start acquiring again."

"I like it empty for a change," said Dinah. "At least for a while."

He nodded. "I'm off to Geneva in a few days. Want to come along?"

Dinah shook her head.

"I know," said Till. "As in 'Don't call me, I'll call you.'"

"Something like that," said Dinah.

Till stepped toward her and put a hand firmly around the back of her neck, his fingers in her hair, pulling her close to him. When their faces were almost touching, he paused, a palpable, unbearable pause, then gently licked her upper lip and kissed her lightly on her nose.

"Bye," he said, and walked away.

"Are you parked in the garage?" Dinah called after him, foolishly.

He looked back at her, amused, all charm. "I have a car waiting for me out front," he said. "Why? Do you validate?"

And he gave her a two-finger wave and was gone.

Dinah dropped into Stacey's desk chair and leaned her forehead on the cool metal surface of the desk. He believed her. Dinah was sure he believed her. He had come to her with suspicions, she had derailed them, and he had left secure again. It had gone well.

Needing some reassurance, Dinah called all the other women, who said they'd come right away—from offices, from home, from the market. And they did, arriving separately and subdued, except for Kat, who strode through the door, looked around, said, "Mmm, cozy," and walked around the room until everyone else was there.

There was little small talk, and when they were all seated on the waiting room sofas, silence. They looked to Dinah, who went right into a detailed recounting of Till's visit that afternoon, leaving out nothing, including his final invitation.

"Thank God," said Polly when Dinah finished.

"You think he believed me?" asked Dinah, looking at each of them for assent.

"Why wouldn't he?" said Polly. "You were good, and it was plausible."

"And he, oddly enough, was easy," said Charlotte. "A very workable combination of qualities. Suspicion, hubris, desire, and the greatest of these is desire."

"Spell it out, Charlotte, spell it out," said Kat.

"Well, there's no question he was suspicious when Dinah mentioned Ginger, a woman now dead. It was a momentary suspicion, not real doubt; this man doesn't doubt his handling of anything, including Ginger's death. He only wanted confirmation that he wasn't connected to the death. You gave it to him, and his faith in himself was justified."

Looking at Dinah, she added, not unkindly, "The desire is something I can't fathom, but you seem to share it. He's a murderer: Get over it."

Dinah put her face in her hands, only simulating shame now. She knew that her friends knew she wouldn't act on the attraction.

"Well," said Polly, "this gives us our first clear look at Milo Till, and we have to keep it in mind. He knew right away that this could be a real threat, and he moved fast. You gotta admit the guy's sharp."

"So was Dinah," said Justine. "Eventually."

They now had an unexpected view of their own situation: Whatever their connection to Ginger Pass alive, no one connected them to the fates of the men involved in her death. In fact, having spent the day fearing they were discovered, they now felt in less danger of discovery. Even Milo Till was concerned only about being discovered himself; there was no indication he had discovered or suspected anything about them.

"Which is what we wanted," Polly reminded them. "We're operating below their radar, on a private and domestic level, and it seems to work for us. You'd think we've been in much worse danger: We've gone to fund-raisers and court hearings. We've crawled into alleys and backyards under the very slight cover of darkness, and nothing's connected us to either Cannon or Reinhart, who caused their own ruin."

Indeed, Milo Till could be the most covert revenge of all, if they could get what they wanted on him. "We won't be climbing any walls," said Charlotte. "We won't trespass. We don't do anything: The IRS does everything."

"Your tax dollars at work," said Polly.

They filed out, talking, laughing. Kat was the last. "Place looks empty," she said to Dinah from the doorway. "You should buy some more stuff."

"So I've heard," said Dinah.

26

"So we're not ruined after all," said Polly to Charlotte as they walked to their cars, parked on the same cross street.

"Doesn't seem so," said Charlotte irritably. She had spent her lunch hour considering that very possibility over a container of yogurt and was therefore hungry and not in a good mood. "In fact, Dinah has answered at least one of our big questions: We now know that her Southwest art collection, paid for by Till's business, is definitely going to his home. Let's hope she doesn't decide to help hang it there."

Later that night Charlotte once again searched the names "Till" and "Till Properties & Development" on various databases, from housing starts to Greek-American fraternal organizations. On several she found the name but no further information. She found Till's name on a number of museum boards and lists of contributors, reread the old news stories on his possible ambassadorship, and reviewed the only financial data available on his privately held corporation, which included figures for total assets but no breakdown.

Charlotte spent a solitary Saturday working on a client's federal estate-tax form. Avery had, as always, gone to his office, so Charlotte took her files of information and financial valuations to the comfort of the kitchen. There she spread everything out on the table, filled a cup from the pot of cold coffee on the stove, and opened a jar of toffees.

By late afternoon Avery was home. They had a retirement dinner that night, a formal hotel banquet with speeches and pretty well guaranteed not to be lively. Charlotte was still working at the table when Avery came in the back door, and she noticed immediately that he was unusually burdened. He had his briefcase, several fat manila envelopes, a big brown accordion file, and an uninterpretable turn to his mouth.

"What?" said Charlotte, turning on the seat of the chair to face him.

Avery set the accordion file down broadside on top of her papers. On that he put the three envelopes, one by one, and precisely.

"What is it?" said Charlotte.

"The last three quarterly reports of Till Properties & Development and the working file for the fourth and final quarter. That includes the tax organizer, plus original materials, plus summaries for the whole fiscal year, which ended November thirtieth." Still his face was expressionless. "Can't guarantee the figures, because the final report's not yet out of the computer, but there's a printout of the draft filings, and the big numbers aren't likely to change."

Charlotte just looked at him, her head tilted back. She put one hand on the pile.

"I don't know what you're looking for," said Avery more conversationally. "In fact, I don't want you to tell me. But the interesting stuff's usually in the gross and net profits, the business deductions, the assets of the corporation, and those are all there. Not that you need any instruction on such things."

"What made you change your mind?" asked Charlotte, surprised that her voice came out both faint and slightly quavering.

"I didn't change my mind," said Avery. "This has always been my mind."

She didn't trust herself to frame another question.

"I'm making a personal statement," said Avery. "Because I trust you and I've always trusted you, and I want to be sure you know I trust you."

"Is that the same as love?" said Charlotte.

"Exactly," said Avery, smiling now. "I never did have your vocabulary." And he left the room.

Charlotte, feeling tears begin, made a move to draw the files closer but then thought better of it. She rearranged them, separated into three piles with some of her client's tax papers on top of each, and went upstairs to dress for the dinner.

The next morning Charlotte moved all the files into her office, leaving the kitchen to Avery, who was starting an all-day preparation of duck-sausage chili. As she gathered up the papers, they talked—about the chili, about his new wines, about the banquet the night before. Carefully, neither spoke of the Till tax files, though she was handling them right under their eyes. Avery moved from cupboards to counters, barefoot and wearing his chef's apron over chinos and a pressed work shirt, assembling utensils and ingredients. Charlotte, still in her bathrobe, stopped only to reheat coffee and then left the kitchen.

The records were much better than she expected. They were as good as she'd hoped. Quickly, she riffled through the fiscal-year filings, feeling excitement rise in her chest.

What they wanted was all there, with nothing hidden, or at least nothing they were looking for. Till Properties had begun only one new housing development in California in the past year—Butte Crest Homes in the unincorporated area of Los Angeles County above Palmdale—with a construction loan taken out the year before. There were only two sales recorded so far. The expenses associated with development were set apart and neatly broken down, with listings for loan service, for land clearing and grading, conduits and pavings, for landscaping and for "Model Homes."

"See Statement 7," it said in parens right next to "Model Homes," and there, pages later, was Statement 7, meticulously itemized. Butte Crest's model homes, seven in all, cost Till Properties $7.35 million. This included $3.8 million for completed construction, $1.6 million for furniture and appliances, $1.1 million for painting and carpeting and drapes and a final $850,000 for "American Southwest Indian Art Objects."

"Oh my God," said Charlotte under her breath. Her feet did a little drumroll on the floor, and she punched the on button to warm up the copy machine. She expected to limit her copying to the Butte Crest expenses, but she found one more note of confirmation before she was finished. Under the year-end assets of the corporation was a listing for "Art," with no breakdown. The tax organizer, however, had all the details and computations with everything named and described, including $850,000 worth of Southwest Indian art objects, "approximately 40 pieces of ceramics, stoneware, and basketry," which sounded wonderfully familiar.

By noon Charlotte had put the Till files back in order and laid them on the hall floor next to Avery's briefcase. Then she wrote "I love you" on a pink Post-it note, stuck it on the briefcase, wondered briefly how long it had been since she'd written such a note, and went down to the kitchen to give Avery whatever help she could.

Alerted to the fact that Charlotte had gotten the Till records confirming the deduction, the women were so jumpy and inattentive at the Monday meeting that Lotte terminated early. She didn't take it personally. All groups worked differently, and this one had a singular personality, a moodiness that affected one and all, inexplicable to Lotte and unpredictable. Occasionally she fretted about it, thinking she should be able to define the particular dynamic, but they were making good progress toward their stated goals and had clearly bonded well, so she must be doing something right.

As a result she felt only curiosity about the day's mood, probed it only gently, and was willing to spend their time considering the nature of retribution—Charlotte's choice of topic, and an odd one. Lotte was often surprised here to find herself discussing Russian literature for the first time since college, a bit of Catholic doctrine (this from Polly), even the mythological views on fate (this from Dinah), but it was all fine, she thought, and with no guilt at all she left early.

Charlotte had been straightforward about how she'd gotten the Till records: They had long ago agreed that sources used by each would become the secret of all, particularly where families were involved. They had also agreed that neither families nor friends should be privy to their plans, and they knew that so far only Polly had made a significant slip. And today they also realized that Charlotte was unusually happy, and that Till's tax deductions were the least of it.

"Okay, let's go," said Charlotte, well before Lotte's footsteps reached the bottom.

Chairs scraped forward on the floor. Kat bounced up and went to lean against the side of the window. Charlotte, in a red jacket, with diamonds in her ears and brighter lipstick than usual, lined up the edges of her papers.

"Well," she said, almost gaily, "Dinah opened it up for us—and I mean that in the nicest way possible. And I have the financial data to confirm it. Milo Till was indeed rushing to buy the art before the end of their fiscal year. As Dinah discovered, he bought it with corporate funds, and the company did indeed write off the whole boodle as a project expense."

The announcement was met with clapping and hooting, and Charlotte joined in. "So, thanks to Dinah," she said over the noise, "we now have the basis of a plan."

"Except that I almost blew it," said Dinah.

"Now that you mention it," said Charlotte, "remind me: What *were* you thinking?"

"I just wanted to see what I could learn," said Dinah, "and it got away from me."

"I don't think there should be any thought that Dinah almost blew it," said Justine. "The point is, she did it. She got information we didn't have and couldn't get and really needed."

"I suppose," said Dinah slowly, "that it still could turn out that I blew it. I don't know if he really didn't remember Ginger's name or was just pretending, but if he is caught on tax fraud with my art collection, he might remember that I mentioned Ginger and make a connection."

She looked around the table, but no one spoke, each trying to decide whether he could make that connection. "I keep asking myself why I was so stupid, and I guess I felt, and a part of me still feels," she added, "that ultimately I'd like him to know he was getting paid back for Ginger, though I certainly won't do anything further to tip him off."

"Forget it," said Polly. "If he gets any inkling we're behind all this, it would be a very brief satisfaction. He's way too powerful. If he knew ahead, he could stop us, and if he learned it afterward, he'd somehow turn it on us and go free. For us, revenge has to be anonymous. We'll just have to pass up that satisfaction."

"But is it really revenge," continued Dinah, "if the person doesn't know why he's punished and by whom?"

"You mean, it's like that old question about if a tree falls in the forest," said Charlotte, "and no one is there to hear it, did it really make a sound? Does it matter? We just want the tree felled."

Justine, who had been particularly quiet, turned to Polly. "Wasn't it your mother who said revenge is a dish best served cold?" She looked around the table. "Maybe revenge is best eaten both cold and quietly," she said. "It should be planned carefully and coldly, and those who do it should stay unknown, if they want to be safe."

"Not just safe but personally removed," said Charlotte, who had been fretting over the issue for some time. "I prefer to think of us as avengers. Taking revenge is usually defined as a very personal payback for some injury, almost demanding recognition. Unlike avenging, which implies a more objective judgment and a punishment well deserved."

"In other words, justice," Kat added.

"We may have to believe that," said Charlotte. "But I wouldn't count on these distinctions in a court of law."

It was Polly who called a halt. "Listen," she said, "the important thing for right now is, does everyone agree we have the best way to get Milo Till?"

Everyone certainly agreed. It was anonymous and feasible. It would interest the Internal Revenue Service, which could audit several years' tax filings of both Milo Till and his company, find the fraud, and gladly mete out justice. And while meting out justice, the Service would get maximum press coverage: The story had not just headline appeal but swarm potential. The initial announcement would get high play, followed by waves of secondary stories, as even more reporters rushed out stories on Till, Till's developments, the tax strategies of major builders, and famous tax frauds from the Helmsleys back to the days of Herod.

The situation also fit what Charlotte called the group's modus operandi. They focused on their man's most characteristic flaw and, working behind the scenes on a very basic and humble level, used it to do him in. With Cannon they'd had his cynical public image, which they manipulated to his disadvantage as he'd manipulated it to gain power. Reinhart, ironically but appropriately, was done in by one of his wives, although Justine and Polly had found the hidden assets they could have used to take him down. Till had worked the government for years, exploiting every law and regulation and tax code he could, and now they would help the government finally and fairly win the game.

"It's like divine judgment," said Polly. "We just help it along, but they called it down on themselves."

"I prefer your mother's line," said Charlotte. "What goes around, comes around."

"That was mine," said Polly.

Charlotte looked at her sternly, pen in air. "Polly," she said, "if you're going to go into your mother's line of work, you need to start using footnotes."

"Okay," said Kat, who had been restless since the discussion turned philosophical, "what do we do now? We have both halves of the IRS guy's question. Do we just turn Till in?"

"Wait," said Charlotte, her eyes canvassing the ceiling. "We've seen the corporate check. We've verified the deduction. Dinah got verbal confirmation that everything was going into his home, but not visual—that is, she didn't actually ball him at his home in his bed in full view of the art objects."

"Didn't ball him anywhere," muttered Dinah.

"Never mind," said Polly. "We can draw a curtain on the scene in the parking garage."

"Which leaves one thing, as I was saying," said Charlotte. "We should at least verify, and by that I mean we should *see* that they're not where he officially said they were—in the model homes."

Kat, who'd sat down, jumped up again. "You mean we have to go up to Lancaster or wherever it is? To one of Till's salt-lick, parched-earth desert communities?"

"Good idea!" said Polly. "It's been over two weeks since the gallery told Dinah the pieces were being delivered and installed, so if that's where they were going, they'd be there now." She raised her hand, waggling the fingers. "I'll go. How's Friday?"

Kat sighed. "I'd go, too, but I can't run."

Justine leaned forward, but Charlotte cut her off. "You did your late night, Justine. I'm going this time."

"What about Polly? She did hers, too," said Justine.

"I always go," said Polly. "Gets me out of the house."

"The only one who really has to go is Dinah," said Charlotte, "because she alone can identify her objects."

Dinah was immediately reluctant. "I'm also the only one who's known to him," she said. "If we're caught, it would really be over."

The idea silenced them. She was right. A minute passed.

"Hey," said Polly, "you could probably say that about every one of our forays."

Charlotte swept the question off the table with her hand and looked sternly at Dinah. "Never mind," she said briskly. "It's the chance we have to take. We need you."

Knowing they'd exchange a lot of phone calls before Friday, they spent only a few more minutes on plans for the excursion, and Polly didn't think about it at all as she drove slowly home in the gathering dark and rush-hour traffic. She kept mulling over the concept of revenge and the proverbial tree in the forest until it became background music to other, seemingly disparate thoughts. She thought about Graham Vere and about Jeremy's silences and about Andrea's current English paper and finally about the letter she'd written on the most recent school fund drive and then put away. It was probably just another of her unheard, unread complaints.

Dear Booster Club:

Looking at the gift wrap I bought in your recent fund-raiser, the one between the T-shirt sale and the silent auction, I'm struck by the thought that there's a good civics lesson here, and it's not about school funding.

I said no to the gift wrap, promising to donate money to the school instead. But the drive leader said the goal was "100 percent participation," adding, "I'd hate to tell the whole school the kids won't get their pizza party because one family didn't participate. Not that I'd name your child, but . . ."

The petty extortion is dangerous enough. More dangerous is the lesson children learn when they're used to sell overpriced trifles to family and friends, and bribed with "prizes" to sell more. But the greatest danger is the insistence on "100 percent participation," the refusal to let parents choose what they'll buy or to let them opt to give time instead of money. And if some parents can do neither, "they shouldn't be here," said one club leader.

Such self-righteousness! Who's to say what others can give or who should be there? More important—and here's the civics lesson—who gets to choose which of all the drives should get 100 percent participation? And what of those who hold convictions that make it important not to participate at all?

Sure, it's just gift wrap, and it's for a good cause. But throughout history great horrors have been perpetrated in the name of good causes, all with that insistence on 100 percent participation. Extortion is the least of them, but it's a beginning.

Sincerely yours . . .

It was a good letter, but she hadn't sent it, overcome by her growing sense of futility. In this case she knew the players well, an entrenched set of parents who held the school in the grip of their officious hands. If they read it at all, they'd shrug it off as the griping of an inveterate complainer. She'd be just another tree making a noise in the forest.

Then out of her musing came an idea, half practical, half semantics. If she wanted to be heard, she had to get out of the forest. She had to take her complaint beyond the limits of the deep, dark wood.

"It's that old poser about the tree falling in the forest," she told Graham Vere later that night as they sat in her backyard looking out over the canyon. He came now several nights a week. They'd each have dinner with their children, then leave them to their homework and spend an hour or two together, usually on Polly's upper terrace. Almost always they sat in the dark, which revealed more of the lights around the hills and somehow concentrated the evening songs of the birds. Occasionally Graham's younger son would come with him and vanish immediately into Jeremy's room to play video games.

"The one that doesn't make a sound unless there's someone to hear it?" he said.

"That one," she said. "It's just me making another complaint that no one will hear."

"Let's see it," he said, but he held her arm and kept her from getting up until he'd kissed the side of her mouth, her ear, and her neck deep below her jawline.

Over the several months they'd known each other, Graham Vere had read a number of her letters, though not all she'd written. Each time he had read carefully, commented thoughtfully, and greatly enjoyed the exercise. He liked her approach. He admired specific word choices, laughed at her wit, and took her seriously enough to offer occasional criticisms, cast as suggestions. Most important, he gave her something that had been missing in her life since Dan died—endorsement. She hadn't realized how alone and exposed one could feel without it.

With Polly holding a flashlight over the page, he read the Booster Club letter straight through, his free arm around her. He laughed once, muttered "Good Lord" once under his breath, and, when he was through, lowered it to his knee and said, "A lot of people could relate to this."

"I hope that's the point of all my letters," said Polly.

"It's really good enough for publication," he said, "not that I haven't had that thought before."

"In the newspaper?"

"It needs reshaping, of course, into a more newspapery form, but for you that should be easy. This one really makes a compelling point."

"Well, I meant it to go beyond school auctions," said Polly slowly.

"Then it should definitely go beyond a school audience."

"That would get it out of the woods," she said.

"Exactly," said Vere.

After he left, Polly sat down with the Booster Club complaint and five days of newspapers, determined to turn a letter into an editorial. The salutation was replaced by a lead: "You never know where you'll find a good civics lesson. . . ." Each paragraph was expanded, as she added examples where applicable and continued thoughts previously only touched on. She made the conclusion more emphatic: "Better to allow people choices and differences. In the long run, schools might even take in more money."

Then she read it over a few more times, alternately pleased and dissatisfied. I can't do this, she thought. It's not good enough.

It's as good as everybody else's, said her mother.

No, it isn't, Polly answered. But if it's a slow news day, it might beat their running a white space.

Sleep on it, said her mother.

That was often her mother's last word, and it usually worked. Polly left the piece on the desk and went to bed.

On Tuesday she changed a few words, actually consulting the thesaurus on one, and switched the places of two sentences. On Wednesday she made some more changes, all minor, and when Graham Vere asked her if she'd sent it to the paper, she said, "Tonight."

Later that night she found a few more changes she could make, all negligible. Then she pulled up her friend Tess's e-mail address at the newspaper and wrote an introductory note asking if Tess thought the editorial page might be interested. She followed that with the text of the revised letter. And pushed the send button.

27

For a change they started in the daylight, if not as early as they planned. The Butte Crest development, which Polly insisted on calling "Butt Crest," was fifty miles north of Los Angeles, up past Palmdale, and even with good traffic an hour's drive. On Fridays it sometimes looked as if half of Los Angeles was leaving for the weekend, so they decided to meet at Dinah's office at two in the hopes of getting there by three-thirty.

Charlotte, punctual as always, came from downtown and was sitting in Dinah's waiting room by one forty-five, working her way through a fat legal brief and surrounded by eerily empty Plexiglas display cases. Polly was late because Jeremy's school had an early dismissal. He hadn't given her the announcement, had missed his car pool or waved it off, and when he called home confused and upset, Polly had to pick him up. It was a quarter past two when she joined Charlotte among the display cases, and Dinah didn't come out into the waiting room until almost two-thirty, having taken a late patient with a staphylococcus boil.

She was still apologizing when they went down to the parking garage. They were taking Polly's car, figuring that someone with an eight-year-old Volvo was more likely to be interested in a high-desert tract of middle-income houses than someone in a Mercedes wagon or a Lexus. As they stood waiting for Polly to unlock the doors, Charlotte looked sideways at Dinah's pressed blue jeans and crewneck sweater, and couldn't resist. "Armani makes jeans?"

"They're Ralph Lauren," said Dinah.

"Backseat then," said Charlotte, since Dinah was already opening the door.

They were all in casual clothing—pants, T-shirts, windbreakers. Where they were going was country compared to L.A., even though it was high desert, more open and empty than the bucolic landscape the word *country* usually implied. The first twenty miles out were clogged freeway, but there was more space between developed areas, the office parks were low and sparse, and the residential centers were intermittent, discrete tracts of controlled architecture—same roofs, same stucco, same lot size, with no visible differences.

They didn't know what to expect of Till's development, although Charlotte had already pointed out that Butte Crest was a contradiction in terms, because a butte was by definition flat-topped and couldn't have a crest. Polly had downloaded a map and directions from the development's Web site, along with some marketing material that she gave Charlotte to read out loud as they drove north, sometimes at only twenty miles an hour.

"'For home buyers who seek a better quality of life,'" Charlotte read, "'Butte Crest offers unique community surroundings that blend rustic refinement with architectural excellence.'" She held up an artist's rendering of undistinguished two-story, faintly Mediterranean homes. "It goes on to describe the setting as 'incomparable, offering desert breezes, end-less sunshine, and a peaceful feeling of isolation and remoteness.'"

"One would think that a liability," Polly put in, "not an asset."

"To go on," said Charlotte sternly, "it says there are seven different floor plans, from twenty-two hundred square feet to thirty-four hun-dred, with a choice of design features. Gourmet kitchens with birch cabinets, trash compactors, and appliance garages, marble master baths, sleeping lofts or dens. Three to five bedrooms, five to seven baths." She looked up: "Is that bizarre?"

"Bathrooms are good," said Dinah from the backseat. "How much?"

"Prices start in the high $300,000s, which probably means $399,999, and go up to a level they don't mention. And if you buy before December thirty-first, you get a membership in the golf club they're putting in later and a free holiday turkey. Every year."

"That's a nice touch," said Polly.

By the time they neared Palmdale, the traffic was moving steadily and there was very little commercial development and fewer residential communities, with the open land between them rocky and bare. Heavy watering kept the Los Angeles Basin fairly green all year-round, but above the basin, where there was nobody to water, the native chapar-ral turned to straw and disappeared entirely as they climbed into the high desert, leaving everything from the roadside to the far horizon flat, beige, and dry.

"Who in God's name lives up here?" wondered Charlotte. "What a commute!"

"Cops," said Polly. "I read somewhere that Lancaster and Palmdale are all cops, because L.A pays them so poorly they can't afford to live in the city they serve."

"I bet they're really fun neighbors," said Charlotte.

"Actually, they're great," said Dinah, a defensive edge in her voice, "and it's really a shame that they have such terrible commutes, although I suppose it gives them some privacy." She shrugged apologetically. "I have a soft spot for cops."

"Another old boyfriend?" said Charlotte.

"No boyfriend," said Dinah without pique. "Just years in the emergency room, where policemen may bring people in if no paramedic's available." She was looking out the window, and her voice was muted. "I've seen them cry over some of the kids they bring us, and they often wait there until they hear that someone's okay. By now I know quite a few of them personally."

"Sorry," said Charlotte.

"No problem," said Dinah, and they drove on. They were in open country now and continuing to climb. There was still an occasional housing development, a patch of new houses marching neatly up the side of a barren hill or filling a notch between two hills, but much of the landscape was empty, and now and then, on an uphill grade, they would go past an outcropping and get a glimpse of rocky terrain stretching beyond for miles. It was the kind of country where the good guys in western movies always tracked the bad guys, or vice versa, riding higher and higher into the upper crags and passes until they had to dismount and stagger on by foot.

"You know," said Dinah suddenly, "I'm not going to fill those display cases in my office." It was so obviously an introductory remark that Charlotte turned around in her seat and looked at Dinah expectantly.

"I'm going to be on call as a ride-along doc for the ambulance service," she said, "so I won't be shopping much."

"Way to go," said Polly, looking at her in the rearview mirror. Charlotte reached back a congratulatory hand.

"And what brought this on?" asked Polly.

"Everything, and nothing in particular," said Dinah. "You know it all. Maybe our meetings suggested it and Reinhart drove it home. And the business with Till clinched it. Anyway, I've applied for another residency in emergency care and trauma, starting next July, and I'll probably get it. I'm not giving up the office or the practice, but we're taking on an associate, which will cut into the waiting-room space, so the cases have to go anyway."

Polly and Charlotte were very pleased for her and eager to hear her plans, so it was ten minutes before they focused again on Butte Crest. They agreed to say as little as possible about themselves, but whatever they did say would contain enough truth so that if they were separated, their stories would hang together. Polly would pose as the interested party, because she was the only one who could even be faintly interested. She'd be a divorcée living in the Hollywood Hills, the single parent of two teenagers and considering marriage to a physician who practiced in the Valley. She'd want to live in the Lancaster area while exploring the relationship, at the same time getting more space for her money and un-crowded schools for her kids.

At a quarter to four, they were there. The town itself, on a county route off the freeway, was called Agua Seca ("How can you have dry water?" Charlotte wondered) and was so sparse and weathered that one couldn't tell if it was a new town or a ghost town. There was an office strip that looked new, a retail strip that looked deserted, and, just beyond, a four-pump gas station and a one-room post office.

Butte Creek was immediately east of this little center on a slight hill. According to the map, it was well situated, a trapezoidal parcel with public roads on three sides, offering easy access to the freeway, which continued north to Mojave, or to the state highway going east to Victor-ville.

As they drew close, they saw a furrowed construction road wind-ing left off the highway and up the hill, probably marking the western boundary of the development. The land was graded and marked off into lots, separated by unfinished streets and dotted with piles of dirt and construction materials. A cluster of buildings was visible farther on, beyond the masonry wall that ran along the county highway a few hundred yards to a double-lane driveway with big gateposts and a guard booth. It was a pretty imposing entry to what was still only an imaginary garden spot.

The wrought-iron gates stood open, and as prospective customers they were waved through. The drive went straight up, bordered on both sides by a strip of shrubs and small, very young palms. At the top were the model homes, three along the front road and two behind them—all finished, painted, and landscaped, strangely complete on the bare hill-top. A few trees were scattered here and there, still in big wooden boxes, and there were more building lots laid out nearby, some with founda-tions and preliminary scaffolding. But if the little group of houses hadn't been life-size and they themselves not so close, it could all have been an architectural model on a table.

"Hardly homey," said Polly as they pulled into the parking lot at one side, "but they're not too bad."

Typical of Southern California tract houses, they were basically beige, in this case close to taupe, with dark purplish brown roof tiles. Their designs differed only slightly. A couple had huge double doors in a two-story entry topped by a mansard roof. One had a protruding entry topped by its own peaked roof. The last two had what seemed to be silos alongside their entries, with a circle of small windows at the top.

"What's with the silo?" said Polly.

"Probably a circular staircase," said Dinah.

"And the gun slits?"

"To light the stairs," said Charlotte. "Or to give the gunners a place to stand."

There was a sales office in a trailer on the parking lot, but there were also a couple of salespeople at the door of the first house—one with a two-story entry and a huge chandelier visible through the window above the doors. Once inside, they were plunged into Southwestern style so thoroughly carried out that it was almost parody. Red and yellow glass chilies hung like prisms from the chandelier, a large painting of a cactus covered the stairway wall, painted sconces shaped like the branches of Joshua trees flanked the doorway, and above the arched entry to the living room three Indian women crouched over their baskets on a long horizontal canvas. Every niche and shelf displayed pottery and figurines, a parade of baskets marched along the recess at the tops of the walls, and the decor, all earth tones, featured puffy round sofas, armless and legless chairs, and mushroomy ottomans.

Visitors were free to wander. Dinah moved methodically from one artifact to another, her face set and noncommittal, her inspection outwardly casual. They knew she was taking mental notes, occasionally putting out a finger to feel the finish on a pot. Polly and Charlotte followed, chatting about the layout and the accoutrements—the counters, the lighting, the best places for Polly to put her piano and her household computer.

It wasn't until they were going on to the third model that Charlotte asked very quietly, "Anything yours?"

Dinah stared. "Are you joking?"

"Not the best stuff, huh?" said Charlotte.

"Please," said Dinah. "I'd be surprised if anything here was made outside Taiwan. The designs aren't bad copies of the real stuff, but the colors, the glazes, the finishes all say machine-made and cheap import. It's commercial—and low commerce at that."

They were in the third house when a woman with a Butte Crest staff badge came through to announce that they'd be closing soon. When Polly asked if they could still see the two back models, the woman said those had already been locked up.

With the car's motor running, the three women watched as everyone else left. One could get to the front drive by crossing in front of the models or by going around behind them and down the other side. People were doing both, and when Polly finally pulled out, she followed a last pickup truck and a van to the upper road. As soon as the others turned down the hill, she checked that no one was behind her and swerved into the driveway of one of the back models. The garages were built under the house, an expensive feature (they had to admit that Milo Till did some quality construction), so when Polly pulled down to the garage door, the retaining walls hid them from both the parking lot and the front road.

While Charlotte and Dinah, bent low, crept from window to window to peer in, Polly crouched by the car, watching from behind the driveway wall. She saw when the four salespeople walked together to the staff parking spaces. She heard their cars go down the hill, and after a silence of several minutes she stepped out to get a better look through the space between houses. The parking lot was empty, except for a blue security car outside the sales trailer.

"Well? Anything?" Polly asked when they were all in the car, Charlotte in back this time, and had eased the doors shut.

Dinah shook her head. "More of the same. But it's interesting that he'd go to the trouble of putting in the same kind of artifacts that he appropriated, if that's the right word. You think he expected someone to check?"

"Did the Helmsleys make any effort at pretense?" Charlotte asked Polly.

"Not that I know of," said Polly, "which makes me think they did it all thoughtlessly, just following their natural inclination to be chintzy and acquisitive and dishonest. Till may be more calculated, consciously covering his tracks with this junk."

"But not well," said Dinah. "The stuff doesn't come close." She sank back into her seat.

"Let's leave," said Charlotte.

"And how exactly do we do that?" asked Polly.

She had been worrying about their exit the whole time she'd been keeping watch. If they just drove down the hill, she said, they'd probably be stopped either by the security guard at the trailer or at the gate, and what would they say? "We were just looking around"? "We got lost behind the model homes"? "I dropped a contact lens"?

"Come on," said Charlotte. "What could they do to us?"

"That's not the problem," said Polly. "Obviously we're not criminals, but we don't want to be noticed. Or questioned. They could ask for some identification, which means that Till might hear that Dinah was here."

While they were holding their whispered conference, they heard a car start up and drive away, and when Polly crept out again to look, she saw the security car reach the bottom of the hill. It paused for a minute on the other side of the gate while the gate swung shut. Was he leaving for good? Going out for dinner? Maybe going to get dinner and bring it back?

In any case, they didn't want to run into him. They studied their maps for another way out. The Butte Crest map showed internal roads exiting on three of the four sides. Choosing the exit on the far side of the development, Polly backed out and drove up and over the hill. The road ended at a chain-link fence along public road. She turned back up the hill to try the perpendicular, a rougher track emerging at the eastern road that went down to the county highway. Here, too, there was a fence, and a construction trailer, but here at least there was a gate.

It was closed, and, worse, it was pretty forbidding. Bolstered with metal crossbars and diagonal struts, it looked like an electric gate, and maybe an electrified fence. Both gate and fence were wrapped with wiring, and instead of a latch and padlock there was a panel with a keypad.

"I'll go look it over," said Polly, opening her door. Just as she was swinging her legs out, there was an explosion of sound and an explosion of movement, and three large dogs, barking and snarling, burst out from behind the trailer and rushed at the car. Polly screamed and slammed the door. Two of the dogs hurled themselves against it, and the third got up on its hind legs and pawed at a window, scraping its nails on the glass. Outside the car, where there had been nothing but flat dirt and a bare horizon, there was now a swirl of black fur and flashing white canines, and all three women pulled back toward the other side of the car, where they could feel the frame shake under the assault.

"Where did those come from?" cried Polly, who had stopped screaming under the pressure of Charlotte's hand on her shoulder and now substituted an uneven series of little yelps. "What are they?"

"Rottweilers," said Charlotte, breaking out in the sweat that follows a surge of adrenaline. "Some kind of rottweiler mix, maybe, but obviously trained to attack."

Still snarling, the dog pawing the window was the first to lower itself to the ground and back off, followed by one and then the other of its mates. There they sat, not a dozen feet away, their three heads of long teeth and foamy lips and glittering eyes fixed on the car.

"What now?" said Polly shakily. Experimentally, she put a palm up against the window. Instantly two of the dogs lunged at the glass.

For the next few minutes, they sat absolutely still, watching the dogs watching them. Every so often someone would make a slight motion— feinting toward the window, wagging her fingers—and the dogs, on alert, would unfold their muscular haunches, advance a few steps, and start growling and barking again.

Then, in one of the lulls, Charlotte said suddenly, "Wait," and began riffling around in her leather purse. Dinah and Polly watched her rummage and watched the dogs. "Okay," said Charlotte, "okay," and she straightened up, slid across the backseat, and, sucking in her breath, put her hand on the door handle.

"Charlotte, what are you doing?" cried Polly, twisting around, but Charlotte had the door open and was stepping out, even as the dogs rose and renewed their din. This time, perhaps sensing that they had their prey on target, they didn't leap forward. Instead two of them, with lower and more ominous growls, bent into threatening crouches, wound up and ready to spring.

Later Polly and Dinah spent some time reconstructing what happened in the next few seconds and in what order. Polly said she saw Charlotte raise one hand to her mouth as she got out of the car, keeping the door half open between her and the dogs. Dinah, watching the dogs, heard the clink of metal, the dogs' growling change to a low whine, and then silence. Both saw Charlotte moving carefully out from the car, fist at her mouth, and the dogs' immediate and eerie reaction. One leaped up, twisting in the air, came down and leaped again, howling. One sank belly to the ground, turning 'round and 'round, whimpering, its tail down and tucked tight under its rear end. The third made not a sound but backed off toward the trailer, dipping its head and swiping first one front paw and then the other over its ears.

Bolder then, Charlotte stepped to the front of the car and gave another blast on what they now saw was a silver whistle. The two dogs twisting and writhing on the ground jerked themselves up and ran to follow the one that had already disappeared behind the trailer. At that, Charlotte walked over to inspect the gate from one end to the other, standing back several feet.

"It's definitely locked," she said calmly as she got back into the car, leaving the door open this time. "A label on the post says 'ElectriFence,' so the fencing is also wired."

"Charlotte . . ." began Polly. It came out a squeak. She swallowed. "Charlotte, what in God's name . . . ?"

Charlotte turned the little whistle around in her fingers as if seeing it for the first time, then opened her hand to examine the other silver pieces attached to the same silver ring. "It's a dog whistle," she said in a faint voice. "From Tiffany. It's a frequency only dogs can hear, and it hurts their ears."

"Did you ever use it before?" asked Dinah.

Charlotte shook her head. In spite of her apparent calm, her face was red and shiny with moisture, and a drop of sweat ran down her cheek, drawing a line to her chin.

"How did you know it would work?"

"I didn't," said Charlotte, her voice stronger now. The collection of little tools, she said, was a gift from Avery years ago when Charlotte worked as a process server while studying for the bar. The job sent her all over town, sometimes to unsavory places to serve unsavory people. Even nicer people in nicer places were not happy to be served, and showed it. Avery had wanted her to have some protection, however miniature: The silver ring held the dog whistle, a screwdriver, a file, a jackknife, and a thin row of four brass knuckles framed in silver.

"I don't expect much from the knuckles," said Charlotte, "but then until today I wasn't sure about the whistle either."

"You may get to test them all before we're done," said Polly dryly.

"How do we find out what part of the fence is electrified?" said Dinah. "Should we throw something at it, like a soda can?"

"You don't want to throw anything at it," said Charlotte. "It's probably meant to set off an alarm somewhere, not electrocute you."

"Maybe it fries you *and* it sets off an alarm," said Polly. "And what difference does it make whether it's all electric or just parts of it? Even if we found a safe part to touch, that wouldn't open it. And if we tried to knock it down with the car, some part of the front end would have to touch some part that's electrified, and there we'd be. Still fried."

"We have to call for help," said Charlotte, looking out the back window, gently swinging her ring of tools from one finger and keeping her eye on the trailer. Only one dog was in sight, submissively flat on the ground at a back corner. "The question is whom to call."

"I know a police detective in Newhall," said Dinah, but before they could ask, as usual, how well she knew him, it became clear that the more immediate problem was how to make the call, any call. All three had cell phones. Charlotte's made a few weak beeps and went silent, displaying an icon that announced the battery was dead. Polly's and Dinah's responded to all efforts at dialing—information numbers, Polly's number, the other cell phones—with the words "No Service" or "Out of Service Area."

"That's it," Polly muttered. "I'm not buying in this place."

Dinah had a PalmPilot, but the message function was "Not Available" because it needed a phone connection. Charlotte and Dinah had beepers as well, but beepers were for incoming calls, not outgoing. While those two were still going over the available equipment, Polly was pawing through the collected junk in the pocket of her door and under her seat. Straining backward, she also felt around on the floor behind her seat and then, reaching past Dinah, opened the glove compartment. Finally she groped around under Dinah's seat, while Dinah pressed her legs against the door.

"Hey!" Polly said, pulling up what looked like a black cordless telephone. "Jeremy's walkie-talkie! But there's only one of them."

"You only use one," said Charlotte. "Another person uses the mate."

"But it only has a range of two miles," said Polly. "I know because I bought it." She pushed the on button, the buttons for various frequencies, random numbers on the keypad. Occasionally she paused, holding up a finger to indicate she heard something on the line, and said "Hello? Hello?" several times before trying another key. A few times she seemed to hear something promising and, pressing her mouth closer, said, "Hello? Is anyone there?"

Suddenly she was waving her hand vigorously in the air, astonishment on her face, and shouting, "Hello, hello, can you hear me?"

She looked at Dinah and Charlotte. "You can hear me?" she was saying. "Where are you?" Pause. "I don't know where that is. . . . Never mind," and she told whoever was there where she was, on which side of the development and how they'd missed the closing and been trapped behind the locked gate. Before she could specify what kind of help was needed, the other person apparently claimed to be on the way.

"No! Don't come!" Polly shouted. "Wait a minute!" But the person on the other walkie-talkie had signed off.

"They hung up," she said nervously. "They're close by, and they're coming."

"What did you expect them to do?" said Charlotte. She saw that Polly was really alarmed. "It's okay. Maybe they'll have a good idea."

Almost to herself, Polly said, "What kind of person has a walkie-talkie they keep on all the time? She said, or maybe he said, his name is Bean. Something like Bean, anyway."

For the next quarter hour, the three women sat stiff and unspeaking. It was past five-thirty, and the sun was already slanting in low from the horizon, so that everything on the ground—trailer, car, fence posts—cast a long shadow. Once, one of the dogs appeared around the side of the trailer and made a tentative step toward the car. Charlotte lowered her window and blew forcefully, if inaudibly, on the whistle. Whatever noise it made was clearly terrible to the dog, which leaped in the air, did a full twist at the height of the leap, and ran back to safety behind the trailer.

Well before it appeared, they heard the sound of a car coming up the road beyond the fence, and then it was there. It was not a car but an off-road vehicle with a loud engine and a whine in the transmission, and it was oddly customized. Basically a dusty brown Isuzu Trooper, it had several two-by-fours across the front, covering the bumper and the radiator all the way up to the hood, and a couple more boards protecting each fender to the door hinges. As it turned off the road and up the five hundred feet to the gate, they could see the windshield. Not only was it pretty dirty, but there seemed to be no one behind it.

"There's no one inside," said Polly in a flat voice.

"What do you mean?" said Charlotte from the backseat.

"There's no one driving the thing. Am I right, Dinah?"

It certainly did seem that there was no one at the wheel, unless it was an optical illusion, a trick of the sinking sun and the slant of the glass. And yet someone's hand had turned the wheel into the drive and someone's foot was working the brake, because the vehicle stopped a few dozen feet short of the gate. The driver's door opened, legs climbed down to the running board, and, with a little hop onto the ground, a boy came toward them.

To Polly's eye he was twelve or thirteen at most. He had a fresh open face, blue eyes under pale brows, a big smile with crooked teeth and braces, a child's rosy cheeks, and light hair an inch long all over his head, like Sluggo in the comic strip. He wore a plaid shirt and a zip-up hooded sweatshirt, and his jeans, wide-legged and low-slung, were cuffed up several times over his cowboy boots.

They got out of the Volvo, keeping an eye on the dogs, now lying quietly in the dirt.

"Hey," said the boy, in greeting, coming to the gate. "I'm Bean. Who'd I talk to?"

"Me," said Polly. "I'm Polly. These are Charlotte and Dinah."

"Hey," he said, hands in his pockets in a baby swagger. "How'd you ladies get stuck in there?"

"We came to see the homes," said Polly, very aware of the fact that the three of them, lined up on one side of the fence, were totally dependent on the child across from them.

"Don't buy here," he said definitively. "Place sucks. Everyone who lives around here is hoping it tanks. How come they didn't wait to let you out?"

"We wanted to see more than they wanted to show us."

His smile broadened, and he gave them a thumbs-up.

"Can you get help?" asked Charlotte.

"Charl," he said, "I *am* help, like I told Polly here when I answered the call. I always keep a receiver open. Lucky you. . . ." He bent in to examine the gate, moving a few inches at a time.

"Okay, ladies," he said, straightening up, hands on hips. "Here's the story. The wheels belong to my brother. He's a marine on call-up, and I'm taking care of his ve-hickle, at his request." He studied them one by one, anticipating questions. "I can drive it, but only around here, given the license problem, okay?"

"Okay by us," said Polly. "Nobody saw you come?"

"Nobody sees me, period," he said. "I got a back way, off-road. Okay?"

"Okay," said Polly. "That's good."

"This here fence is electric, you know."

"We know."

"Some things don't conduct electricity, you know," he said, "like wood and rubber." As if thinking out loud, he put the tips of three fingers in his mouth, probably a baby habit he wasn't ready to give up.

"What do you have in mind?" asked Charlotte.

"Not to worry," Bean said, and he turned to the Trooper. Opening the door, he paused and looked back at them around the edge. "Best stand aside," he said in his child's voice. Hiking his leg way up, he laboriously climbed in and pulled the door shut.

"Bean!" cried Charlotte, starting forward, but he had already disappeared below the dashboard. The motor started, and with a grinding of gears and the tires churning into the dirt, the Trooper leaped backward and in reverse flew the five hundred feet to the turnoff. Once there, Bean tramped down on the brake; the Trooper lurched, rocked forward, backward, and seemed to settle on its haunches. The three women stood frozen on the other side of the fence, like spectators at a racetrack, until Bean gave the horn an impatient little tap. Charlotte and Dinah leaped to one side, and Polly sprinted back to the Volvo, shoved the gearshift into reverse, and, without even looking, ran the car straight back a safe distance and jumped out to watch.

The last strands of sunlight just cleared the hilltop, spotlighting the
Trooper on the bare road against a backdrop of graying sky. The boy
revved the motor a few times, the front end shook like a horse pawing
the ground, and then the tires dug in, kicked back a hail of sand and
gravel, and the Trooper sprang forward, covering the distance to the gate
in seconds.

"Omigod," Polly gasped, and Charlotte was crying "No, Bean! No,
Bean!" when the two-by-fours on the front end of the Trooper smashed
into the gate and knocked it down all in a piece, along with some of the
fencing on both sides. There was a series of flashes and a burst of sparks,
and a ruffle of blue flame fanned out over the wires on the fencing as the
ghostly outline crumpled section by section to the ground.

Bean took the Trooper clear of the fallen gate before he hit the
brakes. This time the back end of the vehicle jounced and landed hard,
and immediately after, Bean, unhurt, opened the door and clambered
down, clear of the wires, which were still crackling, emitting sparks and
thin threads of smoke.

"Wow," he said, surveying his accomplishment. He came over to
them, thumbs hooked on his belt, big proud smile. "Anyone hear an
alarm go off?"

"Do you realize," said Dinah, and her voice quavered, "that you could
have been killed? If there'd been just one loose wire to touch that metal
chassis . . ."

He took a perfunctory look behind him and shrugged. "No loose
wires," he said. "You ladies can cross now."

"Bean," said Polly, who had put a restraining hand on Dinah's shoulder, "you are one fantastic kid." And she reached out the hand, palm
down, and slapped him five and five again, both low and high.

"You are that," said Charlotte, and after a quick check on the dogs,
she handed him her Tiffany tools. "My dog whistle," she said, "and other
stuff. Tiny token of thanks."

"Wow," said Bean again, and as he turned them over one by one in his palm, a phone box on the side of the trailer began ringing.

"Maybe it did set off an alarm," said Dinah.

"Maybe the interruption in current was recorded somewhere," said Charlotte, "and the guy just saw it as he came back from supper."

At that there came the sound of a car on the other side of the hill, still some distance away. As one, all four of them turned and ran to their cars, tore open the doors, and flung themselves inside. As Polly turned on her engine, Bean was already pulling the Trooper forward, made a tight U-turn, and rattled over the fallen gate and out of the development.

"Hold on!" yelled Polly, clamped her teeth and stamped on the gas pedal. All three later admitted that they expected any number of wire endings to scrape against their undercarriage and electrocute them in a spray of light and flame. Instead they flew over the fallen gate as if in a hydrofoil, feeling nothing until Polly braked hard and loud to turn right onto the public road.

Bean, ahead of them, had gone to the left, and Charlotte in the backseat and Polly in the rearview mirror made sure to see him go. The Trooper, once again looking driverless, paused an instant. Bean's forearm came out of the driver's window, waved up and down like a semaphore at a railroad crossing, and the Trooper took off amid swirls of dust and vanished over the hill.

28

The next day Charlotte bought herself another dog whistle at Tiffany, lingering, entranced, over the selection of miniature tools and utensils. There were tiny scissors, nail clippers, and tweezers, lipstick brushes with sterling handles. There were regular whistles, both flat and Phillips-head screwdrivers, wire cutters, a three-sided file, a tiny whetstone, even a wee flint and strike pad. All had holes or rings at one end so they could be hung on a key ring or chain. They were all tempting, but Charlotte bought only the dog whistle for herself and for Avery a disk with a different screwdriver head at each corner. "After all," she told the other women, "we owe him. Not that I told him what we did."

They had been inordinately lucky. After parting from Bean, they had raced over bumps and gullies, sometimes fully airborne, and came up fast on the county highway, where Polly heeled the car into a screeching, two-wheel, ninety-degree turn while they all leaned hard the other way.

Approaching the entrance to Butte Crest, they saw the blue security-service car appear from behind the model homes, speeding over the top of the hill and down the drive to meet another security car on its way up.

Thank God, Polly thought: Bean had gotten away clean. But it was a thought she barely had time to register until later. As they careened past the front gate of Butte Crest Homes, they could hear alarms going off both in the gatehouse and up on the hill, but they had a good lead, a good road, just enough traffic to hide in, and not long after, they shot onto the freeway to L.A.

On Tuesday, Justine met Ray in the lobby of the U.S. district courthouse, where he was attending a trial in tax court. They wasted no time on small talk, although Ray did comment that he had been expecting a call with some sort of tip, if not this soon. Justine quickly laid out what they had on Milo Till, and as she talked, Ray made tiny notes with a fine-point pen on three-by-five note cards.

Justine gave him copies of the Till Properties expenditures on Butte Crest Homes in the fiscal year just ended, the supplementary statement itemizing the specific costs associated with the model homes, and the list of the corporation's art holdings, with the forty-piece collection of Southwest Indian art highlighted. She also had two typed pages of unsigned notes prepared by Dinah, describing the goods actually on display in the model homes, their probable origin, and their likely values. Without looking at them, Ray put the pages in an inside pocket of his briefcase.

"Do you need more from us in the way of proof?" Justine asked.

He shook his head. "Not at the moment," he said, allowing himself a slight smile. "You seem to have been very thorough."

"What happens now?" asked Justine.

"You may not hear anything for some time," said Ray, "and probably nothing directly. The tip is crucial, of course, but it's just a tip. We'll redo everything you did, as if it were our own idea, and we'll go way beyond it. We'll audit the corporate report, which we do anyway, and we'll ask for itemizations and documentation, which we don't always do. Then we investigate, just as you did. And very well, I must say."

"You'll actually go to the model homes?" asked Justine. "To his office and his condo?"

Ray looked at her fondly. "We have cars, Justine, and gas allowances. Uncle even hires art experts, though they're pricey." He stood up. "It could take a while; hopefully, the artworks are just part of a general pattern. Still, as you know, we like to announce a few catches in the early months of the year as a kind of heads-up to taxpayers, to let them know we're not asleep at the wheel. So you might hear sooner."

Justine nodded, gathering up her purse and leather carryall. "Did you look at your African violets yet?"

"That very afternoon," said Ray. "And thank you."

Indeed, the women heard nothing for several months. During that time they resumed their normal lives, though those lives were much altered by small changes they had made while caught up in Ginger's revenge. Some of the alterations came as a surprise, small changes being by nature unnoticeable. They are made more easily than big decisions, sometimes just to put off a big decision, but they can start a process that shifts the whole landscape of a life, like a minor tremor far below the visible earth. By the time it ripples to the surface, what had been a slight adjustment of subterranean plates can become a major event, buckling a whole hillside or raising a new ridge.

The biggest change was this: They had been successful, together and individually. As Charlotte pointed out when they reflected on the changes, they had always seemed successful—competent, respected in their fields, well in control of their lives. But all had felt that they didn't quite have what they wanted and, if they were right about what it was, couldn't get it. Then they had embarked on an impetuous, heartfelt crusade on behalf of their dead friend. They had gone against foreign adversaries in unfamiliar country and had prevailed.

But that was not all. In passing they had refined the skills, the approach, the very assumptions of success. "Maybe success is a habit," said Polly, "and like all habits it's cumulative. You find a little strength, and it gives you more. With each success you get bolder."

"Yes!" said Kat, pumping a fist in the air. "Today revenge! Tomorrow the world!"

"Uh, not quite," said Dinah.

Kat's success came the swiftest. It started with the removal of the implants, which excised from her life a continuing irritant and made her a useful symbol to both Dr. Caen and her teenage charges. Not long after Kat's operation, Dr. Caen had her giving short talks, pointed and personal, about self-image and the difference between beauty and health. As soon as she felt able, Kat was giving "running labs" for teen groups at rec centers, then schools, girls' clubs, even a birthday party. Initially, she admitted, she took a vain pleasure in the admiration she got, but then she began to enjoy the effect on the girls. The first time a group she was coaching entered a competition and came in fourth, she kept grabbing Barnaby's arm and saying, "They looked great, didn't they?" And Barnaby agreed, predictably adding, "So do you."

In mid-February she opened her flagship sports club to teenage runners at a special rate, and then to their parents at a new family rate, and the overnight response of both customers and media proved she had found a fresh marketing niche in the business of sports clubs. The special teen programs filled the club's normally dead hours from three to five in the afternoon, the family rate brought in four or five customers instead of just one, and families were not only more stable as members but, particularly on the west side, much richer than singles.

"In a way I'm still modeling," Kat told the group, "but for a different audience and with a different goal. I want to be a role model, not just an image." She bounced in her seat. "This is going to be really big."

"You'll make a fortune," said Charlotte.

"That, too," said Kat happily.

Justine was, as always, less open about her plans. They heard about her new work in the family business—about the orchid grower she'd signed as an exclusive supplier and about her discovery of a landscape architect who specialized in hydroponic gardening. But she didn't tell them she was leaving the assessor's office until she'd given her notice, quickly assuring them that the decision "was based on all the discussions we had about my situation. The fact that I finally moved on it, moved on all kinds of things, is because of your support."

She had intended to depart by the first of March, after helping to choose and train her replacement. But her office staff wouldn't permit a quiet exit. Many had been with her for two and even three of the four assessors' terms, and they insisted on holding a banquet lunch to celebrate her move. Embarrassed but touched, she accepted, and after two decades of staging farewell lunches for dozens of colleagues, she tied on a scarlet TEYAMA GARDEN SUPPLY apron over a beige silk suit, passed out sixty TEYAMA GARDEN sun visors, and graciously received a two-hour tribute to her own abilities.

Government officials rarely have a light touch, and Justine's thoughts wandered, though later she could perfectly describe the flower bouquets on the tables. The combination, she said, was unusual—several colors of Peruvian lily (alstroemeria) and ranunculus, a half-dozen big roses, fully open, and around the rim an unexpected touch—a fringe of fragrant lily of the valley, which is impossible to grow in most of the Southwest.

"Was Robby there?" Charlotte asked.

"No," said Justine, "because it was a lunch, and no one brought spouses. But he was invited and would have left work if I'd wanted him to. He said so."

It was Lotte who asked if Robby was fully aware of how this had all come about and whether he himself seemed noticeably "evolved" after the experience.

"If you mean has he changed, I don't think so," said Justine, obviously amused but, as always, respectful with Lotte. "But I have. I don't think you can change anyone except yourself."

"Well said." Lotte nodded decisively. "Very well said—a most productive attitude. But it would feel good, would it not, to know that someone gave credit to our efforts?"

It was perfect, an irresistible opening. Justine saw it, and as she responded, looking around the table, it was clear that everyone else had as well. "It's like revenge," she said. "You may plot it, arrange it, and accomplish it, but when you're successful, you don't need the recognition."

Dinah missed no meetings and returned phone calls, but she sometimes nodded off, and when she spoke of herself, it was all about her work, never art or men or even her thoughts about the career change, just the work itself. She was moonlighting two nights a week in a midcity emergency room and on weekends riding along with a commercial ambulance team. She described accidents and the actions the team sometimes had to take when there was no time to think it over. She told them of certain nights and certain cases in the ER, and when she spoke, she looked over their heads and out the window, and they knew she was back in the hospital basement behind the white curtains, leaning over a gurney in a desperate attempt to repel a preemptive strike by the angel of death.

They all wanted to discuss Milo Till, and Dinah's feelings about him, but couldn't take the chance that Lotte might make a connection if his name finally hit the headlines. They had always agreed that Lotte must never know what they'd done; there was almost surely some law that mental-health professionals had to report patients who had taken revenge on someone. It took several meetings until Lotte once again left early, and before her footsteps reached ground level, Polly asked Dinah if she had ever heard from Milo Till.

She had. He had called two weeks after their visit to his model homes, the week after they turned him in to the IRS. "I gave him the usual line," said Dinah, "the feeling-sparer. Said I was looking for something more permanent than he'd want to provide."

"And that was that?" asked Polly.

Not exactly. Till called back before the week was out and left a message on Dinah's machine that he would be "willing to explore that option." She wasn't entirely surprised. It was a refusal calculated to hold out a little hope; she just hadn't thought it would appeal to Milo Till. "Or maybe I hoped it would and purposely left the door open," she said. "Stupid me." She looked at Polly. "Not possible, right?"

"Two words," said Polly.

Dinah nodded. "Ginger Pass," she said.

"So I finally gave him the line-to-end-all-lines," she added with an air of resignation. "I told him I was already involved. And I am: I have a trauma workshop in March and a fire department course for practicing physicians the next few weekends." She shrugged. "You play the hand life dealt you, right?"

"Most people, yes," said Charlotte, "but don't fret, Dinah. Life deals you so many men that you can reshuffle priorities any time you want."

Of all of them, Charlotte's life seemed the least changed, but she herself was the most altered. She was deeply affected by the means and moment of Ginger's death. An expert on dying, she was keenly aware of the difference between a good death and a bad one but had spent little time reflecting on the life to which it put an end. She had never learned, till now, that all you really need from life, and the best you get, is light and warmth and the love of other people. And she began to understand that their need for revenge was a way of making sure that Ginger did not exit from this life unjustified and unloved.

If Charlotte seemed uncharacteristically muted for some weeks, it wasn't because she was unhappy. She reveled in her renewed intimacy with Avery, but she was being very careful, aware that the first flush of change was like the start of a love affair and could as easily end as move forward. So while enjoying it, she watched it closely and was on the alert when it was put to the test at Christmas.

As she told the group, stress was a holiday tradition in her family. Both her daughter and her mother were in residence. Neither traveled light, and they spread their things from one end of the house to the other, with a big central pileup of clothes and papers and personal items in the living room and front hall. The two of them got along very well, but Charlotte was usually pressed into serving their separate needs and wishes—buying particular foods, taking them to particular stores and exhibits, only occasionally protesting the plans or the pace. For his part, Avery would sometimes side with Victoria, who was very like him, and sometimes with Charlotte's mother, whom he disliked. But for him it was more of an intellectual exercise, several simultaneous chess games in which he could play any side.

"Then it came to me," she said, "in the middle of Christmas dinner, in the middle of a squabble. Everyone was being their most annoying, and they were all turning to me, waiting for me to explode so I could be the un-reasonable one. And I suddenly thought of Polly's mother's advice on self-protection: 'Don't react.' You remember telling us she'd say that, Polly?"

"One of her better ones," said Polly.

At the time Charlotte thought she'd find it impossible to follow such advice. Quick reaction and quick retort were her forte and her profes-sional strength, if also her undoing in personal relationships. But at Christmas she started to try, thinking, Don't react, while she made her mouth say something neutral. When everyone looked to her for a sharp comment at dinner, she reached for a roll and said nothing. When her mother said that serving ice cream on apple pie was gilding the lily and none of them needed it, Charlotte said, "Maybe so," and went on eating her dessert. And when later on, in their bedroom, Avery referred to her mother as a "piece of work," Charlotte just smiled and busied herself with setting the alarm.

It could well be, she said, that the little adage as a modus operandi was not simple at all but quite profound. Holding back one's reactions wasn't a matter of subservience or surrender. It was taking the high road, refusing to do battle when battle wasn't necessary. It meant accepting whatever could be left alone.

Polly had told them about her newspaper piece as soon as it was accepted, and they all took her out for a raucous congratulatory dinner. Like her, they were disappointed when her next idea was rejected. Like her, they rejoiced when one of the section editors offered her an assignment, although Charlotte did say, "Boy, I couldn't take the ups and downs of that life."

"I, on the other hand, welcome it," said Polly. "I'm tired of the even keel."

She had already told them she would probably marry Graham Vere, if not immediately. They'd had several days alone together after Christmas when their respective children had gone off to visit their grandparents and Polly and Graham had gone to the desert. It was less a decision, she said, than a realization, and she was surprised when it had come to her. Not when they were in bed, although they'd spent quite a bit of the time there. Not when they walked out on the sand at night, a dome of stars above their heads and heaven to the horizon on all sides.

It was when they were eating long and unhurried dinners and lazy breakfasts, with nothing to do but talk. Inevitably, they'd talk about their children—their problems, their achievements, their particular personalities, or even just what they might be doing at that moment. It was, as Polly told Graham, a little like the early days when she and Dan would get a baby-sitter and go out to a rare dinner, then spend the entire time talking about their children, because they were not just a couple but a family, and permanent.

You see? Good things come to those who wait, had been her mother's response.

God helps those who help themselves, Polly countered, and got an ironic and approving smile.

"It does seem weird that the biggest changes in life can be pure luck," Polly told the other women. "Maybe that's why they say you 'fall' in love, because it's an accident, a totally random occurrence."

Truly random events were rare in life. Dan's death was definitely random: He was in the wrong place at the wrong time purely by chance. Ginger's death, however, was less random, because Ginger had put herself in harm's way, not by chance but by choice. Briefly Polly wondered if she had put herself in love's way on purpose, but she got impatient with that line of thinking.

She thought a lot about Ginger now when she thought of love and death, but Ginger herself remained an enigma. They had only had the vaguest idea of her married life, and while Ginger had told them that what she wanted was power over men, she was kidding herself that she had it. She might even have known that. Polly did think, however, that Ginger was sure of their friendship, as Polly told the other four over dinner one Monday, and probably appreciated its value well before the rest of them, who didn't know the depth of that friendship until she died.

"Maybe that's what revenge is," said Charlotte thoughtfully, "apart from a dish served cold, apart from that damn tree in the forest. Revenge can be a labor of love as well as hate."

"I think so," said Polly. "I hope so."

Justine heard from Ray the third week of February, just before the Internal Revenue Service announced it was seeking an indictment against Milo Till and Till Properties & Development in federal district court for income tax evasion and tax fraud. Everything she had given him checked out, Ray said, and gave the auditors a good idea of where else to look. As a result they hadn't limited themselves to Butte Crest finances or to capital expenditures on the various Till developments and had found a range of deceptions.

When the indictment itself hit the news, it detailed a pattern of fraud that included a wall and gate installed at Till's Malibu home but billed to an Arizona resort development; a full-time Belgian chef at Till's Westwood condo who was salaried by the golf club's snack bar at a Lake Tahoe condominium community run by the Till Properties group; and a thirty-five-hundred-square-foot lake-shore town house and dock in another Tahoe development that were built and financed by the corporation but deeded to Milo Till personally. The IRS gave these and a half-dozen other fraudulent arrangements a value of just over $11 million but reserved the right to add more items that could raise the total to $20 million.

According to the IRS, the action grew out of a "routine audit" of corporate tax filings. The papers carried a response from Till's lawyer, calling the indictment a terrible mistake and declaring that Till had trusted his accounting firm to separate personal and corporate monies appropriately, according to information Till had properly provided. There was TV footage of Till leaving the courthouse, the equivalent of a perp walk. There was also a photo in the newspaper of Till at a political banquet two years ago, on the governor's left, and an inset that looked like a formal head shot from an official publication.

"Maybe it's from his MBA graduation," Polly said when she and Graham Vere were winding up the day with an hour together on her back terrace.

"More likely from an annual report," said Graham.

"They're just mug shots now," said Polly. "*Sic transit gloria mundi,* as my mother would say."

Graham had arrived with an air of suppressed jubilance and an armload of papers—not just local papers, which she already had, but the *Washington Post, New York Times,* and *Wall Street Journal,* which he'd picked up at a specialty newsstand. Since Reinhart's death they had carefully avoided the topic. They talked about the women. They talked about Ginger, and they talked about her death. What they didn't discuss, since that first night in the garden, was what Polly and her friends were doing about it, although Graham knew they were doing something, Polly knew that he knew, and Graham knew that she knew that he knew. Even now all he said as he handed her the papers was "Well, they got your guy Till, and they got him good."

When they finished the papers, taking turns reading quotes and details to each other, they turned off the terrace lights and sat in the dark. The canyon was particularly quiet, with the background hum of the city audible but few birds calling, no barking dogs, just the rustle of the cooling breeze through the palm trees nearby and occasionally a far-off fire or police siren. The night sky was unusually clear for L.A., and they quickly located Castor and Pollux almost directly overhead and at least the belt of Orion. It was a new and shared interest since their desert weekend, when they had on impulse taken along some of their children's old astronomy primers and star maps. The haze of city lights made it impossible now to see any but the brightest stars, so they just skipped over to where they thought those should be.

"Yes! There's Polaris!" exclaimed Polly. "And the Big Dipper! Are we good or what?"

"We're very good," said Graham, putting both arms around her so closely that she was wrapped from shoulder to waist, warmed and protected both front and back. Even nameless, the stars were wonderful; visibility was enough.

"Did I mention," said Graham more quietly, "that I'm not at all interested in how you guys engineered this one?"

"You didn't," said Polly, freeing a hand so she could touch his forearm, "and I appreciate it. It's not important to anyone but us. And Ginger."

"Is it over now?"

"Yes," said Polly. "It's over," and even her mother had nothing to add.

29

There are times in life, and events, that demand ceremony. It had not occurred to any of the women that revenge, a gesture of pure spite, would be one of those, but they all felt the need to mark their success, and with something more formal, more solemn, than a celebratory dinner.

"It wasn't spite," said Kat when they discussed it after a Monday meeting some weeks after Till was indicted. "It was justice."

"Just think how many killers justify their murders that way," said Polly.

"We didn't murder anybody," said Justine quickly.

"Let's not go there," said Charlotte, breaking the awkward silence that followed Justine's remark. "You of all people don't want to go there."

Justine nodded and lowered her eyes.

"It doesn't matter," said Polly. "Remember we used to remind ourselves that this wasn't a detective story? It's also not a court of law: We don't have to justify anything."

They also wanted to include Ginger Pass in some way. At that point they realized they had no idea where she was, and it wasn't beyond all possibility, said Kat, "that Harold just threw her remains out with the trash."

"I'll call him now," said Polly, taking out her cell phone. "With luck, he won't be home yet, and the daughter will tell me."

But it was obviously Harold who answered on the second or third ring, because Polly immediately straightened her spine. She asked how he was doing, asked after Nina, then explained that they had all been talking about "paying our respects" (Dinah groaned quietly and covered her eyes) and wanted to know where Ginger was buried. There was a short pause for a short answer, probably just the name of a cemetery, and Polly asked, "Any particular area?"

That got an equally short answer, because Polly thanked him, added, "Give my best to Ni—" but not quickly enough. He was gone, and she hung up the phone.

"So where is she?" asked Kat.

"Somewhere in Foothill Cemetery, outside Pasadena," said Polly without inflection. "He said to ask at the office and they'll direct us."

"What a prince," said Kat. "As we always said."

They agreed to meet there the next Saturday afternoon, and Polly said she'd go out early, check in at the office, and get directions to Ginger's grave. As a result she was waiting for them at the entrance to the main building that housed the offices and several chapels and viewing rooms. It was a white masonry building with pretentiously tall columns supporting a pediment carved with the name of the cemetery and, under that, in bas-relief, some toga-clad figures in meaningless poses. Cars came up a circular drive, passing the entrance on the way to the parking lot, so each of the women saw Polly before they parked and joined her.

When they were all there but Dinah, Polly said, "Better brace yourselves. This is not a regular grave site."

"Harold put up flashing lights? A marquee?" said Charlotte.

Polly didn't get to answer, because as Charlotte was speaking, they heard the shifting of gears and squealing of tires coming up the hill. As they turned to look, a red-and-white ambulance came into view, tilting to one side and then another as it took the landscaped curves, and in another second it screeched into the circle and jolted to a stop in front of them. It was Dinah, of course, shrugging out of a white coat as she jumped down from the running board.

"Always have to make an entrance?" Charlotte greeted her.

"Sorry. I have a goofball partner," said Dinah, waving her fingers at him as he pulled away toward the parking lot. "He even put on the alarm at one intersection."

"That's illegal, of course," said Charlotte.

Polly led them around behind the main building and down a path between shoulder-high hedgerows, which ended at the gates of a bunkerlike structure, the cemetery's columbarium. It was long and narrow, with a stone floor and a line of benches down the middle. Far above them the high ceiling was made of opaque glass panels that provided most of the light in the room. Fortunately, it was a sunny day so it was well lit, despite walls that went from floor to ceiling unbroken by a single window.

As they moved deeper into the room, they saw that the walls were actually banks of flat, square metal plaques, like the vault of safe-deposit boxes in a bank. Polly led them to the far end of the building and pointed upward, a couple of feet above their line of vision.

VIRGINIA GUNNESON PASS, it said in block letters, and just to the right of the name was a metal bracket holding a skinny vase. Half a dozen wilted roses drooped over the edge, along with a heart-shaped card on a string. Kat reached up and turned it over. "Love from NINA," it said.

"Her stepdaughter," Polly finally said, unnecessarily. "It's just her and us, and she probably thinks it's her alone. I have to call her."

"I will, too," said Kat.

They stood in a line, looking up at Ginger's compact drawer on the huge expanse of wall, and at her neighbors' drawers. Except for the five of them, the place was empty and very quiet. There was only the distant hum of a lawn mower.

"Well, it's no Thornton Wilder churchyard scene," said Charlotte.

"I've never gathered with mourners at a wall of ashes," said Dinah. "It's a little like the Vietnam Memorial in Washington or the wall of names on Ellis Island."

"Nobody buries these days," said Polly. "Everyone knows we're running out of space."

"I hope she's not cold," said Charlotte, looking at the skylight over their heads. "I wonder what time of day the sun hits her niche."

"Funny how you can know rationally she's not in there," said Dinah, "and you still can't help think about things like that." She turned to Charlotte. "But she is in sunshine, Char. Aren't the Elysian Fields outdoors?"

"You're the expert," said Charlotte. "That's myth, not case law."

"Did Harold mention that she'd been cremated?" Justine asked Polly. Polly shook her head.

"We should say something," said Kat, but no one knew what to say now. It seemed they had been talking for months about Ginger's death and Ginger's life, about their feelings for her and their crusade to get her some measure of revenge. Good measure, as it turned out. All they'd hoped for.

Finding it hard to leave, they'd take a few steps away and then turn back. "So we're not going to say anything?" said Kat.

"Actions speak louder than words," said Polly sententiously, immediately knowing that her mother would have a fine time mocking her for such a cliché. But her mother understood: That's always a good one, she said gently.

Before they left the cemetery, they bought a bunch of carnations at the gift shop and filled out the tag with their five names and Nina's. They were assured that the bouquet would be put in the vase on Ginger's niche within the hour.

They got all the way to the parking lot before anyone spoke again. Their cars were parked in a line in the near-empty lot, and now they stood in the noon sun, keys in hand, silent.

"Well, see you Monday," said someone.

Then, having come together from different directions, they went their separate ways.